DEMONIC WORKPLACES
SAFER TO CALL IN SICK!

DEMONIC ANTHOLOGY VOLUME VII
A Dark Humor Short Story Collection

DEMONIC WORKPLACES
SAFER TO CALL IN SICK!

EDITED BY JOSEPH MISTRETTA

ERIKA LANCE	MATTHEW ANDERSON	E. GALLAGHER	STEVE ODEN
ALESSIA LEHUA	F. MALANOCHE	JESSICA HAAS	PAUL LEE	B. C. G. JONES
DW MILTON	KAY HANIFEN	CHESTER ROGALSKI	SANDRA HENRIQUES
J. A. HEATH	ALAN BERKSHIRE	SERGIO "ENTE PER ENTE" PALUMBO

4 Horsemen
Publications, Inc.

Demonic Workplaces
Copyright © 2023 4 Horsemen Publications, Inc. . *All rights reserved.*

4 Horsemen Publications, Inc.
1497 Main St. Suite 169
Dunedin, FL 34698
4horsemenpublications.com
info@4horsemenpublications.com

Cover & Typesetting by Autumn Skye
Edited by Joseph Mistretta

All rights to the work within are reserved to the author and publisher. No part of this publication may be reproduced, stored in a retrieval system, or transmitted in any form or by any means, electronic, mechanical, photocopying, recording, scanning, or otherwise, except as permitted under Section 107 or 108 of the 1976 International Copyright Act, without prior written permission except in brief quotations embodied in critical articles and reviews. Please contact either the Publisher or Author to gain permission.

This is a work of fiction. All characters, organizations, and events portrayed in this novel are either products of the author's imagination or are used fictitiously.

Library of Congress Control Number: 2023944900

Paperback ISBN-13: 979-8-8232-0301-2
Ebook ISBN-13: 979-8-8232-0300-5

Dedication

To all the coworkers, bosses, and friends that helped make work a little less ... Hellish.

Table of Contents

Introduction ix
My Sucky Demon Boss: a Love Story
    By Erika Lance 1
Mandatory Exorcise
    By Matthew A.J. Anderson 13
The Merger
    By E. Gallagher 29
God of Garbage
    By Steve Oden 39
The Cost of Progress
    By Alessia Lehua 51
The Tightrope Walk
    By F. Malanoche 61
Sacrifices at the Cinema
    By Jessica Haas 73
Blood Beast
    By Paul Lee 85
Hostile Takeover
    By B. C. G. Jones 101
Ravenous Little Turds
    By DW Milton 111
Other People
    By Kay Hanifen 127
Vessel
    By Chester Rogalski 137

Good Grace
    By Sandra Henriques 147
The Midnight Grind
    By J. A. Heath 157
Parting Wish
    By Alan Berkshire 167
This Building is For You
    By Sergio "ente per ente" Palumbo 183

Book Club Questions......................... 199
Editor Bio..................................201

Introduction

Demonic Workplaces

Mondays... am I right?

Nothing speaks more to the underlying current in our society than the overall disdain held by most of the workforce for their jobs, their bosses, and their coworkers. Watch a few sitcoms, read a comic strip (yes, these are still a thing in the digital age), or talk to your friends over a few cold ones, and the hidden animosity seeps through the cracked surface.

How many times have you suspected that your boss may be some dark cultist or a "sucky demon?" I mean, without a "Sacrifice at the Cinema," how else do you explain those constantly increasing ticket sales even though people can just wait a few weeks and watch the same movie from the comfort of their home on their own giant television with surround sound and soda that costs less than $5? What about that 24-hour butcher shop that is always open for "The Midnight Grind?" I'm not sure that the demand for quality steaks is that high.

Maybe you're afraid to refuse their requests because you need that job. Sometimes it can feel like a real "Tightrope Walk" determining how much you can say and how much you have to just accept as a part of your job because you are about to quit, and your "Parting Wish" is to just prove how horrible your boss really is.

I know that I have suspected some of my bosses were setting me up for something crazy multiple times when their requests seemed absolutely nonsensical. But I think I may have drawn the line if I were a security guard for an eccentric billionaire who had lots of creepy artwork and randomly asked me to come in and sign extra forms before hosting a bizarre masquerade party as in "The Vessel."

In pretty much any job that involves interacting with other people, we, the poor, little worker drones, are convinced that someone or something is out to get us. Why else would the people we have to come in contact with regularly be so absolutely abhorrent? There must be a more sinister reason than "because." We know we must keep it together because with a little "Good Grace," we might not run into those coworkers that are truly monsters sucking the life out of us each and every day. Sometimes, things are more dangerous than the "Blood Beast" inside that causes our coworkers to do unspeakable things to each other.

Anyone that has spent much time in education knows how draining it can be to constantly see money spent on things that don't make any sense while the teachers, staff, and all the "Ravenous Little Turds" are underfunded and mistreated. It might even feel like the school district and those

Introduction

in charge are enjoying and benefiting from your misery, all at "The Cost of Progress." It's no wonder a few members of the staff disappear every year.

If you know, for a fact, that there are demons and horrible things around you, it becomes part of your normal. You might not enjoy that "Mandatory Exorcise" forced upon the staff because of a little thing like an escaping demon, but you get it, right? After all, "The Merger" between the living world and Hell has made life a bit tricky to navigate while you work away in middle-level bureaucracy dealing with "Other People." It's literally torture for most of the population. Unfortunately, the only solutions that some writers can see are to walk away, sacrifice their coworkers because "This Building is for You," or burn it all to the ground in a "Hostile Takeover."

Even the "God of Garbage" has to deal with this nonsense on a regular basis.

What's the solution?

Grab a drink, settle into a comfortable chair, and read about the misery of others, of course. As they say, misery loves company, and teamwork makes the dream work.

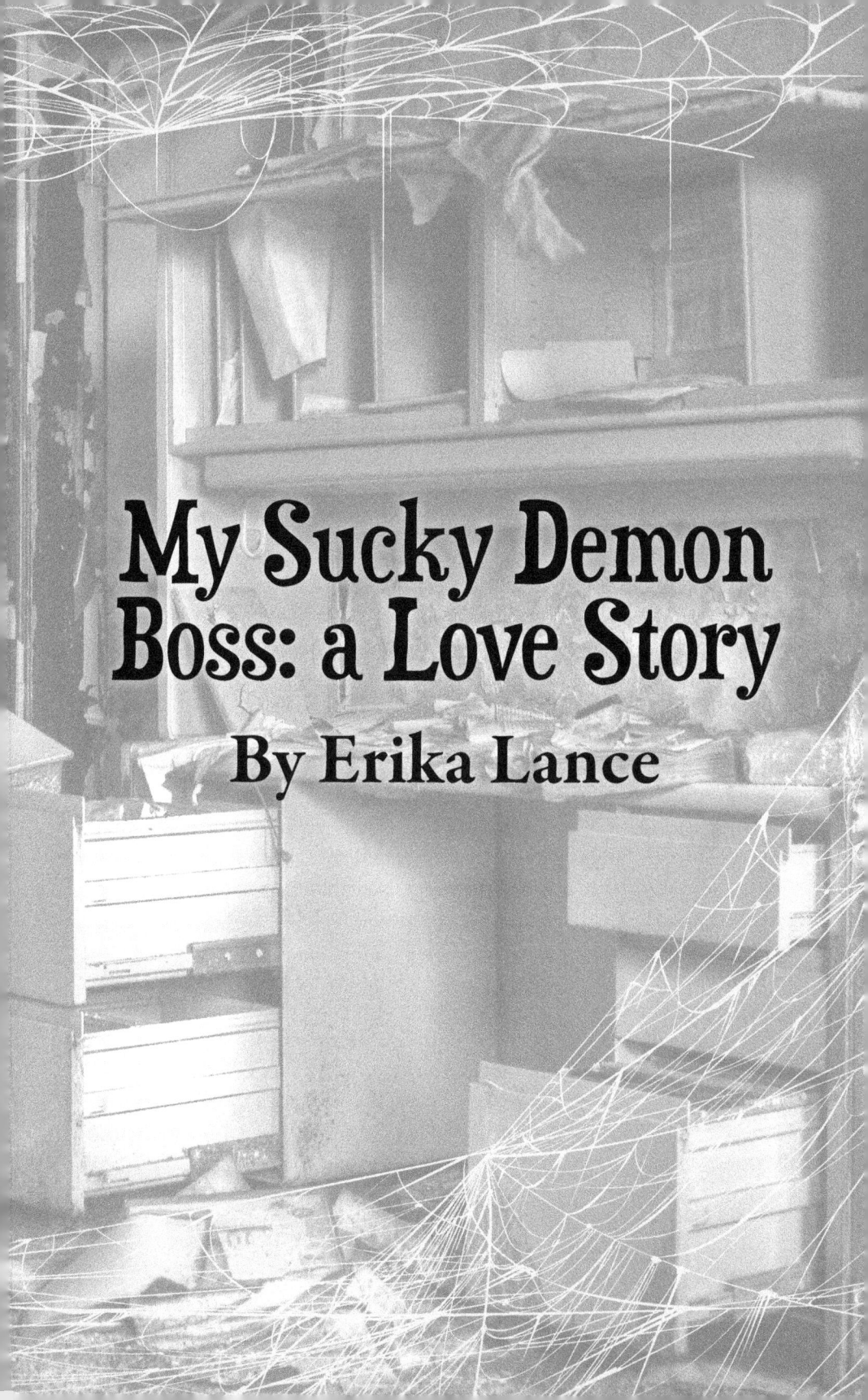

Demonic Workplaces

Some people say that they think their boss is a demon. My boss is quite literally a demon.

You may be wondering how I found out my boss is a demon. Or why didn't I quit when I found out? Or if I am in a mental hospital and I am just unaware of that fact? Possibly you may wonder why he hasn't killed me yet or if Satan really exists. In order to answer these and many other questions you may not even care about, you have to first understand that this is not just a tale of horror and gore, although there will be plenty of that. This is a love story.

Like any good love story, this one begins with me falling for the girl of my dreams. Her name was Angelica Brewston, Angel for short. When we met, I thought she was nothing short of perfection. She is perfect to me in every way imaginable except one, which I believe will become evident to you shortly.

It began on a very hot July day about eleven years ago. I was interning at a large accounting firm in San Francisco while working toward my master's degree in forensic accounting. I wanted to eventually work for the FBI in the White Collar Crime division. My grandfather had been a Madoff investor and had lost everything. I wanted to make sure that those who commit crimes like that against the "little guys" would be fully found out and brought to justice. My dad used to say that I would be a suit-wearing superhero. I wonder what he would say if he could see what I ended up doing instead.

My first encounter with Angel was in the breakroom on the forty-second floor of the office building where the firm was located. Of course, at the time, I thought it was fate that brought us together. It actually was a very dumb person from HR who caused our break room on the thirty-eighth floor to be closed because she over-microwaved one of those mac and cheese bowls you are just supposed to put a little water into and heat for thirty seconds.

Did you know even microwave-safe containers will eventually burn? Apparently, this mac and cheese was put in for thirty minutes instead of thirty seconds. The fire alarm was interesting as well. I found out that if there is a fire in a building with this many floors, they evacuate the floor the fire is on, and the one below. However, the floor above us was evacuated to the floor above them. This way, the people leaving the building do not move in an orderly fashion past the burning floor. Just in case you ever get stuck in a highrise and the fire alarm is going off and they won't let you leave. You have now been informed of the logic.

My Sucky Demon Boss: A Love Story

Of course, when the literal smoke cleared and the offending charred lump was found in the microwave, the breakroom on our floor was closed until it could be cleaned of all the toxic smells from nuked Styrofoam. Therefore, I had to go to another floor for my coffee. Internships, like this one, were amazing to land, but you worked a ton of hours for almost zero pay. I found myself sometimes living off of coffee and free breakroom snacks.

The fancy coffee machine they had on the forty-second floor had just finished and I was reaching for my cup distractedly, thinking about the current project I was on, when she sauntered past. As she moved to be in front of the coffee machine and pushed several buttons to make herself a non-fat, almond milk latte, she turned and smiled at me.

At that moment, I felt a jolt run through my entire body. It was that thing that you see in movies or read about in books. I knew at that moment I was in love. I was completely lost in her smile. And in case you were wondering how I knew I was lost? She stopped smiling and asked me if I was ok. Because, like a creeper, I was just staring at her.

"Hi... My name is Petey... I mean Peter," I said, attempting to reach out to shake her hand that was presently holding two bags of chips, four sticks of beef jerky, and a banana.

"I'm Angel." She smiled back.

"Yes, you are," slipped out of my mouth before I realized it and so, to make the situation that much worse, I did what any grown man would do. I turned and walked out of the room.

I was cursing myself as I hit the button on the elevator to go down when I heard her voice say, "Hey Petey, you dropped this." I turned to see her holding out one of the bags of chips to me. I said, "Thank you," taking the chips as the elevator doors opened. I walked in and turned to press the screen to take me back down to my cubicle, where I could ruminate and shame. When I looked up, she was smiling again. I desperately tried to figure out something to say to her, but the doors closed and she was gone.

Over the next couple of days, I definitely was not one of those losers that went to get coffee a hundred times trying to "bump into" her. I was sure this was one of those cases where I was being very subtle about it until my manager came up to check on me because my projects were falling behind and he had been told that I seemed a bit more jumpy than normal. When you work in a high-demand field and you are more than thirty stories above the pavement, they want to make sure that any twitchiness is not going to lead to being overly jumpy, say, out a window.

Demonic Workplaces

Since it was now four days later, I had not actually slept more than a total of five hours in that time due to my caffeine levels and I had gotten the one and only warning I would receive before my internship was terminated. I decided to head back home over the weekend to take a break.

Driving the six hours up the coast to the small town of Crescent City, CA, I found myself daydreaming about what my life would be like with her by my side. My Angel.

A switch in my brain finally flipped when I started to imagine what my life would be like after we were married. What in the hell was I thinking? I didn't know this girl.

In the past, I had crushes. In the fifth grade, there was a girl named Anna with cute pigtails and a huge smile. She liked dinosaurs as much as I did and sat at my table when we did art in Mr. Martin's class. Then, in junior high, her name was Jasmine, and she played the drums with me in band. High school it was Chrissy, she was a cheerleader and I was the mascot for the team. In each of these situations, me and my crush had reasons to interact. It wasn't until I got to college that I realized that my pining was not ever reciprocated. I had crushes, and that is all they were, and trying to imagine what the person was really like was impossible. Chrissy, as it turned out, was a horrible person and had stabbed her boyfriend in the neck when she thought he was cheating on her. She is now in jail and I could have been that dead boyfriend.

As I pulled into my parents' driveway, I resigned myself that I would keep myself busy in whatever way I could for the weekend to keep my mind off of her.

It turned out that it had been very easy to do just that. My mother had a list of things around the house that needed to be done. I ended up going out with a couple of friends from high school to a party. The weekend flew by and amazingly, the thoughts of Angel were shelved. As I pulled into the gas station before heading out of town, I found myself smiling. It had been a good weekend and exactly what I needed to recharge.

As I finished filling the tank, a car pulled up on the opposite side of the pumps. Normally I would not have taken notice, but it was very unique. The car was a cherry-red Mustang convertible. The paint had an almost shimmer quality to it, like flames. As the car door opened and the driver got out, my jaw hit the floor. It was Angel.

"Oh, it's you," she said, smiling as she slid her sunglasses off.

"Yeah, it is." I stumbled.

My Sucky Demon Boss: A Love Story

There was an awkward pause and then I asked, "What are you doing here?"

"Getting gas," she said, still smiling and biting her lower lips a little.

Any resolve I had established over the weekend completely fell apart at that moment. Her smile made me want to take her in my arms and be close to her forever.

The clicking of the gas pump stopping alerted me to the fact that I had just been staring at her. I looked away and moved to put the pump back into place. I heard a small giggle from her direction and looked up again to find her smiling at me.

She narrowed her eyes a bit as she walked over and touched my arm and she said, "You should have lunch with me".

I nodded. "Yes... Yes, I would."

"Then it's a date," she said, sliding her glasses back on and turning away. Before my brain could tell my mouth to say anything else, she was gone.

Driving home, I found myself back into the realm of wondering the "what-ifs" around the future for Angel and myself. She said lunch. Did she mean Monday? Should I bring something? Will she expect me to simply know what to do next?

In most rom-com movies, the next scene just happens. You do not see all the thinking or planning going into it. I wondered at one point when I was back in my apartment brushing my teeth before laying down to bed if I should keep trying to plan something or just let it happen? I mean, what are the odds of running into her at all in a building that large and again at a gas station after visiting with my parents? As I rinsed the toothbrush, I decided to just let it happen, outside of one thing which I could pick up on my way into work.

The next morning, everything was perfect. I woke up a few minutes before my alarm. I was able to pick up coffee and a breakfast sandwich with several minutes to spare before my train, which ran exactly on schedule. When I sat down at my desk, I knew this was going to be a fantastic day. During the morning, I was able to catch up several parts of my project. I was no longer concerned with when I would see her. Knowing it would happen and that we had a date changed everything.

It was 11:59 a.m. when I felt a tap on my shoulder and I turned my head to see her smiling down at me.

"Ready?" she asked, leaning against the cubicle wall.

I nodded and stood up. She was turning to walk away when I pulled out a bouquet of flowers that I had grabbed on my way into work. She smiled, reaching toward my hands. "Thank you," she said, letting her fingers linger on my mine for a moment before pulling them away.

Her touch felt as if it sent warm lightning through my body. It was wonderful and caressing, as if her warm breath was penetrating me everywhere. As I followed her to the elevators and we ascended up to the sixty-sixth floor, I was feeling a level of comfort and calm that I had not felt in some time. I was happy to be led where she was taking me.

We walked into a conference room and she pulled out a chair. I looked up and across the table was a slender gentleman who smiled when our eyes met. There was something almost off-putting in his gaze, but just as it began to register Angel touched my arm again and said, "Sit down, silly." The playful lilt in her voice pushing any other thought away.

I sat.

"Mr. Johnston." His voice was deep and throaty, "I want to thank you for joining me for lunch today. I hope that Angel chose something you will enjoy." Gesturing in the direction of the plate in front of me.

I had not looked at the food on the plate until he gestured. I discovered that it was a plate of my favorite noodle dish I had found in the city. It was from a food truck near the harbor, which was over thirty minutes away with no traffic.

The food was still hot and very fresh. I looked up toward Angel, who was standing behind my chair. "It's your favorite," she said, as if she had known that the entire time. Looking back down at the food, I was trying to remember if I had ever told her that. I must have told her, but when?

"Mr. Johnston," his voice tore through my thoughts, "I understand you want to join the FBI," he continued. "I think that I may have an offer for you, more tempting than that." He paused.

Gulping down the bite of noodles in my mouth, I asked, "What would... Actually, who are you?"

His mouth opened into a smile again and I felt Angel's hand on my shoulder. "You can call me Mr. Showeran."

"Okay." I nodded, taking another bite of the meal in front of me.

Something was wrong, a voice was telling me and as quickly as I would start to try to define what that was, it would evaporate as I felt Angel's hand move to caress my shoulder.

"I want to offer you a position with a very nice salary, apartment, even an assistant." He gestured toward Angel. "This offer, however, has a very short window." He produced a stack of papers from under the table and slid them toward me. They stopped directly in front of me as Angel was removing my lunch plate.

Was I finished eating? I thought as I watched her walk away. Feeling a little foggy, I shook my head and looked up at Mr. Showeran, taking in the man before me.

He was thin, but not skinny. I could tell he was fairly tall as his knee sat above the line of the table when folded over the other. Skin was light but not pale. He was bald and he had wrinkles around his eyes that were so dark you would not see the outline of the pupil. The suit he was wearing was dark, the same shirt and tie. There was nothing truly unsettling in any of this, but I felt unease as I looked at him.

"I'm sorry." I needed some clarity that I was having a very hard time arriving at. "What is this?" I gestured to the contract and the room. "I am here for an internship. You don't know anything about me."

Angel started to move back over toward me and I held up my hand to stop her. I wanted her to touch me, but the voice was back, telling me something was wrong.

"Mr. Johnston," he began. "Peter. Can I call you Peter?" he continued. "Angel had told me about bumping into you and I, how do I say this, took an interest." The smile appeared at the corners of his lips and a slight chill went up my spine.

"You have good grades, a good work ethic, and more importantly the potential to truly make a difference. To change the outcome of so many things to the way they should be."

He sat forward a little in his chair. "That is what you want, isn't it?"

A question lingered in the air as Angel sat beside me, pulling the contract closer in front of me and putting her hand on my arm. "Just take a look at the contract. This might be your dream job." Glancing at her face, I pulled the documents toward me and she removed her hand.

The contract was thicker than it appeared to be at first, and I began reading.

Title: Snr. Forensic and Operational Risk Manager

Salary: $585,000 and a 30% bonus annually. Annual raise of at least 20%.

Company Provided: Apartment, car service, travel allowance (first or business class), company card, unlimited PTO.

Term: 3 years, with auto-renewal.

This was my dream job.

Demonic Workplaces

I continued to read, but by page two I was skimming and by page five, of the twenty total, I was just flipping pages. When I got to the final page, Angel handed me a pen, and I placed it on the signature line.

Looking up, I asked him, "Are you sure you want me for this?"

He nodded and said, "Very sure."

I began to sign my name, feeling a little sting on my finger. When Angel took the pen, I found a drop of blood forming. Somehow, I had pricked myself. Before I could examine it too closely Angel grabbed my finger sliding it in her mouth. The room began to swim as Mr. Showeran, my new boss, stood up and he was a towering eight feet, and said, "Welcome to the team Peter".

ABOUT TEN YEARS LATER

I don't remember what happened in the room after having my finger sucked. What I can tell you is that I have been working for Mr. Showeran for almost ten years. Most of that time, I would have referred to him with many fun names such as Monster, Jerk, Tyrant, and even an Asshole, but as I came to find out, he is a god damned Demon. Literally.

The amazing contract I signed would be considered great except for the part where I gave the ownership of my soul to him until such a time as he decides to let me out of it. For the record, he never lets anyone out of the contract with a few exceptions.

1) You can die, and if you do, the bad crap you have been doing for him since you signed the contract deems that you go to hell to be tortured for eternity.

2) You can kill yourself, again, if you do, the bad crap you have been doing for him since you signed the contract and/or the fact you took your own life deems that you go to hell to be tortured for eternity.

3) You can go insane, then your contract is simply transferred to another part of his "company" where you will be tortured in life and in death for eternity.

My job, it turns out, is very similar to what I actually wanted to do before this all happened with one fun caveat; instead of finding the bad guys and putting them behind bars, I find ways to help the bad guys hide their deeds and ruin the good guys who get in their way. I suppose there is an irony to the fact I have become the person helping to defraud and destroy people like my grandfather.

Angel, as it turns out, is a demon herself. A kind of succubus. They have the ability to be anyone and anything you want them to be and this helps my horrific boss in his recruitment and, as promised, she has been assigned to me this entire time. I have to say that I am in love, true love. I want nobody more than I want her. I miss her when she is not near me. She makes me smile when I think about her. She is truly my everything and there for my every wish.

She no longer looks like she did when we first met. What she looks like and how she treats me changes as my desire does. I don't sometimes notice it anymore, the way a husband will not notice his wife has changed her hair unless it is something radical. I mean, she does everything I need and knows everything I want.

You may think there is no way she could be somebody I love if she is like a robot to my every whim, but it is not like that at all. The succubus also have the ability to alter your emotional state. I never have to tell her anything, she just knows. I don't have bad days since she makes sure that I don't get upset or angry. Instead of frustration, I am challenged. Instead of loss. I am driven to succeed. Instead of feeling guilty, I feel accomplished with a job well done.

One time, I asked her if she loved me. I mean, she says "I love you, too" when I say it to her, but as a demon, I wondered if she was truly happy. She explained that she feeds off of my emotions. So when I am truly happy, angry, frustrated, sad, depressed, etc that she gets truly full. Apparently, this happens quite frequently and I am just lucky I am not feeling any of it. So for this reason, she never has to worry about her ability to survive with me and this makes her feel the closest thing to love a demon can. It turns out that all demons are not so lucky.

So, I continue to do horrible things for shitty people and terrible things to good people. There is, and will not be, a real end to it. I wish I could tell you that I somehow figured out how to be the hero of my story or the story of those whose lives I am helping to destroy. That I was spending all of my free time trying to find a loophole to this and a way to destroy my demon boss and his minions.

I'm not

Demonic Workplaces

I make a ton of money, have a wonderful girlfriend that makes me happy, and live a lifestyle you see in movies or if you are in the top one percent of people on this planet. I figure I have about fifty or so more years before I have to worry about what comes next. Meanwhile, I am taking a trip on a private yacht to the Maldives next week, which I have no doubt I will have to leave in the middle of to help cover up the next crime some idiot CEO does. Hopefully, I can get a tan before that happens.

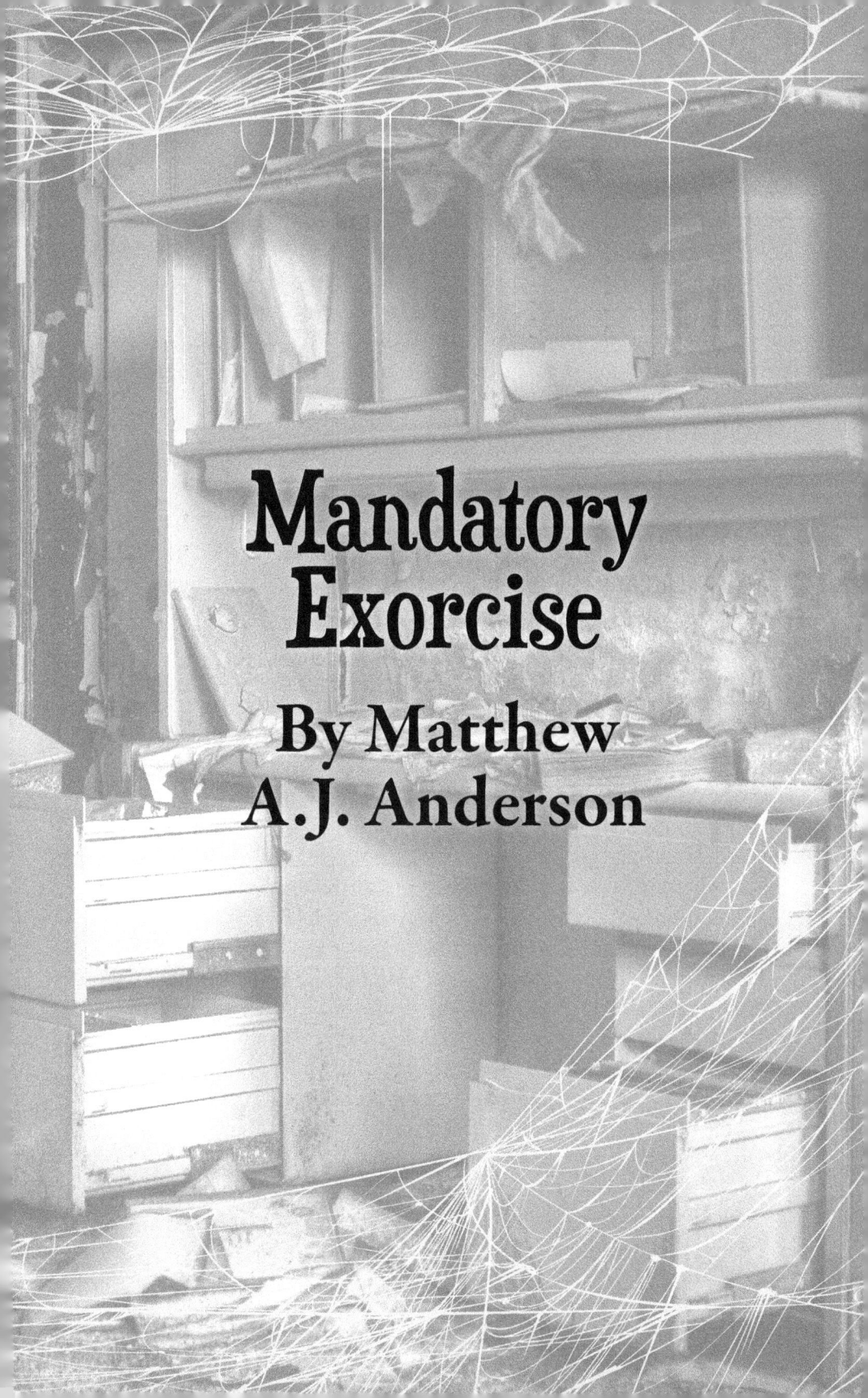

Demonic Workplaces

Even the most unusual work can become mundane over time, whether it be organizing the names of black-listed persons by year, removing all those who had already died, or digitizing the cover-up catalog for the conspiracy department of a top-secret government agency known as *The Kitchen*. Brian had been working in the archives for the "Dishwasher" department for almost a year now, and it had become tedious, but even he had to pause when he recognized a name: *John James Luettgen*.

More commonly known as "The Highway Butcher," Luettgen was a notorious serial killer in Australia in the 1980s. He killed five people before being hunted down and killed by the police.

At least, that's the cover story.

According to the dossier on Brian's desk—a file named "Operation: Black Orchard"—the organization had attempted to create a cover story for some of the many casualties of demonic possession, cult activity, and what the Kitchen colorfully termed "paranormal misadventure." Luettgen wasn't real. His body belonged to an agent killed in the line of duty.

There was a note at the end of the file where the head editor noted:

> "...whilst the media attention was manageable, we failed to appreciate the vigor of the conspiracy theorist community. The interrogator's report (as shown in Doc. 17.) suggests that linking so many disconnected events created conflicting narratives. Whilst the conspiracy theory issue has been neutralized, it is my suggestion that we should not link more than two or three unrelated tragedies so as to maintain a lower profile in future operations."

Brian leaned back in his chair and stared at the ceiling. The fluorescent lights glared back at him. Brian was barely twenty. He'd worked at the Kitchen for two years now, and he couldn't help but ask himself, not for the first time, *What the hell is wrong with this place?*

Brian was snapped out of his occupational consternation when he heard the click of the electronic lock behind him, and he turned to see a man in the standard-issue bulletproof vest that all interdepartmental guards seemed to wear, with a rifle hanging from a strap on his shoulder. He locked eyes with Brian.

"Alright, come on," he said, gesturing for Brian to follow.

Mandatory Exorcise

"What's this about?" asked Brian, not getting up. "I'm in the middle of my work."

"Doin' a sweep, mate. *Come on*," he said impatiently.

"A sweep?" asked Brian.

"Are you *new*?" the guard said, spitting the word "new" like a slur.

"Not really," said Brian.

"Well, it's a mandatory sweep. Orders from the top drawer. All staff, carpark, *now*."

Brian sighed, stood up, and followed the man out of the room. He still didn't understand what was going on, but "top drawer" meant that these orders likely came from the department manager, his boss's boss, meaning it was too far above his security clearance—and pay grade—to argue with it.

"Head for the stairwell. That's a good boy," said the guard as Brian stepped outside and saw the dozen other employees on this floor had been corralled into the hallway and were being led toward the stairwell. He recognized the balding head of Lucas, the lead archivist, and headed over to him.

"What's this about?" asked Brian.

"Probably another screw-up in the Oven. They're always trying to play God and screwing around with sub-dimensionals..." moaned Lucas as he headed into the open stairwell.

"What?" asked Brian, but his voice was drowned out by the echoing footfalls of a hundred standard-issue leather shoes as he entered the fire-escape-cum-stairwell. Brian followed the herd down the grimly lit concrete steps until they reached the bottom and stepped out into the building's underground carpark. There, he saw a hundred or more staff scattered around the blacktop. Brian even recognized David Morrissey, head of the department, speaking with some interns. More people were spilling out of the stairwell, so Brian headed deeper into the clustered people. As he headed further, he saw that someone had put up a cheap barricade blocking off half the carpark. The barrier was just a retractable black ribbon on metal poles, but behind the ribbon were half a dozen armed guards with bulletproof vests, all holding rifles. At the center of the barricade was a windowless van.

Brian approached one of the agents behind the barricade.

"Stay back from the line, sir," said the woman, and Brian saw her muscles tense and her finger curl around the trigger.

"Okay," he said, taking a deliberate step back, so he stood a meter away from the edge. "I just want to know what's going on. I'm *kind of* new..."

"Just follow instructions. It'll be over quickly," she said sternly.

Demonic Workplaces

Brian nodded and headed back into the crowd. Stove Agents were very well-trained, and his own life had been saved more than once by the Kitchen's tactics and defense department, but after working in the Dishwasher archives, he had come across a term: *mental slippage*. Working for a secret organization that dealt with the supernatural, deadly, and outright demonic could be stressful at the best of times, and whilst the term could refer to employees from any departments, it was clear that Stove agents were more prone to "mental slippage." Whilst the documents never actually spelled it out, from the context of some disciplinary documents and black-listed names, "mental slippage" seemed to be the Kitchen's politically correct way of referring to members of staff likely to "go postal."

"Can I have your attention, please? Everyone, please, thank you... we will begin shortly," said a woman, her posh, almost-English accent projected through a megaphone. Brian couldn't see her, but she was near the black van. "Thanks to recent events in the Northern Territory, we have encountered a new demon presence, and as is standard company policy..." Several groans and annoyed mumbles rippled through the crowd, and she raised her voice to drown out, "...we are carrying out an organization-wide sweep of all Kitchen employees for potential demonic possession. All employees must be exorcised. This is mandatory. I repeat, this is not optional. Anyone who does not undergo exorcism willingly will be detained and exorcised forcibly. Thank you..."

There was a high-pitched whine of feedback from the speaker as the woman lowered the megaphone, then Brian heard more grumbling from the crowd.

Brian turned to a man he didn't recognize, an older man in a striped tie.

"Excuse me, sorry, but do you know what they mean by 'exorcise?'" asked Brian.

"Yes..." sighe the man glumly. "First time?"

Brian nods.

"They got a machine they use to suck 'em out," he said, nodding toward the van. "Consider yourself lucky. Years ago, they used to stick the tubes all the way down..." he gestures with a hooked finger toward his throat, "it *still* hurts like hell, but it's not as bad as it used to be."

Mandatory Exorcise

"Alright, we're ready to begin," the posh woman called over the megaphone. "Things will move a lot smoother if we sort ourselves into alphabetical order. Can everyone with a first name beginning with 'A' please come to the front? Then we can get the B's behind them, the C's, etcetera…"

Brian joined the people shuffling to the front, beside the black van. There was some awkward banter as people asked each other their names and tried to get in order—two men were arguing whether "Chris" came before "Christopher"—but he stood in line and watched as the posh woman stood at the front with a clipboard. He actually recognized her. He'd seen her organizing an operation over a year ago. He couldn't remember her name, but she was the department head of the Oven, the research and development department of the Kitchen.

"Adrien Palomar," she said, looking up. The man at the front of the line stepped forward. She knocked on the door of the van, and it slid open. Brian was peering around the four people in front of him, trying to see what was going on. The man disappeared inside the van, and the door slid. After a few seconds, there was a muffled whirring sound inside the van. It sounded like a powerful vacuum cleaner. Over the sound of the machine, Brian heard the sound of screaming. A minute later, the sound stopped, and he heard the sliding door on the other side of the van slide open, and Brian could hear coughing as the man staggered out.

"Next!" called out the woman. "Ashley Valdez."

The next woman stepped up and headed into the van.

"Hey," Brian said, tapping the shoulder of the woman in front of him, a chubby, middle-aged woman with short hair. "Do you know what they're doing in there?"

"I've only been here a week," she said, clearly terrified. "But, I'm *not* a smoker. My supervisor says it's worse if you're a smoker…"

"Next!" called out the woman, as the machine fell silent. "Audrey Cauldwell?"

Brian was nervous, but watching the woman in front shift nervously almost made him feel better. At least he wasn't the only one shitting themselves.

"Alright, next!" called out the woman. "Benjamin Blake."

The woman took a step, then froze, stepped back, and glanced around at Brian.

"Are you Benjamin?" she asked. He shook his head.

Demonic Workplaces

The posh woman sighed and picked up her megaphone, and Brian quickly covered his ears.

"Benjamin Blake! Step forward, please!" After scanning over the crowds of people, she lowered the megaphone and turned to one of the Stove guards. "Find Mister Blake, please. Use force, if necessary..." She then glanced at her clipboard. "Alright... Brenda Vidal?"

As the woman ahead stepped inside, Brian saw her sit in a car seat facing backward just before the door slid closed.

"Brian Lockburn?" the posh woman asked, glancing at him. Brian just nodded, and she looked down at her clipboard. The whirring sound from the van began again, and Brian started shifting on his feet nervously.

"How often do you exorcise a demon doing this?" Brian asked.

"About one in six," she said, sounding bored.

"One in six *people*?"

"No, no," she said, frowning. "One in six *sweeps*."

"Oh... well, how many demons do you usually find?" Brian asked.

"*All* of them," she said sternly, staring at him.

The machine stopped, and they could hear Brenda stepping out from the other side.

"You're next, Mister Lockburn,"

The door to the van slid open, and Brian headed inside, sitting down in the car seat. He flinched when he saw the two rifles pointed at his head.

"Alright, make yourself comfortable," said a bespectacled young man in the lab coat, who was standing between the two armed guards. The guard nearest the door slid it closed, and the scientist reached for a clear, flexible pipe near his feet that appeared to be wrapped in a metal spring. One end of the tube was fitted with a rigid, black facemask with a rubber seal shaped to fit one's nose and mouth; the other end led toward a machine that the scientist was standing over. It was the size of a microwave and looked a bit like a car engine, except it was covered in glass panels and gauges.

"Alright, just do up your seatbelt," said the scientist, and Brian complied. Then, he held out the tube with a gloved hand, the end wobbling toward Brian.

"Just put this on and fasten the strap around your head," he said.

With two guns trained on him, Brian didn't hesitate to affix the mask, pulling the strap over his head.

"Perfect. Now, take a deep breath. This will hurt a bit..." he said.

Mandatory Exorcise

Brian inhaled, and got a lungful of air that smelled like oil and rubber, and held it. The scientist flipped a switch, and the machine burst to life. The sound drowned out all other noise, like sticking your head in a wind tunnel. The pressure immediately increased in the tube, clamping the mask to Brian's face. He felt cold air around his lips and nose, and it started to drag the air out of his lungs. Brian exhaled, but the pressure grew and grew. It felt like the cold air was reaching down his throat. He coughed, but the pressure increased. He coughed more, but he was out of breath. He felt sick. He tried to gasp for air, but he couldn't. He wanted to scream for them to stop, but he was breathless. Voiceless. His chest was hot and cold at the same time.

Then the scientist flipped the switch, and Brian gasped for breath. It was rubbery and stale, and so cold it made him cough, but it was air. Brian went to remove the straps, but the scientist grabbed his hand.

"Not yet..." he said as he looked down at the machine. He was reading the gauges and checking one of the small glass vials on the machine.

"Okay, you're clean. Take it off," he said.

Brian practically ripped the strap off his head, giving it to the scientist, who cleaned the inside with a wet wipe as Brian undid his seatbelt.

"That hurt... like hell..." Brian gasped. The guard to Brian's right approached him with a white plastic strip, wrapping it tightly around Brian's wrist, and used a device that looked like a stapler to fuse it together.

"Keep this on for the rest of the day," he grunted, then he opened the van door beside him. Brian staggered out, taking careful breaths as they closed the door. He glanced at the plastic wristband and saw it was a cheap hospital bracelet labeled with the date. It was still hot where it had been melted together, but it was nothing compared to the ache in his chest.

"Keep going," said a female guard. Brian glanced up and recognized her as the woman he'd *tried* to talk to earlier.

"Where?" he gasped.

"Head up the ramp," she said, pointing to the two-lane ramp that cars used to drive between levels of the carpark, where another Stove guard was posted.

"I have to walk *up*?" Brian asked, weakly. *Had that machine bruised his lungs?*

"You can't break the personnel quarantine."

With a groan, Brian headed toward the ramp. After several painful deep breaths and a few swear words, Brian climbed the ramp, and the guard at the top pointed him toward the elevators. Brian crossed the empty carpark level, where a guard was leaning against the wall.

"Use the lifts, not the stairs," said the guard, pressing the call button.

"Where to?" Brian asked.

"Back to work," said the guard.

"Really? We just..." Brian mimed typing on a keyboard. "*Right* back to it?"

"Yeah, unless you've got a medical certificate or something..." said the guard.

The elevator arrived, so Brian stepped in and pushed the button for Basement Level 1, the Archives. He was finally starting to realize why everyone else had hated this whole process so much since *all* staff had to go through that painful ordeal. It didn't take long for the elevator to reach his floor, but when the doors opened, Brian didn't step out.

All staff... which included the bosses from the top floor. He didn't really want to go right back to work after that, and if he decided to take an hour-long coffee break... who was going to stop him? Brian pressed the button for the highest floor the elevator could reach, Level 35.

O-J, a friend that worked in maintenance, once showed him the rooftop. It had a great view of the city, and it's where a lot of the janitors and maintenance staff went to smoke. Brian thought the fresh air might do his lungs some good.

He stepped out onto the clean management level with its green carpets and glass walls and headed into the stairwell to scale the last two floors. The door was kept ajar by a rusty, dented old soup can weighed down with wet cigarette butts. Brian pushed open the door and immediately felt the cool breeze whipping past as he stepped outside. From here, he looked out at the city. There were a few skyscrapers much taller, and the William Street office loomed large, shadowed only by the clouds in the sky; but below, he could see the Brisbane River reflecting the sun off its brown water, as well he saw the cars along the Inner City Bypass constantly streaming between the South-East and West.

He had to breathe carefully so as not to further injure his tortured lungs, but he slowly took a deep breath. He was actually starting to feel better, but as he looked out over the sunlit metropolis, leaning against the concrete wall that surrounded the edge of the building, he couldn't ignore that thought in the back of his mind: *Some days, I really hate this job.*

Nobody ever *chooses* to apply for the Kitchen. It was top-secret, after all. As Brian had come to learn, by cataloging the human resources files for the

Dishwasher, there were four categories of employee enlistment: Detainees, Recruits, Victims & Witnesses.

"Detainees" were cultists or other "disruptive individuals" captured by the Stove that could be persuaded to switch sides, but few survived long enough to be captured, let alone undergo employee orientation. "Recruits" were people sought out for their innate talents or accomplishments, usually scientists or soldiers, recruited for military or research. "Victims" were persons who had been directly attacked, demonically or supernaturally, and had survived. Brian himself was a "victim," a survivor of an attempted blood sacrifice that killed most of his friends and left him more than a little scarred, and not *just* from the cut on his thigh. Lastly, there were "Witnesses," people who had seen something they shouldn't have seen and couldn't be convinced by the Dishwasher's cover story.

Technically, anyone enlisted to join does have a *choice* as to whether they wish to join... but the choice is usually "you're *with* us, or *against* us," which was an effective incentive for employment, but it tended to negatively affect employee morale.

Brian was brought back to reality as he heard someone trudging up the stairwell and watched the door as a guard pushed it open, holding her rifle at the ready.

"Benjamin Blake?" she asked, aiming at him.

"No, I'm Brian," he said, holding up his hands. He gave his right hand a little shake to show off the bracelet on his wrist. The guard stepped forward, still aiming the gun at him as she closed the distance, the wind catching her chin-length hair.

"Are you alone up here?" she asked.

"Yeah... I haven't seen anyone else," said Brian. "I'm not sure where that guy is."

She finally lowered her gun, and Brian finally exhaled, but she was still glaring at him.

"What are you doing up here?" she asked. She was slightly shorter than him, but he felt small as she glared at him.

"I just needed some fresh air," said Brian.

"You work in management?"

"No... I work in Archives. Dishwasher files..."

"That sucks," she said.

"Tell me about it..." said Brian. "What's this about? Have I done something wrong?"

"No, it just makes it more difficult," she said.

"What do you mean?" asked Brian.

Suddenly, she kissed him.

It was shocking, a little exciting, but mostly confusing. He could smell her sweat and taste the smoke on her breath. After a second, Brian finally reacted, trying to push her off, but the arms around his neck gripped tighter, and he felt the heat of her exhaling into his mouth. Hot smoke, but not cigarette smoke—it was like wood smoke and charred meat—it poured out of her and into him. Suddenly, the guard collapsed onto the ground as the last of the thick, demonic smoke spilled out of her mouth and crept into Brian's throat and nostrils.

Without thinking, literally without even realizing what his body was doing, Brian turned and slammed his head into the concrete wall beside him.

He blacked out.

It's a common misconception that demons, psychics, and other brain-infiltrating aliens are capable of taking control of a person that is "weak-minded," but this is simply untrue. No conscious, living human, even with high gullibility, low intelligence, or a learning disability, is naturally "weak-minded," all human brains have similar voltage and conductivity, which is much stronger than demonic influence. Thus, field research has shown that demons possess their victims by either rendering their host unconscious or otherwise mentally incapacitating them. Whilst there have been rare cases of demons drugging their hosts with sedatives, most use their limited control to inflict brain damage so as to render their victim unconscious or comatose. There are even some cases where hosts have been brain-dead, but this is rare as even though a demon can keep the body alive for a while longer, dead brains tend to rot and liquefy, causing systemic organ failure after a few days.

The next thing Brian knew, he was staring at the road, driving past warehouses and large fences in the early morning, but to his dazed eyes, the road looked like the speckled black of the night sky, and the buildings on either side were made of glass and light. *Looks like I'm in space,* Brian thought. Seeing his fingers on the wheel, he tried to flex them, but only his index fingers moved.

"No, no... not *now*," said his mouth. It was his voice, but not his words.

Must be stiff... cold... like space. But I'm not cold. The ships on autopilot.

Mandatory Exorcise

"Just a few more hours," it said, gritting his teeth, but he wasn't controlling his mouth or his foot as it pressed the pedal, speeding faster down the road that Brian was hallucinating into starlight.

Brian's body drove up to a security fence, stopped, and wound down the window.

No, cold... Brian flinched, his whole body jerking back, then his arm forcefully reached out to swipe his security card in the slot.

"Will you just stop it and go back to sleep?!" the demon growled. The gate opened.

His body angrily wound the window up and kept driving onto the site of a wastewater management facility. *Not stiff. It's fighting me... I can hear my voice...*

"We're almost there. Just sit there a little longer..."

As they drove through the site, Brian started to recognize large water tanks as they drove past them. It reminded him of how his work kept the secret entrance to the secure containment and storage department in a facility just like this one. *How did I drive here? I don't know the way.*

They drove up to what looked like a large, white shed and stopped by a large tree. Still sitting in the car, his hand slid his mobile phone out of his pocket and dialed. After a few seconds, a scratchy-voiced man answered the phone.

"Hello?" the phone answered.

"This is Brian, from the Cabinet, requesting gate access," it said.

No, I'm not... Brian thought.

"Mhmm..." said the phone. "I'll need an authorization code."

"Flock. Puzzle. Amaze. Shiver. Gust."

The phone hung up, and a few seconds later, the large roller door started to go up.

I didn't realize the Fridge was in space... or is it? I can't breathe space...

His foot pressed on the accelerator, and he drove into the building, inside of which was a large ramp leading deep down a hidden tunnel.

"Whoa..." Brian mumbled.

"Stop that," the demon responded. "Just go back to sleep. This is all a dream..."

I woke up from driving... did I fall asleep driving? No, then I'd crash. How did my car get here? Was I asleep? Why can't I remember...?

Brian was lucky to have regained consciousness at all, but his recovery was gradual. The tunnel leading to the underwater facility was almost five miles long, and it took him the whole journey to be able to distinguish his hallucinations from reality. The car drove into the facility's spiral carpark, passing several cars as Brian began to understand.

No, the car is real… which means that you're real. But you shouldn't be here.

"No!" yelled Brian, and he cranked the handbrake. The car screeched to a stop.

"What the hell are you doing?! Are you trying to kill us?" the demon said.

"I want… *you* out," said Brian, a little groggily.

"We're *almost* done…" the demon whined. It sounded pitiful. "Don't fight this."

"Not *ffffuh*-ffffight," he slurred, "I'm luh… *living.*"

"Let's just park the car first, okay?"

Brian didn't respond, but with a will of their own, his hands released the handbrake and turned the car into the nearest car space, then switched off the engine.

"Just relax for five more minutes, okay? Then I'll be done," it said.

"Nnnnnnno…" Brian slurred. "You are a… *demon.*"

"That's what *you* call us," it said. "We're just people your organization hunts down."

"P-p-p… parr…" Brian stammered, forgetting the word. "…I'm stopping you."

"How? You can barely talk," said the demon.

"It's… my *job.*"

"But why? You can't trust the Kitchen. They're corrupt. Don't fight me, Brian. *Help me.* Once I free my friends, I'll go. But if you resist, the Kitchen could kill us both. I just need to hand over the papers, get my friends. Then I'll go."

"Fffffriends?" asked Brian.

"Yes. I just want to rescue my friends that were captured. I need to save them."

"Ssssave them…"

"Yes. Will you help me?"

Brian didn't respond for a few seconds.

"…yesss."

Satisfied, Brian's hand picked up the folder on the passenger seat, got out of the car, and headed into the round central column that housed the entrance. The demon walked over to the desk.

"How can I help you?" asked the young man at the desk.

Mandatory Exorcise

"I'm Brian. I called earlier about resolving a missing record," it said.

"Ohh, yes, the deep-freeze catalog?"

"That's the one," it said, holding out Brian's security card. "I need to cross-reference the vial's detainee number..."

"Alright," said the man, scanning the card. "The floor manager's waiting for you on level ten."

Brian's lips smiled at the man. Then he headed for the elevators in the middle of the room. It stepped inside, pressed the button, and sighed with relief as the doors closed.

"Thank you," it whispered. "I was worried when you woke up, but now... I don't know how to repay you."

"Okay..." said Brian.

The elevator doors opened onto a corridor with concrete floors. There were two Stove guards standing by the door and a pot-bellied man wearing a tailored suit.

"Brian? I'm George. Welcome to Deep-Freeze," he said, offering a hand.

"My pleasure," the demon said, taking his hand.

"I'm... demon," said Brian, and he forced himself to his knees. "Help me."

Brian shakingly forced his hands behind his head as he backed away. The guards looked confused, but after a few seconds, one of them pulled out his gun.

"You heard him. Cuff the man. Now!"

"What are you doing?" hissed the demon. It tried to pull away and get to his feet, but Brian used all his strength to tense his muscles, to keep him still.

"My... job..."

The other guard bound his wrists with zip-ties on his belt and dragged him to his feet.

"No, I was joking!" pleaded the demon. "This is a mistake!"

"No... get it out," said Brian. The guards ignored them both, dragging him to a holding cell.

The Fridge was designed to store demons, not extract them, so it took an hour for Stove Agents to arrive with a portable exorcise machine and drag the demon out. Because of the whole ordeal, Brian had forgotten what it had felt like, but he soon remembered.

Demonic Workplaces

He coughed and choked as the scientist switched off the machine. He could still taste the smoke on his tongue, his chest burned, and his lungs felt like they'd had their veins ripped out. But his muscles relaxed. He felt free.

The scientist removed a small glass vial with a metal cap. It was an inch-long cylinder and only as wide as a marker; inside, it looked like it was full of swirling, grey oil.

"That's it?" Brian asked, looking at the captured demon.

"Well, you'll need a psych eval," said the scientist. "But first, medical. You probably have brain damage."

"Mhmm..." Brian grunted. The scientist stood up and walked over to the floor manager, who had been watching from the corner the whole time. Brian watched them talk, but his vision was fuzzy.

"Get your guards to tail him until he's had a psychic evaluation. Then we'll need a debrief and have the dishwasher trace his steps to see when he was first possessed..." the scientist sighed heavily, "...*and* I have to recommend a mandatory sweep."

"Again?" groaned George, rubbing his chest. "We just had one three weeks ago, doc."

"Yeah... if this one slipped through, we'll have to update the procedure. We're getting sloppy."

"And how many got through before?" asked George, pointing at the vial in the scientist's fingers. "He was headed for demon lock-up. If he popped a few vials, all hell would've broke loose."

"Well, we got lucky this time..." said the scientist, handing the vial to George.

"Don't forget to fill out the paperwork for this," he said, waving the vial.

"Yeah, yeah..." said the scientist, waving his hand dismissively as he left the room.

"Can I go?" Brian asked, rubbing his throbbing head.

"Not yet, mate," said George. "Medical; Psych eval; Interrogation..."

"My head hurts..."

"Probably a brain injury, but don't worry. With rehab, you'll be back to work in a month."

"Work?" groaned Brian.

"Tell me about it..." said George, then he headed out of the room to go find the right paperwork for this kind of situation.

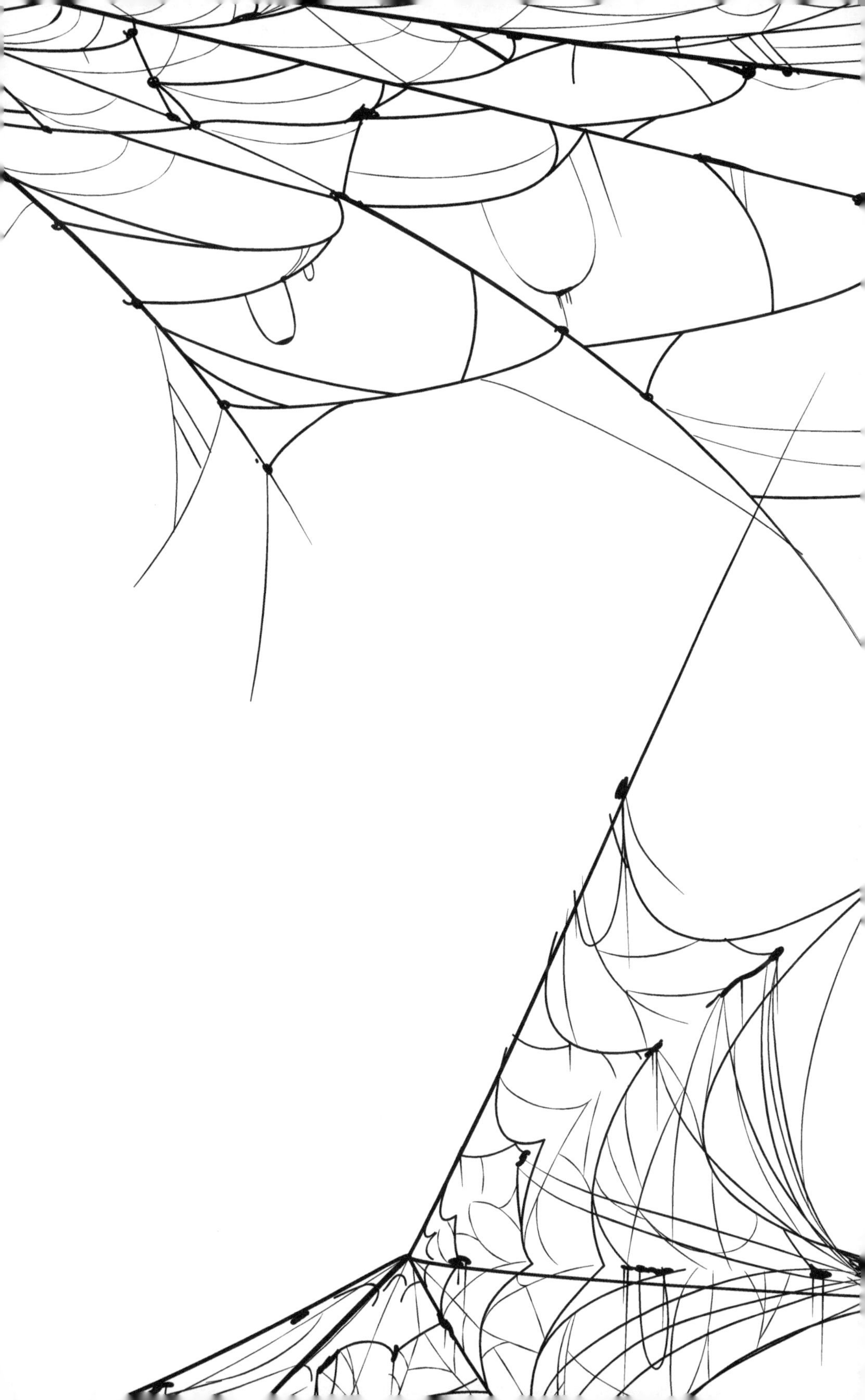

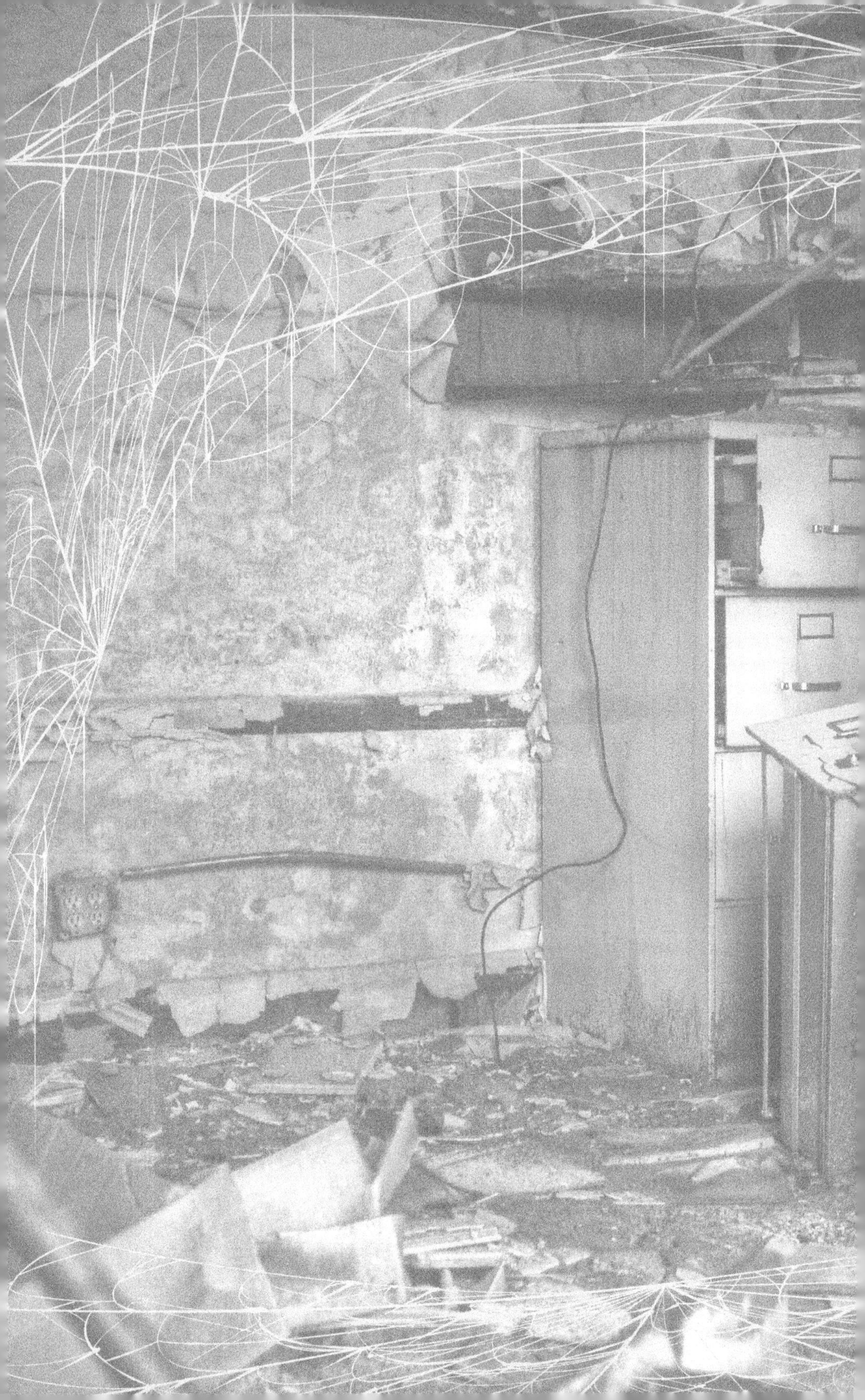

The Merger
By E. Gallagher

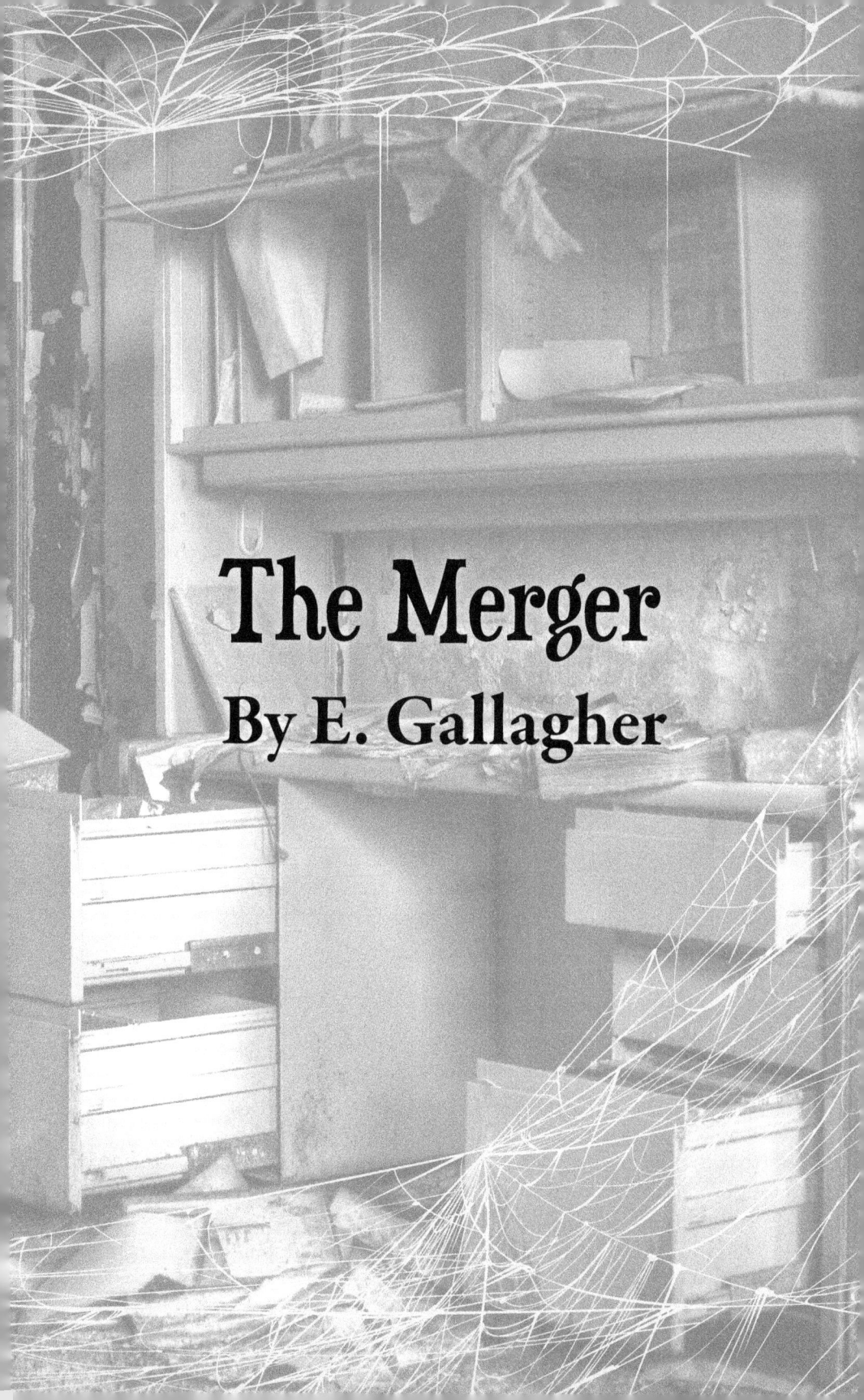

Demonic Workplaces

My morning commute is foreplay to misery. Sunlight is barely peeking through the smog, and East Main Street is already swarming with traffic. Horns blare. Tempers rage. Commuters fester impotently and beat their fists against the dash.

A shimmering Tesla swerves in front of me, cutting me off as the streetlight ahead turns yellow. The driver pauses to flip me off before speeding away as if *I* were the one inconveniencing *him*. I slam on my brakes. Tires screech as my car shudders to a halt. I'm still ignoring that clunking sound. The driver behind me lays on his horn and leans out his window. I hear a muffled, "Hey, asshole!"

I sigh and turn up the radio.

Violin strings shriek above frenzied wails of anguish. I hate this song. The last ninety seconds of this track is just one continuous scream. Asmoday in accounting swears it's the cultural zeitgeist of tomorrow. Honestly, I'm starting to think that guy is a real douche. The bass drops, except it's just tornado sirens and cats yowling. I guess this part is a little catchy.

Asmoday's shitty music has deteriorated into a protracted scream by the time I reach the parking garage. A pair of red eyes glow from within the ticket booth. I dutifully slow and roll my window down. Yes, the clunk was definitely louder that time. The beast inside the ticket booth growls softly as I punch the button and wait for my ticket. Instead of spitting out a ticket, the machine emits a series of shrilly beeps as an error code illuminates the screen.

I jab the ticket button several times in quick succession. A concussive roar erupts from the ticket booth. The volume rattles my eardrums. A thin mist of concrete dust shakes loose from the ceiling and several car alarms go off within the parking garage. I roll forward a few feet, pulling even with the ticket booth window. *Clunk*. The beast is glaring, positively quivering with feral rage.

He hands me a day pass.

I sigh again. Every fucking morning.

I weave my way down to sublevel C and snag a parking spot in the back corner of the garage. Not that we'd have a shortage if any of my coworkers could park between the damn lines. I turn my car off, plunging the area into darkness. There is no way that the feeble fluorescent bulbs down here are up to code. They flicker precariously, stirring shadows between the rows of abandoned cars. I sit in my now-silent vehicle for a few moments, mustering the will to tolerate the day. A hot breath brushes against the nape of my neck as a child's voice begins to sing. The lullaby is slow and hauntingly monotone.

The Merger

It sounds like Asmoday's mellow phase. An ominous chortle echoes above me. Another sigh escapes. I know better than to look up.

My car is filling with discorporate giggles by the time I manifest the will to go inside. Something scuttles along the wall beside me as I pick my way toward the office.

Fucking Mondays, man.

The office is a liminal space labyrinth of cubicles and monochromatic hallways. Tendrils of black smoke curl along the floor, obfuscating the dated geometric carpeting. The walls haven't started to bleed yet, but it's still early in the day. I brace myself as I reach the Office of Quality Improvement.

Malphus is levitating by my cubicle when I arrive. The past year has taken a toll on him. His complexion has a charred cast and his fingers have started to elongate into needle-like claws. Every time I see him, his eyes seem to have recessed further into his skull.

Becca sits in the adjacent cubicle, nervously typing as she pretends not to stare at Malphus. Her homemade barrettes jiggle as she hammers on her keyboard, giving her the vague appearance of a kaleidoscope with palsy.

"Good morning," she squeaks as I approach.

Malphus clears his throat. The sound is like a fork against a glass plate. Becca jumps in her seat behind him.

"Now that our day-shifters have arrived," he begins, "let's have the morning huddle."

Day-shifters. Malphus barely contains his disdain for the human workforce. He is perpetually insulted by our petty need for things like bathroom breaks and sleep, and hates that we lack his suprabiological work ethic.

"Today we have a sync at 9:00. There's a new format for the quality improvement PowerPoint, so make sure that slide deck is updated by 8:00 for me to review."

I look down at my watch. The time is 7:45.

Malphus continues, "Then the staff meeting will be at 10:00. Valefor will ask for an update on the quality improvement survey, so let's make sure we have all our ducks in a row there. That meeting should only take a few hours, so we'll regroup down here at 3:00 for a debriefing."

Malphus chews his lip as his head rotates in a slow circle, trying to recall if he left anything out.

"Oh, and close of business huddle at 5:00. Becca, let's circle back before the sync real quick. I want to discuss your last expense report."

Demonic Workplaces

Becca is visibly trembling now. One of her barrettes, a yellow butterfly, looks like it might take flight. I slump into my chair and open Outlook to search for the new PowerPoint format from Malphus. I'm almost halfway through updating my slide deck when Asmoday slithers into my cubicle.

"Hey, partner, running late on your slides, huh?"

I do not have time for this shit right now. I nod curtly, not turning away from my screen. Asmoday curls up on my desk, oblivious.

"Man, do I have some great new tracks for you to check out. Listen to this one."

The cubicle fills with a symphony of machine gun fire and Gregorian chants.

Malphus rises from Becca's cubicle, hovering near the ceiling as he sneers down across the partition. "What have I said about playing music in the office? This is a professional environment."

"I'm sorry, sir," I mutter.

Asmoday's smirk rips across his face, flesh unzipping as his smile stretches from ear to ear. "Looks like you're busy. But hey, did you hear we have a new PowerPoint template?"

"Yes," I grit out, gesturing toward my computer screen.

"I'll send it to you."

God dammit.

At least the 9:00 sync is relatively uneventful. The PowerPoint update has been updated again. We're going back to Times New Roman in 12-point font, so I'll need to redo the QI deck. Malphus also wants an Excel tracker of the response time for all inter-departmental requests from the past three months.

"We need data points," he says, "to highlight the inefficiency of the system."

I already know I'll have to pull overtime to consolidate that amount of data. An expenditure of time that, I'm sure, is in no way contributing to the inefficiency of the system.

We break out to prepare for the staff meeting, and Malphus floats back to his office. I roll my chair around to Becca's cubicle. She's staring blankly at her computer, chewing the ragged cuticle of her left thumb.

"Hey Becca, can you believe this? Two formatting updates before 10:00."

She lets out a terse laugh. "So ridiculous. At least you don't have to deal with these expense reports. Malphus wants the entire fiscal budget spent before next month. He's still mad that we had an overage last year."

The Merger

I nod. "Oh yeah, I could do without another year of lectures about us asking for budget cuts."

She rolls her eyes and giggles.

"Hey, do you ever get sick of this place?" I ask, "Like actually physically drained by it all?"

"You mean the merger stuff?"

"No, I mean the rest of it. The morning huddle to prepare for the sync meeting, where we prepare for the staff meeting. The debrief to summarize the staff meeting and the close of business huddle to summarize the debrief. I mean, I probably only do about two hours of work every day and I'm *still* pulling overtime because of all these damn meetings."

Becca stares down at the floor, avoiding my gaze.

"Hey, I should tell you." She pauses before continuing, "I think I'm going to put in for a transfer."

"Oh, to another department?"

She looks up, yellow butterfly flapping furiously as she shakes her head no. My heart sinks as I catch her meaning.

"Wait, what? Becca, why would you do that? They haven't even left this building since the merger. You seriously want to be here forever?"

Her lip trembles. "No. I mean, it's just that... look, I really need the money. And yeah, I know I'd be here, well, forever. But I wouldn't *experience* being here anymore. Not really. I think I need that right now."

I gape at her, dumbfounded. I can't account for the way my throat tightens, for the anger that swells in my veins.

"I've already mentioned it to Malphus. We're going to look at a contract this afternoon."

I can't believe it. We both hate it here, but this? Then again, I know she can't quit. Her kid is sick. Something autoimmune and expensive. She probably does need that productivity bonus. I fumble for a response and lamely settle on, "I don't know what to say, Becca. Whatever you need to do."

She smiles weakly. "Yeah, thanks."

I slowly roll back to my own cubicle, head buzzing. I'm still preoccupied when we regroup and head upstairs for the staff meeting.

The staff meeting is held in an elegantly appointed conference hall. The room is dominated by an ornate ebony wood table that probably costs more than my house. Floor-to-ceiling windows line the long edge of the room, which is capped at either end by industrial-sized Smart Boards. Several rows of chairs encircle the central meeting table. I take my customary seat, smashed against the window next to Jeff from accounting. Becca finds a chair along the wall on the opposite side of the room. She catches my eye several times, trying to force a reactionary smile. I redouble my efforts to avoid her gaze. There's something in my anger towards her that I can't seem to look directly at right now.

The room fills with a droning buzz that gives way to disembodied yips and howls. Black smoke twists and rises from the floor. Lights flicker. I guess the boss is here. The back of my chair digs painfully into my shoulder blades. The plush cushions of the chairs abutting the conference table look enviously soft. I do my best not to squirm as the CEO enters the room.

Derrick Hadley III, Senior Executive and darling of Forbes, never wears the same suit twice. He strides in, amicably chatting with a small entourage of demons. Bael stoops on Derrick's left, his cropped horns brushing the ceiling. Bael's kneecaps bend backward, bowing outward at a painful angle as he shuffles along on all fours. The organic orb floating on Derrick's right is Asteroth. Asteroth has translucent skin that barely obfuscates the pulsating of his eerily humanoid viscera. Long tentacles drag behind him, twitching in response to a joke Derrick makes as they reach the head of the conference table. Derrick is ribbing them about something that happened out on the 18th hole this morning. Derrick's secretary is an ephemeral shade that flickers nervously between planes of existence. She darts around the trio, filling their goblets with something viscous and red.

Derrick gathers the silence as it falls across the conference room. Once the smoke clears and the disembodied howls fade, he flashes a perfect real-estate smile.

"Hey, team." That's how he always addresses us, *team*. "I recently had the opportunity to go on a leadership retreat with Asteroth and Bael here. I had time to reflect on all of the wonderful things we've accomplished with the merger."

I groan inwardly. I already hate staff meetings. Staff meetings are the main event of cooperate life, the championship of masturbatory self-promotion and sniping ground for inter-departmental feuds. Nothing drags a staff meeting out longer than a boss who waxes poetic about the art of leadership. I mentally buckle myself in. Jeff slouches slightly in the seat beside me.

Derrick takes a deep swig from his goblet, wiping a crimson smear from the corner of his mouth before continuing, "Three years ago, the job market was imploding. We suffered from a labor force that was insufficient to meet industry demands. Meanwhile, the Great Kingdom below was overburdened,

The Merger

smothering under the seemingly unresolvable constraint of limited space. I'll never forget when the idea struck me, a vision for a brighter tomorrow."

It occurs to me that Derrick is quoting his own Times article. Ugh, this guy. I recall that they had also interviewed a few notable dredged souls for that piece on Derrick. Machiavelli, for instance, had called him "a bit much." I stifle my sigh this time. Derrick is on a roll now, increasingly animated as he recounts the events of the merger.

"This symbiotic expansion has not only alleviated overpopulation in Hell, but through intentional metamorphosis, we have created a workforce that can operate perpetually without biological limitations. This merger is a new dawn of unprecedented productivity, and our team is at its cutting edge."

I stare at my watch as Derrick drones, basking in the thrill of his own brilliance. It takes him twelve minutes and forty-three seconds to use the phrase "the art of leadership." Jeff shoots me a triumphant glance at this. I owe Jeff twenty dollars now.

The meeting drags on. I try my best not to wince as exhausted business jargon hurtles across the room. "Circle back ... lean in ... touch base ... actionable items ... run up the flagpole ... move the goalpost ... hard stop ... game changer ... synergy." Jeff and I have joked about making bingo cards.

At least there are some interesting squabbles to watch. The lagging interdepartmental request process comes up and Malphus gets into it with the employee resources department about who should charter the blame. The finance department ousts a few managers for late expenditure reports. The managers immediately ally and deflect, charging the finance department with poor communication and unrealistic timelines.

Finally, Derrick calls the meeting to a close and asks if there are any further questions.

Of course, fucking Sabnock has one.

His points are irrelevant to ninety percent of the room and could have been addressed in a single email, but the ensuing discussion adds another twenty minutes to the staff meeting.

Derrick closes again. "Okay, team, anything else to add?"

I will literally exorcise Sabnock if he raises his hand again.

Blissfully, no one has anything else to say. I slip Jeff a twenty-dollar bill and head back downstairs to debrief.

I sag into my chair after the debrief. Today has been exhausting. I have about two hours to work on my summary of interdepartmental requests before the close-of-business huddle. This is essentially the only part of my day where I can get shit done, but even that won't be unobstructed. Malphus calls at least once per hour to get a progress report. Sure enough, I've only been working for twenty minutes when Malphus calls from his office.

"I need a progress report on your interdepartmental request tracker."

"I'm 18.6% done, sir."

"I want that in Arial 10-point font."

"Yes, sir."

Click

Another forty-five minutes later, the phone rings again.

"I need a progress report on your interdepartmental request tracker."

"Up to 37.92% done, sir."

"Requests completed within ten days need to be highlighted in green."

"Yes, sir."

Click

On and on it goes. I quote him arbitrary percentages to highlight the stupidity of his intrusive progress reports. He never seems to get the joke. I am making good headway, though. I get so lost in columns and rows of data that I'm startled to look down and see the time is 4:57. I lean back in my chair, trying to stretch out the knots in my back that have been tightening like screws since I got into my car this morning.

Malphus floats out of his office, bobbing softly towards my cubicle. I'm about to tell him that my tracker is 49.834% done when something seizes in my chest.

I gasp in shock. *Becca.*

Revulsion knots in my gut as Becca slowly steps out into the hallway. Her neck is twisted. Her head leans over her left shoulder, hanging at an exaggerated angle. Her eyes are a solid milky white, rotated ninety degrees into vertical slits. The barrettes are perfectly still. She no longer trembles.

"Ah, I see you've noticed Becca's enhancement," Malphus croons.

"S-she's possessed!"

Becca's jaw clicks out of its socket as she tries to speak. Her mouth sags, opening into an elongated and perpetual scream.

"Uhhhhhhhgggggaaaahhhhh," she manages.

"There, there. Let's give you some time to settle in," Malphus says before turning to me. "How far along are you on the tracker?"

"I'm, um, about halfway done," I stammer.

"Good. I want that done by close of business tomorrow."

"Yes, sir."

The Merger

The walls are bleeding as I stumble out of the office. Trails of thick, coagulated blood ooze along the hallways, arranging themselves into a ledger of smarmy corporate motivation.

> Excellence is an unrelenting pursuit of your goals.
>
> Dream it, believe it, achieve it.
>
> Teamwork makes the dream work.
>
> Be the architect of your future.

My eyes are stinging by the time I reach my car. I don't understand why I am so affected, so bewilderingly angry. Becca and I aren't even that close. We gripe about the office, and I tolerate her endless stories about crafting, but that's it. I've had plenty of coworkers take the contract. The exorbitant productivity bonus hasn't ever really tempted me, but hey, to each their own. I just need to forget it. I need to drive home and enjoy a couple of hours of Netflix before I have to come back and re-live this nonsense all over again.

The parking garage children are semi-corporeal now, clawing at my windows as I wind my car up from sublevel C. My car clunks softly as I draw up to the ticket booth. The beast bares his canines and growls menacingly when I return my day pass.

I can't get Becca out of my head. I keep re-living our last conversation. The short exchange circles over and over in my mind.

Finally, I land on it. The thought I've been avoiding. The nidus of my rage.

Becca said she wouldn't have to experience being there anymore.

To be at work without being at work.

I really cannot help but acknowledge the appeal.

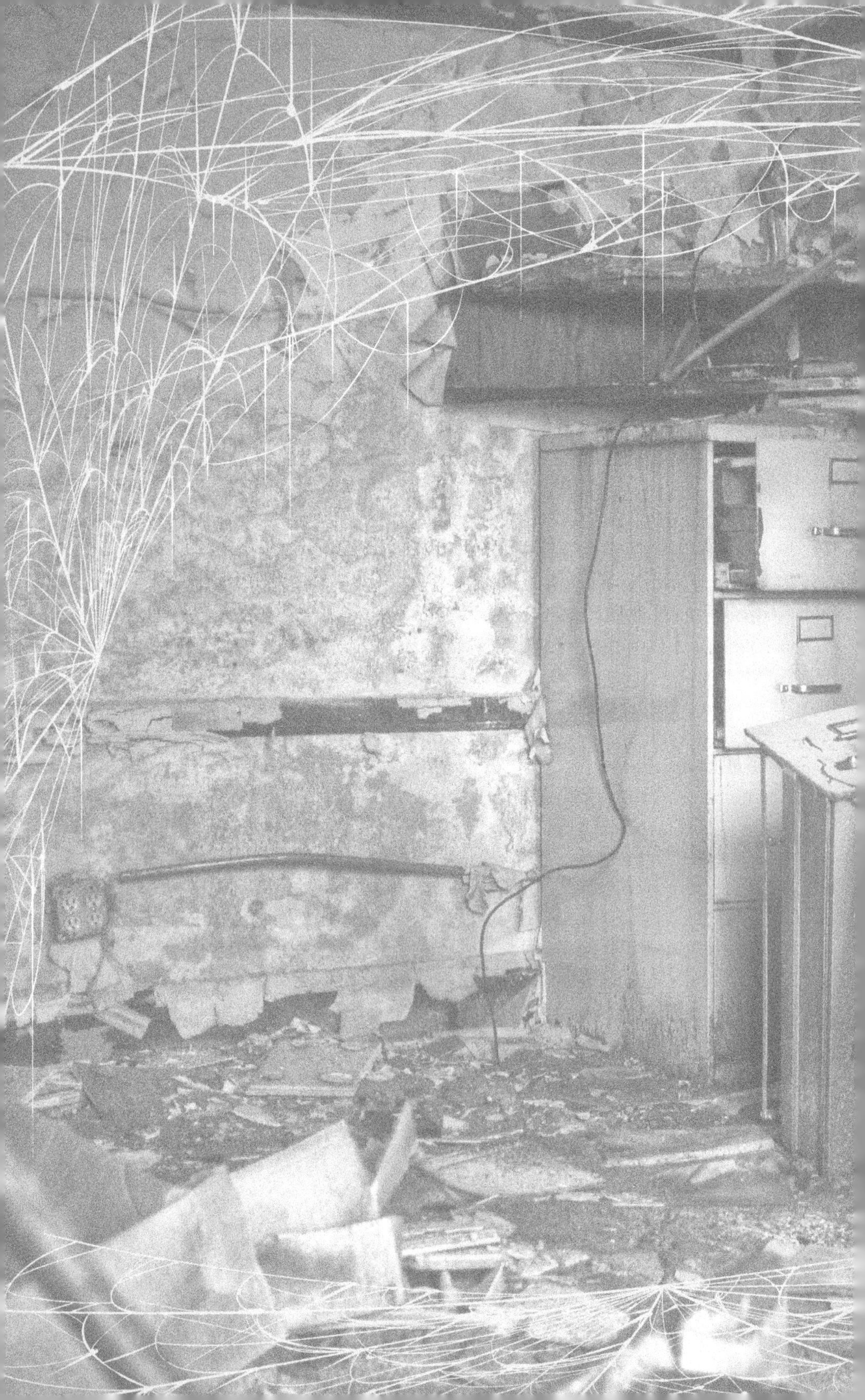

God of Garbage
By Steve Oden

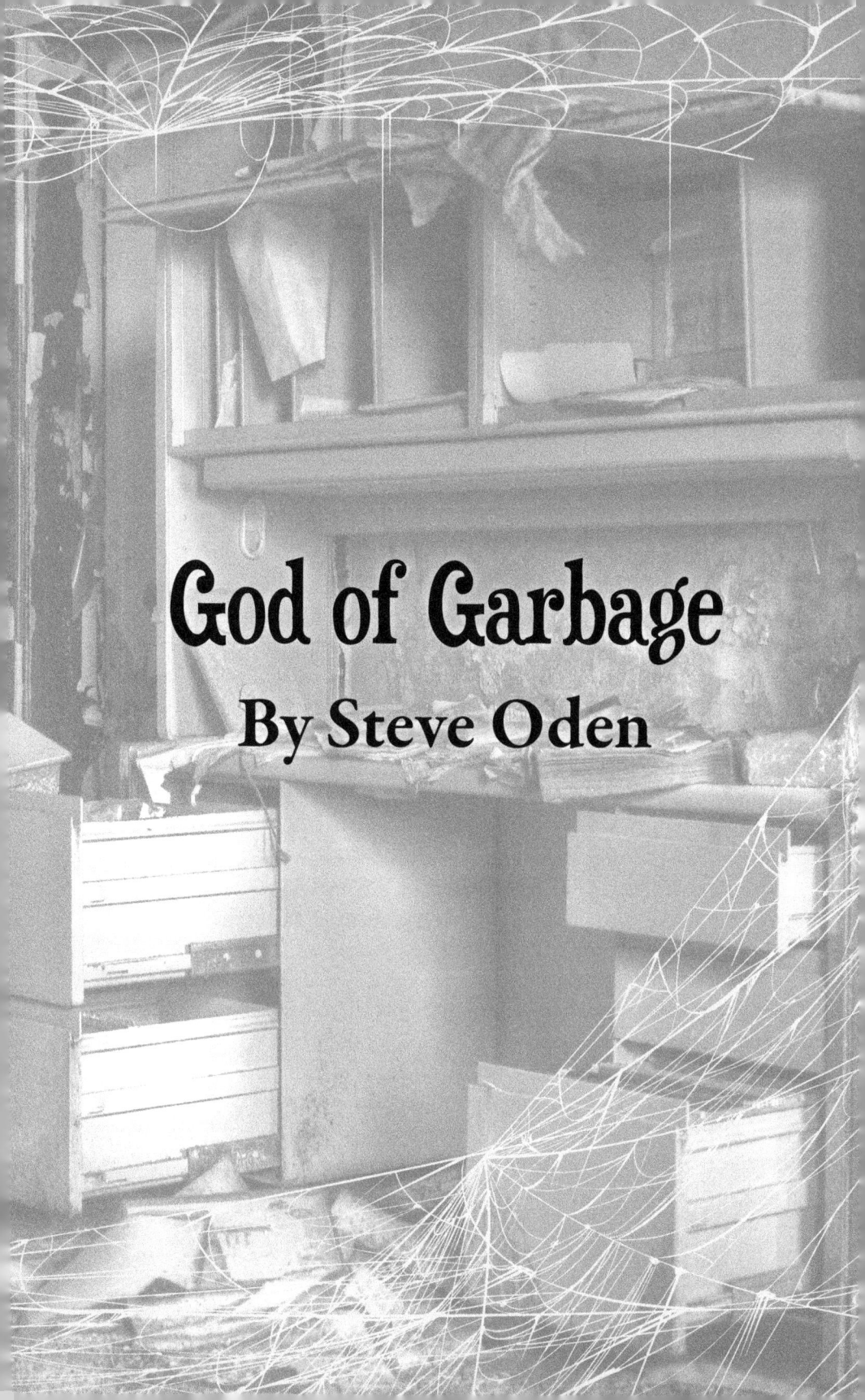

Demonic Workplaces

With a clash of gears and whine of an overburdened engine, the battered garbage truck raced down a street gaping with potholes, along which piles of paper litter and plastic bags formed a corridor. The truck left a trail of leaking motor oil and rancid juices, not to mention a cloud of greasy diesel exhaust.

Peering over the steering wheel, the swarthy driver screamed and cursed each time a tire crunched through the pitted road surface, threatening a load shift that would put the Miss V's Sanitation Service vehicle on its side or upside-down—with tons of garbage strewn in the street.

"Hell-uva way to run a city," the cigar-chomping godling muttered, feeling the rear tires lose traction like a stock car in a curve. Except a racer could rev up the RPMs and let the powerful engine straighten out the slide. If he tromped on the accelerator, the truck was likely to stroke-out, maybe blowing the clattering assemblage of metal and magic that passed for a power plant.

Purgamen remembered the long-ago days when residential waste collection was an honored profession. He had been a respected household deity in those days, a member of the minor pantheon worshipped by common people.

His current boss, Vesta, sat on the board of directors with the likes of Jupiter, Juno, Mars, Venus, Mercury, and other numinous big shots. When the Roman empire went bust and the jealous Christians took control, the gods of myth were banished into retirement: a bunch of impotent immortals looking for a way to support themselves ages before 401ks or investment portfolios.

Minerva, however, played the smart card. She enrolled in an Ivy League university, earned degrees in business management and set up a holding corporation through which all the former gods became richer than Midas, the Phrygian king who turned everything he touched into gold.

Old rules from Caelum, the Roman version of Mount Olympus, forbid they should dirty their hands through actual labor. Instead, they employed innumerable minor deities, demigods, spirits, and demons to get the actual work done.

Purgamen had been lassoed, promised his own cut of the pie, and was turned loose in the sanitation collection business. What he got for his efforts was a fleet of worn-out garbage trucks, plenty of headaches, and a major loss of prestige.

Back in the glory days, the Roman State regulated religion with pomposity and government patronage. Emperors sponsored elaborate worship festivals and built temples for the major gods. The minor household godlings were revered daily in the homes of citizens, however. Common people realized a household's health, good fortune, and happiness depended on obeisance to humble, more approachable powers.

Pergamen didn't mind that his work involved the disposal of spoiled food, broken pottery, ripped and soiled undergarments, bloody bandages, flux-stained hankies, ladies' time-of-month necessaries, and other non-hygienic rubbish. This was stuff that might endanger households if allowed to build up.

So, Pergamen devised and implemented a simple system of collection: all the garbage was thrown in the streets to be collected by his donkey-and-wagon teams manned by dedicated followers. Thus, the world's first solid-waste disposal system was launched.

His brainchild, in one form or another, operated efficiently for millennia, saving uncounted human lives. In modern times, no one acknowledged his godhood or practical importance. He ruled over bloated plastic garbage bags in sprawling landfills.

Purgamen spit on the floorboard. He had little power these days. Not since Miss V had turned his worship into a thriving modern enterprise. She negotiated under-the-table deals for municipal contracts, bought off labor union officials, influenced federal oversight with fat political contributions, and coerced environmentalists whose idealism waned in the face of seven-figure, out-of-court settlements in return for no admission of guilt.

Miss V, surrounded by her squad of vestal-virgin lawyers and accountants, knew whose back to scratch and when. There was gossip that she would attempt to unseat the chairman of the board himself, Mr. Jupiter.

In the meantime, Purgamen became weaker and less influential. He was the forgotten godling who had invented sanitation services to help believers lead better lives. His reputation had sunk to a new low. Today, for example, the godling substituted on a garbage collection route because one of his drivers took sick leave.

He was tired, stressed, and disgusted. The godling couldn't remember the last time he felt the warmth of a prayer in his honor or glimpsed a statuette of himself in a home alcove. His temple was a growing mountain of trash at the waterfront, where barges waited to be loaded for dumping man-made waste in the ocean.

Publicly, Neptune raised hell about the pollution of his waters, but Purgamen knew the hoary old scoundrel was getting a kickback on each ton. Vesta had all sorts of schemes and angles for feathering her corner of the corporate nest. She mainly ignored Purgamen, leaving him to get the job done with a fleet of dilapidated trucks and landfills that were in non-compliance and running out of room.

Truth be told, he was too low on the totem pole to warrant notice... even further down than the deposed Greek gods who'd been carried over from an earlier millennia and used as contract laborers.

He felt another curse boil up when his smartphone rang. The office was calling.

"Hell-o!" Purgamen said, emphasis on the first four letters. "This is the solid waste department vice president of operations. What can I do for you?"

It was a member of Miss V's corporate cabal, a pinched-looking virgin who seemed to regret her career choice. She took it out on everyone around her. There was a betting pool on how long Miss V would put up with her attitude before letting someone zap her with a lightning bolt between the eyes.

Purgamen considered wagers on the virgin's demise a waste of treasure. He suspected his boss delighted in the back-biting and uncertainty this priestess caused up and down the chain of command. The only danger she couldn't avoid was a secret blade in the spine from one of her competing peers. This was, after all, an acceptable way to advance in corporate power and pay grade.

"The Glorious One summons you to a meeting this afternoon at two o'clock in her office on the penthouse level of the Augustus Tower downtown," said the snippy voice. "Questions?"

The godling barked, "Who's gonna drive the damned garbage truck?"

"Just get your fat ass here on time," hissed the vicious vestal virgin, ending the call.

The receptionist, a harpy, made the household godling wait instead of announcing his arrival immediately. She looked human enough but wore loose, ill-fitting garments to hide her wings. Purgamen thought she needed to do something about those scaly fingers and sharp blood-red claws, too.

She finally buzzed him through to Miss V's inner sanctum.

"You're late!" the pair of attending vestal virgins chorused. The goddess only smiled primly and shook her beautiful head.

"Blame that hybrid monster perched on your reception desk," he growled back. "I've been in the outer office twenty minutes. Hell-uva way to run a business, if you don't mind me saying so for the thousandth time!"

The virgins were aghast.

No one talked to them this way, but a stern look from Vesta reminded her retainers to accord the minor deity a small measure of respect. After all, they needed him to keep their garbage business running.

Because Vesta began to bubble and purr in an attempt to smooth over any hurt feelings, Purgamen became even more suspicious. The goddess's mood was too lighthearted and carefree. This meant someone was going to get the stinger, and he knew who.

"Sit, my old friend and faithful servant," she said, motioning to a serving maiden to bring wine.

The godling would rather have had coffee, but Vesta wanted to preserve the traditional form of underling treatment. Give 'em a stiff drink, praise, then the boot... this was engrained in corporate and deity culture.

Purgamen began to wonder where an unemployed household godling might find work.

But it was worse.

"I immediately thought of you when a new business opportunity arose," Miss V said in her most motherly tone. As the goddess of home and hearth, she fancied herself the answer to Martha Stewart: loveable, worthy of worship, but always focused on profit margins.

"Oh, this is so exciting, potential-wise! A chance for the corporation to unload the curse of household solid waste and jump into the energy business," she said.

Shivering in delight, she rearranged her diaphanous robes to expose more cleavage.

Because Vesta wasn't dressed in her usual conservative business suit, Purgamen knew this was an unofficial meeting. The godling got ready for the stinger. *Here it comes,* he thought.

"Sol and I—oh, you remember the sun god and his cult—have been in negotiations. We've signed a memorandum of understanding for the formation of a renewable energy subsidiary. It is called Miss V's Sunbeam Company, and Sol will be a silent partner. We will manufacture, sell and install solar panels, construct solar farms, and install household-sized systems."

She sipped wine from her golden chalice and eyed him over the rim.

Demonic Workplaces

"Think of it, Purgamen! Clean electricity, generated by the gods. No carbon dioxide from burning nasty coal. Global warming reversed. Billions of new worshippers!"

"Umm, what does the chairman of the board think about this opportunity?" the godling dared ask.

Any mention of Mr. Jupiter brought a scowl to Vesta's lovely face. Not this time.

"He doesn't know and never will. This is a private, off-the-books business venture. As long as we continue to furnish tribute and executive perks, the lazy old womanizer will ignore the holding company of which we are a part."

Vesta cooed, "And you will be transferred to help with the startup. In fact, I am making you the chief operating officer!"

Purgamen, whose Latin name meant "rubbish," realized he was being set up to take the fall and eventually be swept into the gutter. Each conniving, greedy business god was involved with underhanded deals. It only required having someone to blame if the scheme failed or was discovered.

"You will oversee getting the solar power subsidiary on its feet. No more nasty garbage collection and hauling," Vesta said, throwing out her arms as if to embrace the future.

"Who'll take over the garbage?"

She held his gaze with those violet eyes that seemed so hypnotic, but he wasn't susceptible to her hoodoo. He had always faced forward in a fight, wanting to see the stinger that pierced him. This time, it sank deep into his heart.

"Oh, we've already consummated a deal to sell the solid waste department," Vesta added. "You're so lucky. This way, you continue your employment with me in a more important role. I know how dedicated you've been to household service all these centuries. Look at this as a chance to save the world from global warming. It's a glorious undertaking, don't you think?"

She didn't mention a higher salary or being allowed more followers.

The vestal virgins sniggered now that the sting had pierced its target dead center.

"You can go now," they said in unison, dismissing the pole-axed godling. "Miss V has another important meeting."

The goddess had already turned her attention to a spreadsheet. On the way out of the office, Purgamen passed Sol. A handsome deity, he wore expensive designer sunglasses, a flowery silk shirt, and baggy surfer trunks. He was perfectly tanned and had a coifed flowing mane of fire-red hair.

Sol didn't deign to acknowledge the minor godling. Purgamen suspected there was more going on between Vesta and her silent partner than met the eye. The virgin part of her image was a branding ploy, anyhow. Everyone at the top and through the ranks knew it.

The harpy watched Purgamen's dejected shuffle through the reception area and out the door. There was a self-satisfied sneer on her beak.

The elevator took an interminably long time to descend. Halfway down, it stopped at another floor. A huge, brawny figure had to crouch and turn sideways to enter. Purgamen heard elevator cables creaking with the stress of the passenger's weight.

Even with his eyes shut in tearful thought, Pergamen knew who it was. The smell of molten iron and burning sulfur gave away his identity.

The godling blinked and beheld a leather apron blackened by foundry sparks and muscle-corded arms marked by burn scars. Clapping the short godling on the back and laughing through an ashy, bristling beard, Vulcan boomed, "Pergy, old boy, I haven't seen you in an age!"

The god had always been one of the household deity's favorites. He worked with those mallet-shaped hands and wore his grime with honor. Purgamen had never seen him in a ritual robe and couldn't imagine the muscular giant dressed for an executive meeting. Vulcan was on the board of directors, however.

"Why so glum, my friend?" he asked, noticing Purgamen's demeanor.

"I just got down-sized. Vesta's got a new scheme, her and Sol. I just found out whose cojones are in the vice when it blows up. Nothing I can do about it."

Vulcan unleashed a basso roar of sympathetic humor, like a volcanic eruption.

"You mean the Miss Holier-than-Thou's sunbeam company?"

That the secret was already out shocked Purgamen. He already felt the vice jaws closing.

"Oh, don't act like you swallowed a bushel of sour olives," Vulcan said. "Those vestal virgins of hers can't keep from boasting about how their goddess has bigger plans than the home-and-hearth business. Gossip travels fast in this organization."

Purgamen drew himself up to his full, not-so-impressive height and looked up at the fire god.

"I am glad at least someone at the top knows the truth because I won't be on the payroll long when Mr. Jupiter finds out," he said.

Demonic Workplaces

Smoke came out of Vulcan's nostrils, and his eyes flamed.
"How long have we known each other, Pergie?"
"Since the beginning, long ago."
"And do you trust me?"
"Of course!"

Vulcan started laughing again—so hard a pile of ashes fell to the elevator's polished tiles.

A dulcet, automated tone announced the bottom floor. The door slid open with barely a whisper. Vulcan squeezed out and called over his brawny shoulder, "Don't worry. You just wait to hear from me, Purgamen. I have a plan!"

"Oh, no..." Purgamen mumbled, sensing that it had taken only an elevator ride to double or treble the danger of his situation. To be the pawn of one god was bad. A power struggle between two of them meant he'd lose either way.

Two winged cherubs carrying heart-shaped briefcases flitted into the elevator. They wore pink bow ties and were naked. One rosy-cheeked servitor pressed the button for Cupid's office. The god of love had turned romance into a multi-billion-dollar enterprise. His operation sprawled over an entire level of the building.

Purgamen slumped in the corner before exiting. The chatty cherubs ignored him.

Hell-uva a way to end a career, he told himself, stepping out as the elevator rose and his hope for the future plummeted.

The next day, Purgamen's crisis weighed heavily on his mind. He didn't even feel like arguing with the maintenance shop foreman about how long it would take to repair the axle on one of the collection trucks. Nothing he liked better than a hearty debate, especially if winning would benefit his worshippers.

He saw no point. This would soon be someone else's problem, and he'd go wherever decommissioned godlings wound up—Limbo, probably. When his phone buzzed like an angry hornet and he saw it was Miss V's office calling, he almost let it go to voice mail. This always pissed off the vestal virgins. So what?

He didn't have anything to lose by giving one of the little twits a piece of his mind, so he answered. But it was Miss V herself.

Purgamen felt his legs go all rubbery.

"What in the name of Hannibal's hemorrhoids has come over you?" she demanded.

"After all I've done for hearth and home, betrayal is the last thing I expected! You're nothing but a pathetic little wanna-be who dirties himself with garbage and filth generated by mortals! Good riddance to you... and I am delighted to see you leave. May bad fortune follow wherever you go, Purgamen. By the way, I won't accept your resignation. You're fired!"

Vesta hissed a curse unbecoming of her public image and broke the connection.

She was really torqued. Must have found out about the information leak and blamed her favorite punching bag. On the heels of her call, the godling's phone vibrated again. It also heated up in his pocket so that he feared it would catch fire. Vulcan, of course.

"Pergie, I presume you are now unemployed? Good! Things are going according to plan," said the fire god in a tone of calm satisfaction.

Purgamen was anything but happy about the situation and told Vulcan to dunk his naked ass in a lava bath.

"Hold on, old boy. You've just received a life-changing blessing! Purgamen, if you could be the immortal authority responsible for reducing the amount of pollution that mortals generate, conserving resources that mankind wastes in pursuit of wealth and material possessions, and eliminating the poisons they pour into the environment, would you take the job?"

The household godling didn't hesitate. "Hades, yes! But we don't have such a deity. Our godly pantheon has never efficiently reflected the social, technological, and environmental issues of the modern world. It's our weakness. That and greed. Present company excluded, of course."

Vulcan nearly blew out Purgamen's eardrum with his laughter.

"Mr. Jupiter, in an emergency meeting of the board of directors, has proposed the creation of a new division of deity. It passed with only two dissenting votes, those being Miss V, who pitched such a fit that she had to be sedated by a clonk over the noggin by Mars, and a certain sun god who is now in eclipse. You should have seen all the commotion!"

Vulcan added, "You are going to be working in the new division, Pergie. I gave you a glowing recommendation, and so did several other gods who recognize what you've done over the centuries."

Demonic Workplaces

"But what will I be doing?"

A screaming comet arced through the sky overhead, stopped, and plummeted to where the confused Purgamen stood in front of the maintenance shop. In a burst of sparks and a cloud of ozone, Mercury stepped forth, the wings on his feet white hot from atmospheric friction.

He tilted his doughboy helmet in greeting, handing a golden parchment to the godling. Then the messenger launched off, leaving a trail of vapor in his wake.

"Read it, Pergie. It's your contract," Vulcan said over the phone.

He scanned the document. The new division was indeed responsible for reducing waste, preserving resources, and cleaning the air and water.

"Renewable energy and reclamation of damaged habitats? Restoration of threatened and almost extinct plants and animals? Green programs and stewardship? This will be quite an undertaking," Purgamen said.

"I would be honored to accept any position in this exciting new division!"

"Just sign the contract, and it's done!" instructed Vulcan before hanging up.

Purgamen marveled. This was indeed a blessing.

He still had a job. Better yet, he'd be helping his mortal followers lead better lives. Scratching his symbol on the last page of the parchment, he read below the line and almost fainted at his new title: GOD OF ENVIRONMENTAL AFFAIRS.

He was now a full-fledged deity with a seat on the board of directors! Not a godling anymore, but a VIP!

"Hell-uva way to get a promotion," Purgamen chuckled.

He ambled into the maintenance garage and—instead of arguing with the shop supervisor about when a broken-down truck would be back on the road—began to develop specifications for the purchase of a new fleet of robotically controlled, renewable energy-powered garbage haulers.

What ideas he had for cleaning up the planet!

Purgamen hoped the other directors would allow him to sit beside Miss V during the board meetings. He'd wear his most stained, rancid, and sweat-soiled coveralls, not bathe or change his socks for a week beforehand. He also doubted whether Vulcan would look or smell any different for the sessions.

The two deities would make a statement about honest labor's toil and how work produced reward. It might be the first step toward dismantling the mythic privilege of power, Purgamen thought.

God Of Garbage

He must remember to eat raw garlic and onions for breakfast and practice leaning over to exhale on the beautiful Miss V several times during the meeting. Vulcan, of course, was infamous for his thunderous flatulence. What if they sat on either side of the goddess? Talk about introducing a common touch to the boardroom!

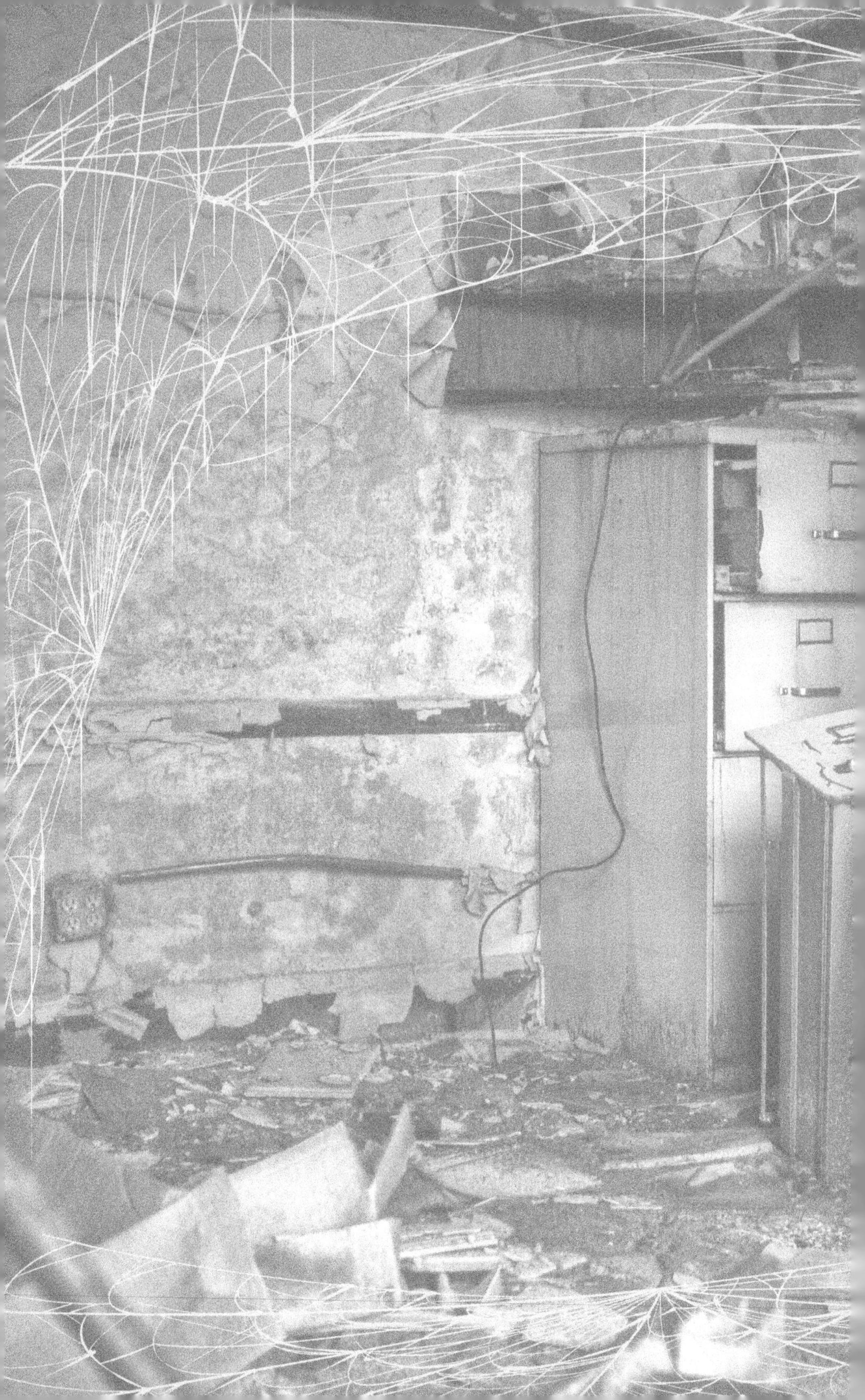

The Cost of Progress

By Alessia Lehua

Demonic Workplaces

Walking in, lights bright, meant to stimulate the brain, to keep employees awake, but serving only to induce an early morning headache, Juniper Miranda groaned at the prospect of another ridiculously early morning meeting.

Coffee used to be served in the faculty lounge, in the before times, but communal food and drink were banned once the pandemic hit; even the office Keurig had been confiscated and replaced with a "no coffee" sign. The small pleasures had been stripped away, leaving only a heavy workload, frequent headaches, and a little devastation.

"Ugh," Juniper groaned, wishing she'd gotten up early enough to stop at the gas station for an ashy cup of low-quality dark roast. Feeling resigned, she walked to the soda machine, the last remaining vestige of comfort, and purchased a 7 a.m. Diet Mountain Dew. "This place is going to kill me."

The faculty had been called in to assemble in a comically small auditorium, packed in much closer than seemed advisable given the sweeping pandemic, for a pre-semester meeting. Often, these meetings were wasteful things that could have been boiled down to a clear bullet-pointed email. Other times, they were maddening, full-morning keynote speakers blathering on about a topic that was neither related to their work nor revolutionary. Today was certain to be more of the same. After the announcement of a 0% raise, they were at least primed for a dismal morning, "This sucks," Juniper said, leaning across the small gap between herself and the next seat over.

"Accurate," Kel replied, joy having been sucked from her bones as she entered the room. "I think these things make me physically ill. I've been nauseous since I sat down."

A loud tapping interrupted their commiserating as the mics were turned on and tested. Their boss, officiously standing there in her bright yellow suit and matching scarf, wore a gleaming expensive-looking smile. "Welcome back, everyone," beamed the disingenuous provost. "I'm so happy you're all here. It's so nice to see our family back together again."

"As if we've been given a choice," Kel said, nudging Juniper with her elbow.

"Ha, yeah." She rolled her eyes, not eager for what was to come.

"Where's Pete?"

"You didn't hear?" Juniper replied, furrowing her brow.

"No, what? Did I miss something?"

"He came down with some weird sickness, some kind of sweeping infection. It rotted him from the inside out."

The Cost Of Progress

Kel's eyes widened. "No way, not again. That's not okay."

"I know. I feel like we've had shit like that happen too many times. Edith, Lara, Brian, and Angie."

Hearing the provost shuffling around, Kel just mouthed "What the fuck?" in Juniper's general direction before the provost's booming voice drew her attention again.

The two women turned their eyes back to the stage as their boss continued her tirade. "I hope you've all had a nice semester break and that you're feeling re-energized and ready to jump in again. Now, I know times have been hard. So, I wanted to share something fun from my life."

Juniper's phone lit up, her co-worker group chat buzzed with disgust.

[Annie: Here we go...]

[Kassedy: I can't wait. Why do we do this again?]

[Kieth: The money, duh!?]

[Juniper: What money?]

[Keith: Oh, yeah. Nevermind.]

[Ryan: Are you all hearing this? She flew to Greece on the company's dime and bought herself a six hundred dollar scarf?!?]

[Annie: WTF!?? Why would she tell that to us???]

[Kassedy: So, they had no money to give us raises but could send her first class to the Mediterranean, where she went shopping? Seriously, why are we here?]

[Keith: This is fucking stupid.]

[Juniper: Okay... Did she just say...]

The chat died down as their provost went on to deliver the killing blow, her gleeful smile morphing to a facsimile of sympathy, "And, now for the bad news... Your insurance premiums are going up $50 per pay period, and, unfortunately, we had to go with a lower-tier plan. We recognize this will be an adjustment for all of you, but we have to make sacrifices to move forward. So, let's not dwell on the negative!" That sparkling smile returned to her face in a split second, her fleeting solemn moment already forgotten. The slick dance between emotions, one of her particular talents, left the room feeling slimy and sallow.

Juniper sat, jaw dropped, looking over to Kel in abject horror, "Did she really just tell us about her fancy trip to Greece before gutting our insurance... during a pandemic?"

"It seems that way, Juni. It seems that way. I wish I was surprised, but we're just bodies to them."

"Seriously, who thought that was a good idea? And we're not going to talk about it? Like, do we just not have any say? Final answer? This sucks."

Understandably, the room remained silent, a whispered hush as everyone processed the blow. These things seemed to happen each year but never got easier to swallow. As a few hundred faculty members collectively mourned both their safety net and their morning, the walls were listening, drinking in the devastation and outrage, filling up as the little sparks of hope dwindled in each faculty member in the room.

The remainder of the morning was an update to enrollment, higher than last semester, tuition, also higher, and new program offerings, along with their plans to expand the college by building a new wing.

"We're not even using the space we have," Kel murmured. "Couldn't they, like, get us working projectors and speakers instead?"

"No kidding. The computer in 110 takes fifteen minutes to turn on, and that's if it even decides to work. Expansion is a joke."

Juniper's brain hurt, thinking about the backward decision-making here, "We don't even have the right equipment to do our jobs. How are the students benefiting from more empty hallways?"

"I don't think they care about the students, Kel, or us. I'm not sure how schools are supposed to operate, but this can't be it. Who even are we serving? Monsters, all of them."

Having tuned out the tail end of the presentation, Juniper was lost in thought. *What am I even going to do? Is this really how things have to be? I can't afford this shit. No one gives me a fucking travel allowance or a company car. I can barely make ends meet.* As things wound down, the group chat picked back up again.

The Cost Of Progress

[Annie: Can someone tell me what just happened? I don't think my brain is functioning anymore.]

[Kassedy: Oh, oh, it is. You heard right. They screwed us and then smiled about it.]

[Keith: So... they had no money for raises, but had money for a Grecian trip, and no money for insurance, but they saved 7 million for expansion? Balls.]

[Juniper: I can't keep doing this. I woke up and drove an hour to sit in a sauna of grumpy professors, and for what?]

[Ryan: Bad news.]

[Juniper: Yeah, that.]

[Keith: But, did you read that last slide? They had 26 million in surplus. They're just using 7 for expansion. They're sitting on a pile of cash like greedy dragons all while crying poor.]

[Juniper: How can any of them look at this and think it's an acceptable thing to present? Like, at least lie about how much money you've got?]

[Ryan: Right!?]

[Keith: Nope, they just want to rub our faces in it. They're soulless. It's evil.]

[Kassedy: That's a good word for it, evil.]

[Annie: You all wanna go get day drunk?]

[Kassedy: Yes.]

[Keith: Yup.]

[Ryan: Where?]

[Juniper: Brother B's?]

Demonic Workplaces

[Annie: Yup. See you all there.]

The lights of the room flared, glowing brighter still as the meeting came to a close. The room seemed smug, satisfied with itself for serving as a vehicle for so much upset. Ready to leave, Juniper felt jittery and uncomfortably warm in the cramped room. Grabbing her jacket and empty soda bottle, she got up to leave, shuddering as she accidentally brushed up against the wall on her way out.

The sour morning mood had leaked into the afternoon as the dejected faculty walked out into the parking lot, shoulders slumped, the seeds of budding migraines blooming in many of their overwhelmed heads. They marched out into the drab day, breathing a collective sigh of relief despite the fall chill settling into the environment.

Miranda and Kel walked in silence along the ivy-covered pathway until they reached the parking lot. "I swear they do this shit on purpose," Kel began, kicking the side of her dented 1984 VW Rabbit.

"Well, even if they do, what can we do about it? We have no power."

"Take it. That's all. We can bend over and take it, or we can leave, but how many of these people are going to uproot their homes and families to move several hours in any direction just to land another teaching job?"

"Yeah, I guess you're right, Kel. It's a lot easier said than done. They know we can't really leave. Hell, I only saw two positions within a reasonable distance pop up all last year. You wanna go drink about it with the rest of us?" Juniper asked.

"Sure, lead the way."

As the two women stepped into their well-traveled clunkers, the building began to hum, feeling a deep satisfaction with the morning's going-ons. The walls, strengthened by the negative emotions they'd absorbed during the morning session, were ready to stretch. As the sun fell, making way for a cool, dark night, the building began growing.

The unique school, built by automated and unexplainable silent construction, had grown many times over the years; drinking its fill in human agony, slowly corrupting people, sucking them dry until they were gray and used up. This time it had plans for a new wing, one that'd house more students, succulent and plucky, ripe for disappointment. They'd come to learn,

The Cost Of Progress

but the building would consume the joy from their lives, empty out their hope, leaving them shells of their former selves. Upon graduation, if they survived that long, they'd shamble forward to be used up by a greedy, soulless corporation, ghouls of their former selves resigned to their miserable fates. This would please the building.

As the structure morphed and grew, a small cadre of administrators watched from inside their lavish conference room, cackling at all of the devastation they'd rained down upon the worn faculty earlier in the day.

"Did you see their faces?" the provost beamed. "The rage and sadness in the room was simply delightful. I wish all days were so sumptuous."

A slick-looking man, the president, in an expensive suit, nodded along. "Yes, you were particularly devastating today. I quite liked the little dance you did showing off that ridiculous scarf." He gave a small golf clap in her direction. "I could smell the desperation on some of them. They won't all make it through the year."

"Well, I hope they die elsewhere. We can't seem to find good custodians, and I don't want to clean up human viscera again," whined their aged HR manager. "I'm too old for this shit. I should be relaxing in hell, forcing the damned to satisfy my every whim."

"You'll do what you're asked, " the provost stated, her voice crisp with finality.

The HR manager, almost afraid, nodded after having been put in his place.

The provost walked over and patted one of the building's original brick walls. "Good boy." She smiled, remembering the first massacre here, trying to recall the scent of all that blood seeping into the school's foundation. "Take your meal and give us more space to fill; Father will be proud."

Reaching up to stretch, the provost finally let her horns pierce the flesh on her forehead. "That's better," she cried, relishing in the pain. The crunch of her great bones echoed across the room as her red wings ripped through the yellow jacket of her power suit.

Her companions, save the human benefits manager cowering in the corner, followed suit, their flesh shedding and falling to the floor to reveal calloused red skin, hooves, and rows of sharp yellow teeth. "Are you boys hungry?" she continued, eyeing the president and HR manager. "I've saved us something delicious for dessert."

Demonic Workplaces

At the end of the morning meeting, Winifred Lucas found herself too dejected to move. The news of the health insurance erosion was too much for her to stomach. *I can't afford that. I'll be homeless by the end of the year. I didn't go to college for eight years to be this poor ten years into a professional career.*

Winifred didn't stand out, keeping her head down and avoiding eye contact whenever possible. So, folks simply brushed past her as they exited the room. The provost knew she was there, but flipped the light switch off anyway, locking the door and leaving the woman to weep alone in the dark. And the building loved it, humming along, sucking out the woman's will to live.

As she sat, feeling more and more dejected, Winifred found herself unable to lift her feet. On a regular day, she might have panicked, but she was so entranced, victim to the school's pull, that she shrugged and slumped over onto the chair.

"Follow me," beckoned the provost, and bring your cups along.

She led them back to the hushed auditorium, unlocking the door as her tail swished in anticipation. "Come along. You'll enjoy this." She flipped on the lights, and the room sprang to life with rows of empty seats, save one. Winifred sat, half slumped in her chair, eyes heavy on her tear-stained face.

"What do we have here?" the president mused.

"A treat. I told you it'd be worth it. We don't get live ones so often anymore."

The HR manager huffed, knowing he'd be scrubbing stains from the carpet in the early morning hours but also drooling at the prospect of fresh blood.

The provost closed in on the depressed woman, one sharp claw outstretched. Pressing the nail into Winifred's neck, dots of fresh blood sprang to the surface. "She's not even going to scream. What a disappointment," she mused before dragging her nail across the woman's throat. She reached up, letting the hot blood flow from the wound and into her favorite mug. Once filled, she stepped aside to allow the others an opportunity to help themselves to the precious life slipping from the woman's neck.

The Cost Of Progress

Winifred gurgled as the three administrators clinked cups and greedily drank their fill. "This one's taking her time to die," the provost noted. "What a gift!"

She hunched in close, pushing Winifred's chin up with her bony forefinger. "Do you want me to help you?"

Winifred's eyes were wild, but she was unable to form words and lacked the energy for much else.

"Hmmm... let's try this. If you want me to make the pain stop, blink twice, but know that I'll own your soul when the deed is done.'

With great effort, Winifred blinked twice.

"Silly girl." The provost beamed as she reached up and broke the woman's neck, ending her life. "You should be more specific when making a deal with a demon. Father will be so pleased."

"You make it look so easy," the president, impressed with the prowess of his brethren, replied. "A soul and a broken neck, bravo."

"Thank you," she replied, curtseying and riding high on the fresh kill. "I can't wait to see how the year unfolds." With that, she sashayed out, leaving the men to clean up and dispose of the auditorium corpse.

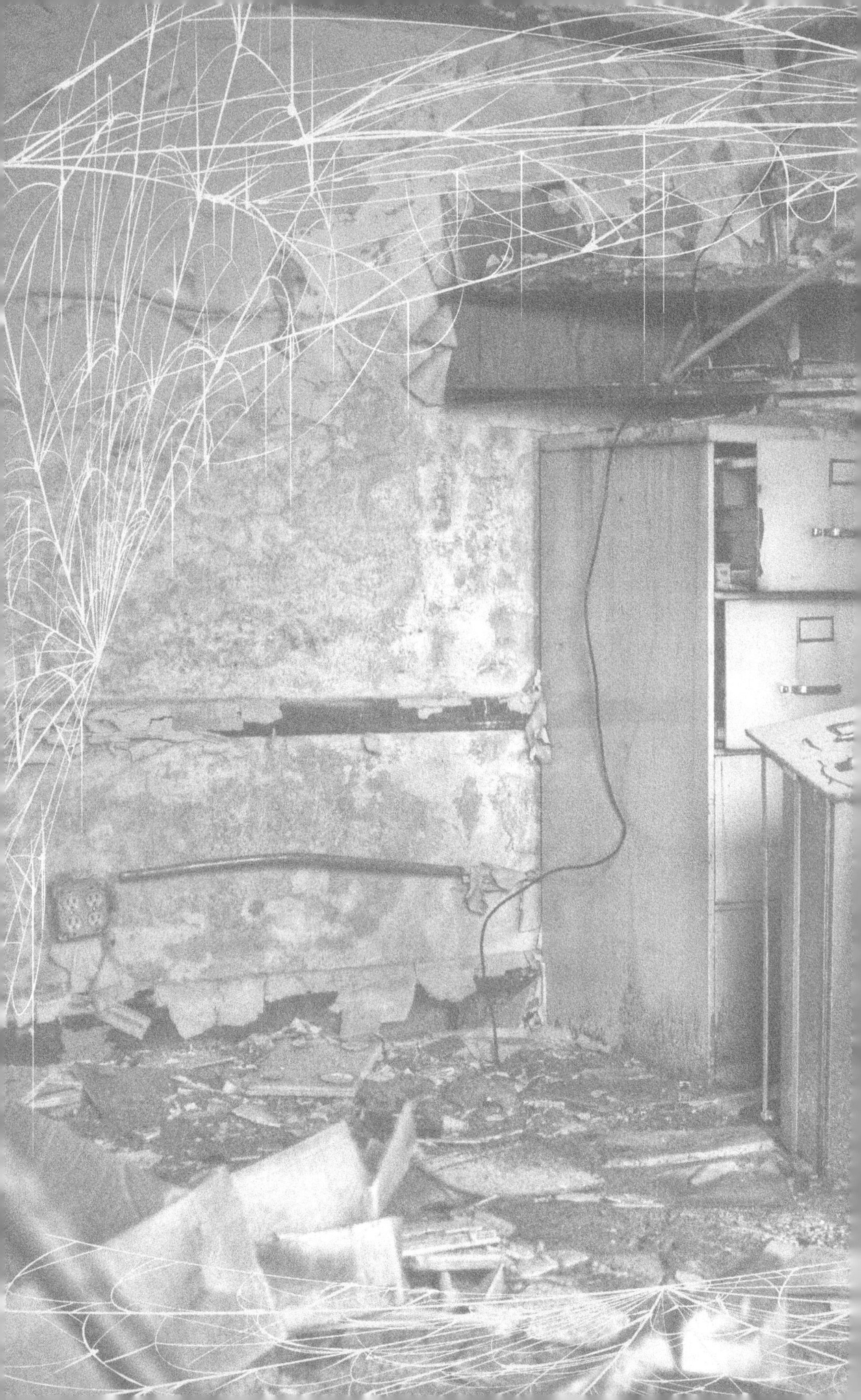

The Tightrope Walk

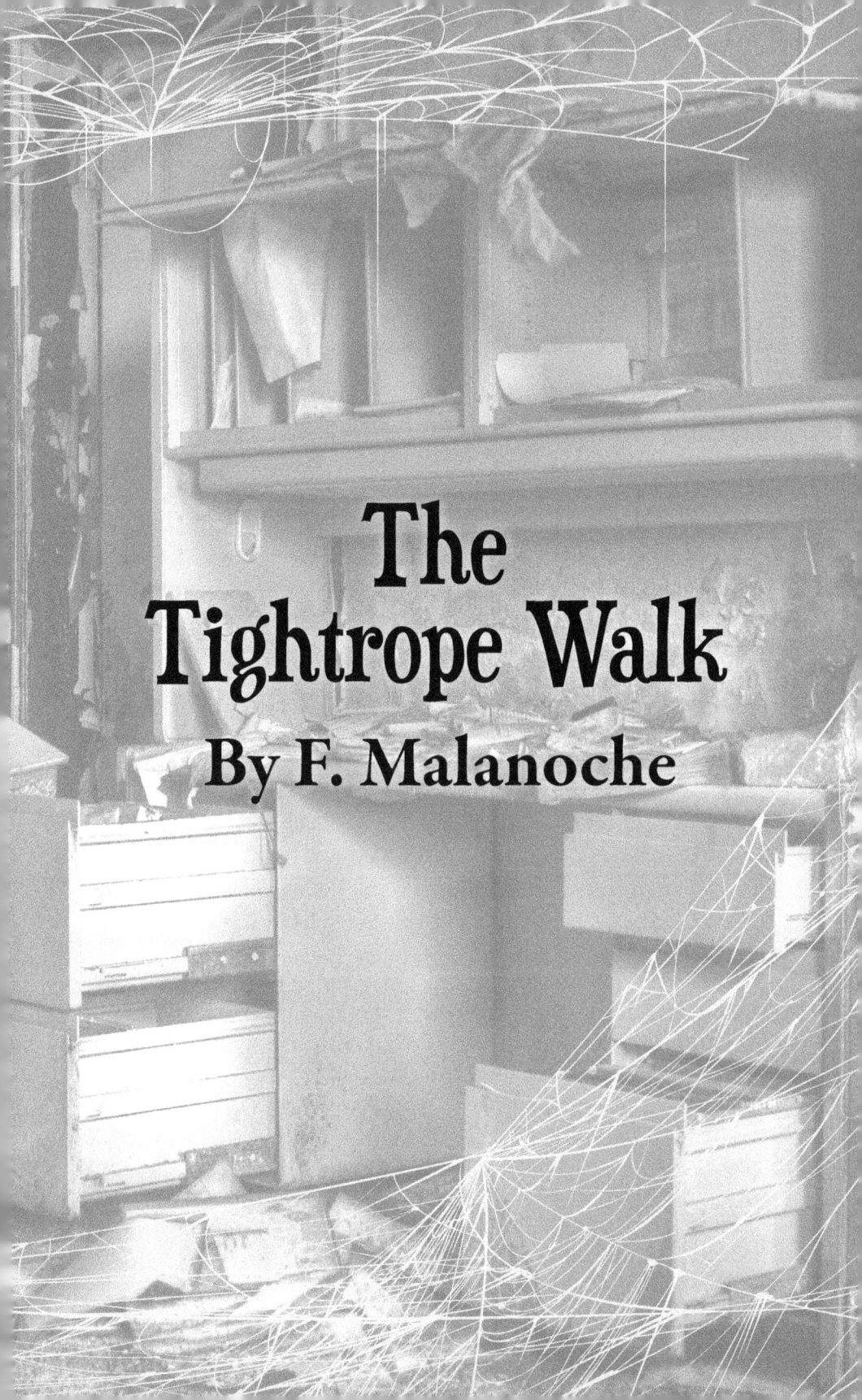

By F. Malanoche

Demonic Workplaces

Marlena looked at the dimly lit faces of the people sur-rounding The Fountain Bar and Grill. A few always showed up just after dinnertime. They typically came for the drinks and seldom paid attention to the food. Warm globe bulbs covered the mirrored ceiling. They were kept low to detract from how cramped the room was. It also gave the clientele the impression they were somewhere different, as they could not see the carpet that looked like art déco had vomited a drink made of orchids and Kool-Aid. This carpet was located over the half of the hotel that wasn't covered in peach tile.

The Fountain Bar and Grill was located in The Embassy Suites hotel in Brookfield, Wisconsin. Though Brookfield was a suburb, it was not without its problems. Nearly a decade prior, the Sheraton Hotel up the street became notorious for the death of seven during a Sunday sermon. From that moment onward, The Embassy Suites made sure in all of its commercials to highlight that Brookfield was a quiet suburb. This tactic, however, became moot a week ago when a man walked into a spa a block up the street from the Sheraton and made new air holes for seven women, including his ex-wife. As a reaction, The Embassy Suites instead highlighted how close they were to Miller Stadium and the Waukesha Expo Center.

Marlena noticed a bit of a change in clientele over the past few days when a handful of people with notepads and phones joined the boozy thirty and forty-somethings looking for a place to get soused. The din of soft jazz flowed into the bar from the speakers placed all over the hotel atrium. A table of four in the middle of the room conversed about what they had written on their notepads. "Look," said the red-haired man with black gauges, "all I'm trying to say is that the taxi driver is complicit."

"How?" asked the girl to his side, a female zombie in a Japanese school uniform tattooed on her arm.

"Oh, come on! What dude goes to a spa wearing camo and carrying a backpack? That doesn't sound the least bit suspicious to you?"

Their conversation was cut short when a man in a camouflage t-shirt walked into the bar, the slogan "This We'll Defend" emblazoned across his chest. A bullet and dog tags dangled from his neck. The man bellied up to the bar and perched on a stool. He ordered a beer. Marlena picked up a glass from the row behind the counter, but he stopped her. "In a bottle," he said.

She put the glass down. "Do you have a preference?" she asked.

"Give me your favorite," the soldier said. She popped the cap off a bottle of Spotted Cow and slid it to him on a coaster. Marlena grabbed a rag on

The Tightrope Walk

the far end of the bar and stood on her tiptoes as she wiped down the surface. To the average customer, she was performing a needed duty. She was actually eyeing the room while keeping the customers at bay. Marlena loved being around people, just not at work. Every moment she stood behind the counter was a moment that she wanted to take a smoke break. The thought of the tingle on her tongue excited her, made her want to grab her purse and sneak out through the loading dock door. She knew she would have to wait for Geoff, the other bartender on staff, to show up before she could make her temporary escape.

The soldier shouted across the bar. "You were right. This is good beer." Her daydream was interrupted. She gave him a tight-lipped smile and walked toward him. Flirtation was the tightrope walk of the job. Too much led to trouble. Too little transformed cash tips into being called a bitch. Marlena had the celebrated misfortune of being the first person she knew to own a D-cup bra. It made flirting easy. It made friendships difficult. She wiped the edge of the bar near the soldier, displaying her cleavage in the process.

His eyes burned into her. She kept her gaze past him on the other customers. He took a long pull off of his beer and asked Marlena, "Do you want to come upstairs and see my room?" She hated the tightrope walk. It didn't matter if she was at work or out for fun, she had to play nice and let him know she wasn't interested. She adjusted her purple frames and said, "I've seen them."

The soldier laughed and scratched the back of his head. He had crossed a line, but he marched on. "I didn't mean it like that. It's just that I got some great booze upstairs—" Marlena wanted to gesture to the wall of illuminated bottles behind the bar. She wanted to slap the man. In that moment, her friend, Andres, caught her attention from the server station. He was a shadow behind the open kitchen door in his all-black uniform. "Hey, Lena, do you have a tea bag? I have some blue hair in the ballroom who is simply dying to have it." Marlena could have hugged Andres at that moment. She smiled in earnest and walked behind the server station, out of view of the rest of the bar.

A steel table contained a dish bin filled with silverware wrapped in paper napkins. Shelves housed trays of sugar, creamer, and straws. Marlena knew there was no tea in the server station, but she drew out looking for it, aimlessly moving around ceramic sugar caddies and searching in cardboard boxes. She apologized to her friend. Andres sighed. "God damn it."

Demonic Workplaces

Marlena couldn't understand his reaction. She asked, "Is it a rude customer?"

"Not exactly." He shifted from one foot to the other. "I'm serving food to a room full of racists."

"What? How do you know?"

"I'm serving the Al Jolson Society. Anyone in there that isn't older than my grandma is a performer or a grandchild brought against their will. And, I shit you not, I am actually trying to get fired today, but nothing's worked!"

Marlena knew she should have watched the bar, but she was fine since she could still see nobody could reach the taps. She preferred hearing her friend talk as long as it got her away from the soldier. "Who's Al Jolson?"

"Some old douchebag famous for acting in Blackface in old movies, and these monochromatic fossils are still losing their shit over him, calling him the world's greatest entertainer. No joke, I straight up asked them about Frank Sinatra or Cary Grant and—" Marlena tried following the words coming out of Andres's mouth as he continued ranting about the party in the ballroom, but she lost what he was saying by the time he said, "Frank Sinatra."

The soldier's voice came from the doorway as he hooked his head over the counter. "Hey, are you coming back?" Andres disappeared into the kitchen, muttering to himself. Marlena returned to her post. She made sure to tell the soldier he couldn't go behind the bar.

"I'm sorry, I'm sorry," he apologized. "Look, why don't I apologize to you upstairs in my room? I have weed. Would you want some?"

At that moment, she heard the Macros computer near her beeping. She looked over, and Geoff was standing next to her, his pencil-thin mustache accentuated the look of boredom on his face as he logged in to the system. He apologized for being late. Marlena said, "I'm going on a smoke break." He nodded as she grabbed her purse and walked through the kitchen doors behind the server station. Jason, the sous chef, leaned over the prep table, watching videos on his phone. She avoided eye contact as she made her way back past the freezer, ignoring the chef in the pantry yelling at the baseball game playing on his phone. She walked through the double doors to the loading dock and out the back door.

The cool night air felt good on her skin. She used an old garbage bag tied in a loop on the handrail to prop the door open before she popped a cigarette into her mouth and lit it. The warm smoke curled in her mouth, prickling tingled her tongue. This was what she needed. She leaned back against the wall and eased herself downward until she felt the cool pavement through her pants.

Meanwhile, in the ballroom, Andres walked from table to table with a pot of coffee in each hand. Those in need of something warm to drink stared vacantly at him with a coffee cup in an outstretched hand. They looked like zombies in Andres's mind. His only weapon against them was his pot of decaf. From behind the microphone at the front of the room, a balding man with beady eyes returned to his seat and asked for regular. Though the balding man wore a black suit coat, Andres focused on his white bow tie. He had never met anyone wearing a bow tie that he didn't wish to deride. It didn't help anything that the man had just been singing a song in the voice of a Looney Tunes character. As Andres poured coffee for Bow Tie, he asked, "So, why Al Jolson?"

The entire table turned to look at the waiter. Bow Tie smiled and said, "Well, he *is* the world's greatest performer." The people at the table nodded as they drank their coffee.

"Sure, but how so?" Andres asked.

Bow Tie turned his body so his feet pointed at Andres. "Well, he did it all. He danced, sang, and acted."

"Didn't Charlie Chaplin do all that as well as act and run a studio?"

"Yes," laughed Bow Tie, "but he was more of a businessman than a performer. He also didn't have songs that top the charts."

"What about Harold Lloyd? He also directed and did his own stunts."

A glimmer appeared in Bow Tie's eye. A smile spread across his face. "You really know your artists, but those guys couldn't hold a candle to Jolson."

With the hint of a long explanation, Andres looked at his nearly empty pot of decaf coffee. The brown liquid swished around the glass that reflected the warm lighting of the room. "Oops! It looks like I need to fill up." Andres walked away and exited through the door to the server's hallway. Cold lighting bounced off of the pale blue tile, taking the luster out of anyone working. He placed the coffee pots on the metal counter next to the coffee machine and walked down the servers' hall until he was in the hall in front of the ballroom, the carpet looking like bleeding flowers. He took a left and proceeded past the bathrooms until he was at the front desk where his friend Peter stood.

Demonic Workplaces

Warm light ensconced the lobby, but the cold blue of the computer screen illuminated Peter's face as he looked up at his friend. "How is it going?" Peter asked.

"This group in the ballroom is really interesting," Andres said. Peter had once told him that there was a microphone placed in the ceiling above the front desk that was used for employee evaluations. Whenever Andres spoke to Peter, he made sure to add the word *really* or *quite* in front of the word he was lying about. Peter responded in kind. "I suspected you would find them quite interesting as well." Short conversations such as these were how Andres made it through work. He turned to walk back to the ballroom and considered a stop in the bathroom on the way, but when he turned away from his friend, Bow Tie occupied one of the armchairs in the waiting area on the other side of the lobby. The balding performer took a slow pull from his cup of coffee and beckoned Andres to come with one extended finger.

Crap, Andres thought.

Marlena stamped out her cigarette butt on the sidewalk and walked back to the bar. When she walked through the doors to the server station, she could hear the soldier. "Where is she?"

"I don't know," said Geoff.

"When is she getting back?"

"Probably when she is done with her break."

Marlena sighed and dropped her purse on the metal table before joining Geoff behind the counter. The bar phone rang. Geoff turned to answer it, raising his eyebrows at Marlena. "Would you like another?" she asked.

The soldier said, "Look, I think you would like to hang out. I can pay you to come upstairs if you like." He flashed a wad of Franklins at her.

Marlena stood rigid behind the bar. She knew how she wanted to react. She also knew how that would get her fired. The words escaped her completely. Geoff grabbed the unfinished bottle in front of the soldier and said, "I think you've had enough for the night." The air grew still. Other customers in the bar tried not to look.

The soldier swiped at Geoff; his fingers curled like claws. Geoff leaned back, avoiding contact. The soldier glared at the bartender. Marlena saw something in the man's eyes, a sort of glowing. His eyes seemed almost red to her. Not breaking eye contact with the soldier, Geoff handed an order slip

The Tightrope Walk

to Marlena and said, "Order's up. I'll need you to take care of it." Marlena grabbed the slip from his hand and hurried away. As she walked through the kitchen door, she could hear someone pound on the bar counter.

She handed the order to Jason and tried to collect herself. She focused on her breathing when she noticed the sous chef staring at her. At that moment, she realized her cleavage was heaving out of her black button-up shirt. She fastened the two remaining buttons. Her shirt was uncomfortable, but no more uncomfortable than the stares. A cigarette called to her. Her smoke spot on the loading dock beckoned her. She knew she should wait until after she delivered the order, but she stepped outside anyway. Sparks flickered at the end of her cigarette, but no flame caught. She hurled the cheap plastic lighter. It clattered in the distance. Deep, heaving breaths of the cold night air leveled off her mood.

Shattering glass and shouts echoed across the atrium. Guests enjoying a drink on the main floor stood outside the bar, looking up to see what was happening. A sound of a crash exploded as a nameless soft jazz instrumental played. Amy had been the night manager for some time, but didn't want to deal with such a situation alone. She radioed one of the engineers on duty, Ryne, to help decelerate the situation. They knocked on the door of the Vice-Presidential Suite on the fourth floor.

The door flew open. A man sporting dog tags and a camouflaged t-shirt that read "This We'll Defend" emerged. He stood a foot taller than Amy. A sneer spread across his face as he looked down at her. Ryne craned his head to look through the doorway. Red wine splattered across the walls. Four slashes ran straight down the painting of a boat at sea. Broken glass lay strewn across the sofa. Amy said, "Sir, we have had a few complaints about the noise." The soldier did not hear her as his eyes were locked on Ryne, flexing his biceps. The night manager continued, "If you wish to stay, you will need to keep the noise down. And you will be paying for the damage to the roo—" The soldier swung at Ryne. Amy held her arm up defensively. The soldier's scratch tore through the arm of her blazer and blouse before the soldier slammed the door shut in their faces. Amy radioed the front desk to call the police.

Demonic Workplaces

The performer sat across from Andres. He finished off the coffee he had and tickled the lip of the cup with his tongue. Andres didn't care for being bothered or for people for that matter. He only wanted to clock out and go home.

"So, you're a big Harold Lloyd fan," the performer asked.

"Not really. I just know a few of his movies."

A long pause lingered between them. The performer pulled his knees together. "Hmm. Maybe you could come upstairs and I could show you why Al Jolson is even better."

"Nah, I'm good. Thank you, though."

"Are you sure? It could be fun."

It was at that moment Andres realized he was being flirted with. For him, the frequency with which he was accustomed to flirting was akin to seeing an eclipse. As much as he wanted to get fired, at that moment, he remembered how hard it was to get a job in the first place. He considered possible responses, but he knew he couldn't get away with retorting, "Thank you, but I prefer vagina." He turned to look over at Peter behind the front counter. Peter, the more diplomatic of the two, could tell what sort of statements his friend was concocting, and slowly shook his head while talking on the phone. Andres sighed and thought of the sort of things he heard when he was turned down. He ended up replying, "No thanks, I'm just planning on heading home and taking a shower."

The performer responded, "I have a shower in my room."

Andres realized the tragic irony of expectation versus reality between men and women. Bow Tie's persistence was admirable and unwelcomed. He wondered how women put up with it all, and hoped he wasn't part of the problem. The urge to walk away was immediate, but he was uncertain if there would be any backlash. He thought of the best lie he could. "I'm afraid I was planning on just going to sleep right after." Two men in police uniforms walked past by and entered the elevators.

There was a brief pause before the performer asked, "So, you're going to go home, take your clothes off, and get in the shower?"

A crack formed in the dam in Andres's mind that held back the river of unadulterated shit-talking. "Yup," he shot back, "that's the only way to take a shower."

The Tightrope Walk

At that moment, Marlena walked toward the elevator, holding a tray with two glasses of red wine and a sundae, and, noticing her friend, changed direction toward him. "Andres, will you help me take this order upstairs?"

Andres, grateful for the escape, said, "Oh, thank Christ, yes" and stood up immediately. The performer stood up as well and walked up to Andres until they were inches from each other. "If you change your mind," he produced a business card from his breast pocket, "give me a call." The performer then slid the card into the front pocket of Andres's work pants. Andres tried his best to contain his anger as he followed Marlena past the front two elevators. He crumpled the business card and chucked it into a planter.

A man laughed wildly on the fourth floor. A crowd emerged from the bar once again to see what was happening. The laughing intensified. Marlena walked toward the elevator in the middle of the atrium. Andres admired Marlena now that he realized her strength. "Lena, why do you need me to help you deliver a sundae and wine?"

"Because," she said, "there is some creep up on fourth, and I need someone to walk with me."

"Oh. Is he tough?"

"He's a soldier, so I would think so."

"Well, we're screwed." Andres looked through the glass exterior of the elevator as it climbed up to the fifth floor. Outside the door of the Vice-Presidential Suite on the fourth floor stood two cops over a shadowy figure writhing in a dark puddle. A flashing seemed to emanate from the shadow on the floor.

"Ha! Those strippers sure picked a weird place to perform," Andres said, pointing to the sight on the fourth floor. "What do you think that blinking light is?

"Those are *actual* cops. They are tasing that guy I was telling you about."

The elevator door opened on the fifth floor. Andres and Marlena exited the elevator and crossed the walkway to the rooms. Two blonde prepubescent girls sat in matching pink nightgowns at the railing, imitating Raphael's *Sistine Madonna*. One girl rested her forearms on the beige railing while the other cupped her hand under her chin; only their gaze was cast downward as the dark puddle expanded around the man flanked by police officers on the floor below. The girls' legs dangled off of the edge of the floor as they watched with interest. The man in the puddle laughed, the sound echoing off the walls, and he shouted, "You fuckers think this actually hurts me?" Marlena shuddered.

Demonic Workplaces

Andres looked over to see the dark puddle around the man had grown to reach the edge of the floor. He assumed the liquid that would go over, would be yellow, watery. Only it wasn't. It was syrupy. It was red. The two cherubic girls stood in astonishment and pointed to the fountain. Andres looked at the red liquid replacing the water from the fountain. Then a crack formed underneath the small pool. The water and blood disappeared. Then came the howl of wind. The wine glasses tipped over, soaking Marlena's sleeves before they rolled off the tray completely. The glass shards trembled on the floor until they were pulled toward the crack in the bottom of the fountain.

"Lena, did I mention I wanted to stay home today?" Andres asked.

The laughing rang in everyone's mind. Marlena covered her ears, but it did nothing to impede the sound. The wind grew so that one of the little girls was pulled over the railing. The lushes outside of the bar found themselves crawling toward the exit of the hotel, but gaining no purchase on the tiled floor. Andres felt himself pulled toward the edge of the floor and grabbed the railing with his right arm. He looked over to see Marlena begin to rise off the ground. He hooked his arm around her like a lifeguard hauling someone back to land and squeezed her and the railing as tight as he could.

The roaring sound of screams and wind masked the soft jazz that played throughout the atrium. Tiles cracked and pulled up from the floor, exposing the foundation. Andres watched helplessly as the barflies, police, and furniture fell into the hole. Vines of the plants whipped wildly in the windstorm from their planters. Then part of the metal railing on the fourth floor came loose. It whipped around the atrium until it was sent skyward, shattering the skylight. The glass rained down to earth. Andres pulled Marlena into his chest and covered his eyes with her head. That was when the railing he held began to wiggle. He looked up between the bars to see the shadowy figure stand.

Wings emerged from the man on the fourth floor. The shadowy figure flapped, but he gained no ground. The pull of the hole in the ground was too much. The shadow was pulled off the fourth floor, its wings flapped with a feral will. Andres watched as the dark being circled the room. A metallic snap sounded from underneath him, then his stomach lurched as he found himself riding the wind five stories high around the atrium on the metal railing to which he clung so desperately. He held Marlena for dear life.

When Andres opened his eyes, the shadowy figure appeared before him. Its wings outstretched, it seemed to be keeping its position in the air as Andres and Marlena headed straight for him. Andres, his arms tired, let go of the railing and doubled his efforts to clutch his friend. The metal railing flipped, smacking the shadow straight into the crack in the ground.

It disappeared.

The wind stopped.

Andres and Marlena plummeted to earth and landed in a long planter on the first floor, the plants and dirt breaking their fall. Andres struggled to breathe through the cloud of dirt that rose around him. As the dirt settled, he could see the moon, a silver crescent in the night sky, through where the skylight used to be. The world was silent for a moment until Marlena said, "Andres?"

"Yes," he asked raggedly.

"I really hate this fucking job."

"Me too."

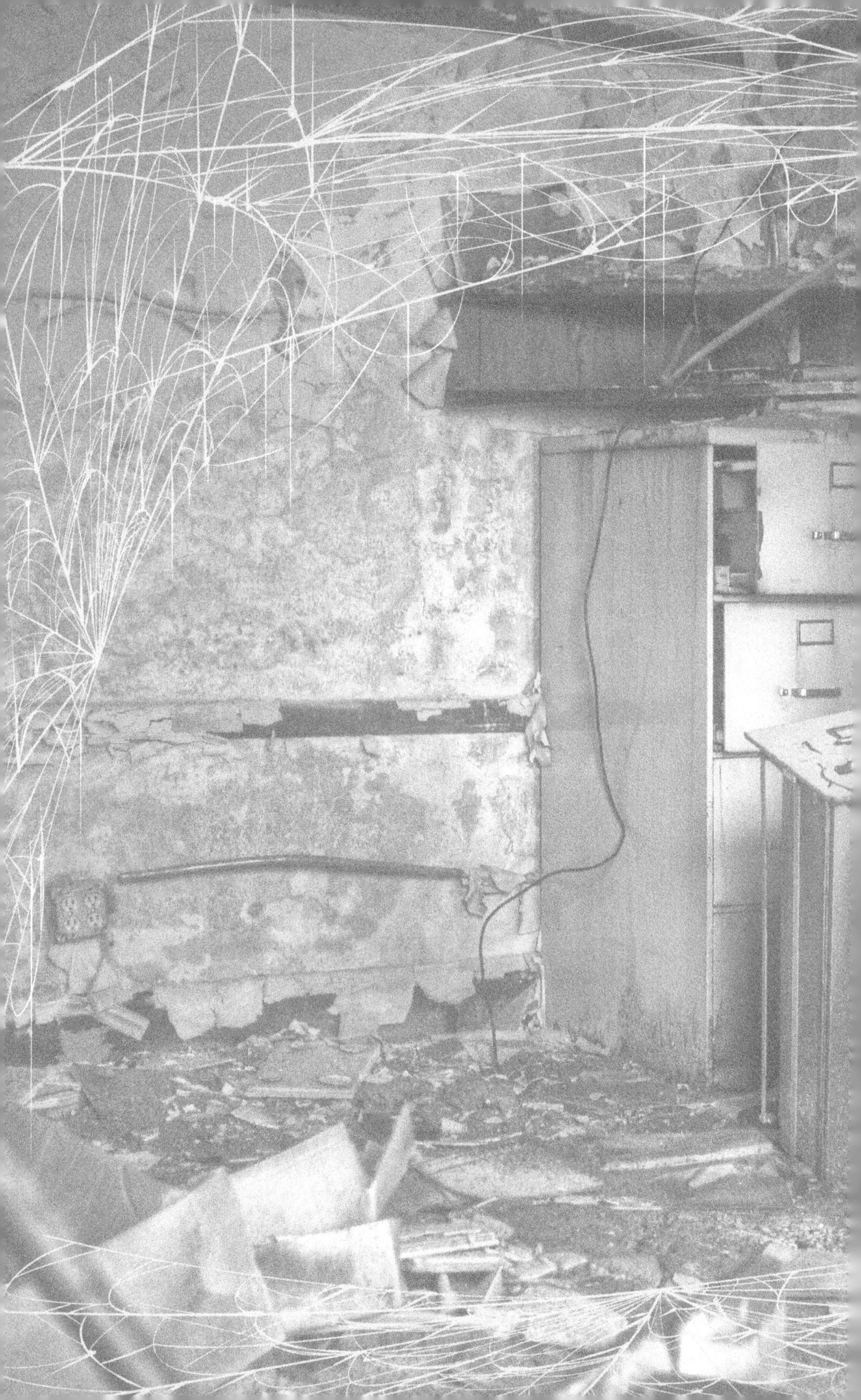

Sacrifices at the Cinema

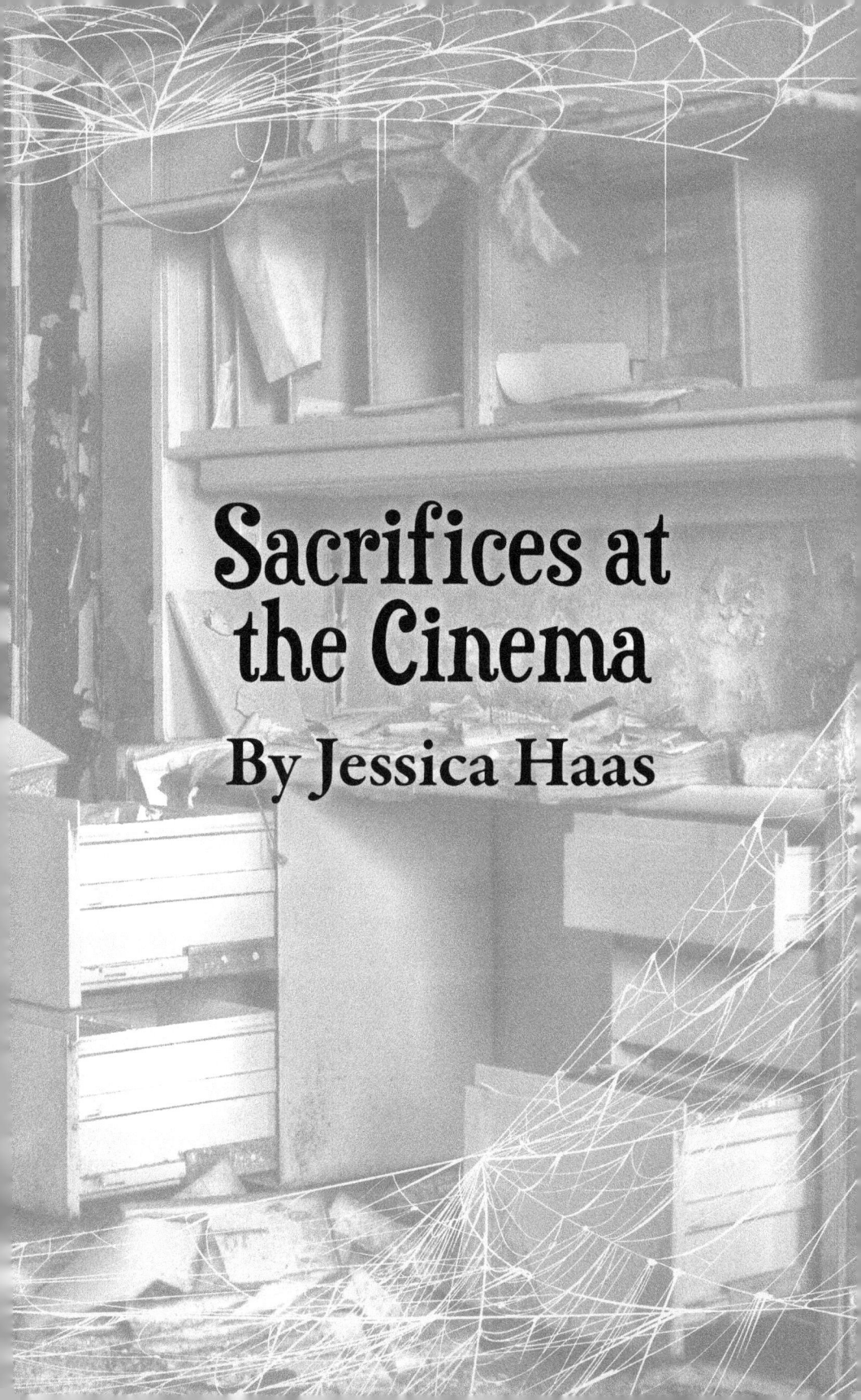

By Jessica Haas

Chanting came from Auditorium 6 with no musical
accompaniment.

I paused in the hallway.

What movie was playing there? A horror flick?

The lack of music meant a person was inside the auditorium. A customer outstayed their welcome. I peeked through the small window of the closed door. I made out the screen on the far left of the room. The ascending wall of seats obscured half of the screen.

A blinding white screen.

The projectionist, Ray, must've left the projector light on with no film running. I've never seen him outside his natural habitat–the circular room of projectors, the all-seeing eye of the movie theater. He seemed nice, always chewing on Red Vines. Did he leave the soundtrack on?

I poked my head through the door.

A man's voice. The words were unfamiliar, but sounded like garbled Latin.

Someone had stayed after the movie ended to sing in the auditorium?

The white screen bathed the room in light. The only other light source came from the small guiding lights along the walkways. A row of trash cans in front of the door were empty. My coworker Juniper was an usher tonight. She should've already cleaned this theater.

Clearly, she didn't do her job fully. One piece of trash remained...

A painful scream ricocheted off the auditorium walls.

I pressed myself against the wall to avoid detection from whoever was inside with me. My heart pounded in my chest.

The following silence was loudest of all.

No more chanting. Dead quiet.

I swallowed, gathering what little courage I possessed, and sidestepped along the wall. When I reached the edge of the auditorium, I poked my head around the corner. I squinted from the bright screen. In silhouette, the ground-level seats and—

I recognized the tall form, long dark hair pulled into a ponytail, and lithe body as my boss Doyle. A knife glinted ruby red in the light.

The knocking in my chest intensified.

He stood in front of the screen next to an elderly man lying on the floor. It was hard to make out where the stab wound was. The man lay motionless.

Doyle raised both hands in the air and let out a high-pitched, demonic shriek that sent a shiver of fear down my spine. He turned around, and I jolted behind the wall. I took off down the hall and flew through the swinging auditorium doors. The garbage can on wheels and the broom were outside, between auditoriums 6 and 7. I sped past them and turned the corner that led to the breakroom. I punched in the code with shaking fingers. It beeped in protest. I tried again. It refused my pleas for entry.

The door flew open, and I gasped.

"Whoa!" Juniper said.

I rushed in and closed the door behind me, and leaned against it.

"You scared me," I said between breaths.

"The door was rattling, so I opened it. What's going on? Someone chasing you?" she joked, taking a seat at the small table with two folding chairs. She took a Tupperware of a beige substance out of the microwave.

She stabbed the beige substance with a fork and put a forkful in her mouth.

"I..." I swallowed.

I couldn't tell her what I saw, could I? Would she believe me?

"I saw Doyle kill someone."

She lurched in her chair, coughed, and spat her mash of food back into the Tupperware. She coughed some more. I raced to her side.

"Are you okay?" I asked.

"I'm fine." She cleared her throat. "What did you say? Doyle killed someone?"

I nodded and explained exactly what I saw. She put the lid on her Tupperware and set it into her locker behind her. It was a tiny break room.

"I don't believe this... It's so dead here... Who'd he even kill? No one goes to the movies anymore. You've got to be joking." She twirled a lock of chestnut brown hair in her fingers.

My story fell on deaf ears. Juniper had a crush on Doyle. She was always flirting with him, and he'd flirt back, but they never seemed to act on their mutual flirtations. Not in my sight, that was. It shouldn't matter to me, but I'd prefer my boss and coworker not to be romantically involved. I swallowed back a twinge of nausea at the thought of them together.

"Let's go look. No body, no crime, right?" she said and jumped to her feet.

I had a feeling she was excited to have an excuse to see Doyle, rather than afraid she'd find him with a weapon and a dead body.

"Shouldn't we call the police?" I said, instinctively touching my pockets for my phone.

I forgot. Doyle had a policy that all workers at the theater leave their phones in a box in his office while working. He said just because it's slow, it doesn't mean we get to act unprofessional at work. So our shifts were boring and slow, with no work to do. No one goes to the movies anymore. I was waiting for it to go out of business any day now. That wasn't a problem for me because I was in college. I could find another part-time job. Did I want to put in the effort to find another job? Not particularly, so I was sticking it out at the theater until the very end. With any luck, I wouldn't have to because I'd be done with school and free to pursue a better-paying job.

"No, wait—"

She opened the door and stepped into the hallway.

Explosions rippled out of Auditorium 3. Melancholic music droned out of Auditorium 5. Most of the auditoriums were clean and ready for our few guests for tonight. I was supposed to work at the concession stand until the last movie started at 10 p.m. I was taking my break when I discovered Doyle. He had told me to take a quick fifteen before the evening movies started.

Juniper's calm demeanor had me questioning whether I should be freaked out or not. I wanted to run away. I saw what I saw. I pulled out my bag from the locker and put my coat on and grabbed my purse.

"Leaving early?" Juniper asked with the door open.

"Yeah, I quit..." I said and frowned at her. Didn't she hear anything I said? She didn't believe a word I said.

"Come on. Let's go find Doyle," she said. "He doesn't have a knife or a dead body..."

"I'm leaving," I said and pushed past her.

I beelined down the hallway to the front doors. The quickest exit out of here. I'd get in my car, drive away, and never come back. I didn't care to give two weeks' notice or that I'd be abandoning my cell phone.

Auditorium 6's doors flopped open. He stood there. His intense black eyes locked onto my terrified ones.

"Doyle!" Juniper exclaimed from behind me. She hurried to meet him, beaming, "Whatcha up to in there? Theater's empty? Guess what Grace said."

He didn't bat an eye. My mouth gaped open like a fish struggling out of water, wanting to interrupt her but not finding the words.

"She said you killed someone in there! With a knife." She burst into giggles.

He smiled that charming bastard smile of his. He upsold customers at concessions with that smile.

"Grace..." His scolding tone made me feel silly and confused and terrified.

"I quit," I said and veered around him.

Quick on his feet, he stepped in front of me, blocking my exit. "Hold on, Grace. I know you're only joking."

"I know she is," Juniper said, pouting because Doyle hadn't even looked at her once so far. "I don't know why she wants to quit."

"I'm serious. I'm leaving," I said, taking a step to the side, but he stepped again, and we were both standing next to the wall.

"Grace, we need you. I have no one else to work at the concession stand tonight. You're scheduled, and I can't manage without you."

I erupted into laughter. He couldn't be serious. The movie theater was a dying breed of entertainment. Hardly anyone showed up. Just elderly folk needing to get out of the house.

He finally acknowledged Juniper. "Don't you need to clean the restrooms?"

"I'm on break."

"You're supposed to be back by now," he said, twirling his wrist to check his watch.

"Right. Sorry! I got distracted by silly Grace," she said and took off where I wanted to go, to the lobby where the front exit was.

I wanted to shout, "Don't leave me alone with him," but she was already out of range.

He was the picture of perfect composure. I eyed his pants pockets. Nothing bulged out, such as a pocket knife. No blood or stains on his clothes or body.

"Stay the rest of the shift, Grace," he said and put a hand on my shoulder. I flinched. "I need you here. Have some courtesy and stay." He steered me toward the break room.

I trembled under his touch.

"Just one more night?" He smiled, revealing a straight row of pearly whites. I couldn't look away or refuse his perfect teeth.

Since there was no evidence that a crime occurred—other than what I recall seeing—I agreed to stay. One more night.

I hung my coat and shoved my purse back into its locker. He waited outside of the break room. He gripped my shoulder with a meaty hand; his lips curved into a grateful smile.

"I can't do this without you. I need your blood, sweat, and tears to go into working concessions tonight, of all nights."

Pandemonium in the lobby awaited us. He escorted me, a helpless prisoner, to my prison cell. People lined up at the ticket counter. They squinted and craned their necks to check out the concession stand menu. The line went out the door.

I'd never seen so many customers at once. On a normal night, there'd be twenty people max. Twice as many lined up tonight.

People still cared.

I got behind the concession counter. After the customers purchased their tickets, they flew to concessions like racehorses freed from the gate.

I handled the first couple of customers smoothly. As I scooped the popcorn and grabbed their drinks and boxed candy, the line grew. I ran out of popcorn buckets, so I had to open a new box from under the counter with a box cutter. I slit my thumb.

Blood.

The first aid kit was under the counter, so I managed to wash and bandage my thumb.

"Hey, what's taking so long?" one irate customer questioned.

"Be right there," I responded, slipping a glove over my injured hand.

Anxiety trickled into my performance. The customers huffed and glared at me in impatience. So many orders with so many items had me rushing to fulfill their needs.

Sweat.

I could see why Doyle said he needed me tonight. How did he know it was going to get this busy? The line lengthened.

"Come on!" One little white-haired woman scowled at me. "This is the worst customer service I've ever experienced." Her jowls wobbled in agitation. She turned to the woman behind her to comment, "You see that? That woman is taking her sweet-ass time." She pointed at me. "This is unacceptable."

Tears.

I turned away from her, willing myself to calm down. The sweet-looking grandmother was anything but sweet. And I wasn't certain she was a grandmother. I put her popcorn on the counter in front of her and rushed to the door. My only exit out.

The knob wouldn't turn. I jiggled the handle and tried to push the door to no avail.

I needed to get out of there.

Above my head, there was a loud smack. Someone flung their box of candy. Everyone stared at me, talking to each other and yelling at me to keep working.

"Hey! Settle down!" Doyle screamed across the tempestuous sea of customers. "I'll throw you out if I need to!"

"Doyle!" I yelled, but my voice died in the din.

A child wailed in the lobby. The crowd parted. A humongous cup—the casualty of chaos—lay dead at the child's feet. Red Hawaiian Punch seeped into the retro seventies carpet.

"M'am, you gotta clean that up," a concerned middle-aged woman said.

"Yeah, I will..." I ran to the door to try again, but someone shouted, "M'am! You didn't give me my popcorn! You're trying to rip me off!"

"Sorry!" I rushed to the machine and scooped a bucket. My forearm burnt on the side of the sizzling hot popcorn kettle. "Ah!"

I gave it to her on the counter and she snatched it away, leaving a few pieces of popcorn on the counter.

"Hey, you!" a man shouted, pointing at the phantom watch on his wrist. "Can you hurry it up? I'm gonna be late!"

"Forget this," I hissed to myself and yanked the door handle. It was no use.

He snapped his fingers repeatedly. "Hey, you!"

I was trapped. The customers awaited, staring at me like brain-hungry zombies.

Doyle stood at the ticket counter. He stared at me with dark, impenetrable eyes, two horns growing out of his forehead. He forced a smile and stuck his pronged tongue at me.

"What the..."

He turned away, back to the customers in line. I've never been in a position to examine Doyle's tongue before. Disgusting. Juniper can have him.

"Can I order yet?"

With a sigh, I slumped to the register and took the customer's order. I abandoned my usual polite smile and upbeat demeanor and focused on getting through the line.

"Hi," I said, defeated.

The demands of the job distracted me from my increasing discomfort at working for Doyle.

People threw their money on the counter. Gave me death stares when I announced their totals. Sighed in impatience as I retrieved their items. I worked through the crowd. The last order was laughable. A box of candy. Easy. I cracked up from exhaustion. The lobby cleared.

Doyle emerged from the box office counter. He sauntered toward me with a devilish grin. Horns gone, tongue unnoticeable.

"See? I need you. Blood, sweat, and tears, Grace."

My bleeding thumb, my sweaty clothes, and the silent tears I shed. I wanted to bolt out the door, but his gaze held me there. My limbs refused to cooperate. The adrenaline bottled up inside made me quiver in place.

"Having a good business requires a sacrifice," he said, drawing out the last syllable like a snake.

A sacrifice.

The hairs on my arms stood on end.

I cleared my throat to steady my voice. I wouldn't let him know how disturbed I was. "Today is my last day. I can close the concession stand, but I'm quitting."

"Why Grace? It saddens me that you leave." He laid one palm on my shoulder.

Juniper crept into the lobby and her mouth fell open, jealousy clouding her features. She couldn't look away from us. Even though I reveled in Juniper's reaction, I didn't want to stay a minute longer.

I stepped back, his hand sliding off. "I need to focus on school." An excuse that sounded weak, even to my own ears. "I'll close up." I turned off the popcorn machine, making movements to show him that I'd do my job for tonight. I wanted him to leave so I could run out the front door.

"We need to talk about this. Come." He held out his hand to me. "Juniper can clean up concessions."

Off to the side, Juniper huffed and stalked off down the hallway toward the auditoriums.

"Come, let me explain," he said and offered his hand. I took it. We weren't standing at the opposite sides of the counter. We stood in an auditorium. The blank white screen on one side, the rows of seats on the other.

"How—" I looked around us.

"I'm disappointed with your performance today," he said, his eyes glowing red and horns reemerging from his head. "I needed you, and you weren't able to handle the concession stand."

"W-well, we were slammed. If we hired more people, w-we could've handled it," I stammered.

He reached into his back pocket and pulled out a knife.

"No, Grace. I'm not hiring anyone else. The only way I will is if someone dies." He shrugged with indifference. "I had hoped it'd be Juniper. But she performed wonderfully. She cleaned up the theaters and directed them to the appropriate auditorium. You, on the other hand... Leave much to be desired."

"Like I said ... I quit. Obviously, I'm not right for the job. If you want, you can fire me." I turned around and ran for the exit. In every theater, there was an emergency exit next to the screens.

He grabbed onto my ponytail. I cried out in pain and he jerked my head back further before pushing me into the theater seats. My back slammed into the hard plastic sides of the seats.

"Good business requires a sacrifice. I'm willing to double my profits and sacrifice you for my evil Lord."

"No!" I hurled myself onto my feet, but he blocked the back exit. My only chance was the door to the auditorium. I eyed the projectionist booth. If Ray was up there, he could see in here. Does Ray know what Doyle has done?

The lights went out.

Darkness swallowed us whole.

I rushed down the hallway to the movie theater's exit. His heavy hoofed steps clomped behind me. I bumped into something hard. I looked up. Doyle stood before me. Instead of running back and forth between the two exits, I zoomed into the rows of seats. Instinctively, my hand reached for my pants pocket for my phone. Empty.

Cursing under my breath, I ducked down and scurried up the steps to a higher level. My only other option was to hide.

I crawled between the rows and stopped, covering my mouth to quiet my breathing.

If I was still and silent, he wouldn't find me. His footsteps shuffled to the door. A pause. My breath was too loud for my ears. My heart pounded in my chest.

The floor felt sticky where I sat. Someone—*Juniper*—didn't clean the auditorium thoroughly enough. Only a spilled drink dried up could cause this. I unpeeled my hand from the floor and crawled back to the side where I left Doyle. If he checks the opposite side, then I could slip out without him noticing.

Light shuffling sounds.

Of course, he could appear anywhere at will. He demonstrated that already. I could only hope that he moved like a human through the dark.

I rose, but still crouched down, and descended the steps as fast as possible. I went for the emergency exit once again and reached to push the door open. An arm slithered around my torso, squeezing me to a halt.

Demonic Workplaces

Guttural chanting filled my ears. I let out a blood-curdling scream that shocked even me. A cool blade pressed against my jugular.

"Hey! That's supposed to be me!" I heard a woman's voice cry from behind us.

Doyle twirled us around, his arm digging into my torso. I took short, panicked breaths into my chest. Juniper charged Doyle. The blade slid off my neck as I fell backward, landing on the hard contours of Doyle's body. The heaviness of Juniper lying on top of me knocked the breath out of me. Warm, wetness soaked the front of my shirt. Her eyes widened as she let out a loud groan. She rolled off me. The knife stuck out of her abdomen.

I sprang to my feet and pushed open the emergency exit behind me. I squinted against the harsh orange street light.

I didn't dare look behind me. I kept going.

He made his sacrifice to increase business.

I refused to give any more of my blood, sweat, and tears to my workplace. A trail of Red Vines guided me away from the theater. I silently thanked my Ray of light. I'll gladly leave my phone and the rest of my belongings behind. It was a small sacrifice I paid to leave.

I quit.

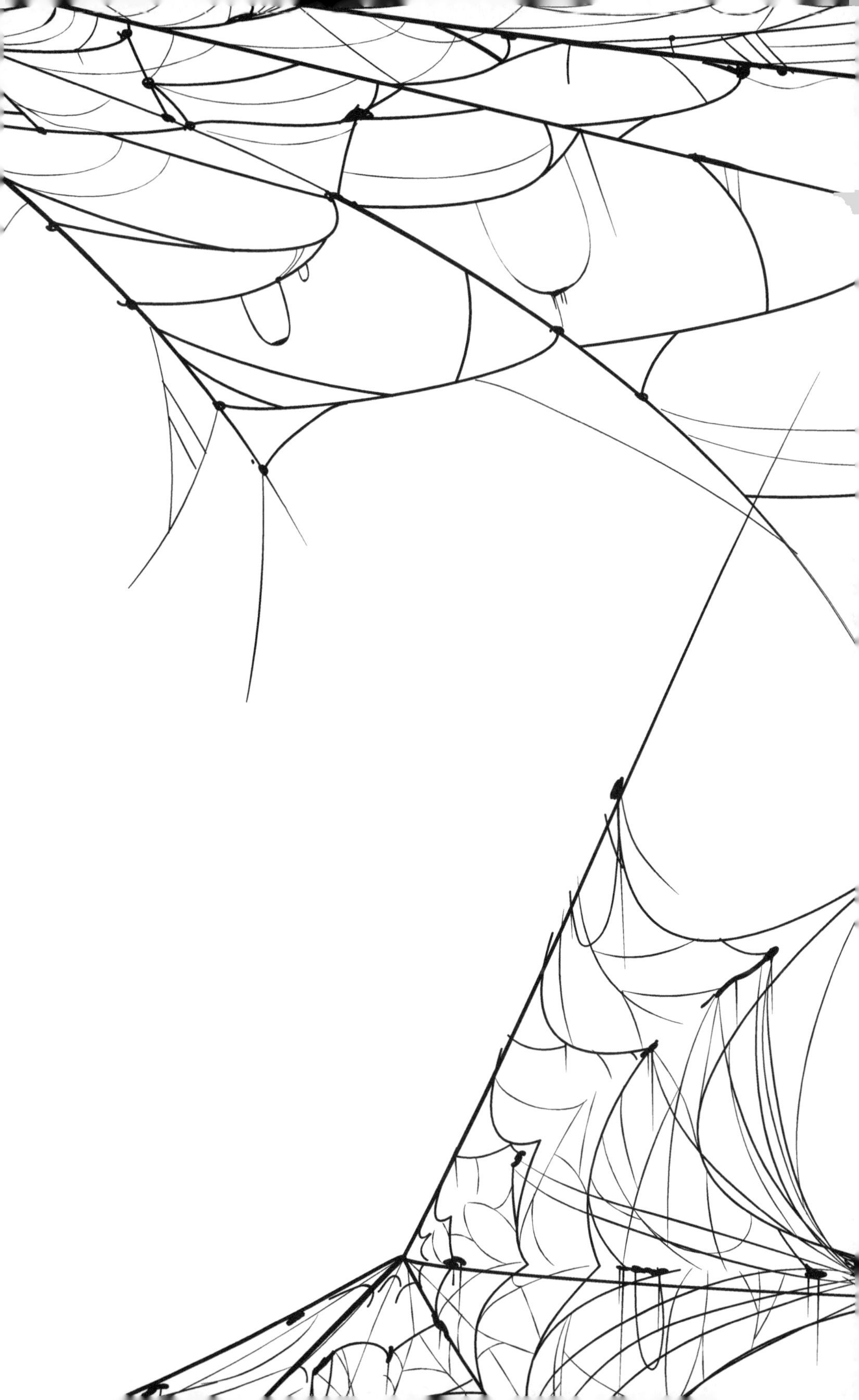

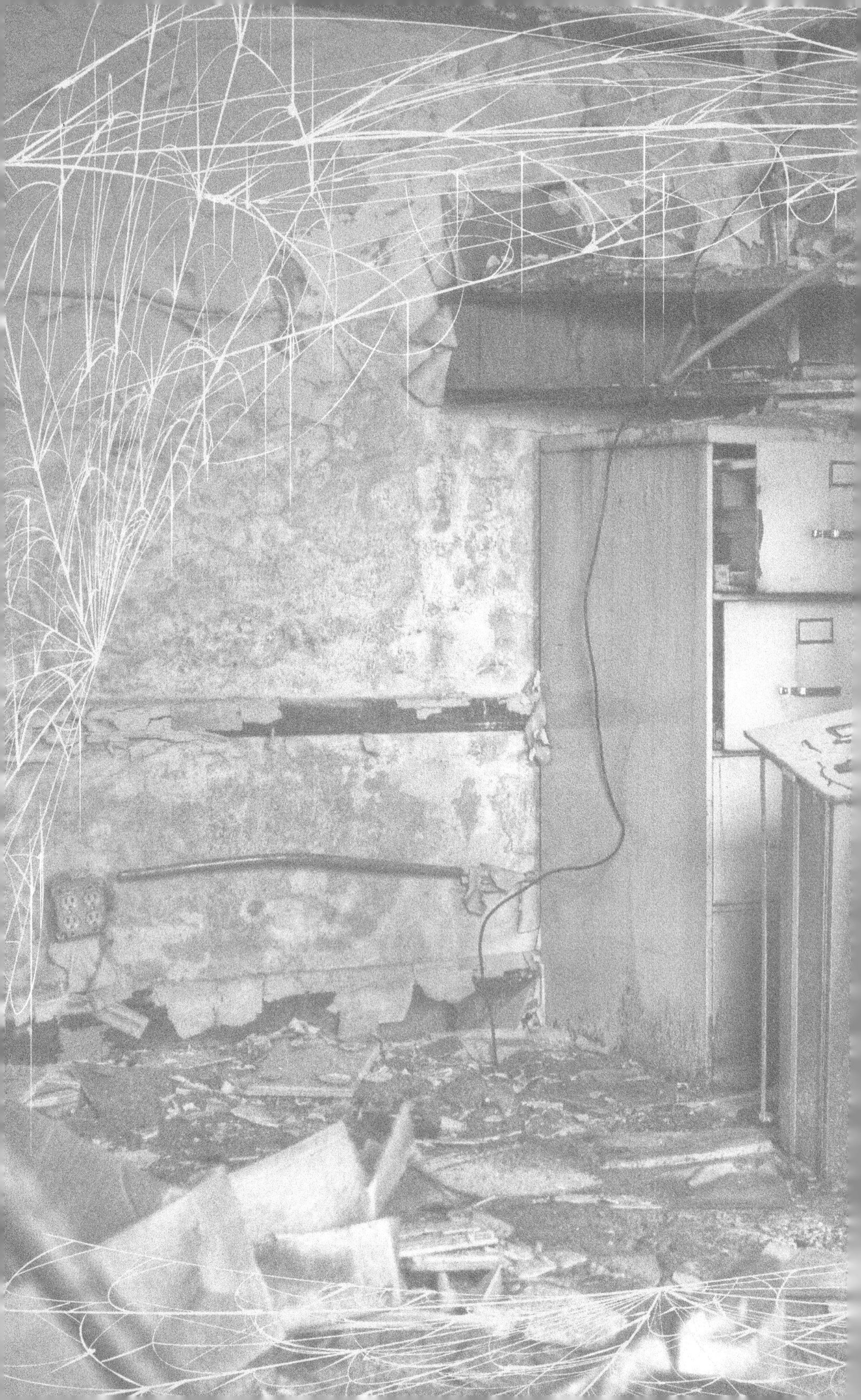

Blood Beast

By Paul Lee

Wind whooshed down from a moon anchored in the night, whistled between terminals, and dived into Drake Daniels's ear. Its cold sting, the sensation of a winter bug, watered his left eye. Papers bent in his hands. The wind pried open their thickness. He pressed his palms against the stack. The paper mouth shut.

Ahead, Tony Rader—wearing a gray suit and puffing a jolly cigar—wobbled toward the wharf. The relics of countless beers dead in his stomach slowed his advance. He removed the tobacco, coughed, and huffed.

His face was an ember.

"Drake, you fool!"

"What did I do this time?"

Gulping, Drake reminded himself to be calm.

"You moved the containers to the *wrong* truck! You've done that twice!"

Coworkers Kelly Rodriguez and Ned Kindle appeared out of the shadows. Ned leaned against a shipping container and grinned. Kelly let the wind realign her collar and said, "Come on, Mr. Rader, give him a break."

Drake's skin warmed. Never had somebody taken his side.

"Shut up and go home!" Tony demanded. "You think you can backtalk to your boss, girl? Beat it!" She looked at Drake. Now more embers burned in this night as cold as ice, as dry as chalk.

Her lips shut, wiggled, then opened.

"Sorry, Drake."

Then she pivoted, shoes sweeping gravel, and walked away.

She was under the gantry—a majestic sawhorse of robotic arms—when Tony barked, "And don't come back!"

She shouted, "This place won't survive much longer, anyway!"

A bar of moonlight bent over the gantry, revealing red flakes of paint seesawing toward her heels.

Tony crinkled his face and jabbed his finger at the air, pointing to Kelly's back. "*That* is who you don't want to be. You know damn well times are tough." He puffed on the cigar. Smoke separated into upward coils, which the night vacuumed into the deeper dark. "And they're tougher when you piss me off."

"Yes, sir," Ned said. Then he shot Drake a quick smirk.

Suddenly, Tony was breathing on Drake's neck. Drake was taller, but his body seemed to shrink.

"From now on," Tony started, "always call me *sir*. Got it, buster?"

Drake swallowed.

"Yes... sir."

His teeth ground behind closed lips.

"I don't like you," Tony said, squinting.

He blew a puff from the red-eyed cigar into Drake's face.

Ned snickered.

The papers shook, almost rattled, in Drake's hand. Tony yanked them into his own.

"The assistant manager was slow. Might be time to replace him." He squinted at both men. "And he knows damn well not to give low-level workers paperwork to hold. Anyways, get out of here. You've got crummy apartments to wallower in." He spit, walked a few yards across the wharf, and threw his cigar. It plopped into the water. "Something for the damn fish to choke on."

He passed the guys and strolled between giant terminals, where wind whistled to the beat of his feet. He was a gray outline, then a shadow, a silhouette, and finally, nothing but a piece of darkness.

Ned left in the same direction. Drake stayed on the outskirt of the wharf. Ten minutes later—after most workers had left the premises—he started for the locker room.

The room was empty except for Kelly weeping on a bench. Her chestnut hair draped her snow-white coat. Drake felt her sadness jump onto his chest and poke his heart.

"I'm sorry about him," he said.

She turned, abruptly wiping tears. Her voice was wet. "Don't be. It wasn't your fault. He's a fucking ass." She shouldered her backpack, rose, and hugged him.

Sniffling, she said, "You're a good guy. I hope you don't have to work here for long."

"I like my job."

"Maybe it's right for you. It's helping your tuition and rent." After a pause, she wiped her eye and added, "But it's not for me."

She left without closing the door.

I didn't tell her bye. This nervousness! I'll miss her. She cared. She cared when the others didn't!

He was putting the last of his uniform into his carrying case when Tony, cigar glowing, stormed in.

That cigar is a fire fed by a coal heart.

"Hey, boy! We got a late shipment coming. Your ass is staying!"

Demonic Workplaces

"I—"

I need to clean my house. The plumber left mildewed plaster in the shower. But... nobody understands.

Tony stepped closer. "*What?*"

"Nothing, sir. I'll stay."

"Of course. You will."

Tony turned and walked out, all hearth, heartless heart, and coal. Drake kicked his locker. Bang! The door squeaked, ajar. He opened it widely. Inside, a brown paper bag was growing, expanding, growing. The string tied to the hook behind the locker handle tightened. The other string, glued to the little square ceiling, flayed. Then *pop*!

Liquified brown showered him.

He vomited waste onto waste. The room smelled of ancient volcanos spewing sewage. Wasn't this simply the smell of a dying world? His body shook. He punched a locker, spraining his middle finger. Or had the world sprained it so he couldn't flip it the bird?

"*Goddamn it!*"

The ceiling light fixture started to swing.

A brownish drop rolled onto his tongue. He tasted 100 toilets and spat them out. Unclothing, he walked briskly to the shower. His filth-caked nails dug into his palms. He considered the various pathogens and diseases the explosion could cause. He imagined maggots blooming, writhing, like weeds inside his stomach, multiplying, colonizing the outskirts of major arteries.

The water gushed salvation. Creeks and rivers of shit slid into the drain. Soap skated across his body, pooling. It was a few minutes before he turned off the Baptism. Drake toweled, walked into the locker room, and changed into his spare clothes. The light fixture still swung stupidly. He hit it. The light died. Dark covered the room. Wasn't this what the world *really* looked like?

Drake exited the building and strolled toward the parking lot. His Ford truck with the corroding battery was the only vehicle, except for the red Camaro pimped out in green neon. The driver's side window lowered. Coworker Jim Toddler was slapping the wheel, laughing, and pointing. Ned appeared in the passenger's seat, laughing with him.

"We got you good!" Jim yelled. "You shithead!"

In a roar of laughter, the Camaro reeved out of the lot. Drake cringed. His teeth sawed enamel. Rage, long bottled, burst forth.

Blood Beast

"Fuck you! You fucking animals! Burn in HELL!"

But they were far gone.

Tears spilled onto the rusted hood of the Ford.

His hand clenched the handle as a *whoosh* filled the wharf. He turned. Behind him, a black mass was docking at the vast platform. He sighed.

Today's been enough hell. I should leave and never look back—not at the ship, not at Tony, not at coworkers! Life's unfair. You give presents and they call you a grinch. You hand out candy and they string you into a pinata. But once my history diploma is framed, I'll be away from the mess we call this job. Tony will fire me if I leave now, and I won't have a chance to pay tuition.

There was time to unload the shipment, right? He assumed the task wouldn't include more than a few crates. Probably a job for one person or a job for none at such a late hour.

He hesitated, then dragged his frown toward the mass, the splash, the creaks. The ship was black and streaked in skeletal remains, some 100-foot-long, with red barnacles strangling the hull. Black masts high on splintery poles were shadows waving at the night. The stern was grooved, and horizontal rows of various bones made its taffrail. The captain's quarters, windowed in crimson, swelled above the sternpost. Beside it, the officers' quarters wrapped toward the port side. Slick oil shined on the deck. The flag leaning on the foremost mast was black with the red calligraphy Blood Beast. Amidship, a grate smoked hellfire.

Drake gaped at the Leviathan.

A figure stepped out of a smoke cloud. The man was neatly shaven, buffalo-buff, in his mid-thirties, and wearing a black cap and trench coat.

"Ahoy!" His voice was as crystal as glass. "Captain Slayer at your service."

Drake scratched the back of his head.

Looking up at the man, he asked, "Did you sail in from the 1800s?"

"No, mate. Blood Beast sails from thousands of years lost. She navigated Greek seas during the Battle of Thermopylae. Her keel sliced the Gulf when the Aztecs were holding beating hearts to the sun and building towers of skulls. Her bow pushed Middle Eastern waves during the dawn of holy wars. She sailed Europe when the land reeked of Black Death ... and circumnavigated the red seas nine times when the whole world was at war." Captain Slayer laughed, and Drake, disbelieving, smiled at the absurdity. "In the dining hall and forecastle," the man continued, "you'll find an etching of every language known, including those spoken by creatures of the deep. Ha-ha! Now, mate, get up here! Let's break our muscles so they come back bigger!" His eyes narrowed. "Like a soul snapped and after its recovery given a knife and perfect memory."

A reef of clouds blockaded the moon. Fingers of gray ectoplasm descended and bled from that reef, like pieces of skeleton pushing toward life. The fingers took a freefall, became a hand, and dripped gray dust across the port.

"This is the strangest night," Drake commented.

"Strange is nothing but the unknown. Ha-ha! What are you waiting for? There's work to do, sweat to spill!"

"How do I get aboard?"

"I already dropped the gangway at the bow! Hurry while night is awake!"

He walked to the bow. A whale's skull grimaced on the front. The captain hurried toward it.

"See that?" he asked. "The skull of a 100-ton whale that sank the *Essex*. The real Moby Dick. Ha-ha!"

Drake closed and reopened his eyes.

I'm not dreaming. This is here. But why? It's a prank, right?

He looked again.

No. Nobody would go through this much trouble, especially for me.

The gangway greeted his feet. He ascended groaning planks. Once aboard, his nose retracted. The deck smelled of copper coated in onions and urine. Captain Slayer stood in front of three crates labeled "Medical Supply Co."

"My apologies for the smell. Our bilge is like a catacomb's butcher's shop."

Our?

"Who else is aboard?"

The captain slapped one of the crates. "Water-Mole!"

The grate behind Captain Slayer wiggled and slid. Out of the smoke came a short figure who was, except for his lower body, encapsulated in a breathing apparatus that clicked, popped, and hissed. The headwear was a transparent bubble welded to gill-like protection. Cylindrical tanks hung on his chrome back. Drake lowered his stare. Wires were stitched between Water-Mole's toes.

The voice was a mechanized nasal. "At your service, Captain."

Goosebumps iced Drake's arms and neck.

"What the fuck?"

Water-Mole frowned.

Blood Beast

"Do not be alarmed," Captain Slayer said. "Water-Mole is harmless. He's my main helper." Water-Mole nodded. "Water-Mole never wanted to breathe like everyone else. He wanted to hold his breath so he could spend weeks under the sea."

"Yes," Water-Mole agreed.

"He can go months in his apparatus. Most of the time, he goes to shore for me. Blood Beast will be miles adrift, and he always swims back."

"Sometimes on the backs of sperm whales."

"Enough talk. The night wants action! Help this good longshoreman move these crates, though they're as light as dead skin."

Face crinkled, Drake looked at the short machine-man, then at the captain.

"It's okay. I can get them myself."

Captain Slayer grinned. "If you insist."

Drake, nodding, grasped the nylon handle of the first crate and dragged it down the gangway. Something inside clattered. Happy not to need the forklift, he pushed the crate into a cargo container used for storage. He returned to the deck and grabbed another handle. A splinter pierced his finger, tickling the bone. Blood welled and rolled. Drake twitched, hissed, and cupped the uninjured hand over its twin.

The captain tipped his cap and chuckled. Drake became dizzy as blood welled.

"I have hemophobia."

Captain Slayer chuckled again.

"Nonsense! Blood is an ancient beauty. Ruby rivers have watered the world for 400 million years."

Drake's eyes narrowed. "I don't know what game somebody put you up to, but I'm moving these boxes, and then I'm not moving a muscle more."

The captain raised his arms in a don't-shoot gesture. "Fine by me. Ha-ha. Night wants us back sailing, anyway."

A wordless Drake finished the job. He stood on the wharf, catching his breath. Captain Slayer was peering down from the gunwale.

"Feeling better?" he asked.

"I could slap someone, to be honest. But I don't believe in violence."

The captain became solemn.

"Violence is *always* necessary, mate. How overpopulated we'd be without it. We'd be sardined smile to smile. You saints ought to remember: there was darkness before the light, and there was storm before the calm."

Demonic Workplaces

"Where do you come from?"

"The passage before time and light, where violence was created for the Big Bang."

A bell tolled somewhere on the ship. A bat fluttered above Drake's head. He ducked as it ascended to the drifting moon. Chains rattled upward, scraped the hull. Water curled at the bow.

Blood Beast dragon-glided out of the dock.

Drake twirled the hem of his shirt around the wound. His head was weightless, his heart racy, his mind jumping rope. He sat on a crate and counted backward from 10 until the hemophobia sank. His mind moved to the crates.

What just happened?

But after the shitshow in the locker room, pranks seemed limitless. For a short while, he debated whether it had been an elaborate prank.

Quickly he drew the conclusion: *Hell no. Firstly, I'm not that important to anybody. Secondly, they don't get aroused unless I'm suffering. Bluebeard's ship or whatever the hell it was didn't torment me. It only confused. What was* it? *One of the elaborate TV pranks shows. That's it! The production crew obtained a replica pirate ship, moved it here, and secretly filmed my confused expressions. It'll air tomorrow night.*

But the ship delivered real supplies! No... those boxes are full of junk, not real supplies. But I never looked!

He went into the storage container and removed the first lid. Halfway down lay a pile of red vials. He grabbed one and brought it to his face. Shifting moonlight trapped his reflection in the glass. There were hollows under his eyes, and his lips were pale. The label on the vial read. "Pharoah X." He had read about the Egyptian Pharoah in the magazine *Lost Empires*. Pharoah X, before the rivers dried below his pyramids, had committed genocide, regicide, and infanticide. The next vial read, "Frankish Knight Godfrey." Oh, yes, Drake knew the name. Godfrey had led the first Crusade to regain the Holy Land from Islamic control. He carried a sac of body parts, littering the streets with feet, hands, and heads.

These are surely fake! Blood doesn't last more than a year! A replica ship delivered replicas...

But he wanted to see the rest.

Chong Wang: the executioner who killed by inflicting 10,000 paper cuts.
Bluebeard: the pirate who impaled his 6 wives with meat hooks.

Thomas Jefferson: a founder of the mass genocide euphemistically dubbed Western Expansion.

Drake brushed aside the vials. They clinked and clattered. Below, his hand touched thin cardboard. He removed it.

The last row of vials waited to be taken.

All had names, most unfamiliar.

Jack the Ripper: London's most notorious serial killer, was nothing but a little red substance.

Lizzy Borden: who took an axe and delivered 40 whacks for one vial max.

He opened the second crate.

Here floated General Shiro Ishii, surgeon of Unit 731, who dissected the living.

Heinrich Himmler: leader of the Nazi SS and concentration camps.

John Wayne Gacy.

Iceman.

Ted Bundy.

BTK.

Digging deeper, he lifted another layer of cardboard.

Eric Harris and Dylan Klebold: mass shooters of a school, smaller than pencils.

James Huberty: the gunman who killed 21 fast-food eaters, turned as tiny as ketchup.

Neither believing nor disbelieving, Drake raised the last lid. A single vial rolled at the bottom. He lifted it above his head. The letters read, "Combined Types." Suddenly the stopper popped out and bounced to the ground. Salty syrup spilled into his mouth. He spit a gush of red. His gums numbed. A stream of the substance was at the back of his throat and dipping, dripping, free-falling. He fell to one knee, jammed two fingers down his throat, and vomited.

His eyes stung mildly, and his teeth ground unconsciously. Dizzy, he sat on his rear, his back against the first crate. His ears smoked as a train of new thoughts chugged over his hills of despair. Here it came, screeching on psychic tracks:

Particles punching and murdering each other had created the Big Bang. Moldering corpses painted the universe black. Gravity broke the bones of clouds to make stars. Rocky fists kept hammering the moon into a bashed skull. Dead matter was cut, rolled, and tossed to make planets.

Demonic Workplaces

Earth spun all red. Fangs ripped jugulars, claws slashed flesh under trees stitched in sinew, where blood watered roots. Dinosaurs stomped in faces and severed veins, until a ball of fire burned them extinct. Humans descended ashen trees and used their big brains to master homicide. They snapped the backs of workers to build civilizations as well as systems of government which led to fast execution of soul, slow execution of body.

War rattled the valleys.

It was on bloodied shields and bleeding limbs that the best saved their families and friends. Through violence, overpopulation was delayed. Through violence, the world was here. And what about the folks in the crates? Many had led to the greatest scientific and technological discoveries. Where would medical science be without experiments on the living? Some of these saints were creators of civilizations and balancers of nature.

Drake gazed at the still water. Somewhere in these deeps, fish were eating each other. The seas were so full that even fantastical ships like Blood Beast occupied their blue mystiques. It was wonderful, he realized, that fish enacted violence to balance the ecosystems, just as bears, lions, and elephants did on land. Through violence, came balance. And only by balance did the world achieve harmony.

In fact, Drake pondered the thermodynamic possibility that violence was the ultimate energy source humans had failed to harness—except for the good folks in the crates. After all, violence had lit up the world billions of years ago. It was God.

O' Violence, glory to Thy name.

He felt blasphemous. He had followed lies and half-truths, propaganda, about peace and love: love was the answer; hate was poison, as if poisons were bad! What did he have to show after walking the bloodless path? A failing job, a red-eyed boss, increased financial woes, an unconquerable college tuition, and coworkers rigging shit-bombs. The latter thought twisted his face like the skull of the dead whale.

Bullies is what they are! I never stood up to them, didn't knock them out, didn't slit their throats!

Bullies would drown in a world washed in blood. Their inferiority complexes caused them to target the weakest links. And *nothing* remained weak when *everything* was violent.

In his mind's eye, Captain Slayer and Water-Mole were steering Blood Beast into a black void, eager to spread enlightenment about darkness. The ship breasted a red swell. The wave heightened, stretched toward Almighty

Violence, expanded across the globe. Witches stirred fish stew in rapids. Bats bathed in shallows. Rocks and sediments sang ancient songs of human sacrifice. Drake peered toward the dead horizon, where a red tsunami pursued the wharf.

His veins jiggled.

Drake's feet, almost skidding water, dangled above the sea. A slit of light was bleeding into the molten silver ripples. He ventured inside the headquarters, which was a sort of hollow water tower wearing a conic hat. He remembered that Tony always kept something special inside his safe. In the early silence, Drake strolled into the office and found what he'd been looking for.

Then he hid it inside the bathroom.

An hour later, the sun was turning into a lemon and smearing sour watercolors. Drake went to meet the elevator. It dinged and creaked. Kelly Rodriguez stood inside. Sunglasses hid her eyes above her snow-white coat. Dark crimson stained the collar. A guitar case hung on her back.

She stepped out.

"Hey, Kelly," Drake greeted.

"Hey. Um, what's wrong with your eyes?"

"My eyes?"

"They're red devils."

He laughed. What else was there to do?

"I haven't checked."

"Why are you here so early?"

"I fell asleep in the locker room," he lied. "What about you? Didn't Tony ... fire—"

"I'm here for my paycheck and my guitar in the locker. That's all that's left."

"Right," he replied. "I should've known."

"You're wondering about my sunglasses."

"I wasn't going to say anything, but, yeah, kind of."

"My boyfriend beat me. It doesn't go over well when you're the breadwinner who loses."

Drake scratched his head.

"That's terrible."

"I know. Well, have a good day, Drake."

Demonic Workplaces

She walked out of the elevator and proceeded to the restrooms. Drake sniffed. The air was thick and coppery. He smelled the locker room. The exploded shit was covering the bench, the three lockers across from his, and a windowpane. But still, he whiffed only copper. He went into the restroom and stared into the mirror. His eyes were as red as Tony's cigar eye. His skin tightened. He remembered reading about looking like this when you busted a blood vessel in your eye. But he knew this was different.

The elevator opened. In the adjacent hall, the side door moaned. Hands high, he pushed back one of the ceiling tiles, gripped a hard handle, and lowered the AK-47. As he unlocked the safety, a dozen feet stomped into the locker room. There was a burst of laughter. Somebody—he couldn't tell who—said, "Oh. My. *God!*"

Ned said, "Prank of the year!"

Jim added, "Tony helped us rig it."

Drake slowed his breathing. He wiped his eye, almost hoping to erase the red. It was electrical. The side door opened again. Jingling keys and periodic coughs informed everyone that Tony Rader was in the building.

Drake's ears perked at the growing jingle. A door yawned, shut, clicked.

Closing his eyes, Drake prayed to Violence. Then, peeling back his blood-ovals, caressing the barrel, he moved toward the locker room.

Everybody was busy reacting to last night's shitshow when Drake entered. There was a second of awe. Then 10 seconds of a piston-engine spilling out of the barrel. Bodies fell like paper dolls. Blood flew in a bloodshow outshining every shitshow. Chunks of pink meat sprinkled in cartilage splattered the lockers.

Gun smoking, Drake advanced to Tony's office. He fetched the key from his pocket and inserted it into the naval of the knob. Tony was under his desk. His voice was shaking away its authority. "How—how did you—how did you get in?"

A grinning Drake held the key toward the ceiling fan. "I've had a duplicate for a while, but never had the audacity to use it." His eyes bulged, red candles shoved into sockets, all lit and melty. "You're going to look at me when I kill you."

"No, *no! God*, please no!"

His voice was red velvet. "I found God last night, Tony. God wasn't what we thought."

"I'll double your pay. Triple your pay!"

Drake lunged. With almost superhuman strength, he tipped the desk, letting it fall on its face. Wood cracked. Tony balled on the carpet, fingers digging into the backing. Drake took the utility knife from his back pocket and stabbed it into Tony's thigh. Tony sprawled and howled. The blade moved to his face and carved jigsaw pieces. His limbs shook violently. Then they kicked and punched Drake's back.

The ember was now a ruby.

The candles in Drake's sockets melted into lakes of blood. They flowed toward Tony's eyes and sizzled there. Crimson oil glinted in waxy water, reflecting Frankish Knight Godfrey. He was in his underwear, wading barefoot through the running blood that reached his ankles. Here was Lizzy Bourdon, whacking an old man's spinal column and singing a precursor to her legendary rhyme. Jack the Ripper energetically clipped the aortic valve of a victim in a rat-ridden alley. General Shiro was scissor-cutting a pregnant woman's stomach as she screamed at crumbling buildings, crumbling people. James Huberty hurled chicken nuggets and more bullets at eaters. And, finally, Drake Daniels was scalping Tony with his knife. The boss's throat rattled, and his limbs wilted until they were motionless roots. The exposed bone was red-tinged gray. Drake grabbed the paperweight on the floor and dented craters into the moon.

Purified in blood, he powerwalked into the hall. Kelly Rodriguez stood at the midsection, pointing an AK-47 at his chest.

She tilted her head, clicked her tongue.

"We had the same idea, Drake. Even the same firepower. And now you've left me with a predicament." She lowered the gun. "Nobody left to kill, except..."

The barrel raised and leveled toward his chest. She squeezed the trigger.

A hot sting pierced Drake's heart. Blood filled him inwardly, outwardly. The lakes in his hollows overflowed.

He fell onto his back.

Kelly descended the back steps leading to the industrial dumpsters, where she had parked her Honda. She took the wheel, lit a cigarette, and sped along the wharf until the tires bounced over the bump in the road which meandered a half mile toward civilization.

The lemon in the sky darkened into a pomegranate. Sirens wailing about better days reached the dock. Police cruisers, armored vans, and ambulances belted the terminals and the headquarters. Before the first responders exited their vehicles, the industrial dumpsters echoed metallic booms. A little machine man scurried behind a row of cargo containers and splashed into the ocean. Only the giant pomegranate saw the star-shaped valve of a tank and the red vial in a webbed hand.

The little glass cylinder read, "Drake Daniels."

THE END

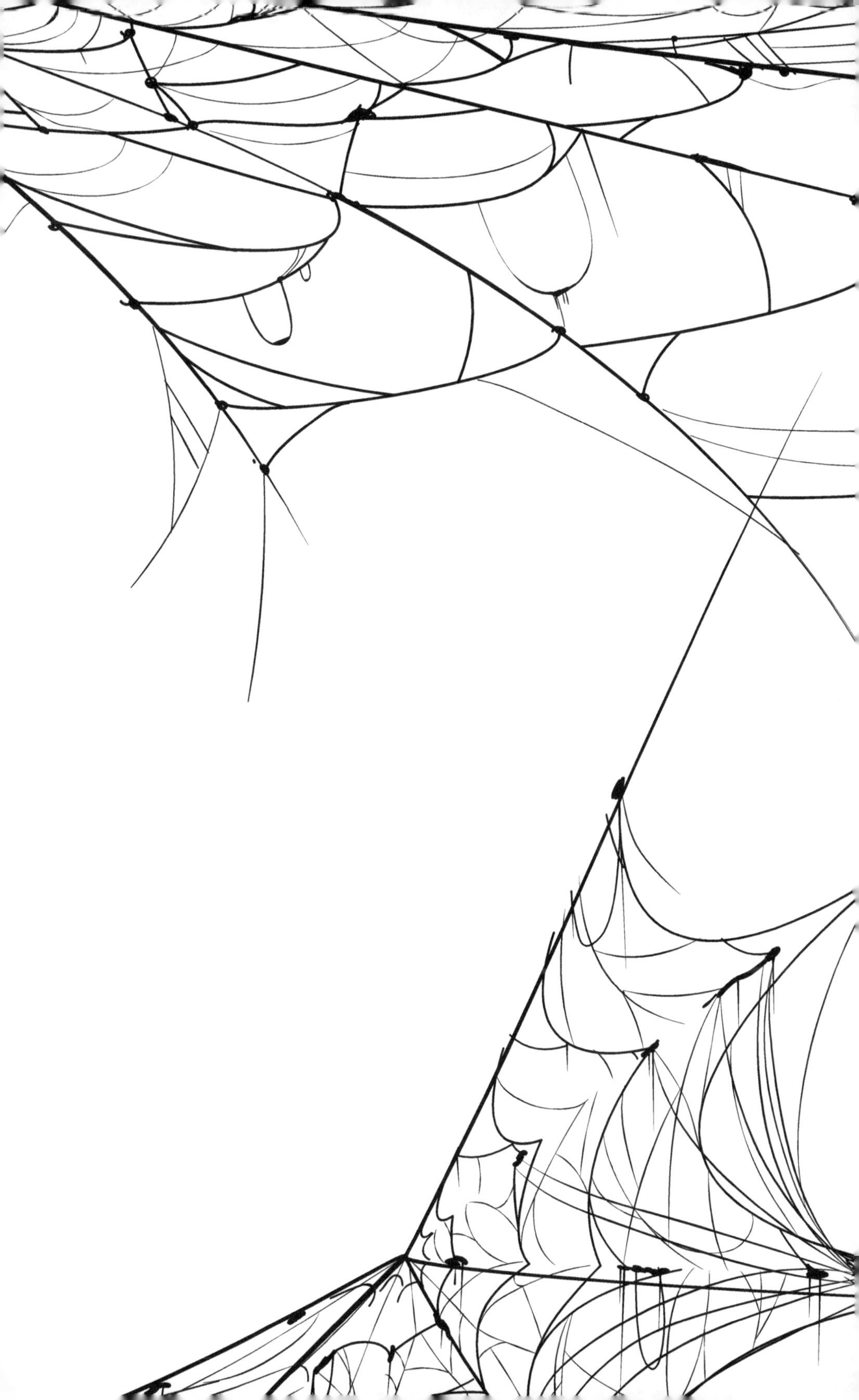

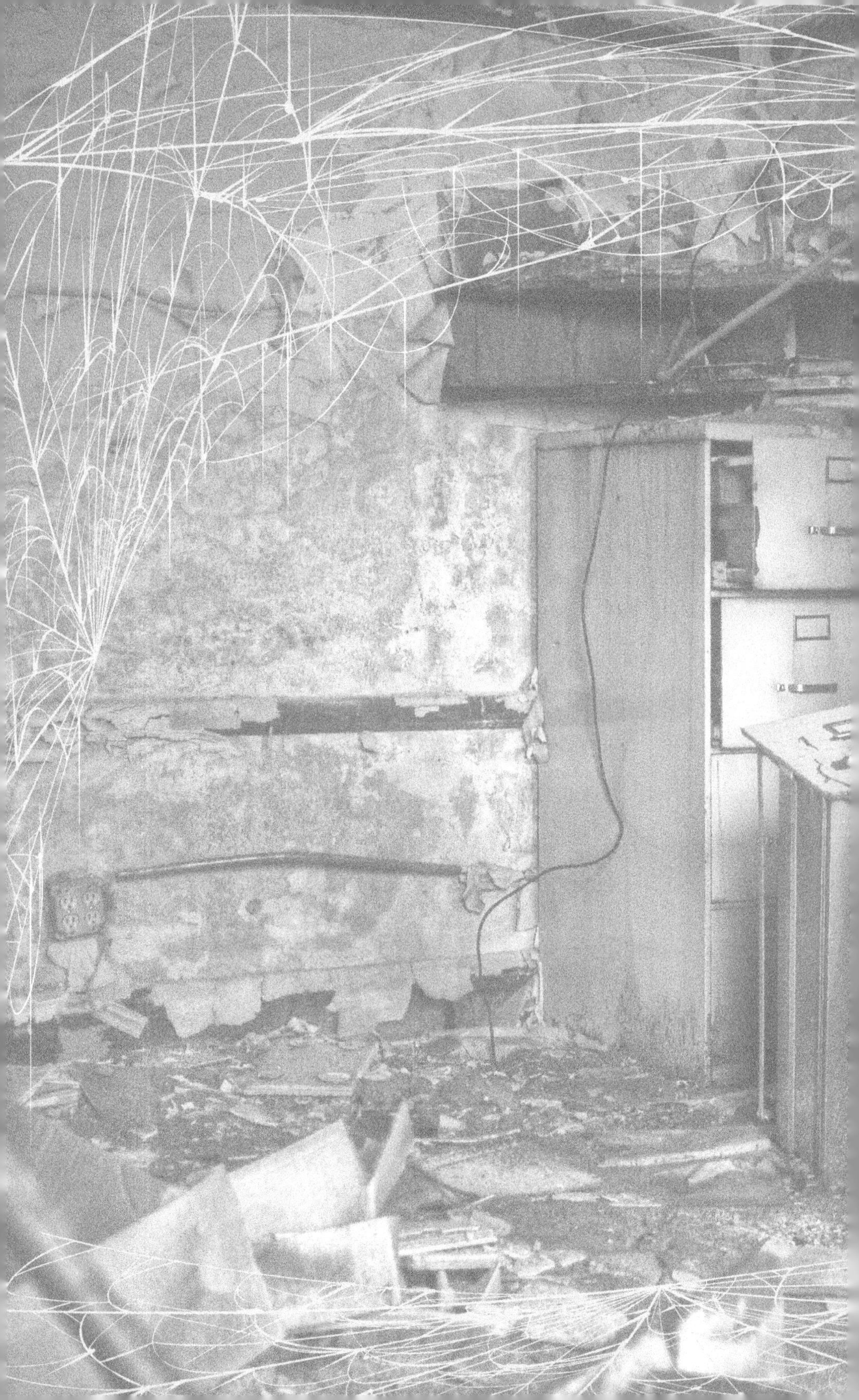

Hostile Takeover

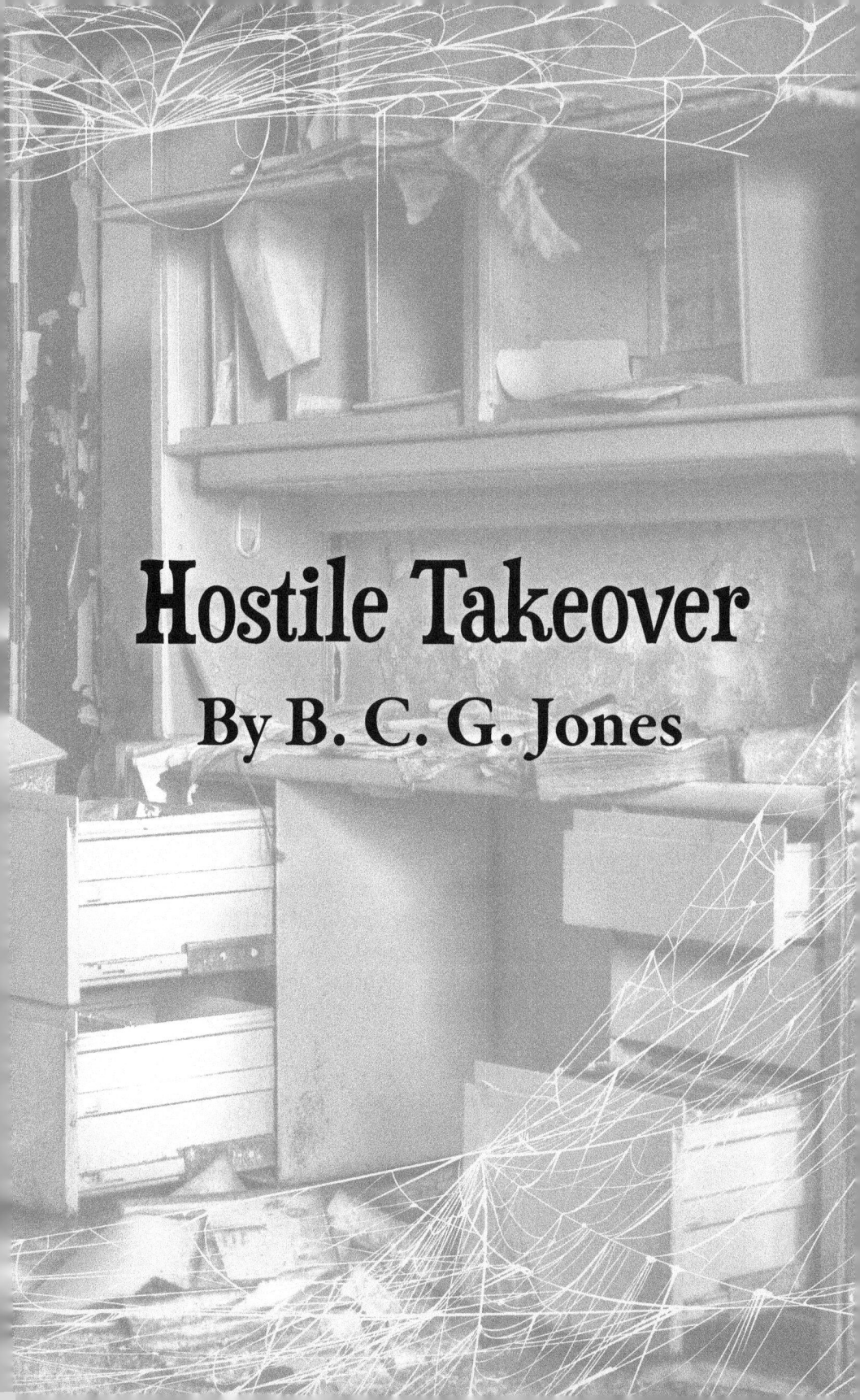

By B. C. G. Jones

Demonic Workplaces

After ten hours doing the full roster of duties at AV Donuts, Laura felt confident that she'd paid her dues. But here she was, driving in again to look at the letter that Pat had dropped ominous hints about. She'd tried to put it off when he'd called her.

"Just take a picture and text it to me, man."

The tensing of his neck muscles was audible, she would swear. "I tried. Comes out blurry every time. And you're the boss."

"Whoa, whoa, none of that. My dad's the boss. I'm just help."

"Well, your dad's out of the country, and this is urgent."

As she pulled into the parking lot, a 737 roared overhead, nose in the air. An expected, even comforting noise when you worked about a mile north of the airport. But once the lights and engine noise had faded into the night, other noises popped up. Crunching steps on the ground, chittering, some insectoid drones. When she stopped to separate the sounds, she found them hardly there, edge of hearing, almost imaginary. And all the more vexing for it.

Once inside the shop, she felt calmer. This place, with its amber light and smells of sugar and coffee, was like home to her. They'd been bringing her in off and on since her infancy, so it damn well should. AV Donuts had been in the family since her great-grandfather and his brother started it before the war.

Pat stood at attention behind the counter, close-cropped gray hair neat, looking every inch the retired cop he was. "Be like dying and going to Heaven," he'd twinkled in his job interview. From under the counter, he produced a standard-size manila envelope and extended it to her. She had a hard time believing it wasn't empty, so little weight did it have.

On thin paper, the letter inside followed standard legal format and identified itself as being from John Smith Capital, LLC. Laura wondered if it might be a frivolous lawsuit or creditors dunning them for an outrageous amount, but neither prospect prepared her for what she found reading it.

> *"Please be advised that we have acquired your business and all assets belonging thereto. This includes the store location in Warwick, Rhode Island and the planned satellite location in Narragansett, Rhode Island.*

Hostile Takeover

"No changes to hours of operation, personnel, or store merchandise are currently planned. We do reserve the right to—at appropriate intervals—bodily consume the patrons of AV Donuts. We will make every attempt to do this in a non-intrusive manner.

"A time of transition evokes many strong feelings, both positive and negative. We expect that to be the case here. But this is also a time of opportunity. In the long run, we see all parties to this acquisition prospering."

She folded the letter, placed it back in its envelope, and laid the envelope on the counter. The paper's rustle alerted her to the tremor in her own hand.

"It's a joke. It has to be."

Rex and Ed looked up from their customary booth. They both tossed luggage at Greene Airport. Rex, older and larger, leaned back and pressed his hands together. Ed, more boyish than he seemed to know, leaned forward and winked at Laura, then blinked out of nerves.

"What's it say?" Rex asked.

"Some nut says they own the place and are going to start eating our customers."

"Damn." Ed scratched his blue t-shirt. "Really?"

Pat nodded. "In so many words."

Shelley sat in the corner, reading a book with cat-eye glasses pressed close against her eyes. She worked as a crossing guard in a nearby school district. This last exchange caught her attention, and she placed a bookmark between the two current pages.

"Well, I'm sure Laura is right, then. Must be a joke. Certainly hope so."

A man appeared out of nowhere and opened the door, giving Laura a start. He wore a suit, well-fitting but faded, with a noticeable hole in the left armpit. Irregular pockmarks covered his sallow skin.

He pulled off a black wool cap, not acknowledging the beige crust that fell from his hat and the hair. His eyes swept around the room in no great hurry.

"Acceptable." His low voice lacked intonation.

"May I help you?" Laura felt the ice of her own smile.

Demonic Workplaces

"I represent the purchasers." He bowed, stiff yet imposing. "And I came to see the investment."

"Oh." Her voice was soft but firm, and the trio of customers leaned in to listen. "No."

"No? I don't understand."

"I know my family, and I know what this business means to us. We're not interested in selling."

Something—not muscle—twitched in the man's face. He tilted his head forward and lowered his eyes.

"It is not a question of interest. This is a thing that has been done. We are the owners."

She felt all the eyes on her, the customers and Pat. She knew that they were on her side, but that they didn't know what she could do. There was only one thing *to* do.

"Get out." She hurled her low voice. "Leave, now."

The man stood, eyes blank, mouth slack. High above their heads, an insect buzzed. Pat came out from behind the counter and closed on the visitor.

"Come on, guy. It's time for you to leave."

The man squeezed the wool cap back onto his head.

"For now, yes. I will return. In the meantime, think. About what is best."

He backed away and opened the door without looking at it. And then he was gone—withdrawn into the dark within seconds.

Dad needed to know what had just happened, and she needed to talk to him. None of this was making sense.

"Hey Pat, I need to make a phone call back in the kitchen. You have everything covered?"

One thumb up in the air, he said, "Uh-huh." Meanwhile, an eye stayed on the door where the visitor had just disappeared.

After her dad's phone rang four times, she expected it to go to voicemail. He picked up just in time.

"Laura? Well, this is a nice surprise."

He was in Greece, touring the places he'd gone with the navy when he'd first met Laura's mother. They hadn't had enough time together, but of course, Laura had gotten even less time with her. What time was it there now? Under ordinary circumstances, she would have looked it up before calling, but this wasn't that.

"Hey, Dad. It's nice to hear your voice, too. You having a good time?"

"Ah, you could say that. This trip isn't just a vacation. But you didn't call just to ask that. What's up?"

"I wanted to know. Did you sell AV Donuts?"

A few seconds of pure silence followed. Then he breathed and then spoke. "Why? What happened?"

"We got a letter. A very strange letter. And then an even stranger man came in."

He sighed. "It's complicated. I'll sit down with you and Creighton when I get home. We'll get the details sorted out." Creighton being the family lawyer.

"Okay." Her hands turned cold. Some big change had happened without her knowing about it. Now she had nothing to hold onto.

"And listen, don't give them any surprises, and they won't hurt you."

"Hurt me? What?" But her father had hung up.

The call had brought her no answers, and she had no real hope of getting any. So the best she could do was go home. She pushed the door open with her shoulder and went back out front. Everything looked the same except for Ed, now grimacing and discolored. He rose, blurring with sweat.

"I gotta..." Instead of finishing the sentence, he pointed at the customer's bathroom.

Laura nodded. "Of course."

Rex sat frozen, eyes wide in confusion. Shelley got out of her seat and reached toward Ed.

"Let me help. We all need help now and then."

Grimacing, he said nothing. Laura opened the bathroom door ahead of him, the light already on inside. But he could no longer walk, even with Shelley's help. He fell to the floor, writhing. Laura worried that he would vomit on the floor.

If only.

Under Ed's left eye, his skin tore open, a ragged diagonal line ending just above his mouth. Well-fed carrion flies dimmed the room's light. More of them than Laura could possibly count. She screamed into her hand so that they couldn't get into her mouth. Shelley, for her part, stood frozen in terror over Ed's twisted body as his head hit the floor with a thud.

Pat jumped over the counter, ran to the front door, and pushed it open. Rex was on his feet now, swatting in a fury. Most of the flies left, flying in a V formation like Canada geese.

Demonic Workplaces

Only two or three carrion flies remained on Ed's very partial remains. On his knees, Rex punched the floor to scare them off, or maybe he was just upset. One fell off immobile and lost a wing. These were the expendables.

His breathing ragged, Rex looked over to Laura. "He was kind of sweet on you, you know. I know, I know, not the time to say that. Stupid."

Shivering, face wet, Laura had trouble coming up with words. "That's okay. I... I guess I knew. He was nice." All she could do now was shrug.

A little messier than usual, and redder in the face, Shelley still kept something like her composure. She strode to the counter and picked up the letter Laura had read earlier and Pat before her. Shelley scanned it once, and something clicked behind her eyes.

"Beelzebub."

Pat said nothing, at least out loud. His patient nod encouraged her to go on.

"Oh, this is an old Sunday school teacher talking," she went on. "But do you really doubt there's something unholy to this, to what happened to this poor young man? And the flies, well, it's a signature."

"Whatever it is." Laura cleared her throat. "Whoever it is, we need to get away from here. All of us."

Nobody argued. Rex carried his fallen colleague across his shoulder.

Her bedside clock's green LCD glow mocked her. She couldn't sleep, no more than two or three minutes at a time. Because she'd see the flies and Ed's broken face, and she'd remember that it wasn't a nightmare, just a memory. Sitting up, back almost straight, swinging her legs over the edge of the bed, she wondered how the others were handling it.

As her feet hit the floor, the board she landed on first squealed. She flinched at the sound, aware that she'd gotten hypersensitive to noise, and that had kept her from getting any decent sleep. That, among many things. At any rate, the sun hadn't even stirred yet, and it looked like she was about to start her day.

Not starting with a shower. Her plans for the day, inchoate as they were, wouldn't wait that long. She just threw on the clothes she'd been wearing when she left AV Donuts, when they'd had to go and take care of the final details on Ed.

Hostile Takeover

She felt the need to walk, walk in order to think. Or to stop thinking, one of the two. And so she went out the door. A chill had set in, a sneak preview of winter, and in that predawn hour, she could feel the bitter cold on her face and neck. Good, she was glad. The chill kept her grounded in the real world, where your friends didn't get eaten from the inside out by bugs. Her face felt hot and wet, then frozen, tears streaming down the center of her face only to stop dead on her upper lip. That was real too, and she embraced it. She pulled her coat a little closer around her. Feeling the cold was one thing, but she didn't want to freeze to death on the way to wherever she was going.

Minutes passed, and she ambled on, accompanied only by the cries of some of the hardier birds. At some point, she came to a pole bearing a white-and-blue RIPTA sign, a stylized bus seen from the front. Laura hadn't taken the bus for years and only a handful of times since she had gotten her license at age sixteen. But this was as good a place as any to stand and watch the dead brown leaves as they tumbled along the road.

At length, a glow rose from the eastern horizon, the sun rising, untroubled by the kind of carnage that had invaded her life. The start of dawn gave her something. Not hope, exactly, but it drove home to her that this was, indeed, a new day. Maybe a day for action.

A bus came along as well. Until it pulled up in front of her, she wasn't sure she'd actually get on. But she did and put a couple of loose bills in the farebox and nodded at the silver-haired driver. At this point, only one other passenger had boarded, a girl wearing a black fleece jacket and nodding along to some tune playing on her headphones. Laura sat across the aisle from her and noticed the youngster giving her a curious look. Was she giving off some kind of aura? In any case, she flashed the girl a peace sign, as incongruous as she knew it to be, and stared out the window.

After only a few minutes and a couple of stops, she saw that she was in a familiar area. The place where she worked, in fact. The center of her world for as long as she could recall. She pulled the cord and got off when the bus came to a stop. It shrunk in the distance, going north to Providence.

In the gray of early morning, she strained her eyes to see if anyone else was around. A few long shadows flicked around, but she couldn't be sure if they were human. Or as human as her visitor had been the night before, anyway. For another few minutes, she waited on the shoulder of the road, waiting to see if anyone would come for her, daring them to do so. No one came out.

Demonic Workplaces

AV Donuts stood squat there, lights off. She took the keys from her jeans pocket and let herself in. Her feet thumped on the floor, and she turned the light on to assess the damage.

So far, there wasn't much. Surprisingly little, in fact. A scattering of napkins from an upset dispenser. A mysterious—or not so mysterious—brown-black scuff on the floor. Otherwise, the place looked as normal as she could expect. But it wasn't normal now. It wouldn't be again. Ever.

It was at this point that the idea gnawing at the back of Laura's brain came to the fore. Only it was no longer just an idea, but rather a decision. She pulled the door open and went back out into the kitchen. They kept the gallon bottles of canola oil on metal shelves. From a shelf at about shoulder level, she hoisted two and unscrewed the cap from one. A carrion fly appeared at the edge of her vision, appearing merely as a dark, moving smudge. It swooped by her ear, buzzing, and then was gone.

She went on, opening and pouring. This would take more than two.

In something like half an hour's time, she had the floor of the kitchen covered. Same with the front house and the tables and booths. Under the register sat a cigarette lighter with U.S. Navy insignia. Someone had left it behind. A sailor, Laura presumed. Heavy for its size, and she knew it to be close to full. A figure appeared in the shadows beyond the counter.

"This would be rash." The visitor from last night spoke with just a hint of tremor. "It was never part of our deal."

She looked him up and down as much as she could stand to. "You never had a deal with me. Whatever else you had, it wasn't an understanding with me."

Then she sparked the lighter and dropped it, which left only seconds to bolt for the door. The man barely made a move to stop her. He stood transfixed by the growing trail of flame.

When she got outside, she could still feel the fire at her back. A back that felt like it would be red and sore for days. A cloud of flies hovered over the shop. Some dropped from the smoke. Others scattered.

The work of three to four generations, gone. There would be time to mourn later.

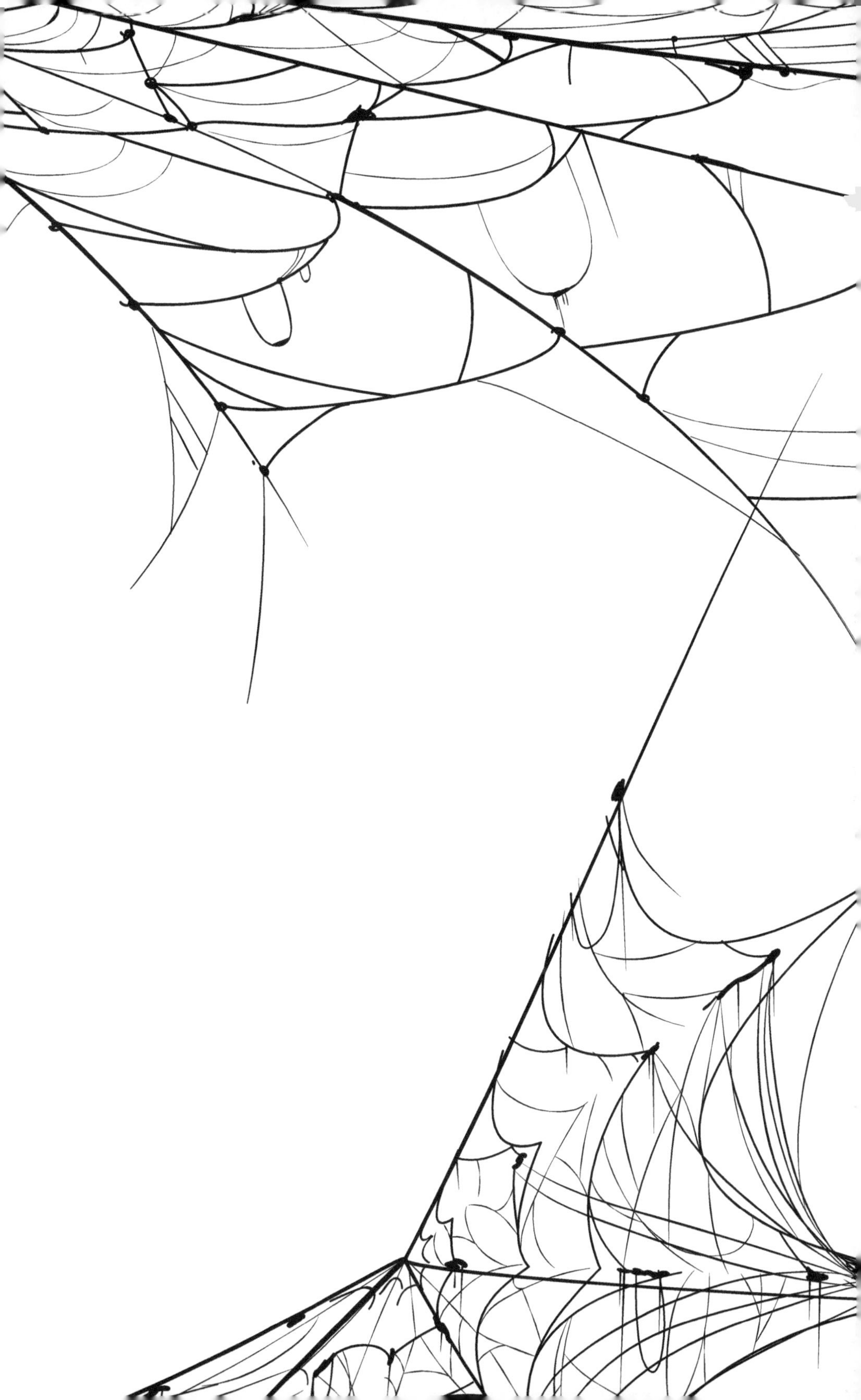

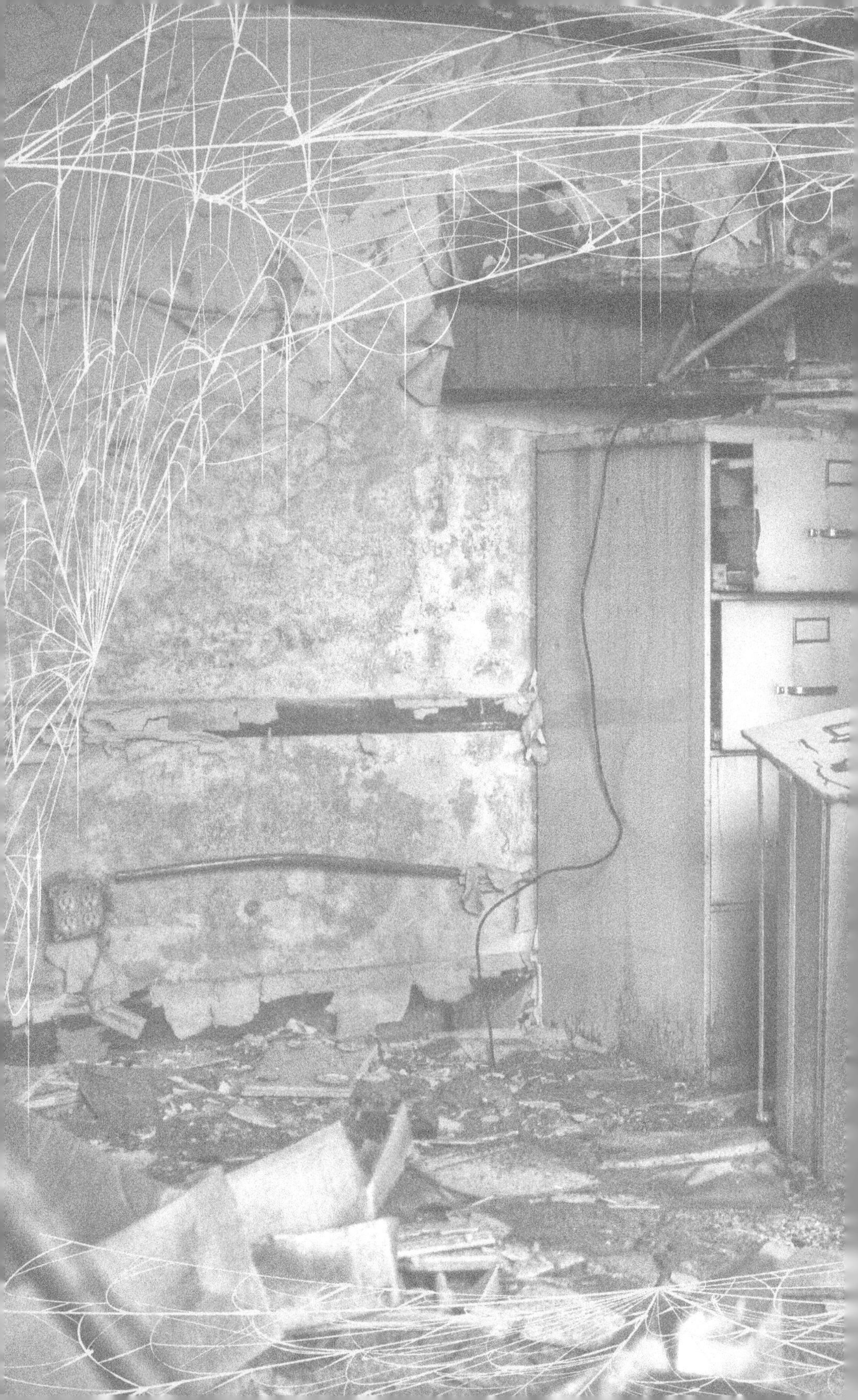

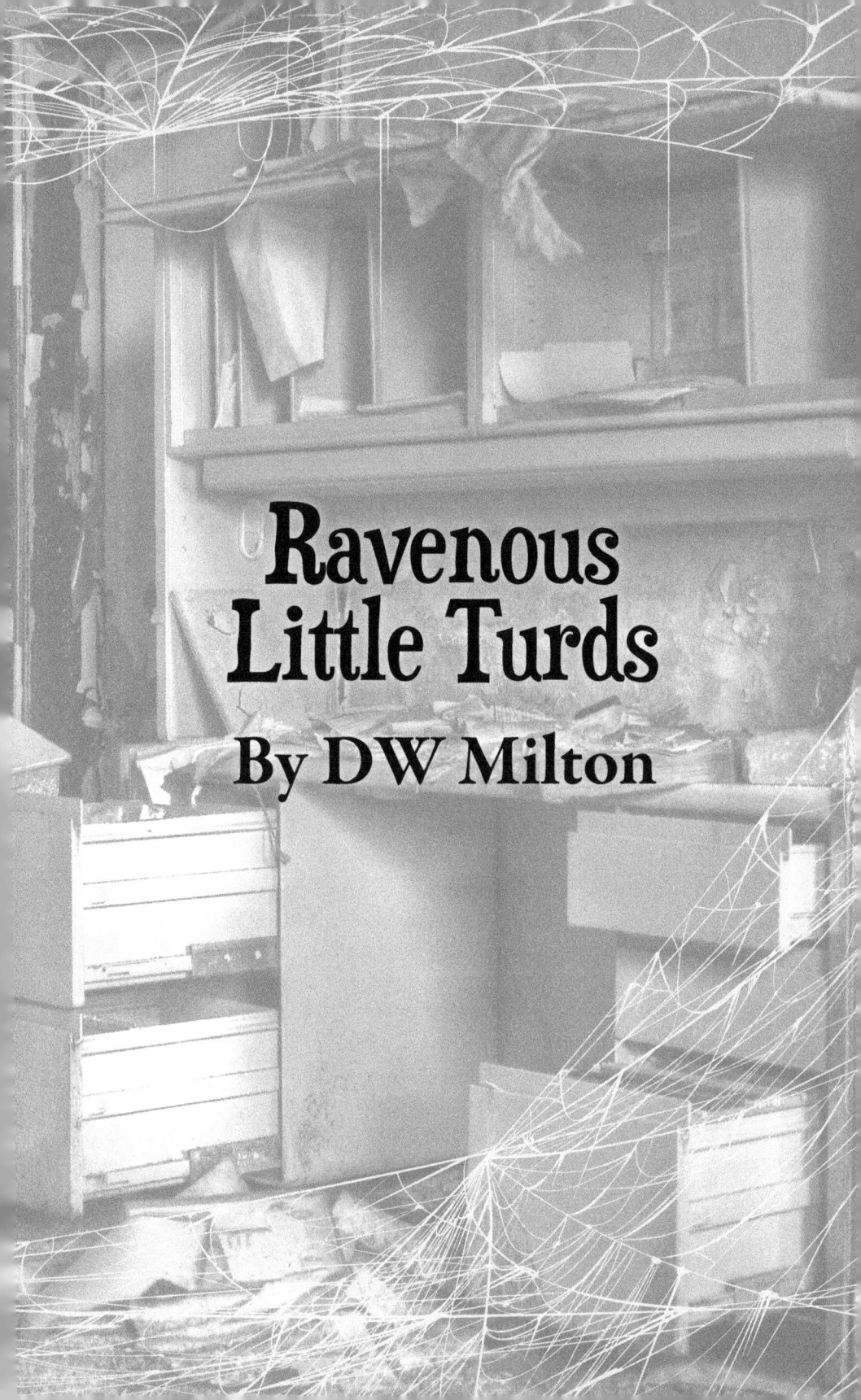

Ravenous Little Turds

By DW Milton

Demonic Workplaces

"Did you hear about Dr. Conover? You know, that fertility doctor who helped father all these little turds." Lexi gestured towards the fifteen toddlers, either spitting up, shitting their pants, or crying about it.

"What?" Maddie hollered over the screaming Patel boy, who despised a diaper change; he would rather sit and marinate. Lexi peeked over her shoulder at the mess.

"God, what a smell!" Lexi gagged and stepped back, swiping on her phone.

The toad on the changing table snuck a finger into his load. Maddie got a clean wet wipe to his soiled digit before it made its way to his greedy little mouth.

Lexi continued, "That gynecologist Jamie's daughter works for. The one who caters to the town's rich and shameless. He was arrested."

The Beckman twins began screaming. Maddie instructed Lexi over her shoulder, "Give Remi the purple one. She's only taking the red because her brother likes it."

Raphe, Remi's older by five minutes, bonked his sister on the head. Remi shrieked.

"Well, Miss Remi," Maddie soothed. "That's what you get when you tease him."

Maddie sat Vishal in the group, then traded Remi the purple block and gave Raphe the red. Raphe, happy as a clam, smiled and babbled at his sister.

"See, Remi, you like the purple one." Maddie flopped on the floor. Lexi hovered with her phone.

"Here on Twitter, 'Local fertility doctor arrested.'"

"What else does it say?"

Maddie was interested. Dr. Conover was a local celebrity. She saw him at the country club on her weekend shift at the bar. He was the current president for golf memberships, deciding who stayed and who played. But the real fan club was his patients—professionals that had forgone their childbearing years for earnings. Childless, they went to Conover's clinic to get their reproductive juices flowing.

"Nothing," Lexi said. "Story at eleven. Tory get that out of your mouth!" The Kepler girl habitually chewed on the wooden blocks.

Maddie tickled Tory, distracting her from the block. "We should just put these away." Maddie tucked it into her skirt pocket.

"Why?" Lexi shook her head. "Her mother is an idiot. Doesn't she know that you can only get rabies from toilet seats?"

Maddie smiled; she never knew if Lexi was serious.

Remi crawled over, straddled Maddie's belly and then farted.

"Aw, disgusting!" Lexi cried. "Did that little beast just crawl over to poop on you?"

Remi smiled a Cheshire Cat.

After the last child was collected, Jamie found Maddie wiping down the room.

"How did it go today?"

"Fine." Immediately defensive, Maddie always kept her answers short with Jamie. Jamie would talk enough for the both of them.

"Dr. Conover has been arrested."

Maddie shrugged.

"I am asking that my employees refrain from speaking with the press. You may get a call or have them come to your door, but please, if you would like to continue working here..." Jamie let her words hang, emphasizing the threat.

"None of my business," Maddie shrugged again.

"Many of the children here, well, their parents were his patients," Jamie stepped closer.

Maddie resumed wiping. "Like I said, none of my business."

Jamie appeared uncertain, then turned to go. "I'm sure Lexi would appreciate it if you could pass this on to her. You know how she is."

Maddie extended her middle finger as the door closed. Jamie just made Maddie responsible for keeping Loose Lips Lexi quiet.

At home, Maddie poked at a bowl of ramen with a stale cracker. Thumbing through her phone texts from the day, she saw that Lexi forwarded her Conover tattle. Local police moved in, closing his office and confiscating medical and financial records. Hints that the FBI was also involved circled the internet.

Conover had tried to get her to go to bed with him, and she did. Once.

Maddie should have sent him packing, but he was an attractive older man. Divorced a few times, but he still had the cash, the car, and the attitude. She hated herself for it, but she had just broken up with Jimmy the Jerk and was feeling alone. The sex wasn't bad, but it wasn't great. He treated her the same afterward, without conscience, without regret, but also without memory. In fact, she didn't think he was that drunk, but he showed no signs that he even recalled them spending the night together.

That was fine with Maddie; as a club employee, she was forbidden from fraternizing with members, and she made good money bartending there.

The following day at the daycare, there were only six demon spawns instead of fifteen, still barely manageable.

"I heard last night that Dr. Conover is in solitary at the main prison. He's not even being held locally." Lexi pulled a wooden block out of Tory's mouth, resulting in an ear-shattering scream. Lexi shoved a *Duplo* at her. "Hush, brat!"

"Where did that imp find that?" Maddie thought she hid all the wooden blocks yesterday. Lexi passed it over to Maddie, who tucked it in her skirt pocket.

"Rumor is they're going to interview his former patients." Lex looked around the room. "All these uppity parents are going to have to spill the beans about their miracle worker."

"Why?" Maddie wondered aloud. "He didn't prescribe drugs except for hormones or Viagra." She looked out the window. "All his stuff was fee-for-service." Maddie overheard many father wanna-bes complain after a third martini about Conover's prices.

"Is it feeding time? The natives are getting restless." No one had gotten a good night's sleep. Cranky parents meant cranky kids.

With everyone tucked into the tables, meatballs, peas, and carrots within reach, Maddie inspected the shredded block. The bite marks were unusual for a toddler, more like puppy's teeth.

Ow! No biting!" Lexi snatched her hand back from Tory. Lexi examined her hand. "Little bitch drew blood."

"Let me see." Maddie looked at Lexi's hand. The bite marks matched. "Like vampire fangs."

"Should I get a shot?"

"For what?"

"Rabies?"

Tory was grabbing at the meatballs, shoving them in her mouth.

Ravenous Little Turds

"I guess she's hungry." Maddie would need to mark it on the daily sheet. "Maybe she's on a growth spurt."

Raphe started bawling. Tory stole his last meatball, so he punched her. Before Maddie could separate them, Remi threw her peas at Tory, who responded by grabbing Remi and biting her arm.

Maddie seized Tory, who thrashed, kicking Vishal in the head, who began hollering.

"What the...?" Lexi swore.

"I'll take care of Tory. Can you calm the Brady Bunch down? Try some music. *Little Genius* is already in the player."

Lexi panicked. "Don't leave me alone with these terrors!"

Maddie carried Tory to Jamie's office.

"Tory, you are going home. I have told you, Miss Lexi has told you, your mom has told you, there is no biting."

Tory stood defiantly, closed eyes, hands fisted, and mouth opened to scream. Maddie noticed her teeth. Tory had a second set, needle-sharp and bloodied, behind her baby teeth. Maddie couldn't tell if it was Tory's blood or from her victims.

"Tory, do you have owies in your mouth?"

Tory opened her eyes and stopped screaming. "Owies?" She nodded her head. "Owies."

"Where Tory? Can you show me?"

"My owth." The two-year-old shoved a finger in her mouth, stabbing the digit on the inhuman dentition. She showed Maddie the new injury. "Owie."

"How about I give you a lolly? No more biting-okay? Pinky promise?"

The little one nodded and held out a pinky finger and crossed it with Maddie's pinky. In the front office, Jamie handed Tory a lolly from the jar and asked Jamie's secretary, Belinda, to call Tory's mom.

"You can't just leave her here," Belinda complained.

"She'll be fine with the lollipop. Besides, I can't leave Lexi alone, or it will be a mutiny in there. Call me on the intercom when her mother arrives."

Belinda hated children and made no secret of it. Maddie left Tory and headed back to the room where everyone was singing *The Wheels on the Bus*.

Demonic Workplaces

Twenty minutes passed and everyone was dizzy from the *Hokey Pokey* when Belinda buzzed in. Maddie took her whole self out into the hall, where she met Jamie.

"Why is Tory's mother here?"

Maddie hoped Belinda had informed Jamie, but payback was a grizzled old bitch named Belinda.

"She's biting again."

"Why wasn't I told immediately?

Changing the subject, Maddie replied, "Tory has got something weird going on with her teeth." Maddie tried to explain. "They are like little needles. Puppy's teeth." Jamie stared, making Maddie nervous. "Maybe it's a congenital thing."

Jamie dismissed her, turning toward her office. "I will handle this. Go back to your class."

Irritated and annoyed, Maddie took her time getting back. Lexi would complain, but she needed to compose herself.

When she opened the classroom door, Lexi hollered over the din, "Where have you been?" The monsters and the room smelled like chaos.

Needing some fresh air, Remi and Raphe sat in the sandbox, babbling in their own tongue. The rest of the jungle bunch slid down slides and traipsed back and forth from the treasure chest to Maddie. Maddie would feign surprise every time a little one hobbled over with a shovel or a plastic car. She was so involved with the game; she failed to notice the twins. Remi had the head and Raphe had the tail of a dead rat. Both were chewing.

Maddie pushed Vishal away to grab at the dead animal. The children grinned. Fur and strands of muscle hung from their mouths. The others, now interested, wanted to share; but the twins greedily hid their find. Maddie wrestled it away and threw the halves over the fence, then struggled to remove the lingering fur and filth from their mouths. They screamed as if she was denying them a treat.

Done with the kids, Maddie vomited over the fence. The children watched wide-eyed as she wretched and heaved.

Ravenous Little Turds

In a weak voice, Maddie scolded, "No eating dead things." The children beamed as if that was the funniest joke ever.

At home, Maddie's brother and his girlfriend, Candi, relaxed on the couch, sharing a pizza and a movie. They offered her leftovers and a spot on the couch. She declined, not hungry.

"It's *Village of the Damned*, the 1960s version. Your favorite," Glen hollered.

"Been there, done that," she called from the stairs.

Lexi could hardly contain herself during the morning report. Jamie eyed her suspiciously and mentioned to Maddie privately, "...keep a lid on Lexi."

"Did you hear? Conover's a total weirdo devil worshipper. I bet all those snotty parents are wishing they had used another baby maker! Serves them right!"

Maddie stared at Lexi. "What are you talking about?"

"The FBI picked him up on tax evasion, but that's how they get them all anyway, but..." she looked around, but the room was empty. Parents wouldn't start dropping off their preciouses for another half hour. "Turns out, he's a total quack! He's been using some sort of home remedy to *induce* the women's ovulation, but then, get this..." She paused.

Maddie stopped stacking diapers.

"He's been using his own sperm!"

Maddie's neck snapped. "What?"

"Yup, all the swimmers were his very own!" Lexi laughed manically. "Who knows how many children he has fathered here and in other towns? Looks like he's been doing this for years!"

"Wait, what?" Maddie was confused. "Devil worshipping?"

"Oh yeah, that was strange, too."

"What, Lexi? What was strange?" Sometimes Lexi was more challenging than the two-year-olds were.

"Supposedly, he is in a satanic cult. Anyway, can you believe all these little shits are related?" She shook her head. "It's going to make for an interesting prom night."

Demonic Workplaces

Maddie stood at the changing table, thinking about her night with Conover. The whole evening was bizarre. He took her to a large estate in the country club. The house seemed staged, as if he was borrowing it. There was nothing personal, like photos or pictures. Other weirdness included a gold pentagram charm, and a mummified chicken's foot on the kitchen table, prompting her to shimmy out the door and back to the parking lot for her car, leaving him snoring.

Tory screeched as she grabbed Maddie's legs, interrupting her thoughts. If Lexi's internet story was true, Tory could definitely be one of Conover's brood; they all could be. The doctor set up practice in town about three years ago.

Despite the news, it was business as usual in the toddler room. Jamie seemed the only one put out. She came by the room "to check on things" more often than usual, but that was it. In the outdoor playground, Raphe somehow opened the latch on the back gate, nearly getting into the woods behind the playground. Jamie would need to put a lock on the gate.

Must be looking for a snack, Maddie snickered but then regretted it, picturing the rat parts hanging out of Raphe's bloodied mouth.

At the end of the day, Lexi noticed a patrol car in the back parking lot. Immediately, she was tapping her phone. "You think they are asking about the kids?"

"I don't know, but stop Lex. Jamie is serious about the reputation of the school and confidentiality for the families."

"Yeah, yeah." Then Lexi's eyes widened, and her jaw dropped. She looked at Maddie. "What if Jamie's in on it?"

"Oh my God, no Lex. Don't even go there!"

"No, seriously, what if?" she repeated. "It's perfect! You need a place to keep all these terrors. Her daughter works for him! Oh my God! I'll bet she knew this whole time!" Lexi broke off, furiously texting.

"Stop, you are going to text your way into getting fired," Maddie warned, but she had to admit, the whole situation was beyond bizarre and getting stranger by the minute. A devil-worshipping fertility doctor who fathered an entire town of children. Sounded like a dumb movie plot.

Maddie waited until she saw the police car leave before visiting Jamie to request a lock for the back gate.

Jamie sat reading from her computer screen.

"Jamie," Maddie hesitated. "We need a lock on the back gate. One of the twins almost escaped."

Jamie barely looked from the screen. "Get a combination lock. I will reimburse you next pay period."

Maddie frowned. "Can I use some of the petty cash? I am a little short this month."

Jamie glared at Maddie and then opened her bottom desk drawer to fish out her wallet. She handed Maddie a twenty. "I want change."

The glare hardened. "I told you to keep a leash on Lexi."

Maddie shrugged, "I tried, but you know…"

"You both leave me no choice. I will have to take care of it."

Maddie left, wondering if Lexi would have a job tomorrow. Great, fifteen little freaks by herself. She would need that lock.

Lexi was a no-show at work the following morning. Maddie texted, but Lexi did not answer.

The kids were unusually well-behaved. Even Tory was helpful. Maddie was unnerved. Especially when Tory came over to Maddie during naptime, pointed at Maddie's belly, and said, "Baby."

Following work, Maddie flew down the road to Lexi's house. Lexi had never missed a text in her life, and all her social media was quiet. Dead, in fact. No additional posts after "someone is at the door." That was at 10 p.m.

As she drove up, Maddie instantly knew something was wrong. Lexi's car was in the garage, but the door was left open. Lexi never did that. The interior door was also ajar. She entered. The house appeared empty. It was not until Maddie found Lexi's phone lying on the floor that she began to panic. Lexi would never go anywhere without it.

The cracked screen suggested someone had dropped or smashed it. Maddie swiped, and it glowed, indicating it still worked. Punching in Lexi's passcode, the screen brightened, returning to Lexi's Twitter account. Nothing since ten last night.

Demonic Workplaces

Sitting on the edge of the bed, she brought up Lexi's search history. A plethora of items popped up, all about Conover, including his address at the country club. Lexi had Google-mapped the address, and a corresponding satellite photo came up on the screen. Maddie panned around. She had not realized the house backed up to the same woods as the daycare.

A knock at the front door surprised her, and she almost dropped the phone. Sliding Lexi's phone into her pocket, she opened it to two police officers and a squad car blocking her car.

"Are you Alexandra Blume?" one asked.

"No, a friend."

"When's the last time you saw your friend?"

"About six, we left work. She didn't come in this morning, and I could not get her on the phone."

"How did you get in?" the partner asked.

"The garage door was open."

"Please step outside, miss, and let us have a look."

Maddie obliged while the officers went inside. Stuck, she waited.

They returned. "No one is here."

"I know." Maddie was impatient. "And I don't know where she could be. I want to file a missing person's report."

"Too soon," one stated as they pushed by her, exiting the front door. "You'll need to wait 24 hours."

The other remarked, "Don't worry too much about your friend, miss. I am sure she will turn up."

Maddie watched them go. In her car, she pulled out Lexi's phone and she refreshed the Google map image. There was some sort of clearing in the satellite photo with a strange structure just behind the daycare. Maddie had never realized it was there, but she had a feeling about it. Maddie started her car and headed back to the daycare. Lexi and her theories were one thing, but maybe Lexi was right, for once.

The building was dark, with no cars in the lot. Climbing the steps to the side door, she peeked in, but all was quiet. Then she heard something out in the woods.

Walking past the gate that needed the lock, she saw a glow deep in the thicket. Maddie got closer. Hidden behind a large tree trunk, she stood staring in disbelief. Torches outlined the clearing filled with chanting, cloaked figures. The figures surrounded a structure that looked like a large stone altar jutting out from the ground. Behind the stone loomed a massive oak tree. Branches stretched into the darkness. Hung, just above eye level, facing the gathering, was an inhuman skull. The blackened horns twisted and curled into the night. The bleached bone emanated its own sinister light.

A hooded figure stepped between the stone and the skull. The chanting quieted. The person threw back the hood, revealing Jamie's face, flickering in the firelight.

The others followed, showing their identities—Jamie's daughter, Belinda, Tory's mother and father, and the other parents of Maddie's toddlers.

She panicked.

From the darkness, another covered figure carried Lexi's unconscious body and laid it on the stone like an offering. Behind waddled Tory, the twins, and Vishal—her two-year-olds. Maddie watched in horror as the children marched to the front of the stone, their backs toward her. The robes closed in.

Unable to see, she crept in for a better view. Finding a break in the trees, she crouched. Lexi lay there as if asleep. Maddie took the phone out to call 911, but before she dialed, Jamie spoke.

"Faithful brothers and sisters. I stand here in place of our brother Stephan Conover, who has sacrificed himself so we may go on."

The followers murmured their thanks.

"For we are the chosen. We have, through our brother, received these gifts from our Father, The Dark Lord!" She gestured to the babies in front of the stone, sitting calmly, as if waiting for a treat.

Maddie had not noticed Jamie remove a dagger from the folds of the cloth until she rammed the blade down and into Lexi's chest.

Maddie couldn't scream; all the air had been sucked out of her lungs. A small whimper escaped before she slapped her hands over her mouth. The scream from Lexi masked it. Maddie would never forget that sound; tears rained down her cheeks.

Jamie carved Lexi up like a butcher. As if throwing scraps from a feast to wild dogs, Jamie tossed organs and parts of Lexi to the wanting mouths waiting expectantly below. Tory slurped on Lexi's heart, blood dripping down onto her PJs. The twins fought for and tore at the intestines in a gruesome tug of war. Vishal sat shyly, nibbling at a brown, slimy kidney.

Crawling on their knees, the adults cooed and awed at the little ones, chanting again. Maddie's chest heaved with a sob, and if things could not get any more insane, Jamie turned and spoke to the skull.

Demonic Workplaces

"We have brought you your kinder, Dark Lord. We have fed them on a non-believer, as you instructed. How may we serve you?" Jamie folded herself in a subservient bow.

The skull replied, "Bring me the woman with whom I have lain. She is with *my child*."

The voice sank deep into Maddie's bones. Petrified of discovery, she backed away. Once Maddie thought she was out of earshot, she ran for her car.

No one noticed Tory looking over at the far trees. She removed the mangled organ from her mouth and she said, "Baby."

Home, Maddie locked the front door.

"We're out of milk?" Glen called from in front of the TV.

Maddie rushed to the kitchen door, and locked it, pulling the curtains closed, then raced by him to the living room to pull those curtains closed.

"What's eating you?" Glen rubbed the TV from his eyes.

Maddie rummaged in a lower kitchen cabinet. "Lexi's dead. Do we still have Mom's good whiskey?" Finding a large bottle containing amber liquid, she grabbed a tumbler from an upper cabinet, poured, and then repeated, "Lexi is dead."

She began to cry.

"What? What are you talking about?"

"Jamie carved her up like a Thanksgiving turkey!" Maddie's shoulders heaved.

"Here." Glen grabbed the glass with the fiery liquid. "I'll drink. Then maybe you will start making sense."

He waited for Maddie to calm.

Maddie took a deep breath. "Lexi didn't show for work today, so I went to her place when she wasn't answering her texts. Her house was empty, but I found her phone. The police came but wouldn't let me file a missing person's report. I used her phone to follow her searches and wound up in the wood behind the daycare."

She took another deep breath. "Lexi told me that Conover has been accused of inseminating his patients with his own sperm, fathering the kids at the daycare."

Glen sighed; he had also heard that.

Ravenous Little Turds

"I think Lexi was wrong." Maddie took a deep gulp of the whiskey, cringing. "After what I saw in the woods, I think they are all devil worshippers. Conover, Jamie, Jamie's daughter, Belinda—all the parents. But," she hesitated.

"But what?" Glen asked.

"I don't think Conover is the father."

"What?"

"Satan is," answered Maddie.

"You think Satan is their father!" Glen began laughing. Tears sprang to his eyes. "The Devil spanked his wank, and Conover inseminated the mothers with his semen?" He howled, "That has got to be the grossest thing ever!"

He stopped laughing when he saw his sister's face. "So you're suggesting that Conover is like that Atticus Finch actor who played that Mengele doctor and made all those Hitler youths?"

"Gregory Peck," Maddie replied.

"Yeah, that guy, and got the Stepford Wives pregnant with Satan's sperm? So you are like working at a daycare full of Rosemary's babies. What could be worse?"

"That they ate Lexi! Consumed her like a pack of ravenous little... turds!"

Glen put his head in his hands and sighed. "Oh shit, does this mean if the Devil is here, that Heaven is real? God, Maddie, we haven't been to church since Mom died. We are so screwed!"

With nothing more productive to say, Glen declared, "Tomorrow, we start going to church!" He then left the table, slinking out of the room.

Maddie sat, woozy from the alcohol and ebbing adrenaline. Lexi was dead, and her boss, a co-worker, and clientele worshipped Satan, which, in essence, made her Satan's nanny.

Lexi, the one into conspiracy theories and creepypasta was finally right. *Who knew?*

Maddie wiped her eyes. *What if everyone knew?*

"Maddie, Maddie!" Glen burst back into the room. "We gotta get out of town. This whole place could be crawling with these crazies! If the cops know you know Lex is missing, and now she's dead, oh man, we have to go! Get your shit together!"

For once, Maddie was in total agreement with her brother. All she had in her wallet was Jamie's twenty.

"Where are we going to go?"

Demonic Workplaces

"Candi's uncle has a hunting cabin in the woods in New Hampshire. We can fall off the grid there."

"Let's go!" Maddie grabbed her bag. She could get a toothbrush later.

Jamming north out of town, they were going to pick Candi up on their way, but a mile from Candi's place, a squad car pulled out of nowhere, inserting itself behind them.

"Pull over," Maddie said, "I'll handle this."

Glen slowed and stopped on the shoulder. He reached across Maddie to the glove box for his license and registration. The gun fired before he sat back, removing a large chunk of brain and scalp, the bulk of which fell into Maddie's lap with the rest of him.

Maddie hyperventilated. The world began to spin. Her brother and her best friend were dead.

Too calm for what he had just done, the officer ordered Maddie out of the car.

He didn't have to ask twice. She climbed out of the car and almost into the arms of the second officer, whom she recognized. He was one of the pair from Lexi's earlier.

"We found your friend," he snickered. "Well, parts of her anyway." Both laughed.

Unable to look at the carnage in the car but overwhelmed by the smell of gunpowder, blood, and gore, Maddie fainted dead onto the pavement.

Maddie awoke lying somewhere familiar, but her head hurt and it was hard to focus. Bringing a hand to her brow, the pain intensified. Eyes adjusting, she realized where she was. The events of the evening came smashing down on her. Closing her eyes, again, she wept.

Jamie entered her office and sat. Rolling her chair slightly, she inquired, "How are you feeling?"

Maddie was silent except for an occasional sniffle.

"I am sorry about your brother. Jamieson and Polk are, at times, a little too zealous."

Maddie rolled over to face the back of the couch.

Ravenous Little Turds

"Lexi," Jamie sighed. "Well, with Lexi, you can't say I didn't warn you. I don't doubt that you tried, but that girl was always too much up in everyone else's business."

It was too much for Maddie. She exploded. "What the hell are you talking about? Everybody else's business? What does everyone else have to hide that is worth killing innocent people! Tell me!"

Sarcastically she continued, "I guess everybody in this fucking town is a homicidal devil-worshipping psychopath that feeds innocent people to demon spawn."

"Yes," Jamie replied, unfazed.

Maddie sat stunned. *Well, that was unexpected.*

Belinda opened the office door. "Parents are beginning to arrive." She looked at Maddie. "Good morning." Leaving the door open, Tory waddled in, chewing a lolly.

Maddie picked up her feet, sliding back on the couch as far away from the child as she possibly could.

Tory climbed up on the couch, pink drool slobbering down her chin from the red lollipop. She crawled over to Maddie and smiled a toothy grin, sugar caked on her lips and gums. Tory reached through Maddie's crossed arms to touch Maddie's belly.

"Baby." She smiled.

Jamie stared at Maddie, then a huge smile spread across her calculating face. "So, it is you. You have the Dark Lord's child."

Dumbfounded, Maddie watched the little toad slide down the couch on her belly, her butt sticking out, and then saunter out the door.

END

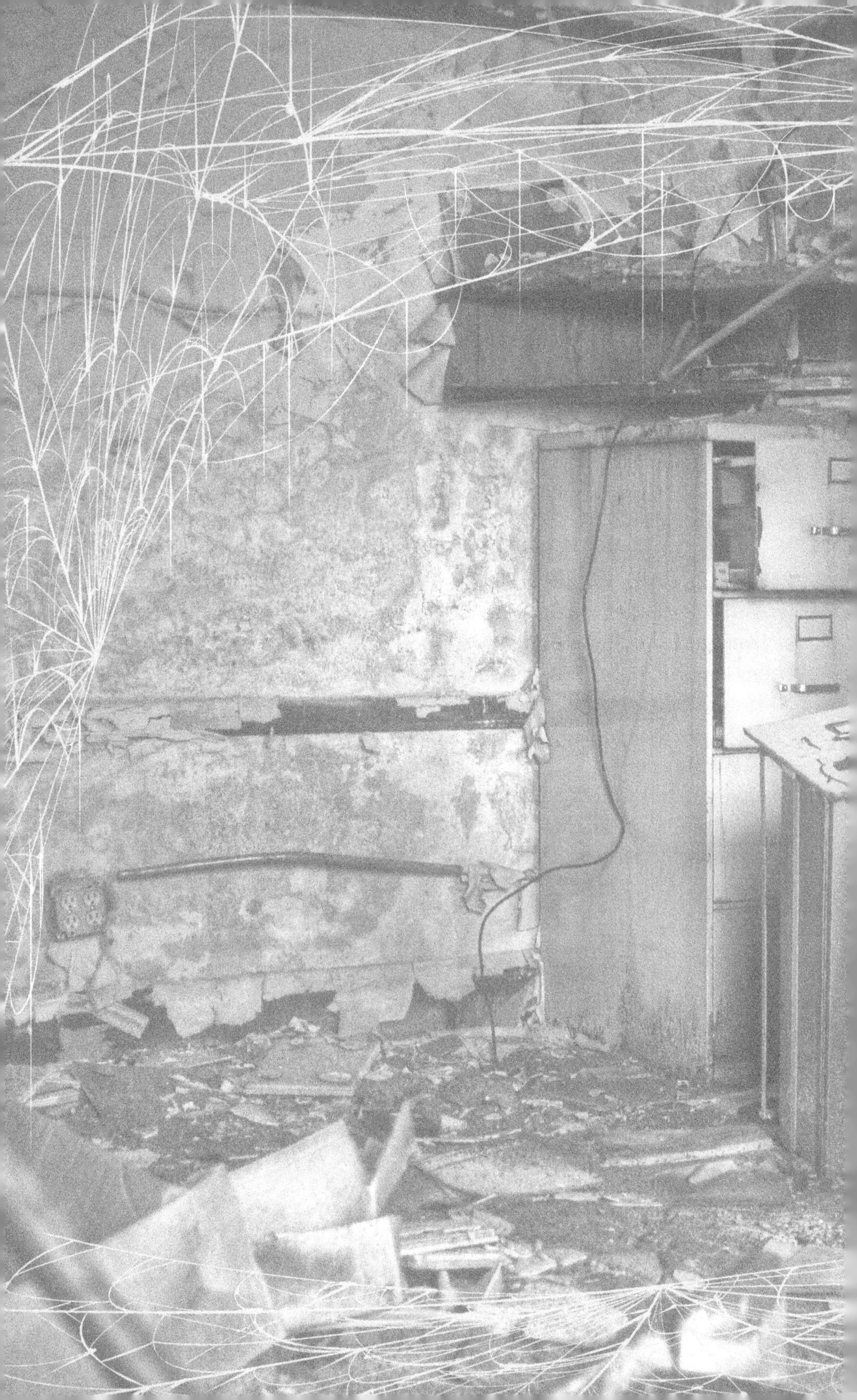

Other People

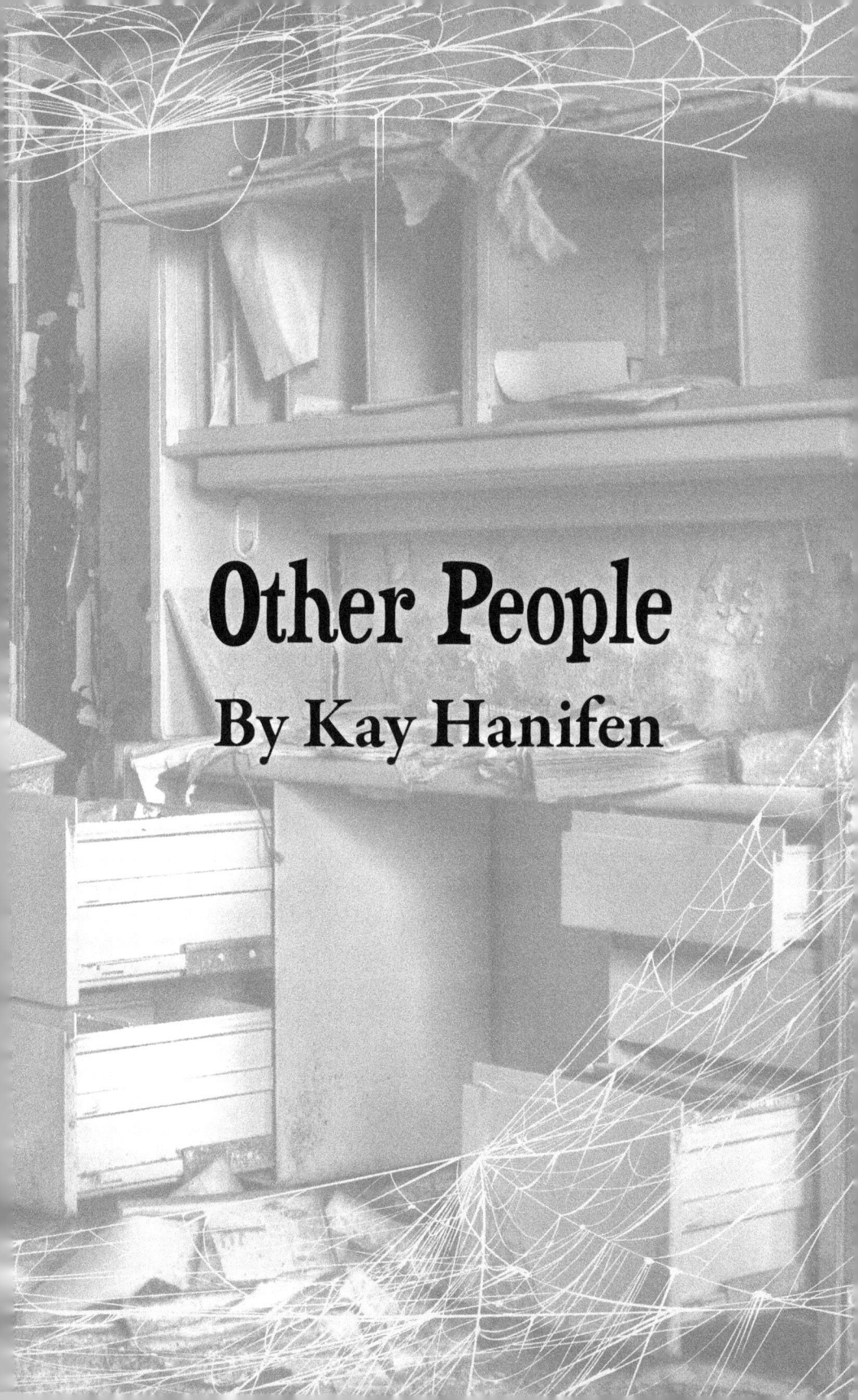

By Kay Hanifen

Demonic Workplaces

The office chair had a loose spring. It jabbed into my ass, keeping me from sitting comfortably as people came up with paperwork for me to sign. My wrists ached from carpal tunnel and my eyes burned from staring at computers and tiny print. I looked up at the clock. Though it felt like hours, only a couple of minutes had passed between now and when I last checked it.

A new arrival placed a pile of papers in front of me. His eyes shifted anxiously around the room at the impossibly long lines of people bisecting and intersecting one another. "Name," I said, skimming the legalese on the papers. It was all nonsense, but I had to check that he had been through all the proper channels. My boss would get angry if I gave him my stamp without making sure that he'd gone through all the others first.

"Name?" I asked, not looking up at him. It was easier that way, easier to focus on the paperwork instead of the haggard faces of the people hoping desperately that this was the end of their quest to dot every "i" and cross every "t" so that they could finally move on. But it didn't work that way. It never does because someone always finds one mistake, one missed stamp, or an incorrect signature.

"Mark Lewis Wood," he replied.

"Reason for being here?" I asked, even though I knew the answer: petty theft and a drunk driving incident that left a college student permanently paralyzed. He never tried to make amends or stop drinking. In fact, when he died after wrapping his car around a tree, his blood was twice the legal limit.

"I-I can't remember," he replied, unable to meet my gaze.

Yeah, this one wasn't ready for the final stamp. And lo-and-behold, the penitence department had not signed off on his release. I pointed this out to him.

"Penitence department?" he repeated, his eyes wide and fearful. "No one said anything about a penitence department."

"Floor 616, second door to your right. You can't miss it." He headed toward the elevators, forcing me to call out, "Wait!"

He paused, the irritation obvious on his face. "What?"

"The elevator's broken. I'm afraid you'll have to take the stairs."

Turning around, he shouted, "Are you fucking kidding me?"

I placidly shook my head, doing my best not to feel bad for him. I had been in his position once, dashing from department to department, trying and failing to finally be released. I also had to walk the 616 flights of stairs to the Penitence Department, where instead of being flayed alive and having my insides devoured by a rat king, I was assigned this desk job, going from the citizen to the bureaucrat standing in the way of their freedom. Like I'd chewed out all those waiters and retail workers, I now had to face the irate citizens of Hell and let them take all their frustrations out on me. The punishment certainly fit the crime, and it was better than an eternity of torture. In that sense, this was more of a purgatory than Hell, a place where souls are cleansed of their sins before moving on. No one was meant to be trapped here forever, but with all the lines and red tape, it certainly felt like it to the ones jumping through these seemingly infinite hoops.

To be fair, things weren't exactly a picnic for us, too. Hell made a point of making sure that all our chairs were always uncomfortable, our pencils always dull, our customers always irate, and everything just a little bit miserable. I couldn't remember the last time I took a break. If he ever caught us slacking, the boss, Asmodeus, would punish us on the basis of the three-strikes rule. The first two were a warning, and the third would send us right back into those lines, waiting to be processed with aching legs and growing rage.

Another soul set down their paperwork. This one, though, I recognized. They had to be sent to the Department of Mortal Sins to get a murder expunged from the record. Sure, it had been premeditated and especially cruel, but there were mitigating circumstances. It wasn't an act of self-defense committed in the moment, but the other soul would have killed them, eventually. That other soul had been sent to the Department of Violation to get a taste of what he dished out to them on a daily basis.

"Name?" I asked, skimming the stack of paperwork.

"Ember Flask James," they replied.

"Reason for being here?"

"I killed a man by drowning him in a boiling pot of spaghetti." They said it matter-of-factly, showing no signs of remorse for their actions. I checked their papers and found that the Penitence Department had signed off on them.

"And have you done your penance? Are you truly sorry?"

They met my gaze with a steady one of their own. "I've done my time. I'm sorry that it ended that way, and I hurt the man I loved, but I'm not sorry for being happy once he was gone."

I nodded. Apparently, that was enough for the paperwork. Every "i" was dotted, every "t" crossed, and for the first time in a long time, someone was cleared to move on. With a flourish, I pulled out the dusty stamp from the back corner of my drawers and slammed it down.

REDEEMED

They took on a heavenly glow as they floated toward the exit opposite the hall. Everyone gazed in awe and jealousy while a heavenly chorus sang a lilting tune. Opening the exit door, they gave one last salute before vanishing into What Comes Next. Perhaps one of the cruelest tortures that Hell had to offer was the hope of heaven.

But you just can't help yourself. Watching a soul be redeemed gave me hope for myself. Maybe… just maybe, it would be my turn to leave one day. Maybe I'll have learned my lesson and done my time and could know a peace beyond this bureaucracy. I was reminded of Pandora's Box, the story of the woman who unleashed all the evils on the world—pain, suffering, starvation, illness, death. And after they were all gone, and she was about to close the box, a final emotion escaped: hope. The reason why depended on the story and the storyteller. Optimists will tell you that hope's release was a good thing. It gave humanity something to cling to even as it suffered. Pessimists will tell you that hope was the cruelest manifestation of all. Without hope, people would simply end their suffering as soon as possible.

I wasn't sure which camp I fell into. I wanted to believe that hope was a strength, something that kept us from giving up, but watching the soul's redemption, I acutely felt the poison that hope carries in its fangs. It was a reminder that this might not be how I spend my eternity, setting me up for disappointment when it turns out that I was never worthy of redemption.

Another soul stepped up and placed their paperwork on the desk, her eyes full of barely contained hope that soon she would be freed like the one before. That poisonous hope became an expression of devastation when I informed her that she still had to make amends with her mother-in-law.

This is why I didn't dare hope anymore. Instead, I fell into my miserable rhythm of rejecting requests for redemption. Some were pleasant, others furious, and most were devastated that they had to go through the whole process all over again because they didn't catch that their name was misspelled, and therefore the redemption belonged to someone else at the moment or that they failed to get a stamp from the proper departments with the right number of witnesses.

After a time—I don't know how long—a young soul approached. She looked to have been in her early twenties, and, like the others, she was visibly irritated. I suppose I shouldn't be surprised anymore. "Name?" I asked.

"Evelyn Carla Walters," she replied, setting the papers down on the table. "I've been to every floor, every department, every single one of you bureaucrats to get you to let me leave."

I ignored her complaint. At this point, I'd learned to thoroughly tune out the rants of the frustrated souls. "Reason for being here?"

"I'm—I *was* an addict. I robbed and threatened and stole to maintain my habit." She squinted at me as though I was a puzzle that needed solving. "I don't understand how you can do this."

"Do what?" I asked mildly, studying the paperwork so that I wouldn't have to meet her intense gaze.

"How you can help them torture us? You're human, but you won't even look at me like I'm one, too."

I sighed and put down the paperwork. "Do you think I'm here because I want to be? This is my penance, an ironic punishment for someone who always treated waiters and retail workers like they were beneath her."

"So, you're stuck here as much as everyone else?" There was something in her eyes resembling sympathy.

I was torn. On the one hand, if I kept talking, that would hold everyone up, making them even more irate with me. The boss wouldn't mind that—hell, he'd probably applaud me for drawing out their torture—but it would be another pain in my already sore neck. On the other, Evelyn Carla Walters was the first person in a very long time to acknowledge my humanity. Sure, she wasn't happy with me either, but unlike the rest, she did more than throw abuse at me.

"I am," I replied, returning to skimming her papers. "You've heard the saying 'Hell is other people,' right? Here, it's very literal."

"Tell me about it," the soul muttered. "I think the bureaucracy is worse than the torches and pitchforks."

"Don't speak too soon." I pointed to page sixty-six of her paperwork. "You need a signature from the Temple of the Body."

"Thanks," she said, snatching them up and heading toward the elevator.

Demonic Workplaces

"It's out of order," I yelled to her. "You'll have to use the stairs."

"Did it ever work at all?" she called back as she course-corrected to the stairs.

"Not that I know of." I watched her go before turning to the next in line. One of the worst features of Hell's bureaucracy is the random spontaneous combustion. Sometimes, the paperwork will erupt into flames, usually when someone is holding it. When this happened, the unlucky soul would have to start the process all over again.

I can't say that I felt particularly bad for the latest victim of exploding paperwork. He was a serial killer who enjoyed murdering sex workers purely for the pleasure of it. As he held the stack out to me, the papers erupted into flames. He yelped and dropped it, his hands already sporting blistery second-degree burns. "What the fuck was that?" he demanded.

"It means that you have to start it all over again," I replied as I brushed some of the ashes from my desk.

His eyes widened, jaw muscles twitching with barely contained rage. "Are you for real right now?"

"Unfortunately. I don't make the rules. Sorry."

"I'll fucking kill you, bitch!" He lunged at me, fingers ready to wrap around my neck. You can't die in the afterlife, but believe it or not, getting strangled or stabbed isn't at all a pleasant experience.

"Hey!" a familiar voice snapped. We both turned to see Evelyn Carla Walters in the doorway near the stairs. "Leave her alone. She has as much control here as you do."

I shot her a grateful smile while he scowled. "This is none of your business, bitch," he growled.

"Did you ever consider that not being a dick would make your sentence shorter?"

Her steely gaze met his, and his expression went from outraged to nervous. "Fine. I'll go back to the start, but this better not happen again," he muttered as he stalked off with his tail between his legs.

I stared at her with eyes as wide as saucers. "Who are you?"

"I'm a person, just like you." She shrugged. "I've been thinking, and a part of what makes this place Hell is the dehumanization. I know what it's like to be treated like a waste of space and thought everything would be more bearable if I remembered that we're all trapped here together."

I watched in awe as she made her way back to the end of my line, patiently waiting and chatting with the person in front of her. It took a moment, but then the other began to talk back, laughing and gesticulating wildly. I smiled to myself, and it stayed on my face for the next person in line. "Name?" I asked, meeting his eyes.

"Alexander Stephen Jameson," he replied, seemingly taken aback by my smile.

"Reason for being here?"

"Theft, murder, and drug dealing," he replied and then squinted at me. "Why are you smiling?"

Embarrassed, I skimmed through his papers. "I thought I'd try something different. Something to make us all feel a little more human."

"Oh, uh..." He rubbed the back of his neck, apparently unsure of how to respond. "Thanks"

"I can stop if you want."

He shook his head. "No, no, I like it. I, uh, can't actually remember the last time someone smiled at me."

"Neither can I." With a sigh, I spotted a discrepancy. "I'm really sorry, but Beelzebub misspelled your name on page twelve, rendering it void. You'll have to go through the Field of Flames again."

He groaned. "That place was the worst."

I nodded sympathetically. "Yeah, it really is."

It took some time, but Evelyn Carla Walters finally made it to the front of the line again. She smiled at me. "I think this time's the charm." But the moment both our hands touched her paperwork, the stack burst into flames. We both watched in horror as her hope for something better was reduced to ash. She would have to start all over again on her path to redemption.

But then, instead of rage and grief, a look of determination crossed her features. "You know what? Fuck it. Has anyone ever checked if we could just leave?"

I shook my head. In truth, I had never seen anyone try. Like the assumption that we had to be miserable assholes to one another, I guess I assumed that the door was locked.

Seeing the expression on my face, she made her way across the room and to the door. The crowd watched, as awed as I was by her, whispering among themselves and wondering if she was insane. Maybe she was. Or maybe she was the bravest soul in Hell.

Evelyn Carla Walters hesitated at the door for just a moment, glancing over her shoulder at the rest of the damned souls. And then she turned the handle, pushed it open, and crossed the threshold. There was no heavenly chorus to greet her, nor was there a lake of fire for her to fall into. No one knows where she went.

Now, there are some who choose to go through that door, willingly leaping into that great unknown because it is better than here. But most choose to keep waiting in lines, though we're less miserable. We try to be patient with one another, and there's nothing the demons can do about it.

Maybe soon, I'll open that door, too.

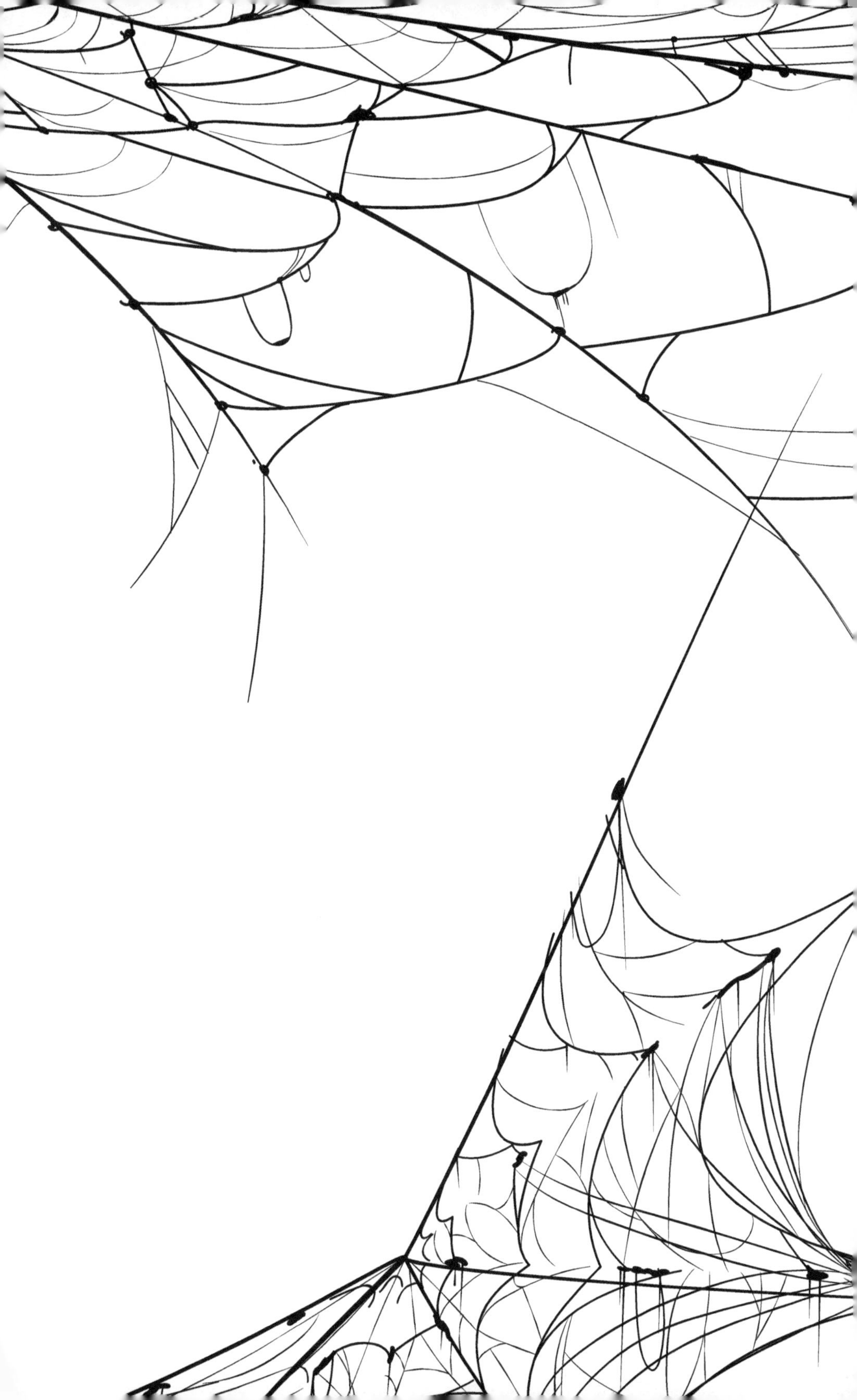

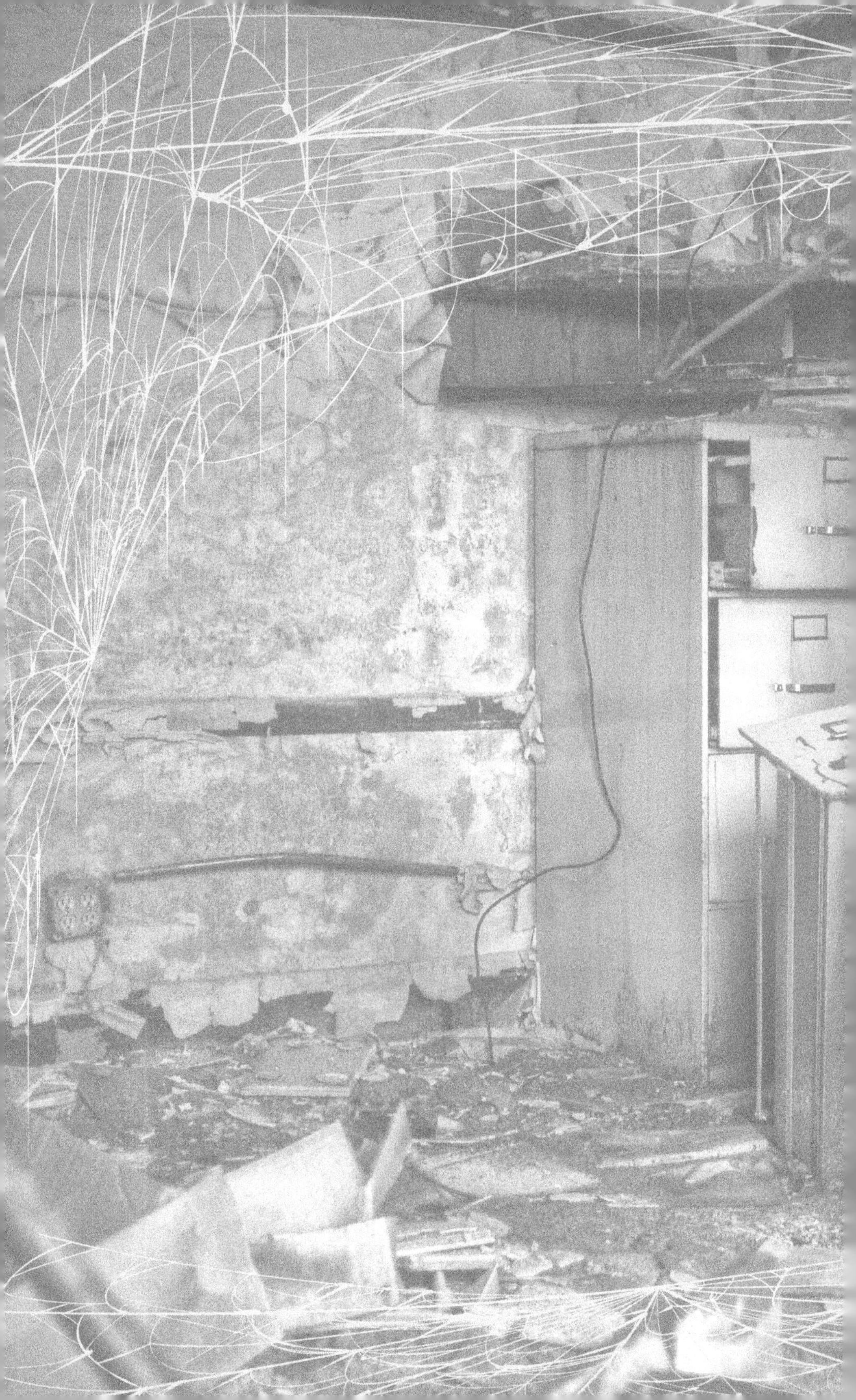

Vessel

By Chester Rogalski

Demonic Workplaces

I'm writing this from a Comfort Inn somewhere outside

Ossining, New York. No continental breakfast here. Remember those? Cereal in tiny colorful boxes with your favorite characters on them. Little handles. Good times. Those used to be a thing when I was a kid. My parents would take us down to the Jersey shore, and Mom would fill up our beach bag with them from the motel lobby. Took all the croissants, too. Tony the Tiger, that green frog whose name I never remember, heads poking out amongst baked goods, trying to catch a glimpse of the ocean. Look at me now, Mom. Sitting in a motel with all the pages of Gideon's bible ripped out and stuck all over the windows, anything glass, anything to keep the face out. I can't escape it. But this professor says he can, or at least give me some kind of explanation. So, I've got this legal pad and a lot of time to fill, to organize my thoughts.

I consider myself to be a serious person. Call me Jake. I don't rattle. Spending four years in the United States Marine Corps as an 0311, grunt for the layman, will do that to you. Or have you howling in the middle of the night and reaching for the bottle, the pills, the needle, anything to escape it. That's not me, though. Not that I would ever judge the way a man deals with those kinds of demons and the hell we faced down together in the sandbox. I've heard it described to me by a buddy of mine who struggled with severe PTSD as a projector in your head being on a constant loop replaying the fucked-up shit you saw over there. Buddies getting shot, blown up. Civilians mangled, gunned down over fucked rules of engagement. A literal hell, full volume, live in technicolor. I was lucky that it didn't happen to me. You never could tell who it would afflict. The biggest, baddest on the outside, only to be found having hung it all up when the shit got heavy. I put rounds down range, and they were put right back at me, and I came home and got out healthy as a horse. Mentally and physically. Tip-top shape. Big time fucking lucky and that's really all there was to it. Dumb fucking luck.

I kept my nose clean while plugging away at a degree in economics and living a modest, uneventful life on the GI Bill. Enough money rolled in that I didn't have to work and was able to live okay. Rent was cheap in Newark, for good reason. Nearing graduation, I realized the GI Bill party was nearing the end, and it was high time to find a job. I found work at a prominent executive protection firm based out of New York City, packed up my studio apartment, and headed for the big apple. The training was a two-week course, and afterward, I was posted in the home of an extremely (extremely) wealthy businessman in New York City. It is important, to me at least and for my safety, that I do not divulge details about who the client was and where this home is located. I can't go into much about the location and describing the home's exterior would very likely give away where the home is. I have enough on my plate right now.

I took to the job well and got along with the clients and the house staff. There was a rotation of a handful of us alternating between nights and days and weekdays and weekends. Everyone worked alone and everyone besides our boss, we'll call him Tom, had been there less than six months. They were all Tom, Jim, Ed, John, Chris, Joe, seemed to me that you got promoted, and the first rite of passage was to chop off half your name.

Since I was the newest addition, I worked the night shift, where there were minimal interactions and less of a chance for something to go wrong. I did rounds hourly, starting from my guard post, which housed all the security cameras, alarm panels, fire suppression systems, and other various security equipment. I always started from the bottom of the home and went upwards. The sub-cellar housed all the boilers, cooling, plumbing, and laundry rooms. The kitchen, wine room, pantries, and staff quarters were on the cellar floor. The first floor, or the ground floor, had the large dining room where formal dinner parties were held, along with the foyer, my guard post office, and the estate manager's office. Above this was the second floor, where the study, recital room, and reception room were located. Floors three, four, and five all had guest bedrooms, the master bedrooms, and a living room with a large skylight. If you couldn't tell already, they live in a fucking palace.

About two months in, I got an email from Tom that the clients were having a party that night and to make sure I wore a black suit, white shirt, and black tie. Okay, Roger that. The email went on that this was a formal party they held every year on March 20th and that I would have to sign an additional NDA about what I might see that night. Okay, fucking weird. But okay. I arrived on site fifteen minutes early to make sure I got all the information I needed from Tom. I walked into the side door that the staff used, which led into the hallway where our security office was located, along with the service elevator. Tom and the estate manager, Helen, were waiting for me.

"Jake, glad you got here early. We have some things to discuss before everything gets started," Tom said, clasping both of his hands as he spoke. "Helen has the NDA I mentioned to you as well that you'll have to sign before your shift."

I looked at the both of them briefly before I spoke. Helen had a wide smile on her face. She was a middle-aged box blonde that always looked far to put together, born in a pantsuit, lots of peach and salmon colors, making her pale skin look washed out. She didn't say anything at first. "Why do I need to sign another NDA? We have a standard company NDA that I agreed to, stating that I won't divulge anything client related," I asked.

Helen stepped forward, widening her grin before speaking as if she was trying to look more friendly; it wasn't working. "This is for us to keep on file. The attorneys, you know how they can be, they're requiring us to get one from you. It's a whole bunch of legal mumbo-jumbo. Don't worry too much about it," she said as she waved her hand and scoffed. They both stared at me, waiting for me to take the pen and sign. Tom smiled and nodded his head toward the document. I relented. I signed.

"Great! Well, that takes care of that. Tom will give you the details of what's needed tonight." She grabbed the document off the desk and scurried out the door leading into the house. Tom gave me a quick rundown of what I had to do that evening. Standard access control and occasionally roaming around the party to keep an eye on things. He told me it was supposed to be an easy night. He didn't look me in the eye the whole time he spoke and hurried out the door, giving me a quick wave in the window with his back turned as he pulled the gate open and left. The iron gate smacked against the maglock. An ominous symbol of finality. If you haven't noticed, there were quite a few fucking red flags.

Guests began arriving a little after 8. Helen stood at the main entrance door, checking them in while I watched over the security cameras. Everyone arrived in evening wear holding something in their hands. I couldn't make out what it was. The camera was up too high to see. Approximately a hundred and fifty guests were expected. By 10, everyone had arrived. Before making my rounds through the party, I realized that they all had on a mask, that that's what they carried in with them, masks. Rabbit masks, specifically, I would soon find out.

I pushed open the door leading into the house and stepped out into the dining room, where I saw a handful of guests milling around, speaking with one another. Each of them had on an ornate rabbit mask, the ears jutting straight up, bedazzled with rhinestones and different colors. I received nods from the group as I walked by, returning their nods with what I'm sure came across as a very uncomfortable smile.

An older man in a gold and green rabbit mask stepped in front of me and grabbed me by the shoulder. "So glad you could make it, my dear boy, so glad!" he said before walking quickly away. I didn't have time to really react, or quite understand what the hell he meant by that. He disappeared up the stairs and into the party. A large arrangement of flowers was placed in the center of the foyer. It looked expensive and planned well in advance. Vines of flowers went around the handrails leading up deeper into the festivities. I went up the stairs and saw more lush green plants and flowers on the landing and on the entryways to the study, recital room, and reception room. The door to the study remained closed while the others were open.

I took up a post in the recital room, and from where I was standing, I saw, not quite sure how to describe them, small child-like adults playing instruments. They were dressed in white with crowns of vined flowers around their heads and spotlights shining on them. They weren't kids. Up close, their faces appeared much older. The instruments they played were unfamiliar to me. I believe I saw a harpsichord, flute, a small drum, and maybe a fiddle or violin. The music was awful, sounding out of tune and, to me, like they had never played them before until that night. Guests circled around them though and watched as if they were witnessing a grand performance, clapping off and on even if the song hadn't ended. A white bassinet was off to the side, and I saw guests get up occasionally to drop things into it. I figured it was likely money.

I made my way over to the reception room next to check on what was going on in there. A bar was set up in the back and I took a seat on a stool next to the bartender to survey the activity going on. Guests walked up and gave me a nod before ordering, smiling with their rabbit masks on. I was starting to get uncomfortable, asking myself whether I was going crazy or did everyone there fucking know who I was? I left my seat to find Helen.

She was in her office on the ground floor, off to the side from the foyer. The glow of her computer monitor was the only light on as I walked in. She was looking out her window with a cigarette lit in her hand, through Venetian blinds overlooking, well, let's leave it at that. "Rough night?" I said from the doorway. Helen didn't look over and continued to take long pulls off her cigarette. To tell her smoking wasn't allowed inside would have been moot. She knew the rules. "Where are the clients? I haven't seen them tonight at all."

"They flew out hours before the party started, some type of emergency down in Louisiana at their family home. Too much was already in motion, and they didn't want to cancel. Why don't you just relax in the security office? I think it's all under control," she said. She ashed her cigarette on the floor and I left it at that. I went back to my office to watch the activity from there, sufficiently weirded out.

Little did I know the party was only just beginning.

The party lasted until a little after midnight, and cleanup by house staff took roughly another hour. Helen waved at me from the foyer and left without saying a word. By about 1:30 in the morning, I was the only one in the house. I sat in the office and thought about the strange night's events. Party in the house, the clients left town before it began. It's all strange music, rabbit masks, held every year on the same date. What the hell is even today? I did a quick search online and found out that it was the spring equinox. Some kind of spring party, I thought. That's not that crazy. I made myself a pot of coffee and put on a movie, hoping this shift would end quickly.

Around 4:00, I got an alarm in the study for one of the paintings. All of the paintings in the house were worth quite a great deal of money and were equipped with motion detectors that would cause an alarm to go off in our office if someone moved one of them. Typically, this was because one of the maids dusted a little too vigorously and set it off. I looked at the camera in the study, which was where the alarm was coming from. The lights were off, so I couldn't see much. I'd have to go and take a look to make sure nothing fell off the wall. That was one of the first stories Tom told me, how a former member of the team ignored an alarm for one of the paintings on the night shift, only for it to be found by the client the next morning. Boom. Fired. I grabbed my flashlight and made my way toward the study.

An important fact as well is that lights in the house operate on a timer, and any messing around with the light switches manually messes up the timer. I'm not sure how accurate this was or is, but I believed it at the time and always kept the lights off and used my flashlight to get around. It was pretty fucking bright, anyway. So don't think I'm a moron because I didn't immediately go for the lights.

I got to the door to the study at the top of the landing and opened it up, the towering dark wood doors looming over me as I entered. My flashlight lit up the study, shining light on the rows of old books spanning the entirety of the room. The alarm was for a painting I hated, the screen of the art alarm system gave a picture of the painting that needed to be checked, which in this case was of a nun with yellow eyes. To me, it was a nun based on how she was dressed, in black and white with some type of headdress on. The thing that always got me was the yellow eyes and the fact it was perched on a stand in the middle of the room facing the door. I stood about fifteen feet away from it. It looked fine to me. All clear. I turned and walked back toward my office. And slammed that goddamn door closed.

I grabbed a cup of coffee from the freshly brewed pot and sat down in my chair to resume the movie I was watching. As I hit play, I realized that the light in the study had turned on. The screens were small, so I had to get up to look and see what was on the screen. The camera faced the center of the room where the painting was. Except something was off about it. It was blank. The painting was there, but there was no woman in it, just a blank canvas from what I could see. I sat back down in my chair, dumbfounded. Not fully realizing, nor wanting to believe, what exactly I was seeing. I went to the DVR controls to play back the cameras, still not sure what exactly I was going to see. We kept a log of whenever we left the area after hours, so I rewound to the time I had entered into the log and let it play. I was only gone for about five minutes, so there wasn't much footage to go through. I put it on double speed and hit play. The footage began and was black, and then out of nowhere, the lights go on, and the canvas appears on the stand. Blank. As I stood there looking at it, another alarm went off. This time it was a chiller alarm in the sub-cellar. These chillers (Air conditioning, I think? Not my forte) were on the older side and were prone to flooding. It was just another thing we had to check, and if it was bad enough, inform the house manager. I grabbed my flashlight and walked over to the service elevator, feeling like I was on autopilot, being directed.

I arrived at the sub-cellar and pulled out my flashlight, turning it on to light up the pitch-black ahead of me. I walked out and turned the corner, pointing my flashlight down the long hallway leading to the rest of the sub-cellar. At the end of the hall, I saw it. There was a tall figure dressed in a black shroud, hunched over. The ceilings down there were maybe seven feet, and this, this thing, was hunched over considerably. Down where it was standing was the laundry room. As I pointed the light at it, I realized that it was wearing a black wedding dress and veil. Its limbs were unnaturally long. Its neck was bent, the side of its head flush against the ceiling. I heard over the hum of the chillers, boilers, and plumbing at work down there the figure humming. It was a low and deep hum that made my chest vibrate like I was standing too close to a subwoofer. It still hadn't realized I was there, and my flashlight was shining on it. I was terrified to turn it off and lose sight of it. I was frozen. The humming continued, and I put it together. Whatever it was, was humming "Ave Maria". I stood there with my flashlight still pointed at it. I was dripping sweat as the song ended. I held my breath. The figure turned, and I saw a pale face with two black chunks of onyx for eyes and a long jaw. I heard a groan as it lumbered toward me, its feet pounding on the ground, shaking the floor and walls around me as it made its way. The humming started again, but faster, louder. It moved slowly, as if its feet weighed hundreds of pounds. Its jaw was drooping and elongating toward the floor as its feet thudded and shambled. I dropped my flashlight and turned, and ran toward the elevator behind me. I heard heavy footfalls thundering toward me, quickening. I dashed inside and hit the 1st-floor button, never realizing until then how fucking slow those doors were.

I got out of the elevator and locked it in place, unsure if this would actually do anything to stop the creature from getting to me. I went to the camera feed in my office to see where it was. It appeared again in the study, standing fully erect and staring directly at the camera. The figure stared straight at me, somehow knowing I was watching. It walked slowly toward the camera; I felt its heavy feet thudding from my office as it moved. The figure walked straight until it was out of sight beneath the camera. I kept watching. I saw on the feed the top of its head slowly appear on screen; it continued to climb up until its full face was in view. It was the nun with the yellow eyes. She smiled on screen. Her eyes and the holes that held them turned black. So did her mouth until it was the face of the pale creature that I saw in the sub-cellar. It began to appear on each of the screens in the office. I ran out the door.

I sprinted to the gate and pushed it open. I was out on the sidewalk when I saw a group that was standing there cheering and clapping quietly in hushed tones. I heard voices calling out, "You did it," "She's back," "You brought her to us. Oh, bless you, Jacob, bless you." I sprinted to my car as the group continued behind me. I got in and pulled out as fast as I could. The sun was coming up, and I was on my way home to tell Tom I quit. I quit so fucking hard. I stopped at a red light when I saw it. The nun's face was forming in my windshield. I pulled over and got the fuck out. I took out my phone to call Tom. I saw her face on the black screen of my phone. I put it back in my pocket and pulled it out again. There it was. I stared at it for a second. It didn't move. The face was just there. I got back in my car; she was in the windshield. Motionless. I thought I was losing my mind. I got back to my apartment and saw that her face was appearing in every window, everything glass, in fact. Fucking crazy. I thought I was fucking crazy. I pulled out the drinking glasses that I had. There she was. Bathroom mirror, that horrible fucking face was there. Staring at me. I realized if I made eye contact long enough, the face would form a wide smile, revealing black teeth. Hell of an Easter egg.

I didn't sleep for three days. Still haven't. They called me Jacob. How did they know me? I went by Jake, always. I pulled open my laptop and did what research I could with her fucking face in the glass of the screen staring back at me. I must have sent three thousand emails. I got a reply back from a professor at Yale, who, for whatever reason, only wants to talk in person. So, I'm on my way. I just need some sleep. I ripped out the pages from the Gideon's bible in the dresser to cover up all of the glass here. I just need sleep. That's where she appears, and she's beginning to taunt. Sticking her tongue out if I see her too long, disjointing her jaw, and letting it drag open. I just need a couple of hours to make it to Connecticut. Answers lie there.

I just woke up, got maybe three hours of sleep. It's 0436. She's talking now. Vocal. Standing in the corner of the room. She's too tall. I hope you find this.

She needed a *vessel*, and I was *there*. She needed a *vessel*, and I was *there*. She needed a *vessel*, and I was *there*. I needed a vessel and there you were. I needed a vessel and there you were. I needed a vessel and there you were. *Vas mihi opus erat, et ibi eras. Vas mihi opus erat, et ibi eras. Vas mihi opus erat, et ibi eras.*

We have to go now.

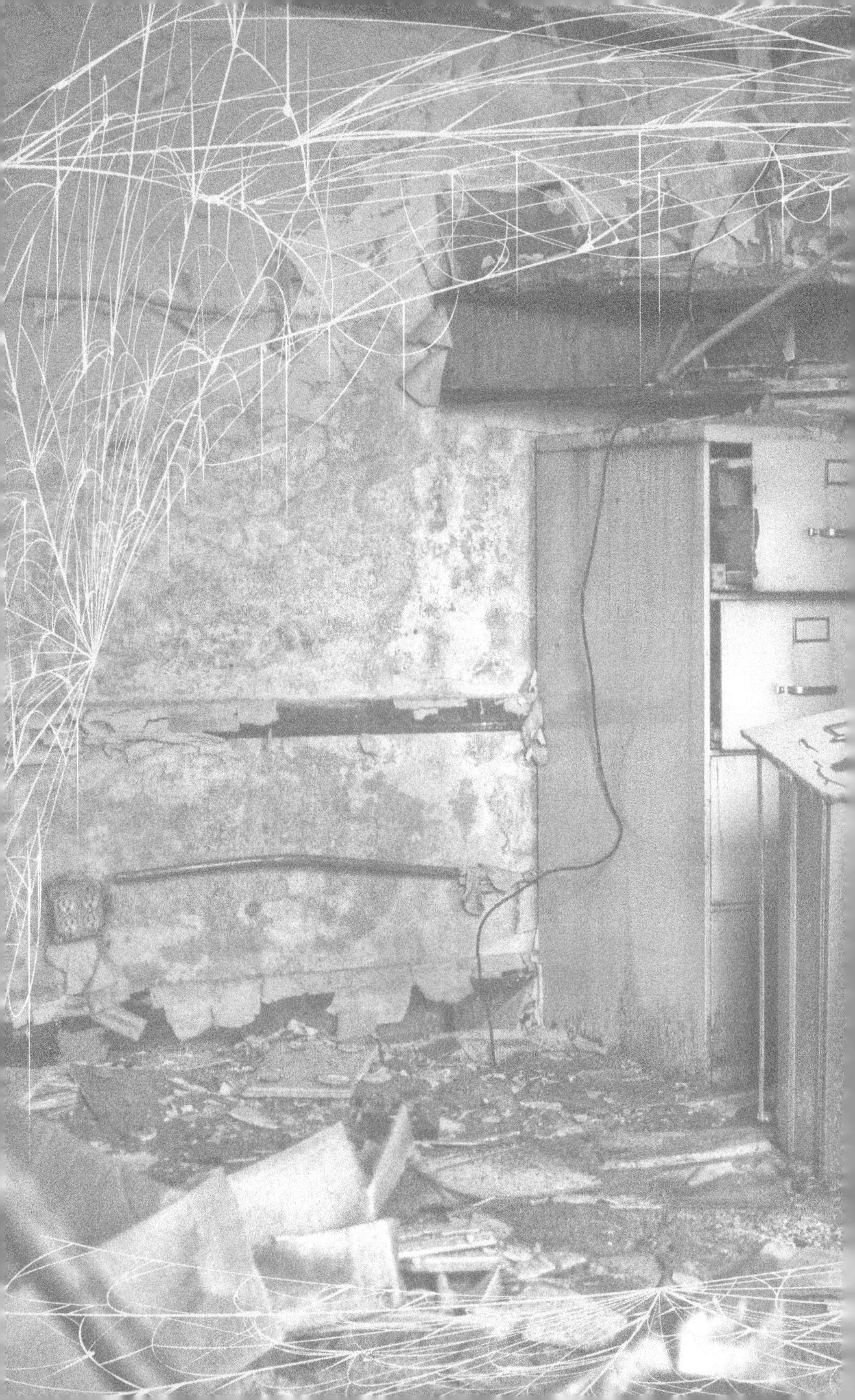

Good Grace

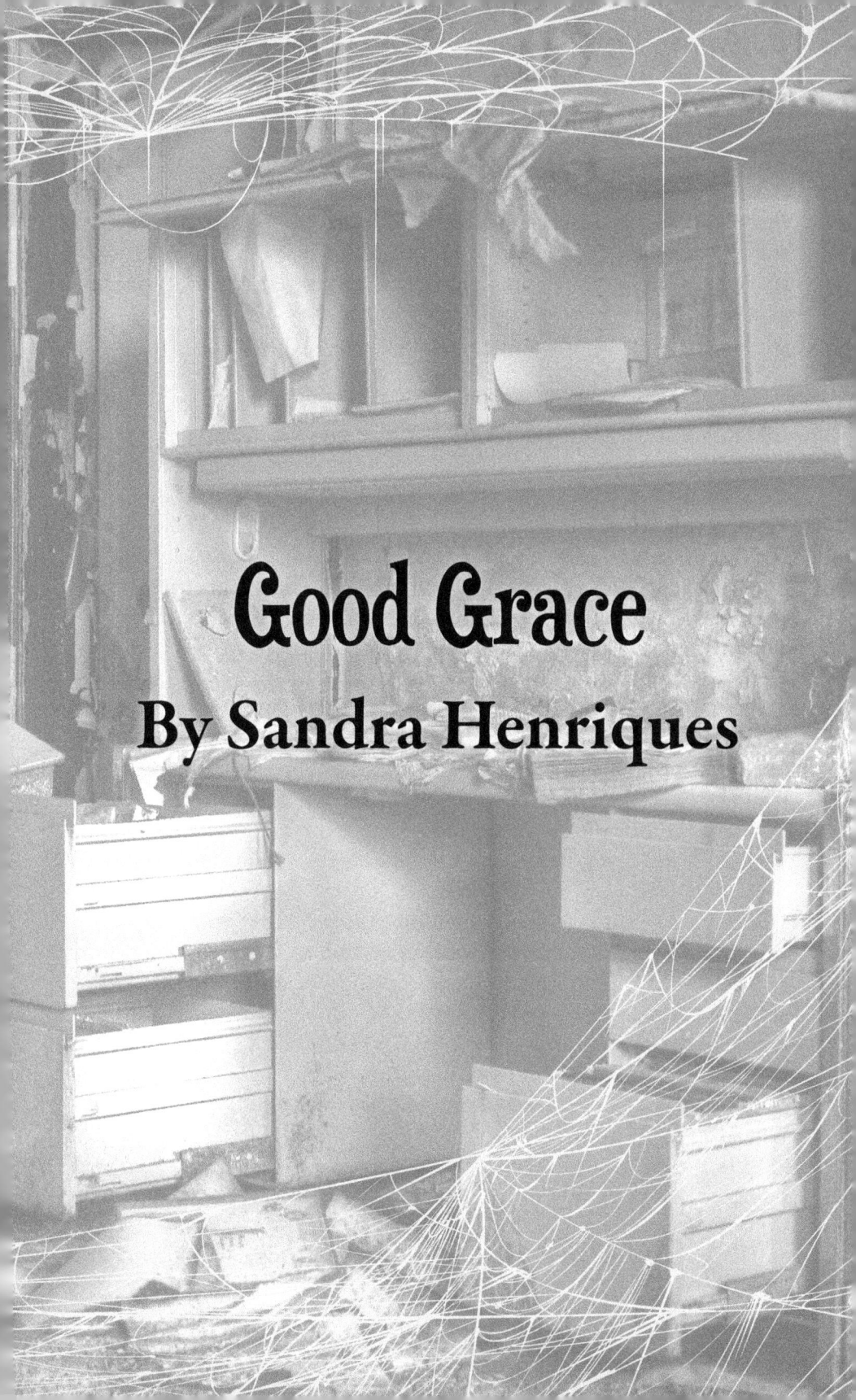

By Sandra Henriques

"Red velvet cake?"

She handed me a plate, with her thumb too close to the cream cheese frosting for my liking and her warm smile lighting up her face. Grace was new to the office and eager to please. Every Friday, she'd bring a treat for the team: cake, cookies, once a loaf of her special homemade bread for each of the eight colleagues on our floor, and last month *amigurumi* of our favorite cartoon characters to celebrate her first week on the job.

"So sweet of you, Grace! Maybe later?"

"Of course! I'll keep it in the fridge for you."

She scribbled, "Please don't eat me! I'm Jane's ☺" on a sticky note, winked, and headed to the kitchen. Sweet, kind-hearted, warm, lovely Grace, wearing her brightly colored blazer over a white cotton t-shirt and a pair of dark jeans and casual sneakers. Thirty-something, married, no kids, and highly career-focused and results-driven. Any company would kill to have her as their head of marketing, but she had chosen ours. Lucky us.

I, on the other hand, would kill for her replacement. John had been a far better candidate, much more qualified, with an impeccable track record working for multinational corporations in Japan, Germany, and Portugal. His handshake was firm; his answers were absolutely spot on. And his business case presentation? My god, it was the most flawless case study I had ever seen in years!

He was reliable and had worked at each of those companies for at least ten years. A stable employee leading the marketing department was what we needed. I thought Grace was too young, had far less experience, and her longest tenure was six months managing her best friend's lifestyle social media accounts.

"I get that you liked John, and in some things, I agree with you, Jane." Robert had leaned over the conference room table to soften the blow. "But Grace is a better fit for the role. She understands the market; she has, like… an intuition, you know? And the rest, she'll learn."

"Is that how we are hiring people from now on? Based on how much of an intuition they have?"

"Don't fight this. Grace has mine and Barbara's vote, so the decision is final."

I threw my hands in the air, nodded, and left the conference room, doing everything I could to avoid looking too defeated. "She has an intuition, my ass."

"I'm sorry, what?" I hadn't noticed Geraldine standing at my office's door.

"Don't mind me, Gigi. Apparently, I'm an old hag complaining about stuff for no reason."

"Ha! Robert and Barbara forced their CEO and CFO uninformed decisions on you again?"

"Yeah. I guess I should see it coming by now, but I never do, you know?"

"Yep. But you have to let it go. Do the work, collect your paycheck, and enjoy your perks. We're both too old for this crap." Gigi's loud and bright laugh lifted part of the weight off my shoulders.

I called John first—a short and firm conversation without any attempt at consolation in my voice. I took a deep breath before contacting Grace. *Focus, Jane. It's the standard "you got the job" call. You don't even have to be friendly. Just nice enough to make her feel welcome.*

Her phone rang a dozen times, and she picked up just when I was getting ready to leave her a message.

"Hello." Grace didn't sound like herself. Her voice was croaky and dull.

"Hum, is this Grace Richardson? It's Jane Williams. I interviewed you for the head of marketing position at..."

"Oh! Jaaaane! Yes, hiiiiii." Ah, there she was, good old Grace, squealing over the phone.

"Yes, hi. I want to congratulate you and officially welcome you to the team. You got the job."

"Oh my gosh, thank you! I was so sure John was gonna get it, but I'm glad you picked me! I'm so, so, so stoked!"

"Yes, we are quite happy to have you on board, too." I lied through my forced wide smile and rolled my eyes. "I'll e-mail the onboarding documents as soon as we end this call, and we'll see you here next Monday morning. Tell Mike at the reception to let me know when you arrive, and I'll meet you in the lobby with your credentials."

"Oh, Mike is an absolute sweetheart. I'm sure he'll let me right in. Did you know we attended the same school? Well, different years, of course. But I somehow looked familiar, and he asked me if we'd gone to school together, which was weird. How can he remember someone who *went* to the same school but at *different* times, right? He DMs me all the time. He's so sweet. Oh my god, oh my god, I am so excited, Jane!"

She was like a human machine gun spewing nonsense phrases!

"Grace. Yes, alright. Grace, I have to hang up to send you the documents. Please E-Sign your contract and return it to me by the end of the week. I'll see you Monday. Have a nice day."

Demonic Workplaces

"Th..."

I hung up the phone before she finished her sentence. My head throbbed, and without much consideration, I sent Robert a message on the company chat tool informing him I'd be going home earlier that day. "Migraine acting up again, Rob. Do you mind if I go home after I send Grace the onboarding stuff?"

Asking him was a courtesy and for my records if he ever tried to use it against me. "I have a migraine" was code for "I don't give a shit; I'm leaving work now." I didn't need his approval anymore. Not after he had grabbed my ass at the company's team building retreat three weeks ago. *Asshole.*

Of course, Jane. Feel free to take the rest of the day off. You did well today.

Now, that's what I call material worthy of a top performance evaluation. I should get it framed before the next meeting. The thought of being alone with him in his office sent a shiver down my spine. But I was a powerful, successful, self-assured professional who had learned how to curb men's advances at the workplace. And when I couldn't, I always kept as much evidence as possible to have the upper hand. *Good old Jane*, I noticed them whispering behind my back. Good. Old. Jane. Indeed, boys.

She sometimes got a little under my skin, but I couldn't help noticing that Grace was the life of the office. After a while, I almost forgot I'd prefer to have hired John instead of her. She had impeccable work ethics; she excelled at managing conflict with clients, and (*goddamn it*) she baked well. My stomach grumbled when I remembered the slice of red velvet cake in the fridge with my name on it. *I could definitely use the break. These late hours are killing me.*

Everyone had gone home, but the kitchen light was still on, and I could see Grace's computer screen glittering in her empty office. The door was open, and I peeked in. Her desk was a mess of papers, colorful pens, sticky notes, cookie crumbs, and coffee-stained napkins. *Not the untidy person I imagined she was.* Her coat and purse hung from the rack by the door.

"Grace," I called to the empty corridor. "Are you here?" No one replied.

I gave it half a second and went into the kitchen, not expecting an answer. My slice of cake awaited in the fridge, untouched, the ink on the sticky note fading. The sink was full of forks, spoons, cups, and empty, dirty plastic containers with employees' names scribbled on the lids. Ricky, Stephen, Melanie. I stuffed a piece of cake in my mouth to fight the urge to do other people's dishes. *Fucking privileged pricks.*

Good Grace

The sound of glass shattering came from the bathroom down the hall, and I instinctively grabbed my fork as a spear. Not entirely sure of what good that would do against an attacker who might be stronger than me.

"Grace?" Still no response. "Grace, is that you? Please say something!"

A foul, thick smell suddenly permeated the air, forcing me to pinch my nose. *What the hell is this?*

"Please help m...." A fading, gurgling voice echoed in the hall.

I stood up, grabbing the fork, ready to stab whoever was out there.

"Boo!" Grace jumped out in front of me, blocking my passage. Her pupils seemed dilated, her hair was a little disheveled, her lips were bright red, and the tips of two large fangs poked out of her mouth. I continued to hold the fork firmly above my head. "Hey! Don't kill me!" Grace burst out laughing.

"What the hell are you doing?"

"I was trying out some costumes for Halloween. What do you think? I call it *office drama*."

She squealed when I smiled.

"I knew you'd like it, Jane!"

"Well, yes. I guess it's funny. Maybe lose the fangs, though."

"Yeah, I thought the fangs would be a bit too much. I'll remove them in a bit; they're kind of... stuck. But I'm keeping the fake blood as lipstick. What do you think?"

"The fake bl... Okay. Maybe we have to run it by Robert tomorrow."

"Why?" Her facial expression suddenly hardened, and she stared into my eyes with an ice-cold gaze. The joy was gone from her voice, too.

"Because he's the CEO."

"And what the fuck does the CEO have to do with what we decide to do for Halloween, huh, Jane? Good. Old. Jane?" She turned her head at each word.

Her voice had lost that high-pitched, always happy, and vibrant tone I'd gotten used to. She sounded raspy again, like the first time we spoke on the phone. My heart pounded in my chest, and I felt the urge to run away suddenly, but I was, surprisingly, able to remain calm. I guess I also had... an intuition. I bit my tongue not to laugh.

Grace smiled and licked her lips, smudging the fake red blood around her mouth. I noticed it had started to dry on the corners of her mouth—the brownish speckles of dried goo made her look like a kid who had shoved their face into a pile of chocolate fudge and poorly rinsed it off to avoid being reprimanded by a parent.

Demonic Workplaces

"Well, Jane? Do you want ass-grabbing Robert to decide that for you, too?"

"I don't know what you are talking about, Grace."

"Sure, you don't." Her smile widened, and the brown specks cracked. She came closer and whispered in my ear. "It's simpler not to deal with it and let the other bitches at the office fend off for themselves, right? But everyone knows."

I began to shiver and stopped a tear from trickling down my cheek with the back of my hand. *What the fuck, Jane. Get a grip. She's grasping at straws.*

"I'm sorry. Did he do anything to make you uncomfortable, Grace? That's a very serious accusation, but as the head of the HR department, I can give you instructions on how to file a complaint."

"Why, Jane?"

"So that you can get proper legal assistance."

"No. Why didn't *you* file a complaint?" she shouted, and I was taken by surprise.

"I... I don't know."

But I did know. After the incident, I had managed to escape him and head to the hotel bar. I spent the rest of the night there, sipping from the same glass of red wine. Gigi asked me something I don't remember, and I said my migraines were acting up again and that sipping wine slowly was helping. What a load of bullshit. I never suffered from migraines. Ever. But that night, I decided I would always have the upper hand with Robert. I would keep any lawsuits at bay as long as he did as I told him. But he had to go and hire Grace, didn't he?

"Did Robert do something to you, Grace?"

"No! Of course not. But you know how it is. Not all men, but men. If not Robert, some other asshole. Like Stephen, Ricky. Or even Mike, the security guard, always funny and always kind and always willing to hold the door open for you." She grinned, and I noticed spots of red on her (*fake?*) fangs. "Did you know that's why Melanie hangs out with the dudes? 'Cause if she's one of the boys, then she's safe?"

I nodded. I planned to keep her talking, calm her down, and maybe invite her for dinner so she could clear her head. I could not afford to let this unhinged woman jeopardize the balance of the office.

"Do you mind if we sit, Grace? My feet are killing me. And I want to finish eating your wonderful cake, too." I smiled warmly.

Good Grace

She shrugged and pulled a chair. I forced myself to eat another mouthful of cake and make conversation. Another whiff of the foul smell hit my nose again. Grace took a deep breath and started laughing.

"Oh my. I have to do something about that, don't I?"

"About what?"

"The shit show in the bathroom." She burst out laughing again, tilting her head back. I noticed a few darkening bruises on her neck.

I took another bite, trying to look as relaxed as possible.

"I know you didn't like me, Jane. I could sense your discomfort throughout my interview."

"It's true. I didn't. But I was wrong. You don't have the experience, but you have the willpower to learn and the courage to bring a fresh perspective to the table." I lied. "The company appreciates that."

"The company appreciates that." She mocked me. "How's the cake?"

I swallowed with effort. My throat felt as dry as sandpaper.

"It's delicious! Love the frosting! You should give me the recipe sometime. There's a flavor I can't quite figure out, but it's lovely." I sounded livelier than usual and feared she would notice.

She ran her hands through her hair and smiled. Her eyes were again fixed on mine as I took another bite of the cake.

Grace stretched her arms across the kitchen table and grabbed my left hand. Her long fingers felt warm and sticky. I hid my disgust the best I could. "I really like you, Jane."

We sat in silence for a while, while she stared out the window into the half-lit parking lot. She seemed hollow, but I felt more fascination than empathy for her. I finished eating and placed the empty plate inside the dishwasher.

"Time to head home. It's been a long day. Are you coming?"

"In a while. But go ahead, Jane. I'll clean up."

I returned to my office, grabbed my bag, and shouted, "See you tomorrow, Grace," from the elevator. She didn't reply.

I walked by the empty reception and started heading across the parking lot, which was empty besides my car, the one I assumed to be Grace's, and a third one with a bumper sticker for Trump 2024. *Mike's car. Definitely Mike's*, I thought and sneered.

My car keys, damn it. After fumbling through my purse, I closed my eyes and visualized the keychain on the pristine glass top of my desk. The thought of going back made my skin break up in goosebumps. It took me a few minutes of deep breathing to gather the courage to reenter the building. *Elevator. Office. Keys. Leave. You better be quick, Jane.*

The ride in the elevator was slow and painful, so I counted the floors under my shallow breath. The door opened with a long bleep, and I noticed all the lights were now on. There was a strange buzzing energy in the air. Instinctively, I removed my shoes and ran the short, carpeted distance to my office to grab my keys. Soft moaning and slurping sounds came from the bathroom, and the foul smell hit me again, stronger now. Like a weird mix of spices and expired cheese curd.

Leave right now, Jane.

But I couldn't help it. I keep records of everyone.

I walked slowly toward the restroom, covering my nose and mouth with my forearm. The stench grew more potent and more unbearable with each step. I looked down when my bare foot slipped on something viscous that made me gag. It was a streak of blood leading inside one of the toilet stalls. Shards of a broken mirror were scattered all over the floor.

"Grace. Is that you?" My voice trembled, and I could no longer disguise it. I let the tears run down my face. "Grace, please. Are you okay? Are you hurt? Let me call you an ambulance. Or Mike."

Her laughter echoed through the room and then abruptly stopped.

"Good old Jane, yes, let's call Mike." Her voice sounded deep and coarse.

She opened the door and stepped out of the stall. Her face and hair were covered in blood, and she was naked from the waist down. The security guard sat motionless on the toilet, with his boxer shorts and jeans around his ankles and his chin leaning against his chest. When she grinned, I noticed her yellowed teeth were sharper, like the fangs of a wolf. Little pieces of tissue hung from them, and her eyes were bloodshot. She held out her hands with freakishly long fingers and claw-like nails. Mike's torn-out tongue rested on her palms. My stomach churned, the acid burning my throat.

Grace dropped the tongue on the man's lap and pressed her right index finger against her lips. *Shhhhh.* She leaned against my ear and whispered, "You won't say a word, right Jane?" And she walked away, leaving bloody footprints on the bathroom floor.

I remained immobile until I heard the bleep of the elevator. Back to her chirpy voice, Grace yelled, "Tomorrow is Friday, Jane! I'll make apple pie!"

The elevator doors closed, and I fell to my knees, shaking and vomiting chunks of undigested red velvet cake.

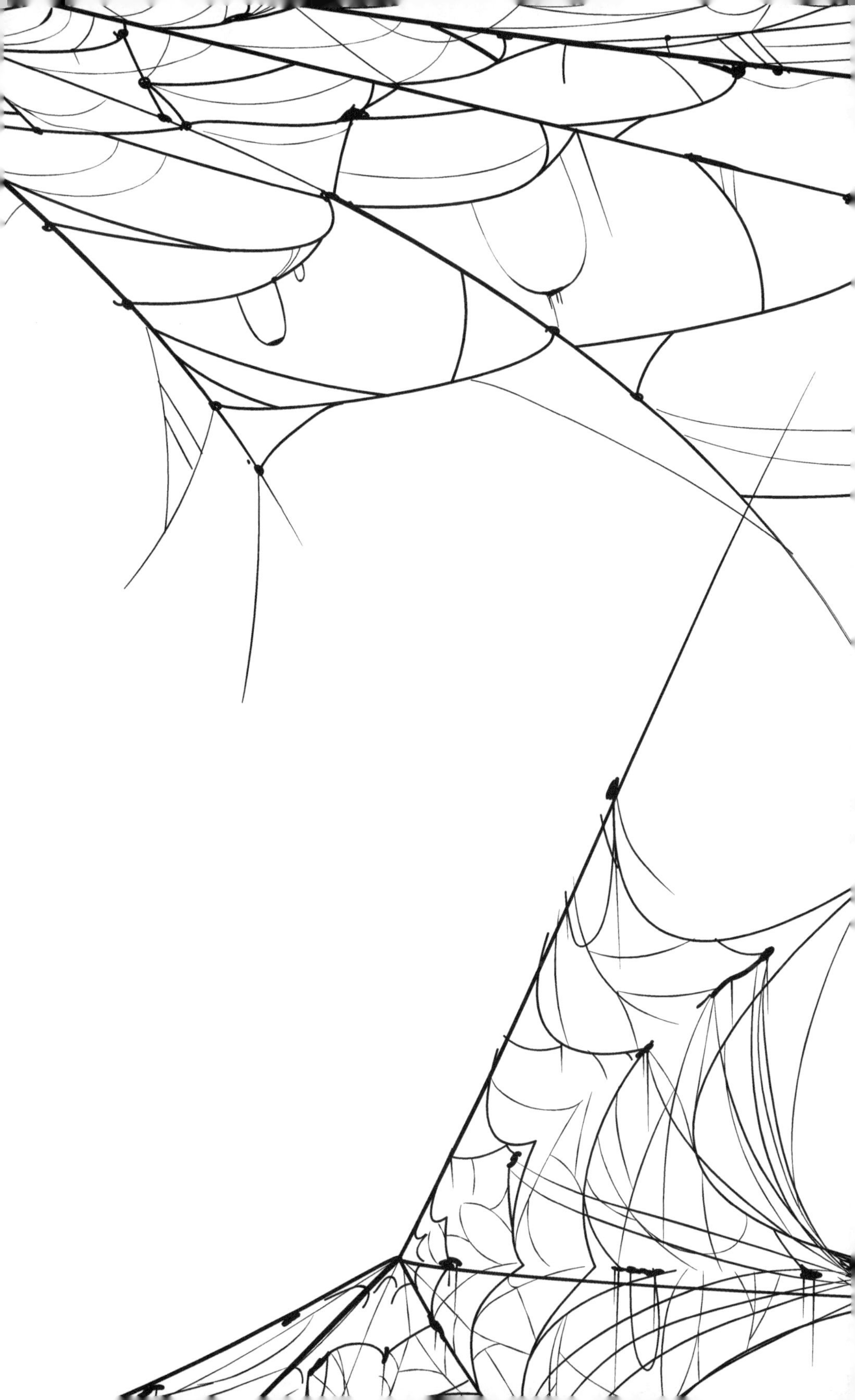

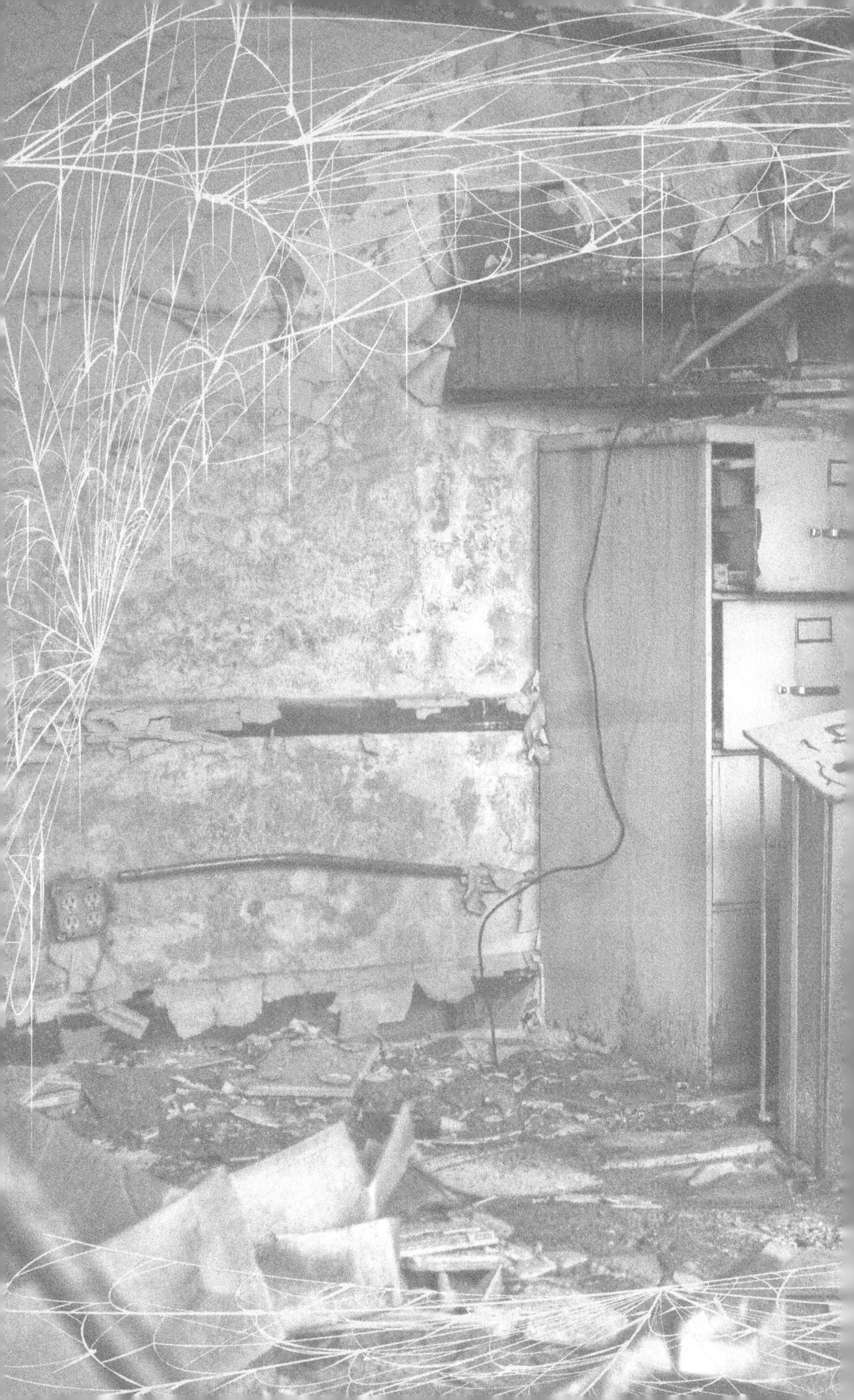

The Midnight Grind

By J. A. Heath

Demonic Workplaces

Brett pulled into the parking lot. He could hear the crickets chirping their nighttime lullaby as he got out of his car and headed straight to the employee entrance. *My shift begins at eight. Let the fun begin.* It was his first time pulling an all-nighter, and the timing of the shift still seemed foreign to him. Brett yawned as he arrived at the door and quickly punched the code he had been given into the security box. The box beeped, unlocked the door, and he opened it and went in.

The apprentice made his way to the meat department as he passed the manager's office. *First one here.* He arrived at his workspace and immediately headed to the coat rack. As Brett removed his jacket and traded it for a white smock and vinyl apron, his boss, Tom, arrived.

"Ready to work?" Tom asked.

"Oh yeah, just trying to get used to the idea that it's going to be morning when I get out of here." The two chuckled between themselves and continued to prepare for the shift.

Being a small butcher shop, it would just be the two of them for the overnight. Tom owned the Sav-A-Bunch butcher shop and requested that Brett work the shift with him. He gave Brett the spiel that "an apprentice has to learn every part of the job, even the least desirable." He added that since tomorrow was the day before the Fourth of July, the overnight was necessary to give the shop the best chance to sell as many products as possible.

Brett accepted the offered shift, but knew he didn't have a choice. He needed the money. If working overnight meant getting in favor with his boss, then he was all for it. *I hope this gets me a raise.* The uniform of a butcher wasn't the career path Brett had initially expected, but it was a job he had come to love and appreciate. Besides that, it was one of the better-paying jobs in the small town he had come to call home. It's pretty hard to turn down good money, after all.

As the young man pulled and tied his apron into place, he heard the phone on the wall begin to ring. Brett hurried to the phone, hoping it wasn't another coworker calling out for the morning shift. Reluctantly, he picked up the phone and brought it to his ear.

"Thank you for calling Save-A-Bunch; this is Brett in the meat department. How can I help you this morning?" The apprentice hypnotically said, having come accustomed to repeatedly giving the introduction. He paused to listen for the reply. Instead, Brett was met with the sound of rugged, heavy breathing.

"Hello?" he tried to coax the obnoxious noise into a conversation. An awkward silence followed, forcing him to wait longer. After a prolonged pause, the voice finally spoke.

"Yes, this is Karen Freeman. Is Tom there? May I please speak with him?"

"Yes, he is. Hold on, just a moment. I'll go get him.," he replied with a cheerful disposition.

"Thank you."

Brett placed the phone down, walked to the cooler door, and looked inside to see if he could find Tom. He walked in, the chilling temperature of the room wrapped around his neck like an ice-cold hand, squeezing his breath away. He peered down into the distance, looking past the hanging beef. The cooler, with its picture of death, still felt unsettling to Brett. He hadn't acclimated to the thought of decaying animals being the solid foundation around which the life of a butcher revolved. Something about dead animals hanging on meat hooks just felt unnerving to him.

Nothing.

He exited the cooler and shuffled back to the phone. The apprentice brought it to his ear and asked Ms. Freeman to hold for a moment longer.

"I'm sorry, ma'am. I know he's around here somewhere. Please, give me just a moment longer. I know he's here. I apologize for the wait," he said, trying to appease the woman he felt was becoming irritated with him from the prolonged wait.

He placed the phone down once again and headed for Tom's office. When he arrived, he saw Tom slumped over his desk, looking at the sales numbers from the past week. Tom's brow was bent in solid concentration.

"Hey Tom, there's a woman on the phone. She said she needs to speak with you."

"O-Ok. I'll be right there," Tom replied as he pulled himself out of a financial trance.

Brett nodded and returned to the department, where he began to work on putting the grinder together to make hamburger meat. He had just lifted the forty-pound auger into place when Tom entered the room and picked up the phone.

"Thank you for calling Sav-A-Bunch; this is Tom speaking. What can I do for you?"

Brett listened out of the corner of his ear as he heard Tom's side of the conversation.

Demonic Workplaces

"Hey, Ms. Freeman. How's my number one customer doing?" Tom chuckled as he began to talk with the familiar voice.

"No, I'm afraid we don't have any specialty meat available right now. I don't have another delivery due until two days from now. It's gotten pretty expensive, so I try not to keep much of it on hand."

Tom stood with a long pause as he listened to Ms. Freeman.

"Ah, I see. I'll tell you what, since you're my favorite customer, you can come to the store here in a couple of hours. I'll prepare something special just for you. How's that? Does that sound good to you?"

Brett looked over his shoulder towards Tom to see him smile.

"Yeah, I've got just the thing picked out for you. I'm sure you'll love it. It just got delivered today," Tom said.

"Ok, good. See you in a few. Goodbye now," he said as he hung up the phone.

Tom placed the phone back on its hook and looked over at Brett. He held the same smile from the conversation he had just finished. The owner walked over to the apprentice and leaned against the wall beside him as he continued to tray the hamburger meat.

"What do you think about being responsible for making our number one customer's evening?" Tom asked.

"I'd love to," Brett replied with a smile.

"I've known Ms. Freeman for a very long time now. I only serve her the best and freshest meat I can offer. That's how you're supposed to treat good friends, don't you think?"

"Yes, sir. Friends can be like family," Brett said.

"I suppose you're right about that. After all, friends can know just as much about us as family does. Shoot, some people even say they owe their lives to them. If it weren't for Ms. Freeman, I would have never opened this butcher shop. Now that I think about it."

"You two must be very close."

"I guess we are. I guess you could say I owe my life to Ms. Freeman. She's supported me through thick and thin. Even cut a deal with me back in the day."

"Well, that was nice of her. She sounds like a nice lady."

"Oh, she's to die for. I'd do anything for that woman. Now enough of this sappy talk. We got to get to work. Ms. Freeman won't be here until much later. She's a bit of a night owl and lives most of her life at night. I

The Midnight Grind

guess all those years of working the graveyard shift became a habit. Anyway, let's get to it."

Brett went back to grinding out the hamburger meat. Tom walked into the cooler and returned with a beef quarter. Resting it on his shoulder, he walked to the cutting block and flung it onto the table. The large piece of meat made a loud thud as it bounced on the cutting block and came to rest. Tom pulled a trimming knife and honing steel from his scabbard. He began to run the knife's blade across the steel, truing up the point. The sound of the cold steel running against one another gave Brett goosebumps. After several passes, Tom re-sheathed the honing steel and began to cut into the large piece of beef.

Tom worked with precision, a true craftsman of the trade. As he cut and trimmed, he trayed several different pieces of meat. Steaks, stew meat, and roasts all came from the massive quarter of the deceased bovine. He continued to remove one piece at a time as he whittled down the quarter, merchandizing it into cuts that the customers would fight over. He worked his way down to the bone and discarded it. After wiping the block clean of myoglobin, Tom returned to the cooler. He re-emerged with a second beef quarter, repeating the process as Brett finished up the last bit of hamburger.

The apprentice cleaned up the grinder and set up a cutting block to begin processing chickens. Poultry was the first and most straightforward meat new butchers learned to merchandise. The process was simple. Each chicken produced two drums, thighs, wings, and breasts. Brett went into the cooler and walked over to where the cases of whole chickens were stored. He loaded four cases on his cart and turned around to return to the door.

Brett looked over at the hanging beef. Tom had already cleared a hook from the two quarters he had retrieved. The light reflected off the sharp meat hook, its tip still covered in residue. It reminded Brett that everything a butcher worked with had to die first to make it here. He felt a shiver crawl up his spine, forcing him to exit the cooler quickly.

He pushed his cart to his station and was about to begin unloading a case of chickens when Tom turned around from his block. The old butcher placed his knives down and walked over to Brett.

"Hey, we need to take a moment to get Ms. Freeman's order ready. She called me while you were in the cooler. She's on her way now. I don't want to keep her waiting."

"Ok. What can I do to help?"

Demonic Workplaces

"Just go in the cooler, walk down to the end, and get me the last quarter of hanging beef. That's the best one. I know it'll make Ms. Freeman happy."

"Ok," Brett said.

The apprentice made his way into the cooler. He walked down the row of hanging beef. *They die for our enjoyment.* He pushed past the thought of dead animals. *It's for the customer.* As an apprentice, he'd have to work on them at some point. It didn't make sense for a butcher to be uneasy about slaughtered animals. Sooner or later, Brett would have to get over the thought of death. He continued, passing quarter after quarter until he finally neared the end.

As Brett came to the last hook, he was shocked to find nothing on it. He started to turn around, but before he could, he felt a sudden excruciating pain come from the back of his head.

His sight went black.

When Brett finally came out of his daze, he could feel a cold, wet substance slithering down the back of his neck. *Blood!* He tried to move his hand to investigate the liquid and see what it was, but quickly realized that his hands and feet had been tied together. He found himself hanging on the meat hook inside of the cooler. The rope binding his hands had been looped over the hook, leaving him unable to stand on solid ground. He could not move except for the short side-to-side swings that he made when he panicked from the new reality.

As he hung from the hook, his feet dangled. The sound of the cooler fans running began to sound like screams in his ears. A dark figure emerged from behind a piece of hanging beef.

Tom.

"W-Why Tom? Why am I bleeding? Is this a joke?" Brett asked, confused.

"No. It's not a joke. Listen, I don't enjoy doing this. But, you remember when I said Ms. Freeman and I cut a deal? Yeah, about that."

Tom paused for a moment as if he was contemplating even telling the rest of his story to the young apprentice.

"I guess it doesn't matter. I'll tell you," he began. "Ms. Freeman works for a rather unsavory character if you will. A lot of people don't even think he exists. Rightfully so, I suppose. Most people will never meet him until it's too late."

The Midnight Grind

"W-Who are you talking about, Tom?" Brett pleaded. "You're not making any sense."

"Oh hell, I'll just cut to the chase." The butcher leaned up against the piece of beef that was hanging next to Brett.

"A while back, I had a run-in with the bandsaw blade. Call it careless, but I slipped on some stray beef fat and went head-first into the blade. Cut clean into the middle of my brain. It killed me, stone-cold dead. Imagine my surprise when I ended up in Hell." He paused again. "Yeah, not what I expected either." He began to smile. "But the strangest thing happened. A demon in that fiery pit of misery pitied me and decided to strike a deal with me." He chuckled. "Can you guess what that deal was?"

Brett realized that what Tom was about to say next wouldn't bode well for his current situation.

"Tom, it doesn't have to be like this," the apprentice begged. "Please, just let me go. You'll never see or hear from me again. I swear."

Tom began to cackle with excitement as he shook his head.

"Don't try and talk me out of it! I-It's not that easy, Brett. I've got to hold up my end of the deal, you see? You're my end of the deal. I hate it for you. I do. But this is the way it has to be. I supply the demons with fresh meat, and in return, I get to keep living. I get to be immortal. Isn't that awesome? Once you make a deal with the devil, your body stops aging entirely. I still look as young and spry as I did in my fifties. That's a heck of a sweet deal. Be honest. You wouldn't turn down an offer like that either, would you?"

As the two faced each other in a deadlock of emotions, a knock came from outside the cooler.

"Ah, that must be her," Tom said. Brett tried to scream, but the insulated casing that housed the cooler muffled every sound from within. The roar of the fans mocked the apprentice.

Tom moved to the door of the cooler and opened it. A seemingly plain woman stepped into the cold. She neared Brett and began to look him over. The apprentice looked down at the woman, noting the grotesque, jaundiced eyes that her face held. Terror flooded into his body. His heart began to race as she glared at Tom and then looked back at the apprentice. She moved closer to him, coming within inches of his face. Brett squirmed as he tried to put distance between her and himself. She reached out her finger and ran it across the back of Brett's neck. Ms. Freeman pulled the pointed digit to her face and looked at the crimson liquid that coated the tip of her finger in awe. She opened her mouth, put her finger in, and then sucked the finger clean with a pop.

She began to grin until her smile reached from ear to ear.

"Oh yes! That's lovely! He's perfect. He's so sweet and full of youth. Tom, you've surely outdone yourself this time," she said as she began to walk back toward the refrigerator door.

"Make it quick. The meat always tastes better when there's adrenaline still in it. The others prefer it that way," she said. Tom nodded with a smile as she shut the door behind her.

When the door had fully closed, Tom pulled a skinning knife from his scabbard. He began to move toward Brett, his blade leading the way. The apprentice panicked and started swinging his legs together to try to release himself from the meat hook. Tom lunged toward Brett with the knife, grazing the apprentice's rib cage. Fueled with desperation, Brett powered through the pain and gave everything he had with one more swing. The young apprentice felt the loop of the rope loosen from around the hook as his body fell to the floor. What he hadn't planned was what happened after he freed himself from the hook.

Unable to catch himself, his body fell to the ground with a concussive thud. Brett lay on the concrete cooler floor in a growing pool of blood, his ears ringing from the bounce of his head against the concrete. Brett looked up at the ceiling in a daze as his consciousness was fleeting. The last thing he saw was Tom standing over him, shaking his head.

"Like I said, son. I've been doing this for a long time. You'd think after a hundred years of living, I'd seen it all. But I'll be honest. You're a wily one. You're the first one ever to make it off the hook." Tom smiled as he pulled the honing steel from his scabbard and began to run his skinning knife across it. The sound of the steel blade going against the honing steel was as cold as the concrete floor.

Brett felt a sharp sting as pain poured into his body. He screamed out in agony as he came to his end. The sounds faded, and an hour later, Ms. Freeman walked out of the butcher shop, a delighted customer. Tom looked up at the clock on the wall. It was midnight. He cleaned up the mess from Ms. Freeman's order and put the grinder back together to make more hamburger meat.

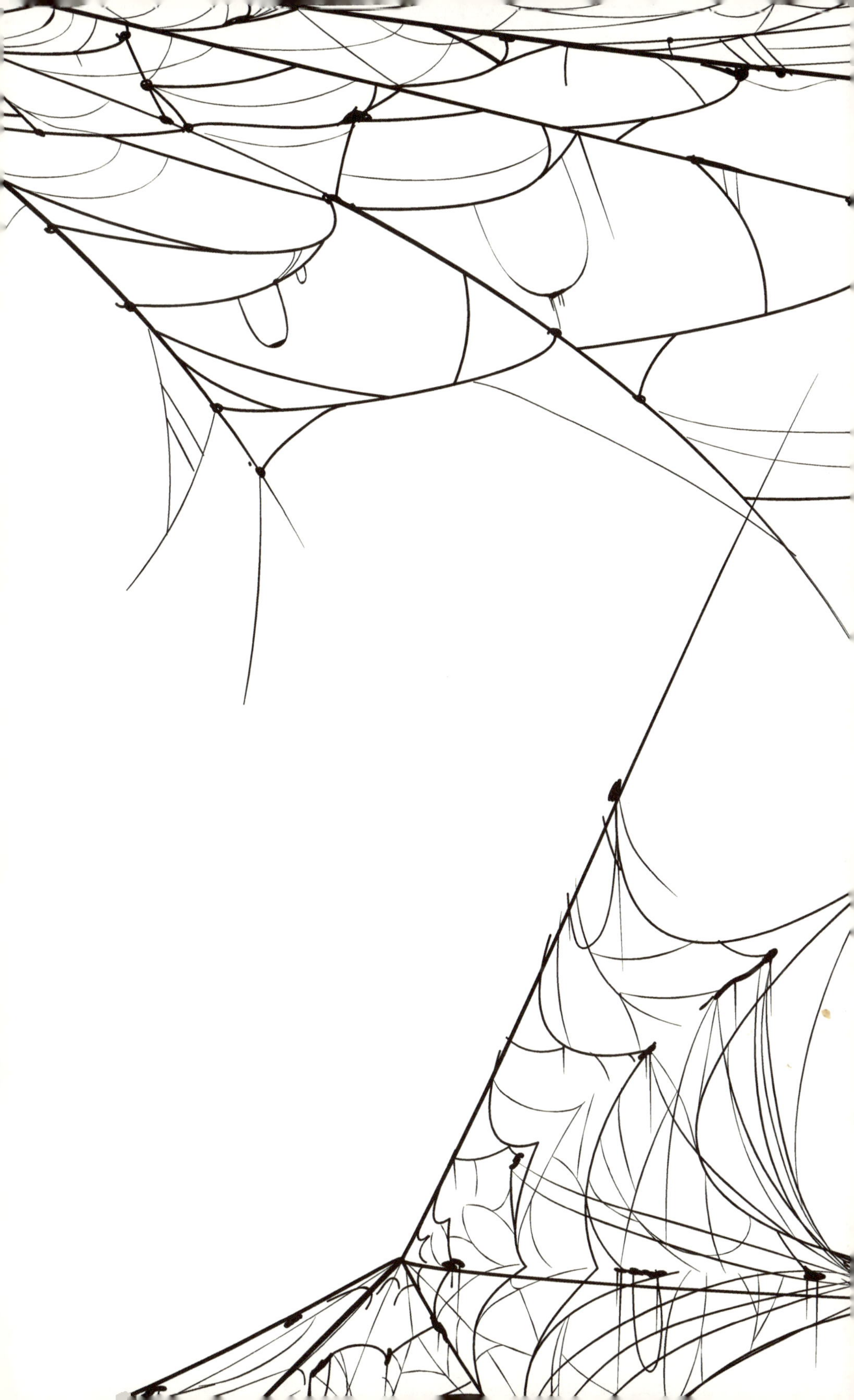

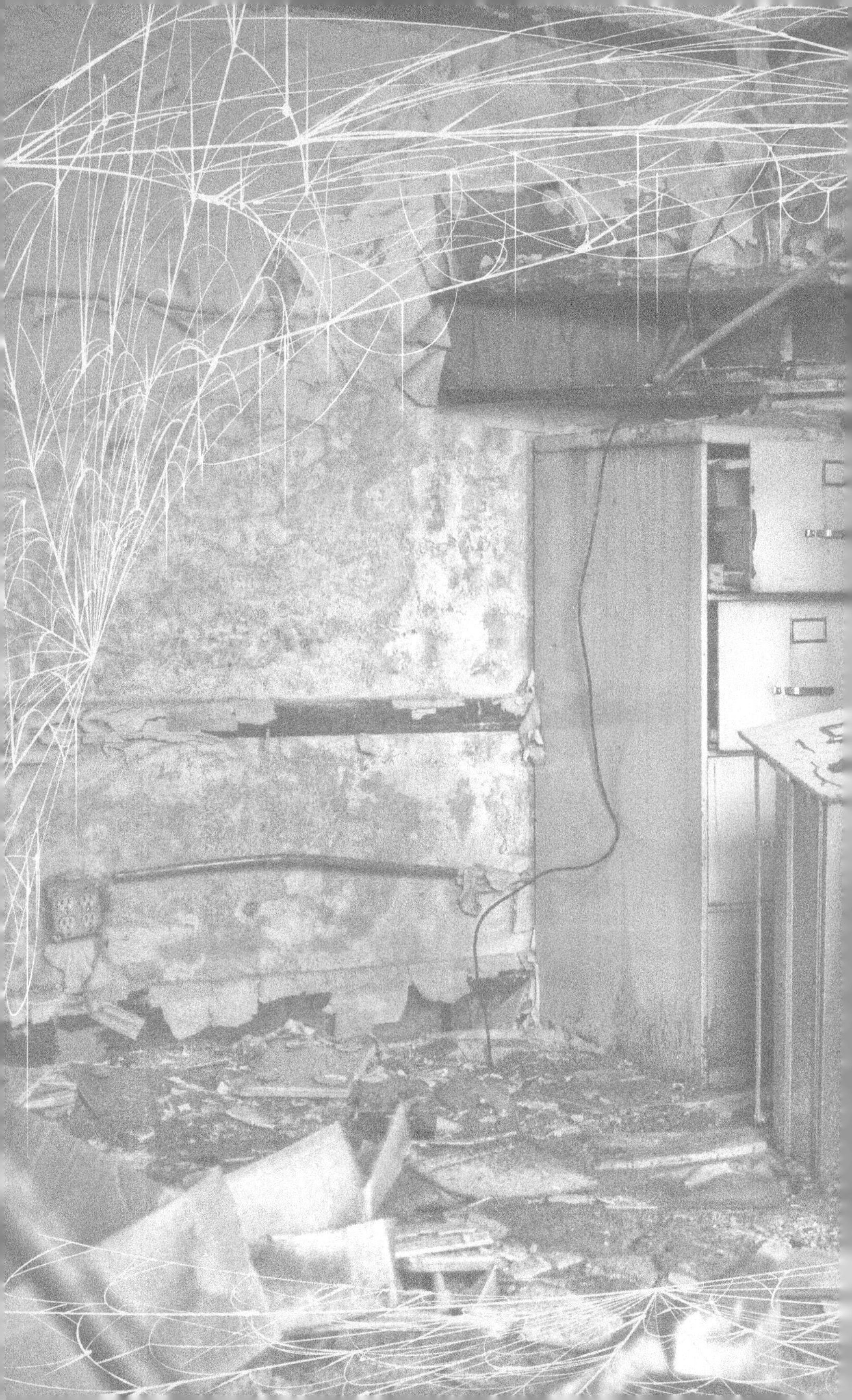

Parting Wish

By Alan Berkshire

Demonic Workplaces

Parkes and Son had been trading for over one hundred and eleven years, passed down from father to son over four generations. They were well known and respected by all the locals, always dependable to give the deceased a good send-off. Like this afternoon's service: Mr. Blenkensop, seventy-eight years old, good life, big attendance. Everyone praised Parkes and Son for their respectful and sincere handling of the whole service, the go-to funeral home.

Jeff Newberg, though, wasn't happy.

"I know it's a funeral, Jeff, and we have to keep a somber and appropriate demeanor, but your face is like thunder… What's wrong?" asked Ashley Lombard.

Jeff pulled off the dark grey cravat and undid the top button of his pristine white shirt, sighing heavily.

"I don't know, Ash," he said, slumping down into the staffroom chair, looking down at the floor.

"Well, it must be something," Ashley said, sitting opposite him. "Come on, spill it."

Jeff looked up at her, gazing into her light gray eyes. She was a pretty girl, two years his junior, twenty-three years old, with light brown hair and soft brown eyes. "Haven't you noticed anything odd over the last couple of months?"

Ashley's brow furrowed. "Like what?"

Jeff shook his head. "Things haven't been right, nothing major, just little things."

"You're going to have to give me more than that," she encouraged.

Sitting back in the chair, Jeff briefly closed his eyes. He had seen things, odd things, out of kilter. But now that he was giving voice to his concerns, he was starting to have doubts.

"Several times over the last few months, I've found Reggie in the preparation room. He said he was just checking to make sure everything was in order."

"He's the boss's son; it's part of his job, especially now that he's taken over from his father," pointed out Ashley.

"But that's just it. Mitch complained to me that he's found the latch pins unfastened on the coffins several times; upon checking inside, the pillow fold was disturbed, or the lid fastenings were loose. A couple of weeks ago, I went into the prep room and I'm sure Reggie was just closing the lid on a coffin."

"What are you saying?" asked Ashley.

"I don't know," Jeff said, shaking his head dejectedly. "I didn't give it much thought till today."

"What happened today?" said Ashley.

"Mr. Blenensop's funeral," said Jeff.

Ashley huffed. "Well, I know that."

"What you don't know is that I'm sure the coffin was the same one we used for Mrs. Peabody's funeral two weeks ago."

Ashley gasped. "That's impossible."

"Ash, I was front left pall-bearer at Mrs. Peabody's funeral, just like I was today at Mr. Blenkensop's. I noticed a small v-shaped scratch just below the handle on Mrs. Peabody's casket, nothing big or really noticeable, but it was there. Today I saw the same scratch on Mr. Blenkensop's casket."

"You must be mistaken. Mrs. Peabody was cremated."

"I know," agreed Jeff. "But the handle was three inches from my face, Ash. I know what I saw. It was the same casket."

"But how?"

"That's the question," Jeff said darkly. "How?"

He got up and paced the room.

"I mean, look at Reggie, he's what, one hundred and twenty pounds soaking wet? Mrs. Peabody was at least one hundred and eighty? I know. I helped carry her."

"Are you saying Reggie somehow switched coffins? That's crazy," blurted Ashley.

"Is it?" said Jeff. "That coffin was top of the range. It cost £4956.00. I checked. That's a lot of money just to burn."

"I can't see how it's possible, especially for a little weed like Reggie," said Ashley.

"That's what I can't work out," said Jeff. "He obviously has help. But who? Once the inspector checks the coffin nameplate against the cremation order, there's very little time to make a switch. It has to be someone inside the crematorium."

"I don't know, Jeff. I think you're treading on very thin ice. Even if you're right, how are you going to prove it? Old Man Parkes will have you out the door before you can say 'Grave robber.'"

"I know," sighed Jeff. "And you can bet your bottom dollar Reggie has his tracks well covered."

Jeff stopped pacing. "Come on, let's change out of these clothes and go to The Green Man. I think we need a drink."

Reginald Ian Parkes sat back in the armchair and gloated over the large box placed on the coffee table in front of him. The Amazon Prime logo on the side grinned back at him. The overhead light reflected off the many jewels crammed into the box, highlighting the gold and the silver, like a pirate's treasure chest, which, in effect, it was. Rings, brooches, bracelets, necklaces, pearls, there were even a few World War One medals in there somewhere, one or two of them very rare.

A small fortune, gathered over the three years since his father handed the reins of Parkes and Son to him whilst he went into semi-retirement. The best thing the old fool ever did. He was always too prissy, too "hands-on" to allow Reggie any opportunity to relieve their deceased clients of their valuables.

Well, reasoned Reggie. *What's the point in cremating it all when I will be able to put it to far better use? Seemed such a waste.* And when Seth Burroughs, assistant chief administrator at the crematorium, came up with the idea of recycling caskets, it gave him something else to think about... How could he refuse?

They had met in the pub one evening by sheer chance. Seth had been drinking and got a little bit loose-tongued. The suggestion was tentative; the discussion followed the lines of what a waste it all was: expensive caskets reduced to worthless ash. What was the point? *Sentiments after my own heart,* thought Reggie. The "discussion" took on a serious note, then they started to make their plans. It took a bit of working out, and it wasn't something they could do on a regular basis—just play it by ear as the occasion arose. It was lucrative, though. Very lucrative.

"If I could just get a photograph. Catch him at it," said Jeff. "Concrete proof."

"It would cost you your job," said Ashley.

"I don't think I want to work for a funeral director that robs its clients," said Jeff. "Do you?"

Ashley sipped her Bacardi and Coke. "I guess you're right."

"Of course I'm right," Jeff said hotly. "It's wrong, Ash, on every level—totally bloody wrong. I thought of confronting Reggie, one on one when no one was around. Let the little shit know I was on to him. Threaten him with the police. But it's pointless; there's no evidence, it would only be my word against his, and he's the son of a respectable funeral director. All he would have to do is say I was just a disgruntled employee."

"You should just let it go, Jeff. There's nothing you can do, really. Sooner or later, Reggie will get his 'comeuppance.'"

Jeff looked moodily at the pint of Guinness sitting on the table in front of him. "I can't, Ash. It goes against everything I stand for. The public trusts us to do right by their loved ones, to treat them with respect—not rob them blind.

"No, I'll just bide my time, keep an eye on Reggie. Sooner or later, he'll make a mistake, and when he does, I'll be right there, waiting..."

Flora Merryweather stood in the reception of Parkes and Son, quietly waiting to be noticed. The room was tastefully decorated: plain light green walls with dark oak wainscoting and matching table and chairs. Dark green carpet covered the floors and soft ambient music played in the background. In the middle of the table sat a shallow copper urn filled with dried leaves and flowers, all in shades of autumn.

"May I help you?" asked Ashley Lombard.

"I hope so, dear," Mrs. Merryweather answered. "I'm here about my friend, Phoenix Sunflower."

"Would you like to sit down and I'll take some details?" offered Ashley.

Ashley respectfully waited until Mrs. Merryweather was seated before sitting opposite this extraordinary-looking woman dressed in a sleeveless flowing dress of purple silk, throat to ankles, a beautifully made shawl of fine black cotton draped over her right shoulder. Mrs Merryweather was slim and tall, with dark flowing hair, raven black, cascading down over her straight shoulders and narrow back. Ashley noted her hair wasn't dyed; it was her natural color without a single strand of gray showing. Her eyes were a lively green, twinkling with a friendly light, and she had a full mouth with a touch of discreet pale pink lipstick. Several jewels adorned her fine long fingers and wrists, jade, amethyst, intricate silver bracelets and rings. A dark green emerald set in a lovely silver mount surmounted by a small crescent moon hung around her long neck by a fine silver chain.

"Okay," said Ashley, producing a leather-bound clipboard. She was finding it hard to take her eyes away from the amazing tattoos covering Mrs. Merryweather's left arm. An intricate design of vines and ivy leaves interspersed with cryptic sigils and runes, light grey and black, delicately trailing the full length of her arm.

"What can Parkes and Son do for you, Mrs. Merryweather?" Ashley asked with difficulty.

"My best friend, Phoenix Sunflower, passed recently. It was her wish to be cremated," she said in a soft voice.

"My condolences," Ashley said sincerely. "I'm sorry for your loss. We at Parkes and Son offer several options, services to suit every taste…"

"A service will not be necessary. The appropriate service and rituals have already been observed. All Phoenix requires is the cremation," said Mrs. Merryweather.

"Oh, I see," Ashley said, somewhat surprised. "You wish to choose a casket, then?"

"No," said Mrs. Merryweather. "Phoenix and I have that in hand. We made our own. All we require is a vehicle to pick up Phoenix from our home and transport her to the crematorium. Can you accommodate that?"

"Yes, we can," said Ashley. "It will be our privilege…" Ashley hesitated, "…may I just say that Ms. Sunflower's name is very unusual…"

Mrs. Merryweather smiled. "Yes, it has often been commented on. Ever since we were at school together. We have been friends almost all our lives, sixty-eight years. Her name always suited her." Surprisingly, Mrs. Merryweather chuckled. "She always said she would rise from the ashes."

Ashley was amazed. She had placed the beautiful woman sitting opposite her in her mid-fifties, perhaps younger. Yet if she had met her friend in school sixty-eight years ago, that must put her in her early seventies at the very least.

"Well, you look amazing," Ashley said. "You must tell me your secret."

Mrs. Merryweather laughed again, the soft, rich sound somehow comforting.

"I don't think you would believe me if I told you." She said.

Parting Wish

"It's beautiful," said Ashley in awe.

"They made this by hand?" Christopher "Mitch" Mitchell asked.

"That's what Mrs. Merryweather said," replied Ashley.

"It even smells good," remarked Jeff.

"Chrysanthemum," advised Ashley. "And tobacco."

The two men looked at her.

"Mrs. Merryweather told me. She gave me a whole list of things she required us to do before the cremation tomorrow. The candles surrounding the casket, the hydrangeas to ward off negativity and cleanse the air, the white linen shroud, and the white flowers.

"She asked if the clock could be stopped and all mirrors covered, as well as a window left open in here. Seeing as the only mirror is in the reception, I told her it wouldn't be a problem."

"Odd requests," commented Jeff.

"It's part of their belief system. They're Wiccan," Ashley informed him.

"Wiccan? You mean witches?" asked Mitch.

"Yes," answered Ashley with a quiet smile. "Though not the Disney type witch, all warts and wrinkles."

"I can see that," said Mitch, looking down at the cadaver in the intricately decorated willow-work casket on the plinth. "She was beautiful, especially her hair. What a lovely shade of auburn."

"I don't know how they even managed to weave those flowers into the wickerwork. The horse is amazing,"

"So are the stars and the crescent moon. It's a bloody work of art," admired Mitch.

Phoenix Sunflower lay in quiet repose, dressed in a simple white shroud that covered her from head to toe. Her slim hands were folded over her breast, adorned with several rings, jade, amethyst, and opals all set in silver, just like Mrs. Merryweather's, thought Ashley. An identical amulet hung about her neck, a dark green emerald, twinkling in the discreet overhead lighting, surmounted by the same silver crescent moon.

"What's that?" Jeff said, indicating a golden statue nestled in Ms. Sunflower's hands. About six inches tall, it depicted a young woman carrying a bow with a hunting dog standing beside her.

"That's Diana, the Huntress, one of their deities. It's to be cremated with her," said Ashley.

Jeff frowned but said nothing.

"Look at this," Ashley said, moving around the casket. She picked up a large wickerwork lid. "Look at the work on the tree."

"Oh, wow!" said Mitch.

The lid showed a tree, every branch, every twig, and every leaf, set in the middle of the lid, just below a copper nameplate. The whole thing worked in wicker, reeds twisted and woven, without any other fixings except the wicker itself.

"That must have taken weeks," said Jeff.

"And it fits perfectly, snug and tight. The whole thing is a complete work of art, right down to the black and white ribbons," said Ashley. "Mrs. Merryweather told me the tree is a symbol, the connection between life and afterlife. It's very sacred.

"Every part of the funeral furniture means something, the designs, the sigils, the colors, even the smells. She is relying on us to make sure everything is just right, and I promised her we would."

"Absolutely," said Mitch.

"There are still one or two things that need to be attended to, the final one being the car. Mrs. Merryweather requests that the car circles the crematorium three times, sunwise, before entering, then the cremation can begin."

"Sunwise?" queried Mitch.

"Clockwise," said Jeff.

"I saw your expression," said Ashley. "Are you not comfortable having a service for a witch?"

Jeff looked at her in surprise. "Hell, yes!" he said. "I think it's great. That's not my concern."

"Then what is?" said Ashley.

"Did you see the jewellery?" he said. "That gold statue? It's got to be worth five, maybe six, hundred pounds alone, add the rings and bracelets, and that necklace... There's a small fortune sitting there."

"You're worried about Reggie," said Ashley.

"Absolutely. He's not going to be able to resist," said Jeff.

"What are you going to do?" asked Ashley.

"I'm going to stay overnight. Keep watch. I'm not going to let that little bastard rob this client, no way. I'll get some sandwiches, and there's tea and coffee in the staff room. I'll settle down in the armchair in reception. Reggie will have to pass me to get into the viewing room."

"Isn't that a little drastic?" said Ashley.

"Prevention is better than cure," said Jeff. "And I haven't got a cure, so..."

"Do you want me to sit with you?" she asked.

"No, I'll be fine. I'll have Stephen King's latest to keep me company."

Avarice glowed in Reggie Parke's eyes as he slowly walked around the wickerwork casket in the viewing room. He regarded the jewels, the rings, the necklace, but especially the gold statue of the woman and dog. He knew quality when he saw it.

He had read the instructions left by the client, a Mrs. Flora Merryweather. His employees had seen to most of the requirements. The only immediate item left was the closing of the casket at dusk, and Jeff Newberg and Ashley Lombard already had that in hand. Reggie smiled to himself. There were no fastenings on the wickerwork casket, no locks or screws. The ornate lid just fitted over the top like the lid of a shoebox. It would make his task all the easier.

He would wait until late that night when he was sure everyone had gone home, then he would pay a little visit to the shop, and no one would be the wiser.

Easy, risk-free money.

2345 hours.

Jeff put down the paperback and rubbed his eyes. Everything was quiet. He figured if Reggie was going to come, he would have been here by now. The man was intrinsically lazy, always looking for the easy way out, leaving all the work to Jeff and his colleagues. Jeff had been thinking of moving on from Parkes and Son for a few weeks now, regardless of the situation with Reggie. He had thought it was a good career move when he came here four years ago, but over the ensuing years, he had realized he had made a mistake. To quote a little grave humor, it was a dead end as far as his future prospects were concerned. Reggie was just the final straw. He was a nasty piece of work; sly, underhandedly charging for services never performed was just the tip of the iceberg. The recent events just compounded the situation. Jeff thought about the letter of resignation sitting in his desk drawer. It was time.

He yawned and stretched. Drowsiness suddenly stole over him. His eyelids felt like lead weights; the reception area felt warm, stuffy.

"Maybe just for a minute or two..." Jeff muttered, laying his head back against the armchair.

The key rattled in the lock, the door swung open on well-oiled hinges, and Reggie Parkes stepped into the reception area.

"Shit!" he gasped as he saw Jeff Newberg sitting in the reception armchair, highlighted by the small lamp on the occasional table beside him.

Words choked in Reggie's throat; no excuse why he was at the funeral home this late came to his guilty mind. Then he realized Newberg was asleep. He looked closer. No, not just asleep; he was fast asleep. Reggie clapped his hands, a sharp, loud crack. Newberg didn't stir. A golden opportunity.

Quickly, quietly, Reggie closed the front door. On silent feet, he moved across the reception, his gaze never leaving the sleeping man. He swiftly opened the door to the viewing room, passed through, and closed it behind him.

The candles surrounding the casket threw a flickering light around the room, a soft, calming ambience accompanied by the sweet smell of hydrangeas. The casket rested on its plinth, the lid in place. Reggie's eyes gleamed.

An owl hooted, momentarily startling Reggie. It sounded as if the bird was actually in the room! Reggie peered into the dark corners, chiding himself for being an idiot. Passing through the circle of candles, he stood before the casket. Despite his cynicism, Reggie had to admit it was a beautiful thing. Tentatively, he stroked along the lid, snatching his hand back when it felt unnaturally warm. He realized the wickerwork wasn't wood; it was tactile and absorbed heat, not like the cedar and oak of ordinary coffins, but still, it seemed to be generating a lot of heat.

"Ah!" Reggie jumped back.

Something had brushed against his legs. He scanned the floor. Shadows moved. He thought he saw a shape moving along the wall at the base of the wainscoting. Something feline—Then it was gone. Had Ashley allowed cats into the viewing room without asking permission? Another one of the damned woman's "requirements?" If she had, there would be words tomorrow!

The window was open. Impatiently, Reggie strode across the room. He grunted as he pulled on the lower casement. It refused to move. Taking a firmer grip, he pulled harder. The window stubbornly remained open. Stepping back, he frowned at the window. A gentle breeze wafted through the open portal. They were brand new, well, almost. His father had all the windows in the funeral home replaced just over a year ago. Top of the range, they had never stuck before.

Reggie turned back to the casket. Time was passing. He had no idea how long Newberg would sleep for, and he had no idea what he was even doing there. It didn't matter. Reggie would take what he came for and be out of there before anyone noticed. Perfect. He hesitated before touching the lid again. The warm sensation he had felt before had been unpleasant. He hadn't expected it. Now he did. With a grimace, he took hold and eased the lid up and off the casket.

The fluttering of wings made Reggie jerk, almost making him drop the lid as he whirled around. Someone—Something—whispered in his ear, so close he could feel the sweet-scented breath against the sensitive skin of his neck.

"Thief... Desecrator..."

Reggie whirled again, facing the open casket. Ms. "Whatever her name was" lay in calm repose, the thin white silk shroud covering her face unmoving. Candlelight glinted on the gold statue clasped in her white hands. The emerald resting on her breast shone a verdant green.

Something tugged at Reggie's mind. He was drawn to her face, made filmy by the white silk. She looked so calm, so serene. Then her eyes opened and looked at him, a vivid violet gaze that held just a hint of reproach.

Reggie screamed, dropped the casket lid, and bolted for the door. He twisted the handle. The door remained firmly shut. Using both hands, he pulled frantically. Using a fist, he pounded on the door, throwing fearful glances over his shoulder.

"Newberg! Newburg, help me! The doors stuck, Newberg!"

There was no response.

"Newberg! For God's sake! Open the fucking door! Newberg!"

Reggie turned his back to the door, his thin chest heaving, eyes fixed on the casket. He was expecting to see the woman rising from her resting place, the violet eyes glaring at him, fingers beckoning... But there was nothing.

Demonic Workplaces

From where he stood, he could clearly see the body still lying in the casket, looking as if it had never moved. *Her eyes had opened, looked at me. They had!*

Trying to still his jangling nerves, Reggie hesitantly approached the casket. His mouth was dry, his heart beating hard against his ribs. He could see her face; even through the veil, he saw her eyes were definitely closed.

"Idiot!" he cursed.

How many times had a corpse "moved," flexed its fingers, looked as if it were breathing, and, yes, opened its eyes whilst being prepared for viewing? That's why the eyelids were glued shut to prevent such a thing from happening whilst being viewed by loved ones. Before the implication of that thought could take root, laughter filled the room, mocking, soft and gentle but mocking.

"Who's there?" Reggie peered about. Shadows danced. "Newberg, is that you? Stop playing games, or you can collect your cards at the end of the month. See how funny you think it is, then."

The laughter continued.

The slim arm floated out of the air behind him, encircling his throat, the soft hand clamping over his mouth. Wide-eyed Reggie gasped, fixating on the delicate tattoo's swirling up the forearm to the shoulder, vines and small ivy leaves interspersed with sigils and runes, grey and black. Rings glittered on the long fingers closing over his mouth, pulling him gently but inexorably back against the side of the casket.

With a fluttering of gossamer wings, two tiny figures hovered above the coffin, their eyes twinkling, their laughter soft, melodic, like miniature angels, or maybe cherubs, hovering in the semi-darkness, their outlines glowing with a silvery radiance. One dipped down, and though he could feel nothing, Reggie's legs were raised as the cherub effortlessly hoisted him up and settled the terrified man into the coffin next to Phoenix Sunflower.

"Familiars…" whispered the soft voice in his ear.

The cat landed on his chest, purring, its green eyes boring into Reggie's, as black as ebony, its outline depicted in an ethereal radiance. It cocked its head on one side like an inquisitive puppy, its tail curling sinuously in the air.

It was there, Reggie could see it, but there was no weight on his chest. He couldn't feel its paws even as it disdainfully turned and slipped over the side of the casket, out of sight.

"Please, please, let me go… I'll never steal again, I promise to God! Please, let me go—"

Parting Wish

The words were muffled, unintelligible through the hand over his mouth. He tried to struggle, to break free, but his limbs wouldn't respond. He just lay there beside her, together like star-crossed lovers. The fluttering of wings drew his attention, and Reggie screamed. The two cherubs, the *familiars*, hovered above the casket; suspended between them was the beautifully woven lid. Tears streamed down the helpless man's face as the lid began to descend. Reggie kept on screaming—

"Hush... Hush..." crooned the soft, gentle voice.

"He's late," said Ashley, looking at her watch.

"It can't be helped," said Jeff. "We'll have to proceed without him."

They looked at each other as they stood in the reception of Parkes and Son.

"This is my last funeral with this firm," said Jeff. "I think enough is enough."

"He didn't turn up last night, did he? Everything was alright," said Ashley.

"That's not the point, Ash. Having to stand guard over our clients? It's the last straw. I can't be here anymore."

"Jeff..." Ashley nodded towards the door.

Mrs. Flora Merryweather stood quietly, dressed as elegantly as before. A dark veil covered her face.

"Good morning," Jeff said.

"Good morning," she answered. "It's a beautiful day."

"Just a sad occasion," Jeff said.

"Oh, no." Smiled Mrs. Merryweather. "It's not sad at all. Just another milestone on our path."

"That's a lovely way to look at it," said Ashley.

"Our lives don't end just because we pass from this world," Mrs. Merryweather said.

"Everything's ready," Jeff said. "We've placed Ms. Sunflower in the car and she awaits your pleasure."

Mrs. Merryweather smiled. "Oh, and I would like to thank you, young man, for sitting with Phoenix last night. She really appreciated the company."

Jeff looked surprised. "How...?"

"We have our ways," Ms Merryweather said with a knowing smile. "You fulfilled her parting wish."

"I did?" asked Jeff.

"Yes. It was always her wish to have someone with her when she began her long journey to Summerland." She touched Jeff's hand and smiled. "You made that possible."

ENDS.

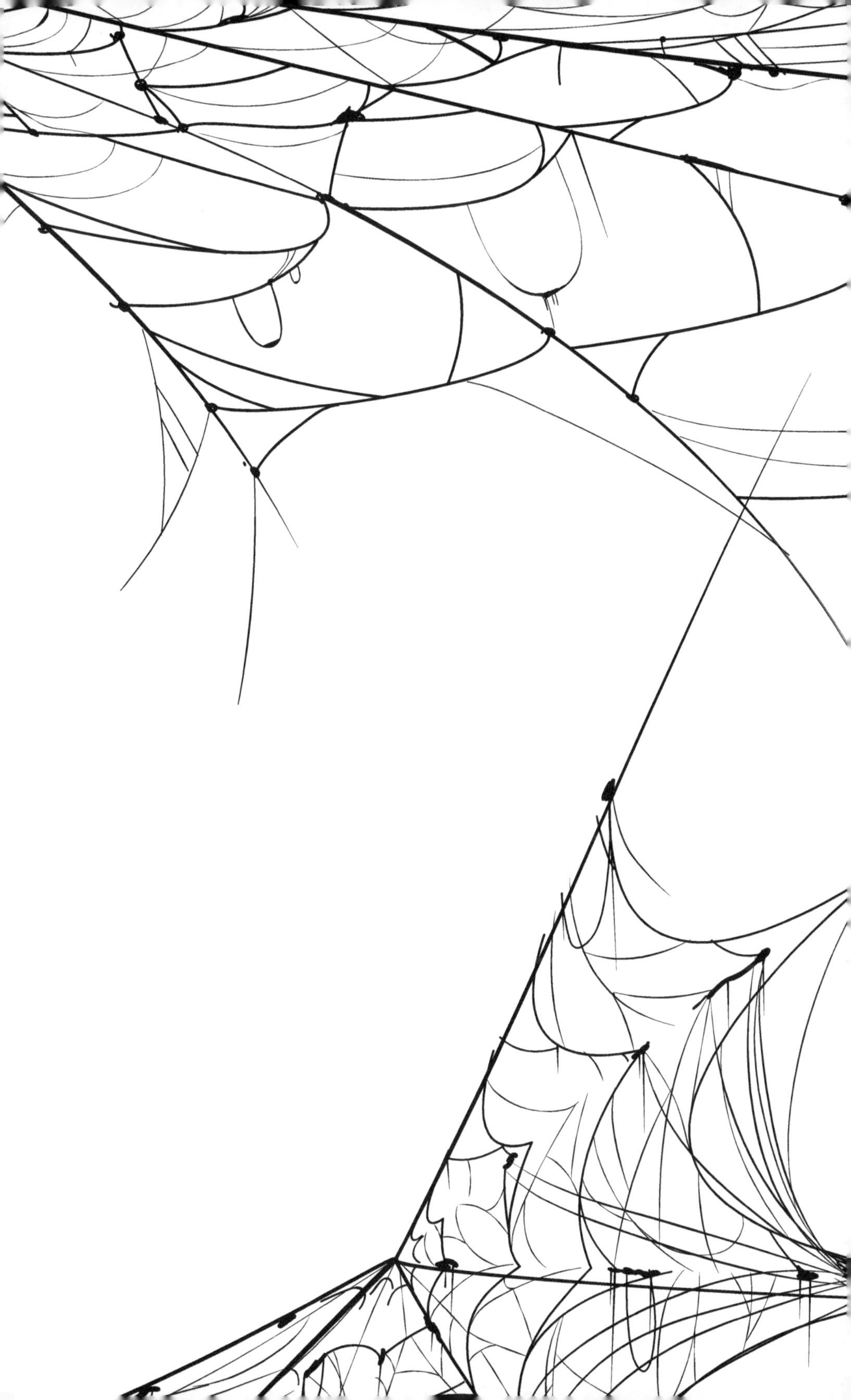

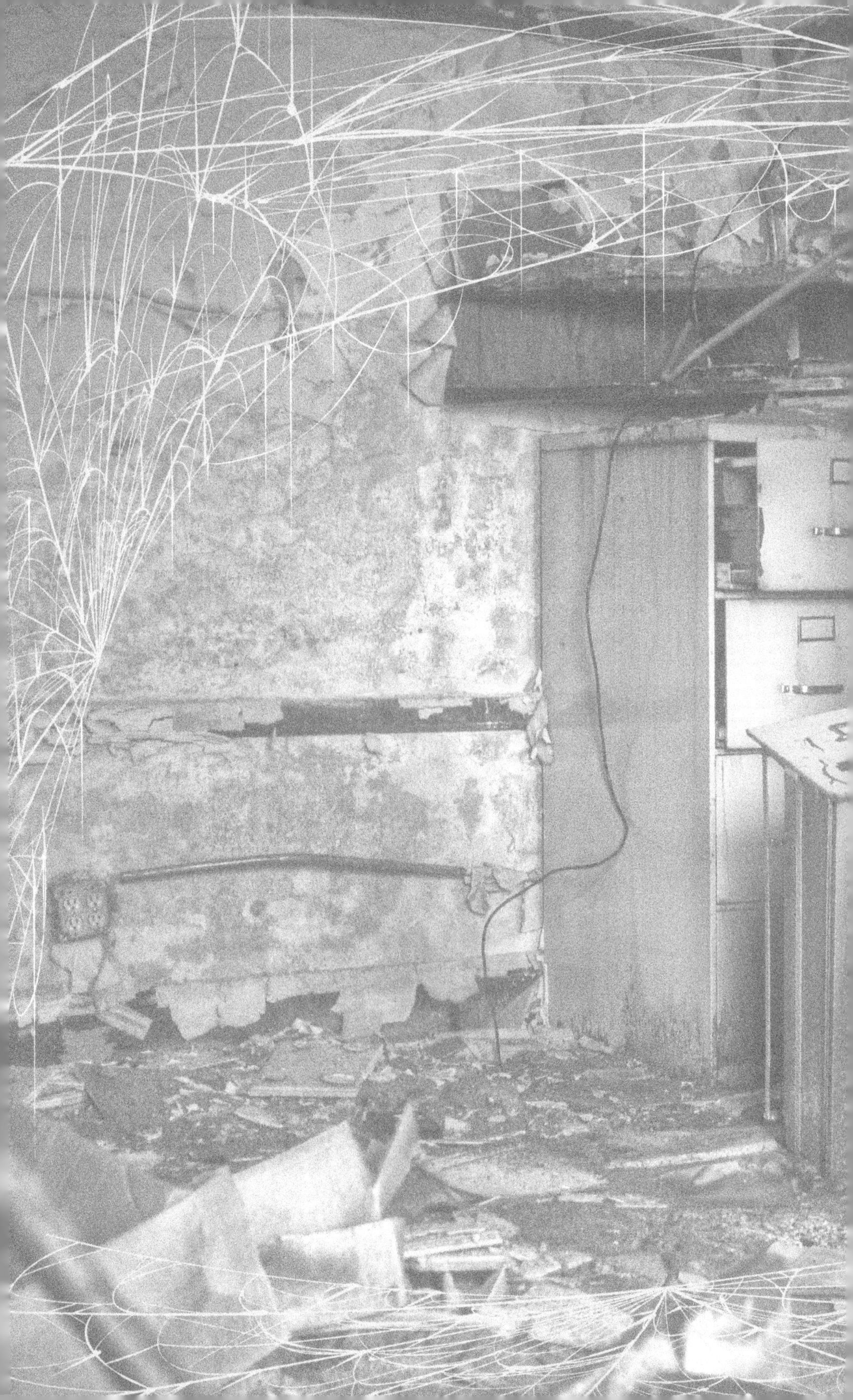

This Building is For You

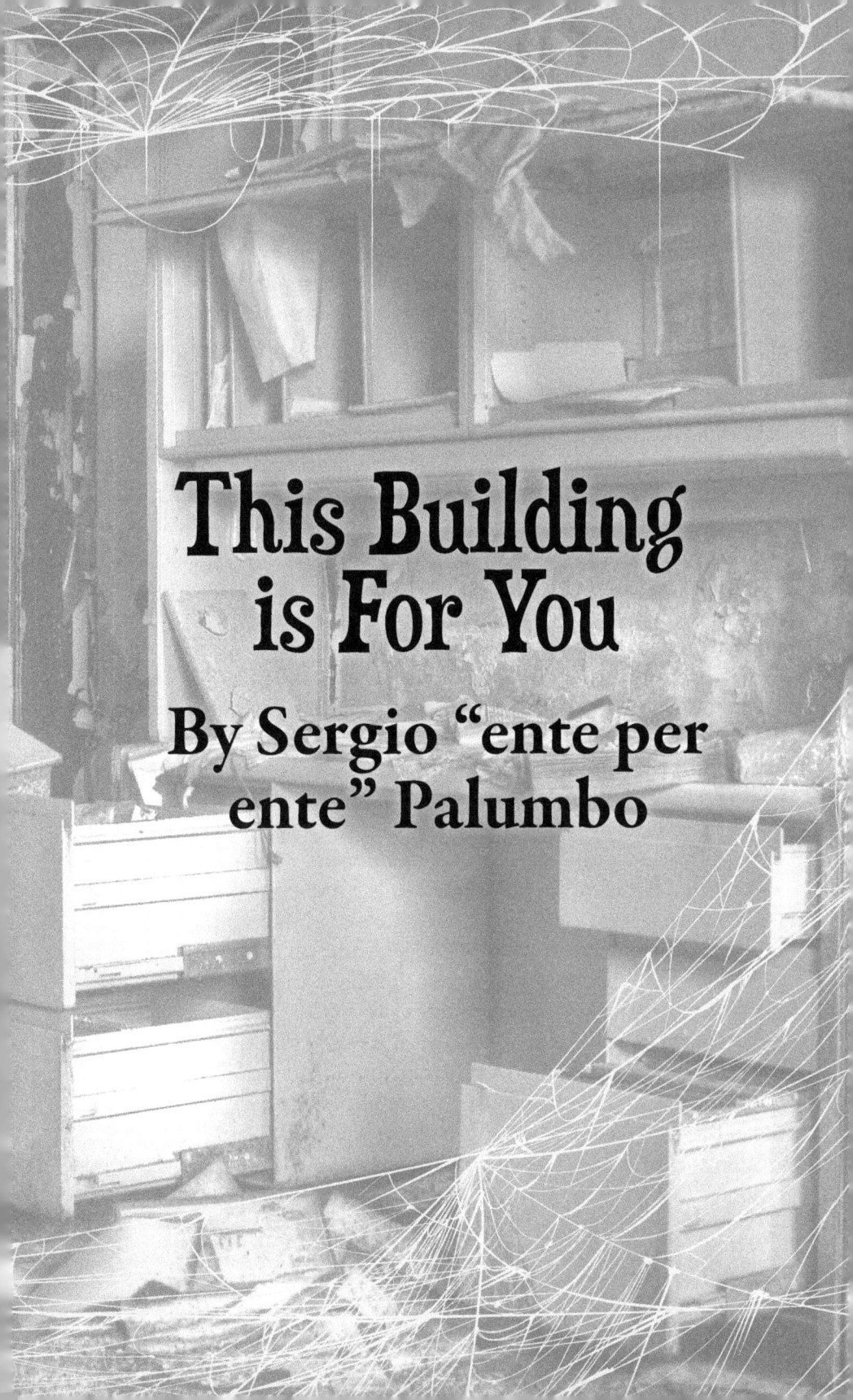

By Sergio "ente per ente" Palumbo

Demonic Workplaces

The young man wielded the knife he had been given in complete silence and stepped ahead at a trembling pace. The time of the ritual had come, and he had been told, more than once, what was expected of him.

His black eyes stared at its blade, every inch of it covered in the dirty gray liquid he had just taken it from a moment ago. Now it was blessed—if blessed might be the correct word under the dark circumstances of this cruel act of today—and prepared to do what it had been built for many decades ago, and it had already achieved on several occasions in the past.

And then, he eventually smelled the scent of the blade as it floated through the air. It didn't smell like anger or regret. It smelled like fear. It was something he had never imagined he might sense, or think about, one day in his lifetime, undoubtedly. The air almost froze around him, but he had to move on regardless of the cold and the sadness he undeniably felt inside.

He remembered how many high hopes he had when he was at school and what he wanted to do in the years to come, after his graduation in Economics, then after his Master's in International Trade, and so on. The wait for a quality job had arrived sooner than expected, and he believed the results he had long been fighting for, hoping for, were in his hands, and he had just to pluck their fruits. But they hadn't manifested. No, there was still that last step. The longest, and the most difficult, probably. It might be possible that everybody who was at all a constant dreamer, like he was, had had at least one experience of an event or a sequence of circumstances that had made them face how different the real world was. Many of those dreams were broken at times by absurd and fantastic incidents, which put them out of bounds in regard to their subsequent fulfillment, and forced someone to look, and be astounded, at how ghastly reality could turn out.

But, hell, not like this! *Not like this...* he told himself again.

"We command you to do as we ordered, and kill the body that stands before you now, closing the door of the past behind you and opening another that leads to a beneficial future for this place and all of us!" This had been spoken by the group of people, made up of men and women dressed in their matching garments, who stood around him and their next victim.

The young man's heart sank at that command. He knew he had to continue. The day outside was warm, as it always was in that season in the urban area, and an intolerable oppression reigned in this place despite the air conditioning. But it was his hopelessness that seemed to be dragging him down, without the chance for any real change at present.

This Building Is For You

There was something awful in the room and the overall circumstances he was in, along with that strange group of people surrounding him, and the killing he had to do.

The young man forced himself to go on, trying to regain his bearings and remove his trembling, as he slowly distanced himself from the others who were studying him, watching his actions while evaluating his uncertain behavior. The deadly silence succeeded by another deadly sentence.

It had to be done, he knew. And the man, in reality, could never escape that fact.

This was simply to make clear, if possible, to the unknowing people walking the streets now (how deeply he would have preferred to be one of those passers-by at that time!) that they couldn't even imagine what horrors lurked behind the glittering windows of a tall, rich, modern building in that city. Behind these glass walls were unimaginable horrors that could easily consume everything and everyone.

This while the poor captive was weakly struggling against the oncoming end of his life.

Frank Berstaf was walking the streets of Sydney, and he stared at those high-rise buildings all around him: modern skyscrapers, tall towers, and other similar structures. As a matter of fact, Sydney, the largest city in Australia, was said to be home to 1,168 completed such structures, more than any other city in Australia, and 47 of those reached a height of at least 490 feet! Moreover, there were sixteen other great structures rising at least 510 feet in height currently under construction in the central business district and immediate surrounding areas.

As home to some of the most noteworthy companies in the most expansive period of the city's growth, that area also had historical importance, indeed. Those buildings had brought a modern maturity to the cultural initiatives of the city's founders, highlighting the urban area's unrestrainable ascent from an old town with European-like features to the country's most important city today.

The dark-haired, dark-eyed man in his mid-twenties had always been attracted to old tales about strange and almost impossible—at least, impossible to common human knowledge given the lack of experience and studies in that field that most men had—buildings like those skyscrapers. Those structures seemed to rise too high to be real. But this might also be said for edifices of the past. Think of those old bridges, for example, supposed to have been built by devils—like the Ceredigion bridge, in Wales, that he had read some news about, consisting of three bridges built on top of each other: the original bridge was medieval, dating back to 1075–1200, while the second one was a stone bridge from the 18th century. Even the three bridges of Andermatt, in Switzerland, seemed impossible: the first one had been built over the Ruess River in 1230, while the locals built the second after the first bridge was badly damaged during the Napoleonic Wars and then the last one in the 1950s. The legend goes that back in the 13th century; the villagers found it a difficult task to build a bridge over that river. That's why they asked the devil, who, of course, demanded the soul of the first man to cross it. The local people outsmarted the devil, anyway, simply by sending in a goat first. The devil was said to be upset due to that trick and wanted to immediately destroy the bridge with a large rock, but an old lady with a cross stopped him.

Legends of old, indeed!

Perhaps you might think that he had read a lot about such tales. Well, in a way, Frank had always had an interest in such things. Anyway, while looking again at those tall skyscrapers of great architectural quality—some of them being from the postwar building industry—he thought of something he had long been considering in his mind. *Well, you know, such things were really high. Come on, how could they be there, and how could anyone have built them?* Of course, he hadn't ever been an engineer, or he would certainly know how those were made. From his point of view, he just thought there had to be something unnatural in those. *What if they had been made thanks to other means than human technology? There might be something unearthly in their shape and the way they kept standing! So, what was it? Could sorcery, or even dark practices, be involved in the way those buildings had been constructed?* Frank had doubts about it. Actually, it might be so, but he would probably never know one way or the other. He wasn't stupid, after all, he had a Bachelor of Arts in Economics and a Master in International Trade, so he was well educated. He had spent most of his youth in the countryside near Blackheath, which was not far from the Blue Mountains, full of rolling forests and giant boulders. But he enjoyed exploring other branches of science, history, and the arts. That was all. This was why he thought it was better to have an open mind and to always remember that there were many things still unknown in the world. It had always been like that.

This Building Is For You

And when he approached the last street he needed to walk that day and entered the tall tower where he was expected, he knew he might be right, undoubtedly. This was an important day for him, a day he had long been waiting, of course!

The central business district where he was going to work from now on was wonderful. To its west lay Darling Harbour, which included Sydney's well-known Chinatown and a great diversity of architectural styles.

Just a few yards and he would arrive at his destination: a tall skyscraper, gray-colored with more than 50 floors—that was where the main offices of the famous Kamlolub Limited stood. Though almost conventional in structure in comparison with the super-modern and much taller buildings that had appeared over the last fifty years, this structure still looked attractive. The building had a main entrance where glass had been used very creatively, with a very high window built that enlightened the lobby. On each side, triangular structures with a strange design added to the effect, and the metal decorations of the glazing bars were a nice touch that was perfectly in accordance with the entrance door below. The tower itself was endowed on the top with large spire details, which were a late modification to increase the height of the tower, at least according to what he had read about that. He imagined that building must have been made to be impressive at night when the number of skyscrapers of the vivid downtown simply stood out against a glowing background. This was the place he had to enter, and the starting point of his promising career, or so he hoped.

After taking the lift, the young man got to the 10th floor, where he was expected. "Good morning. I'm Frank Berstaf. This is my first day here!" he told the attractive secretary/receptionist sitting at the entrance of the floor itself, before the many doors of the offices that were all around.

The chestnut-haired woman smiled with lips that looked whitish in color—the current fashion—and gestured for him to sit on an armchair. It didn't take long before someone was there to greet him, a graying man with vivid blue eyes. Maybe he was about fifty. "Pleased to have you join our company. I'm Abdullaev Wuerch, the public relations man here at Kamlolub Limited. And I am always tasked by our CFOs with the duty of welcoming our new employees here."

"I can't say how glad I am to be working at this company, Mr. Wuerch!" Frank told the other man while smiling his best smile.

"So, let's see what the e-papers I received say about you." The public relations man had a look at the gray tablet he had in his hands and then sneered. "Well, this says that you are here to start today in the Marketing Department! So, do your damnedest, don't prove that whoever chose you for this job was wrong."

"Sure thing, I will not disappoint you!" Frank exclaimed, convinced that he would be a success indeed.

The first weeks at Kamlolub Limited were really easy for Frank, and he had begun to like his new job. And the company itself, of course. In the Marketing Department, they had twice-a-week consultations and a lot of hurried paperwork that came unexpectedly or had to be set at the last moment. For the rest of the time, he seemed to be completely qualified for that role. There were a few tricks he had to learn about how to properly address the right superiors about the varied matters and problems—there always were some. He learned the right way to the bathrooms—there were many on that floor—and to the other offices of his colleagues who worked in that same area of business. But he only had a few moments every day to talk to them. In a way, his work duties occupied about eighty percent of his time while on the job. Whenever he had some free time, he found himself standing in front of a window above the busy streets; he didn't even know why. Maybe it was due to that new and wondrous city sight. Sydney was very different from what he had been long accustomed to during his life.

The young man was surprised when, early one evening, he unexpectedly spotted Mr. Wuerch again on his floor—as he hadn't seen him since that first day. And he was even more stunned when he saw him going to his office. Apparently, the public relations man wanted to have a talk with him.

"What brings you here, Mr. Wuerch? I thought you were a very busy man who never had the time to revisit the humble offices of newbies like me after their first day." Frank smiled and seemed to kindly make fun of his presence there. "I hope nothing is amiss."

"No, there is nothing wrong with you or your work. You can be sure of that." The other man looked at him with a sneer. "And, yes, I rarely find the time to get out of my office once an employee is in service, especially after our last transport going lost last week. That shipment was later found in a military hangar with no explanation from the shipping company in the end. We, on the other hand, had to give a lot of explanations, even to the media, of course. Such things always make a bad impression, you know."

This Building Is For You

"Oh, I heard about that. Sad occurrences are bound to happen. Never take for granted that your parcels, and their deliveries, are safe—as a shipping company says to be the rule for them, as it is not true. This was what one of my uncles always told me while he worked in the shipping business."

"Well, we have finally dealt with it. So, how was your first month here? Did you get your first paycheck?"

"Sure thing... 5,260 Aussies, and I can only imagine the faces of my uncles when I tell them about that. They will be happy, though they didn't approve of my choice of fields when I entered college."

"Oh, they'll be delighted, of course, though this is just your first month, and after your first year with us, things will improve over the course of time. The combination of different models with one good overall strategy in the field is what makes Kamlolub Limited the great business it is today. It is also a wonderful fit for the type of activities of the company." Then Wuerch told him, "By the way, you said that you're going to tell your uncles about your paycheck. What about your parents? I thought you would tell them first..."

"Well, you know..." Frank visibly saddened and made a strange look. "Both of them have long gone. My uncles are the only ones left of my family."

"I see... and I can understand that they are important to you."

"They are, surely," Frank replied in a happier tone of voice. "In a way, I still need to settle into my new home here in Sydney, and so I've not invited them here yet. Oh, by the way... given that I am talking with you today, I have one question."

"Please, go on..." Wuerch said.

"What are those pictures of men and women in that windowless room in that direction? I saw that almost nobody goes in there, even though there are many chairs and a large desk. Seems like an abandoned room. Are those the pictures of people who founded this company or that got great renown during the years?" Frank asked.

"Actually, those are pictures of our past colleagues, those who went missing," the public relations man said.

"Oh, my! There are twenty pictures in there, if I remember correctly. How is that possible?"

"So, you went in there. Well, by chance, are you aware of how many missing people there are here in the city of Sydney every year? On average, 28 people go missing every day in New South Wales. In Australia, more than 38,000 missing persons' reports are received by the police each year."

"So, are those former employees who died?"

Demonic Workplaces

"No one knows... they simply disappeared over the past years, so we don't know what happened to them." Wuerch stared at him and looked saddened. "They were good at their jobs here, so this is why we, and the others who worked here before us, simply decided to honor them and put their pictures on display. Such terrible things happen, unfortunately. This is sad, but don't think about it too much. In the U.S., the average of missing persons is even higher than here."

"I imagine it is..." Frank nodded. "But it's worrisome, anyway."

"Yes, it is... but we can't do anything about it, you know. So we try to ignore it."

"I usually never think about such things. When I walk the streets, I feel really comfortable and safe here in Sydney. Of course, it's a different world from where I grew up near Blackheath because here it's crowded with ceaseless traffic, cars parked end-to-end for as far as I can see, and the sidewalks look more or less like rivers of pedestrians who don't seem to know or care about what is happening. But what you have told me about this is sad! And I imagine that such occurrences are always unexpected and seem worrisome."

"Yes, you're right. It should never happen. But the police have never solved the cases, or at least they never reported back to our company about the outcomes of their investigations over the course of time. So, I think they are still investigating. You might call them cold cases. Or maybe they don't know yet where they went or how they disappeared, which is even more troublesome."

"Yes, it is." Frank appeared to be pensive and disappointed, actually. "Such things should never happen."

The first year at Kamlolub Limited had gone by quickly, and Frank believed he was lucky to be accepted to work there. In a way, the rest of his life was going well as well. Most nights were spent with some of his new colleagues—not that he had really befriended many, but a few—among beers and mixed drinks in pubs. They often enjoyed great courses that were a mix of local seafood and Asian flavors at some excellent restaurants. More uncommonly, there were dinners with handcrafted pasta and coffee from abroad, with strange names enjoyed at the home of somebody he had known during those long first months in the city. Then, there also was that young woman named Henrietta, whom he had just started to know better, and he was hopeful it might lead to a more serious thing, maybe a long-term love affair. But it was too early to tell about that at the moment; only time would reveal exactly where it would bring them, of course.

That morning he had met with Tadeusz from Information Technology about a problem with his office notebook to be solved. After that bald man had been busy activating some new applets and working on some updates for a few minutes, like a diver wrapped in a sort of completely invisible virtual suit that forgot about everything around him as he was working, things seemed to be going okay, and the computer was restarted as usual. "We're here to solve all of your computer problems," Tadeusz said with a large smile before walking away. "But for all the other problems that pertain to your job, we can really do nothing. That's up to your skills, as our expertise is only about information technology, you know."

"Of course, *this is the way*..." Frank nodded and sneered while funnily quoting a famous phrase from a character of a well-known Star Wars™ TV series.

The other looked at him as if he had figured out that funny meaning and smiled again before taking leave of him.

Then, it was Wuerch that appeared on his floor, reached his desk, and seemed to be willing to talk to him. "So, is everything okay? You have probably seen your annual earnings, and I trust you are satisfied, Frank."

"Yes, I am. 62,535 Aussies," he said. "How could I not be happy? Working here is a dream for many young men like me!"

"There is one thing though, Frank," the other said in a more serious voice. "Here at the company, there are some hearsays, people on the higher floors, and our CFOs, who think we—maybe—have too many workers at present, mainly due to the crisis worldwide. Our last financial reports showed our profits were not as high as we'd like this year. I mean, this had to be expected. It was in the predictions we made, but in the end, it is a bit disappointing."

"So... is the work of my section to blame? Or perhaps my work, in particular, Mr. Wuerch?" a trembling Frank asked and stood silent.

"Well, not exactly. Lower profits were the results we expected. And, as I told you, this was due to the worldwide crisis and there was not much we could do to prevent that from occurring."

"So, will there be a cut in the workforce?" the young man asked, staring at the other.

"It is possible, and we'll know about it in the next few days. So, this brings me to you."

Demonic Workplaces

"Me?" Frank considered those words. *So, my dream of continuing to work here is going to end soon...* he thought and was afraid of what Wuerch might say now.

"Well, I'm telling you that we are not going to eliminate the whole section you work in. We're happy with your work and think that you are valuable even if still very young. In the next few weeks, however, some difficult decisions will be made."

"So, are you telling me that they are looking at my performances and then trying to decide if I'm worthy of being kept, maybe?" Frank looked a bit doubtful.

"Exactly! This is why I'm telling you about that. They're looking at your work, and they want to know if they can trust you on certain things," Wuerch went on.

"I'm ready to up my game. What are these certain things you mentioned? I'll do my best to fulfill your expectations."

"I am so happy to hear this from you. Please, follow me ... and I'll show you how you can be of help to us, and to yourself as well."

"Right now? Today?" the young man was surprised but also full of many hopes.

"Yes, right now. Today... why wait any longer? Leave your smartphone on the desk. You'll not be needing that for a few hours."

Tall towers like that of Kamlolub Limited were high-rise buildings similar to small cities packed into a single structure. An edifice like this was heated with temperature control that involved ventilation and air conditioning systems in addition to heating, offering improved uniformity of temperature control over the structure. The most modern skyscrapers had large enough pumps and heat exchangers, a single system with a cooling tower, and a chiller plant on the roof that was able to service the entire building. On the other hand, this tower didn't happen to be so modern, dating back to the early 1970s, maybe even before, and its system needed heavy infrastructure, with pumps, which were laid out beneath the streets. Central heating systems like this, as far as Frank knew, operated by having a localized plant that heated water that was pumped to heat emitters, such as radiators, convectors, and perimeter heaters. The heat emitters were located to heat spaces as required.

This Building Is For You

On the ground floor of that building, where he was brought that day by Wuerch, below all the many offices and the streets, they entered the so-called mechanical room. This was where the heat was distributed throughout the entire skyscraper, typically by forced air through ductwork, and there they found an armchair and a hooded man tied to it. He also noticed that the armchair on which the unfortunate man had been left was surrounded by a group of people, men and women, whose faces he had already seen in the building. Those who worked in the higher offices, different from his. So a disconcerted Frank was told about what would now be happening.

"Here we are," Wuerch said, looking at his surprised younger colleague. "You know, a building like this can't only live on profits due to the many expenses to be paid every year and can't be simply maintained by a common central heating system. Something else is required."

"What do you mean? What is that hooded, tied man doing here?" Frank stared at it all in full bewilderment, not understanding the very strange turn of events.

"You see... that man, under the hood, well, he is Tadeusz. Maybe you have spotted him before. He is from Information Technology at Kamlolub Limited, and his value was being questioned, too. But the higher floors thought you might be of more value than that man. So, tell me, Frank, really, were they right, or were they wrong about you?"

"Whoa. I'm confused. Certainly confused! I can't figure out what you're saying," answered Frank, looking uncertain. "This looks bad. It looks like madness."

"Well, you see, it is this simple," Wuerch added in a deep voice. While the confused man tried to understand what was going on, a pistol unexpectedly appeared out of Wuerch's suit and was pointed at him. "It's that this building, the profits of Kamlolub Limited, don't only rely on the business results we've received all these years. There's much more to be done. In a way, we have to revive the building and thank those who gave it into our hands to be managed and make it grow more and more. So, there's a strange fuel it requires from time to time. And that fuel is a sacrifice. A human one, you see. This is why you are here today. To kill him..."

"What... are you? Get real... this is not possible!"

"So, are you saying that our superiors are really mistaken?" the older man sneered. "Well, you know, that tied man to be sacrificed might have been you today, but I asked the higher floors to think about it twice." The other people in the group nodded in full silence, and Wuerch kept talking. "In my

Demonic Workplaces

opinion, you would be a more valuable worker for us than Tadeusz. Think that it might have been you there, hooded and tied and on the point of being killed for the good of us all. What do you have to say?"

"This is real, deep madness... what makes you think I could do this?" Frank cried out.

"So, were we all wrong about you? Should I have chosen Tadeusz instead of you? Maybe we should let him go free and see if he would be willing to immediately sacrifice you now. What do you think his answer is going to be?" the other pressed him.

"What? Now stop, please. Think about what you're asking me to do."

"What are you going to do, Frank? And, sure thing, we have carefully considered it all, before we came to this decision. This is why Tadeusz is hooded and also tied there now, and not you. But we can make things change immediately if you don't agree to it, obviously. Think twice before making your next move. Just choose to walk through it, leaving behind the dead body of this man once you have put an end to his existence, and leave your doubts with it. Without this unearthly tradition going on, if we move against the devil's deal once made by those who created this business, Kamlolub Limited might reach disruption and disorder as the company collapses! It's exactly like on Earth: the soil that supports and sustains our beautiful planet over millions of years of evolution and adaptation has made the beings who live on this world grow and develop into incredible life forms. So it is in our business: the field of commerce is where it's important to make more and more money by producing or buying and selling products or services, activities meant for profit. The fertilizer, you know, it's blood, the sacrifice of others, and our deep cruelty that is going to let our ability and right to control people or things be strengthened and become bigger with the passing of the years." Wuerch looked cold-minded. "How do you think things work in this field? How do you imagine other old and famous buildings like that of Kamlolub Limited, which are in the city, great businesses like this, have survived and have made profits until today?"

"So, what is it? Do I have to choose if I want to kill him or allow him to kill me? Is this what this all is about? Against any rule of law and common decency? How could all of you ever think that this is knowledgeable and civilized?" Frank was really surprised. He was afraid of what might be next... and he also thought he now knew what might have happened to the many missing people in the pictures he had seen in that empty room since his first days here. They had been killed. They had been sacrificed!

This Building Is For You

"You have been working for us for a year. Remember when you saw your first paycheck from the first month you worked here? And your earnings from your last year? Think twice before you act. Do you think that an important job like this is given to a young employee like you, though with a good graduation and a noteworthy capability, simply without the required cost? That there is nothing else to be sacrificed to keep it? The devil built such a place, and the high-ranking managers that came after followed this tradition to have the building fortified and revived, the same as their profits, when the time came. The founders of this business were given this, and they would lose it certainly for no reason. Whatever the cost—and you now know what the price is—Death by ritual is the thing that keeps this place all-in-one-piece, and the blood of the next corpse, the man sacrificed, obviously will be giving fuel, sorcerous fuel, immediately to this building, and for the few years to come. It's just like air-conditioning makes the days cooler in summer, and the heating allows the edifice to be warmer in fall. The skyscraper will remain the same, but it will also be restored and better than before once everything is done. Renewed, in a way... After all, even some of the best-known architects of the past stood ready to achieve the same goal. This is how they built ancient temples, impossible bridges, markets, and so on, in order to ensure their own good in an unearthly way over the others. If you want to keep your earnings and let them grow over the course of time, you know what needs to happen next." Wuerch was serious. His blue eyes looked like two icy moons from an alien world without life. "And you must know that there is only one way you can exit this room alive today. Which is all the more reason for you to stay here with us and do as you are told. On the other hand, you could put everything to waste, and then another one, like our Tadeusz here, will be kept working for us here. So, it's your choice."

"My choice... to live or to die. If I don't kill him, it will be my life that comes to an end... No return home," Frank considered.

"To live and be richer and richer year after year, or be dead and allow others to be wealthy instead of you," added the cruel Wuerch. "Take it as a fight for survival and for getting your right to be someone, to become a person much more powerful than you presently are. Is this clear?"

"You... how could you?" the young man was almost speechless now and stared at the other men and women in the group. "This is how you want me to agree to follow the orders of the forces of the most evil darkness!"

"The higher floors are ordering you to do so, on behalf of the old devil that gave it to them. This is the rule. Do as ordered and then live a long

Demonic Workplaces

life full of money, and you'll also find it will be easy to forget about today's killing. This is exactly as we all did when we were told of the rules. So, what do you plan on doing? Ah, and if you think about going to the police, you must know that no one will be listening to your charges there. Our power is really noteworthy, and it has been reinforced for years. Well, before I forget about this, you must remember that, of course, we'll be filming your actions of today to remind you, in the future, if necessity comes, of what you did and why you did it. This also is the rule, Frank!" Wuerch insisted while facing him.

Frank stayed motionless for some moments, his eyes lost apparently, as he fought in his own mind a sort of battle to choose between responsibility, and humanity, and the aim of getting a rich life, and also how to keep that. Then, he also thought of a way to keep living and get away from that place as quickly as he could! But the pistol of Wuerch was still aiming at him.

"Now take this old knife and bathe it in the liquid inside that vase." It was one of the other men who surrounded him now, and that Frank recognized as Paytov, the Chief of the Virtual Office Department, that gave it to him.

"What is inside that vase? What is that gray matter?"

"Don't worry about what is in there. Just think about doing as you are ordered," was the immediate reply. Even Wuerch stared at him and studied his next moves.

So, the young man kept the knife he had been given in full silence and stepped ahead at a trembling pace. Then he put it inside the vase until it was submerged in the dirty gray liquid.

"Now the knife is just blessed for its purpose," the same Paytov said in a sort of awe-inspiring tone.

If blessed might be used as a sort of correct word under the dark circumstances of this cruel act of today, the young Frank thought in silence. It took him some moments before he could do anything else. After having smelled the air, that smelled of fear, that smelled noxious, he remembered how many high hopes he had when he was at school and what he wanted, or better, what he liked to do in the years to come, after his graduation in Economics, after his Master in International Trade, and so on. How different was the reality of the very cruel business compared to what he had long dreamed of!

"We command you to do as we order. Kill this body that is before you now, closing the door of the past behind you and opening another door that leads to the good future for this place and all of us!" said the group of people dressed in their suits that stood around him and the next victim.

This Building Is For You

The young man's heart sank at that voice. Frank forced himself to go on, trying to regain his bearings and remove the trembling, as he slowly distanced himself from the others that were studying him, unceasingly watching his actions and also evaluating his uncertain behavior. The deadly silence succeeded by another deadly silence.

It had to be done, he knew. And the man, in reality, might have never escaped his inevitable death.

Once done—that bloody act—the lifeless body of Tadeusz was untied from the armchair and hit the ground, dead.

"This is not over, Frank." The words of the cold-minded Wuerch sounded like sandpaper in the young man's ears because he knew something more had to come. "Not yet. We need to burn the corpse in that vat and let it be slowly consumed in the next few minutes. We have deactivated the fire alarms in this part of the building for this purpose today, and the sprinklers that are in this room don't work right now, of course."

So, poor Frank did that too, regretfully and in full silence. As the dead body burned, its smell lingered like stinking carcasses in the air around him. The young man saw—or simply thought he saw—in the disgusting smoke the first steps of his new future, a future of great wealth, unlimited earnings, and many other pleasing accomplishments in his life to come. The air was full of scenes sneering at him that quickly appeared one after another, among the swirling vapor that still came from the vat, as if his actions of that day had let him walk into this new world, their promise becoming a reality through that opening he had made possible, and that he would soon savor, in a way.

The same was true for the whole company he worked at and the other men and women who surrounded him in that room. Until the next time someone else would have to do the same cruel thing so as to have the skyscraper revived and refueled again in a sorcerous way. The way of evil defilements of a human body to get a different good for a few others who lived on such gruesome tradition of blood and thrived because of it, of course.

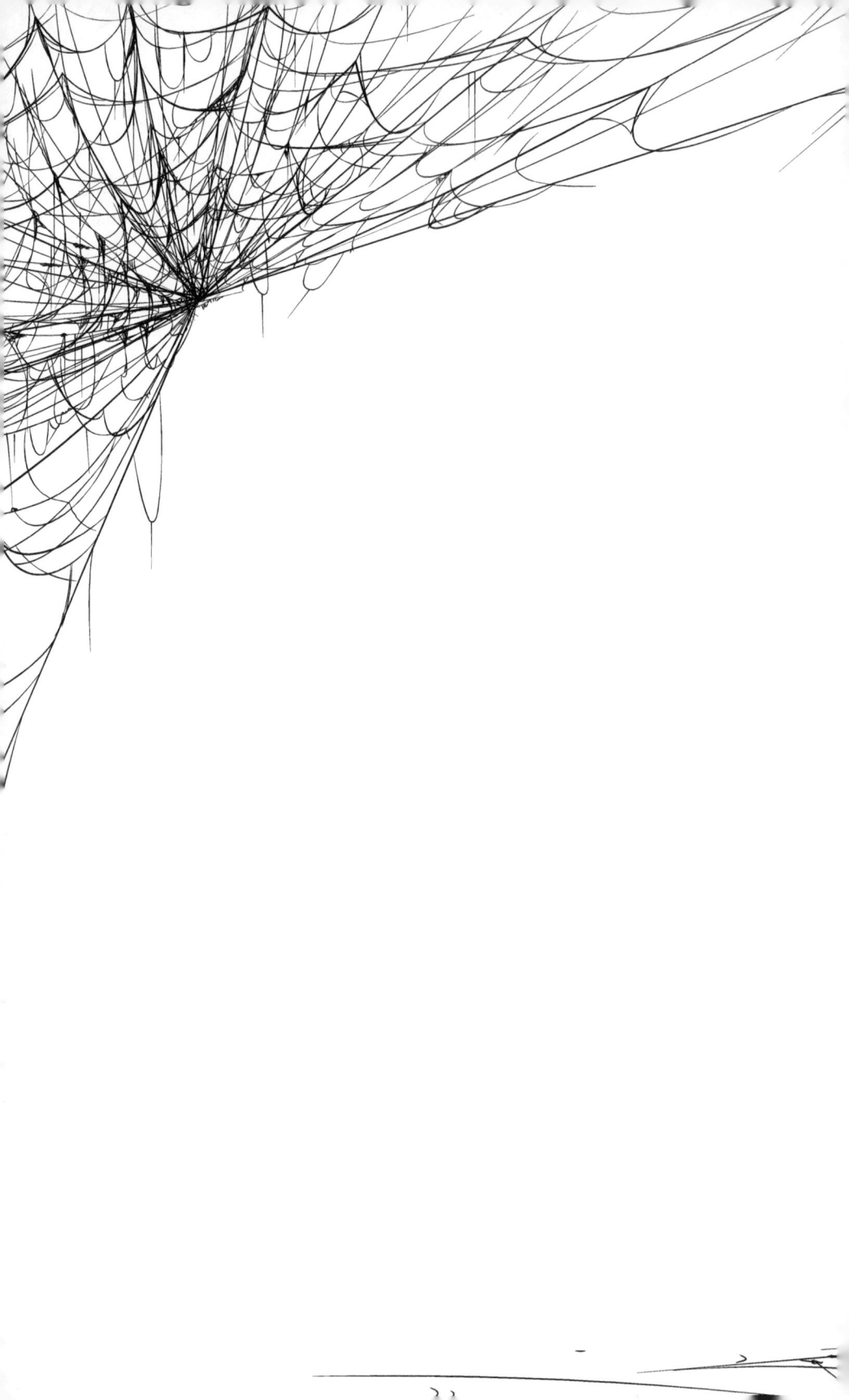

Book Club Questions

1. Which story did you feel a connection with? Why did it resonate with you?

2. Do you ever suspect that your boss or co-worker is in fact a demon? Which one(s)? Why? What kind do you think they are?

3. How well did the stories included meet your expectations for this anthology theme?

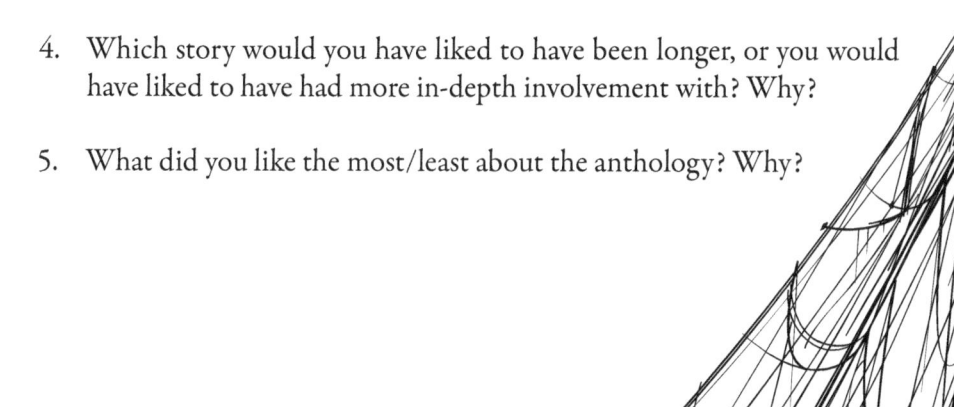

4. Which story would you have liked to have been longer, or you would have liked to have had more in-depth involvement with? Why?

5. What did you like the most/least about the anthology? Why?

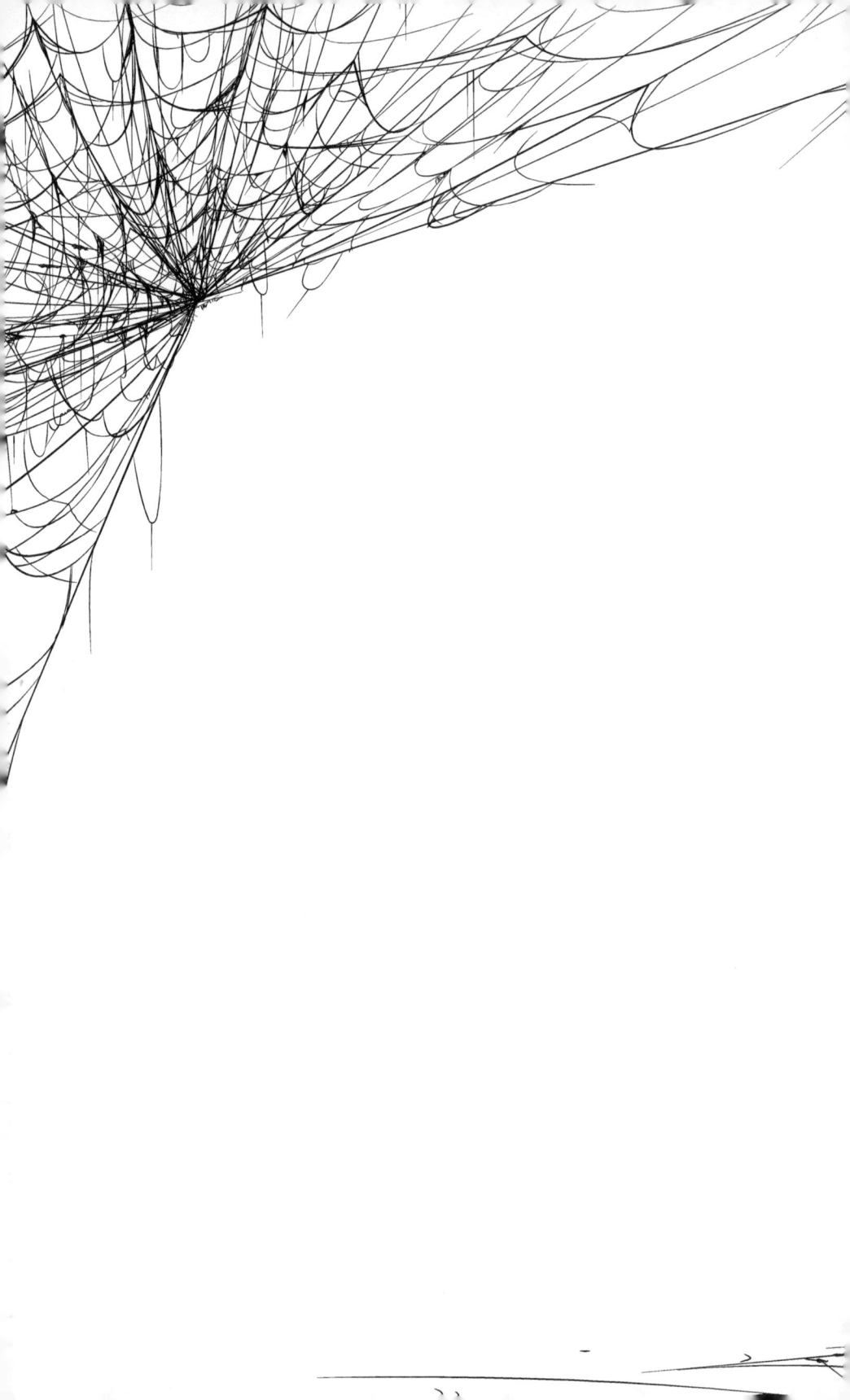

Editor Bio

Joseph Mistretta is a born and bred Chicagoland native. He edits manuscripts of various genres, such as steampunk fantasy, epic dark military, murder mystery, and more. When not fixing comma splices or recommending word choices, Joseph enjoys spending time at the Orlando theme parks, museums, and restaurants with his wife or online gaming with friends.

More books from 4 Horsemen Publications

Horror, Thriller, & Suspense

Alan Berkshire
Jungle
Hell's Road

Erika Lance
Jimmy
Illusions of Happiness
No Place for Happiness
I Hunt You

Maria DeVivo

Witch of the Black Circle
Witch of the Red Thorn
Witch of the Silver Locust

Mark Tarrant
The Mighty Hook

Steve Altier
The Ghost Hunter

Anthologies & Collections

4HP Anthologies
Teen Angst: Mix Vol. 1
Teen Angst: Mix Vol. 2
My Wedding Date
The Offices of Supernatural Being
The Sentient Space

Demonic Anthologies
Demonic Wildlife
Demonic Household
Demonic Carnival

Demonic Classics
Demonic Vacations
Demonic Medicine
Demonic Workplace
& more to follow!

XXX- Holiday Collection
Unwrap Me
Stuffing My Stocking

Discover more at 4HorsemenPublications.com

Milton Keynes UK
Ingram Content Group UK Ltd.
UKHW040820161123
432684UK00005B/329